The Boy
in Formaldehyde

Also by Michael Antony

Non-Fiction

The Masculine Century (A Heretical History of Our Time)
Part One: Sex, Art and War in the Twentieth Century

The Masculine Century
Part Two: From Darwinism to Feminism: The Rise of the Ideologies of Aggression

Fiction

The Apocalypse Syndrome

Poetry

Visions of Kali

Website: www.michael-antony.com

The Boy in Formaldehyde

Michael Antony

authorHOUSE®

AuthorHouse™ *UK*
1663 Liberty Drive
Bloomington, IN 47403 USA
www.authorhouse.co.uk
Phone: 0800.197.4150

This is a work of fiction. All of the characters, names, incidents
and dialogue in the novel are products of the author's imagination
and any resemblance to any living person is fortuitous.

© 2016 Michael Antony. All rights reserved.

No part of this book may be reproduced, stored in a retrieval system, or
transmitted by any means without the written permission of the author.

Published by AuthorHouse   04/07/2016

ISBN: 978-1-5246-3096-6 (sc)
ISBN: 978-1-5246-3097-3 (e)

Print information available on the last page.

Any people depicted in stock imagery provided by Thinkstock are models,
and such images are being used for illustrative purposes only.
Certain stock imagery © Thinkstock.

This book is printed on acid-free paper.

Because of the dynamic nature of the Internet, any web addresses or links contained in
this book may have changed since publication and may no longer be valid. The views
expressed in this work are solely those of the author and do not necessarily reflect the
views of the publisher, and the publisher hereby disclaims any responsibility for them.

1

Camilla glanced through the pages of the art section of *The Guardian*. There was an article on an exhibition at the Tate Modern called "Masters of the Monochrome — a Hundred Years of Blank White Paintings." The reviewer was lyrical in his praise:

> This is a long overdue tribute to the great Modernist and Postmodernist tradition of painting canvases entirely white, and for the first time allows comparisons to be made between Malevich, Klein, Manzoni, Ryman, Rauschenberg, Reinhardt and two dozen lesser-known masters of the white monochrome painting. This exhibition not only allows us to admire the subtle differences of texture and brushstroke between thirty magnificent blank white paintings never before seen together, but also shows the extraordinary persistence of this revolutionary exercise in originality — which has been repeated now for nearly a hundred years,

ever since Malevich's epoch-making breakthrough in 1918. Decade after decade, rebel geniuses have been inspired to plaster canvases with a uniform wash of white paint, in a daring protest against art, against life, against having any sort of subject or expressing anything at all — a brave and original challenge to our preconceptions of what art is about. Many of these paintings (of which there are now several hundred) hang in the greatest art museums of the world — each one defying our imagination all over again to see a picture which isn't there, a subject which isn't there, a vision which isn't there. This is the expression of absence, of nullity, of nothingness. It is the essence of modern art.

She yawned and her eye moved down the page. Then the headline of an article at the bottom caught her eye. It read: "Boy in Formaldehyde at Grafton Gallery." There followed a review of a daring new work by an up-and-coming, controversial artist called Piers Bendigo.

In a bold revisiting of Damien Hirst's classic works of a shark in formaldehyde, a sheep in formaldehyde, half a cow in formaldehyde, and various species of fish, Bendigo has placed a boy in formaldehyde. The boy, who looks about ten years old, is suspended in a glass tank as though in the sea. He is naked except for a pair of black swimming trunks and his face is partly covered by an old-fashioned, green-tinted diving mask. His body is at a slight angle to the horizontal so it seems to be swimming upwards from the seabed, represented by a layer of sand and shells and pink coral on the floor of the container. The boy's arms are half-extended in a sort of dog-paddle as he struggles towards the surface. One can make out a series of fine wires keeping the body in place, though it looks from a few feet away to be floating freely. Of course, nobody seriously believes this might be an actual dead boy, but the extraordinary verisimilitude of the installation is nonetheless disturbing. It succeeds brilliantly in giving the macabre impression of a real body, and the sinister element of doubt it plants in the mind (what if it were?) is what makes this work both so morally challenging and so electrifying. The installation is attracting crowds to the gallery and has given a boost to the reputation of Piers Bendigo, who has struggled for the past two years to produce anything as exciting and controversial as his debut work. It seems only a matter of time before this masterpiece is snapped up by a major collector or a museum.

Camilla put the paper down with a grimace of revulsion. Then she picked it up again and checked the address of the Grafton Gallery given at the end of the article. She glanced at her watch. She still had time to make it. She put on a jacket and slipped on her purple boots. She wanted to take a closer look at this Boy in Formaldehyde. She put her Ricox digital camera into her jacket pocket, as well as her Weihai Galactic smartphone. As she walked out the door she felt a slight shiver down her spine.

2

Romain Lagarde sat in his studio flat in Camden Town staring at the screen of his four-year old Lanova laptop. The same page had been up there for half an hour and he hadn't got anywhere, apart from tweaking a few sentences, chipping off a word here and there. This was a story that wouldn't come. Who the hell were these characters? What did he care about them? He suspected it had been a mistake to start from an intellectual formula — basing each character on a cliché turned on its head. His fictional creations had promptly rebelled against their artificial conception and were sullenly refusing to come to life. They remained walking abstractions. They had no souls, no inner world. He couldn't hear them think.

He stared moodily out the window at the crumbling brick wall opposite. Was this just another passing creative crisis or something more serious? He wondered if it was a hopeless task for a foreigner to try to write stories set in London. Of course he was writing in French for a French audience (so he hoped) but even so his writing must lack authenticity even to a French reader. He hadn't captured the real atmosphere of London in this story. It was always seen through the eyes of French exiles, because he didn't trust himself to get English characters right. He reflected gloomily that French bookstores were filled with translations of English books. Surely French people with a hankering for stories set in London would turn to them, the real thing, in preference to his own second-hand stuff. In short, he was back at square one, in the same predicament in which he had found himself in France.

By some peculiar stroke of fate he had been born in the French Overseas Territory of New Caledonia. He had got out of that Pacific backwater and to the true centre of the universe, *la France métropolitaine*, as fast as he could, but he had soon found his ambitions to write stymied by his outsider status. What did he know about France and the French? He was a foreigner there. He had the perspective on France of a foreigner, and this was a mental aberration which even the most enlightened Parisian publisher was apparently not yet ready to forgive. Of course France was "diverse" and multicultural now, and some authors wrote with exotic voices, but you had to represent an exotic culture, oppressed by French colonialism, which gave you a recognized viewpoint and preferably (for the leftist chattering classes) a chip on your shoulder against the old colonial power and its wicked racism. He had none of that. He was a blue-eyed Frenchman born at the other end of the earth (his grandfather had gone there after the French were thrown out of Algeria, and his mother's people had been there ever since the Germans annexed Alsace and half its inhabitants fled to the colonies.) He had nothing against France. He had worshipped it humbly from a distance all his life. His familiarity with its history and literature was only exceeded by his ignorance of the life that went on in its towns and cities — its moods, its mentalities, its subtle social codes.

The trouble was that the mode of acutely observed social realism which had become the default form of serious modern fiction — in contrast with all the other arts of the modern age — made his ignorance of the myriad tiny facets of daily life in France a crippling handicap. Nor could he get round it by writing instead about the island where he had grown up. If he had come from some hellish Third World warzone, bringing with him, like Aeneas from Troy, a horror story to appal the world, French readers (and the publishers who anticipated their desires) might have shown a morbid interest in his grisly narratives. But he came from a place of almost monotonous tranquillity, and his natural creative impulse was not to tell the huddled masses of Europe his story but to tell them theirs. This seemed to strike them as a pointless, if not an impertinent, exercise. He felt that the Parisian publishers he sent his stuff to were puzzled that he should be trying at all. What on earth could he possibly have to say to them — they, the denizens of the most wonderful city on earth? He knew nothing about their lives and he was a man from nowhere. He felt oddly as if he had no ground to stand on, no standpoint from which to see the world. Without solving that problem he could not find his voice, his style, his angle of attack on life.

It was this that had persuaded him to leave Paris after three miserable years teaching in a sink secondary school in a ZEP (a *Zone d'Education Prioritaire*, the official euphemism for an immigrant ghetto of graffiti-daubed tower-blocks ruled by gangs of surly drug-dealers.) He tried Montpellier and then Bordeaux, and found both of them rather stuffy provincial towns of depressingly parochial outlook. He had thought the south might be a bit nearer in lifestyle to the sun-drenched, laid-back island he came from, but he found it if anything even more closed and suspicious of outsiders and more resentful of the wider world. Despite all his efforts he couldn't whip up any sense of belonging, and his writing was no more successful than before. He had now dropped out of the National Education Service and supported himself by irregular supply teaching in "sensitive" secondary schools, where the teachers averaged one nervous breakdown a year and the white children were adopting Arab accents in order to sound tough and streetwise. There was a series of unimaginative girlfriends, who looked forward eagerly to a married life of do-it-yourself stores on Saturday and do-it-yourself chores in a never-finished dream home on Sunday. What on earth could he say about any of this that wasn't obvious to everyone? The state of France was so depressing it was difficult to believe anyone would actually want to read about it. Finally, he thought he would go somewhere that would seem exciting and fascinating even to the French.

London! The place so many of them dreamed of moving to in order to escape the economic morass of France — the deadweight of taxes and regulations, the endless strikes, the stifling little world of Parisian snobbery and literary incest. As a teenager he had spent a year in Australia on a high school exchange so he spoke English fluently. At first he found the move across the Channel an adventure, but in terms of writing he soon found himself faced with the same problem as before. He was an outsider in London, ignorant of its social codes, its street life, its bewildering Third World tribes, the confusing fault-lines of its Byzantine class system. He could only guess at what was going on there. And once again, as he addressed a Parisian literary audience, he thought he heard the eternal question: But who *are* you? You are a foreigner in London, but what sort of foreigner? Where are you from? What are you comparing this with? His characters were all expatriates and outsiders, but he couldn't define exactly what it was they were outside. They had left something behind but he couldn't describe what. He was only familiar with that in-between state, the state of exile, of expatriation, of not being at home, and neither where they had come from nor where they had ended up was within his power to portray with any conviction. He once had a dream that he was sitting trapped in the transit lounge of Heathrow Airport, trying to write about the world as it passed through. What went on beyond the doors in any direction he could only guess at. This dream stuck in his mind as an image of his situation.

The advantage of living in London was that he could survive by giving private French lessons. But this now threatened horribly to become not merely his "day job" as he struggled with his art, but the sum total of his prospects in life. He seemed doomed to live out the next forty years as an impecunious French teacher. How on earth would he ever be able to support a family doing that? Where would the money come from for the do-it-yourself stores and the do-it-yourself dream home? He was thirty-three years old and earning just enough to eat out at a pub once a week and pay the rent on this poky studio flat above a tattoo and piercing shop. ("The area is quiet," he liked to tell people, "apart from the odd scream.") Three novels and a collection of short stories had been turned down by every publisher, and in despair he had self-published them. Two or three copies of each sat on his shelves leering down at him, while a whole boxful more lay under the bed. He had managed to give one copy of the collection of short stories away to one of his students. There had never been any feedback.

That reminded him that the very student he had given the book to was due right now for a lesson. He saved his short story and switched off his computer. He glanced around the flat. Was it tidy? He needed not merely a tidy table but a tidy floor, as this student was special. She paid him not in money but in yoga lessons. She was a person like him, in short, struggling to survive by various shifts and expedients. She was in her late twenties, not bad-looking, and he rather fancied her, but there was something a bit reserved, self-contained, and faintly melancholy about her that kept him from making any advances. He decided she was either one of those world-weary English feminists who have given up on men, or she was recovering from a disastrous relationship, or she was still suffering from some traumatic event in her past that had spoiled her appetite for living. Whichever of these scenarios was true, it seemed insensitive to make any sort of pass at her. He swept some papers off his table and stuffed them into a folder on a bookshelf, brushed the table clean of dust with his sleeve, and looked at the floor. There was only a pair of jogging shoes and sweaty socks to be thrown behind the plywood partition that closed off his bedroom. He made sure the plastic curtain was pulled across to hide the dirty dishes in the tiny kitchen alcove. He took out the French book he used with her and turned to where they had got to so as to mentally prepare a lesson. The doorbell sounded a minute later.

He opened the door with a cheery "Bonjour, entrez," automatically assuming his French teacher persona — a jovial bonhomie combined with intellectual other-worldliness, which he had unconsciously copied from a favourite lecturer from his student days. She stood there for a moment as though posing till he had taken a mental photograph of her. She was dressed in a rather worn dark jacket, tight faded jeans and purple boots. Her face was slender and elf-like and framed by a tangle of wavy auburn hair. He had the impression that a few years before she must have been strikingly pretty, but they were the sort of looks that fade quickly as the skin loses its glow and its tightness over light bones. There were already tiny wrinkles where once there would have been the smooth, silky skin of a film starlet, and she wore no make-up to hide them. Was this laziness, ruthless honesty or some form of spiritual asceticism? He was still trying to figure her out.

She shook hands, walked in past him and sat down in the chair reserved for pupils. She slipped off her light jacket in the same movement and hung it over the back of her chair. She made herself at home quite casually, since she had been coming there every Friday for the last three months and their relationship was easy-going and familiar. If they had been in France he would have called her *tu* already, but the exact nuance of this would be lost on the English and he didn't want it interpreted as a sexual advance. He was paranoid about violating the norms of a more puritanical and reserved culture, or even being accused of sexual harassment in the motherland of militant feminism. He contemplated her slim, neat figure as he sat down on the chair opposite.

"Can we speak English for a bit?" she said unexpectedly. "I need to tell you something."

"Sure. You can correct me for a change."

He wondered if she was going to announce the end of her visits, a move to another city or abroad. He felt a slight tension, as though readying himself for a sinking feeling of disappointment.

"Something has happened that has rather scared me and I don't know too many people I can tell," she said awkwardly, as though embarrassed. "I need your advice, but I hope I can trust you not to tell anyone else without asking me first."

"This is all rather intriguing," he said, somewhat relieved not to be losing her as a student. He had begun to enjoy the yoga, mainly for the opportunity it afforded to watch her adopt various improbable postures that showed off her sylph-like figure to advantage. "Of course you can trust me and I'll help you in any way I can."

He studied her. She looked a little agitated, which was unusual for her. He knew nothing about her private life and it both surprised and flattered him that she saw him as somebody she could confide in. He had just assumed that she was well-integrated into one of London's myriad but impenetrable social circles, with hosts of friends, and that he was a very peripheral figure in her life.

"I thought of you because you once told me you used to be an aikido teacher," she said.

"Yes, one of my high school teachers was an aikido black belt and persuaded me to try it and I got hooked. I taught it to kids to help pay my way through university. It's not an aggressive sport, because it uses the momentum of the opponent."

He felt he was prattling on, as if trying to justify his mastery of a martial art that she might disapprove of. Then he realized she wasn't really listening. He wondered why she had brought that subject up. A thought struck him.

"Camilla, you're not in some sort of danger, are you?" He tried to make it sound like a joke.

"I don't know. Not yet, but I could be in the future." She looked serious. "I'm thinking of doing something a bit dangerous."

"Really? Tell me about it."

She hesitated, as if pondering the best way to begin.

"I think I mentioned," she said slowly, "that I have a website and web-forum."

"Yes, something to do with child abuse. A support for victims, you said."

"The Paedophile Files. People write in who have been victims of sexual abuse as children and ask for advice about going to the police and so on. I sometimes meet them to talk about their cases." She paused. "I may not have told you but I went through something of that sort myself when I was young."

"I'm really sorry," he said, not knowing quite what else to say. He wanted to touch her hand or arm but wasn't sure how an English girl would take this. He had suspected something of the sort lay behind her interest in this subject — as well as the subdued, oddly melancholy character she had, as if she was living her life under a shadow.

"That's all a long time ago now, but this case I've just stumbled on is something a bit frightening."

"Tell me everything from the beginning."

She took a deep breath and began to tell her story.

The previous week she had received a disturbing message on her website, The Paedophile Files. It came from a young Ukrainian woman called Ekaterina, who suspected that her son had been abducted. The woman's story, sketchily told, seemed dramatic enough for Camilla to agree to meet her. She was not disappointed.

Ekaterina was a good-looking, willowy blonde of thirty-one. She had arrived in England at the age of twenty, on a visa to visit a man she had met on an internet dating site. In the flesh she did not find him attractive enough to marry or even to go on seeing, so she left him. She overstayed her visa, went underground and became a freelance domestic cleaner. One of her clients was a Middle Eastern businessman, who lived alone in a house in St John's Wood. One day while she was cleaning, the man dragged her into the bedroom and raped her. She fled the house in tears. She did not go to the police because she feared deportation for being in the country illegally. But the man owed her money, which she desperately needed to pay her rent, so she went back to see him, taking care to carry a knife in her jacket pocket in case he attacked her again. He said he would only pay her if she had sex with him, and then he grabbed her and tried to tear her clothes off. She pulled out the knife, and when he tried to take it off her they fought. She stabbed him twenty-six times in a frenzy of fear and hatred. She explained tearfully to Camilla that once she started stabbing him she couldn't stop, because she had to break free of this horrible bloody spectre that was still holding onto her and trying to strangle her. She ran out of the house but was seen leaving and was tracked down days later by the police. She was unable to prove her story of rape, which the prosecutor poured scorn on. Why hadn't she gone to the police? Her English was too poor to explain herself in a convincing way and the court interpreter was incompetent, she said. She was sentenced to eighteen years for what the judge described as a particularly vicious murder.

She was sent to Holloway Prison where the medical staff discovered she was pregnant. They tried to persuade her to have an abortion, but she adamantly refused. She had moral objections, partly because she was a Catholic, like many western Ukrainians from provinces that used to belong to Poland — in fact her mother was Polish-speaking. Even though it was the baby of her rapist (she did not have a boyfriend) she saw it as innocent and not deserving death. They told her it was cruel to have a baby that she would not be allowed to keep, but she replied that her baby was the only living thing that needed her and she was not going to kill it. Then they tried to persuade her to give the baby up for adoption immediately after birth, but again she refused. When she was due to give birth they moved her to a mother-and-baby unit in Bronzefield Prison in Surrey, which had just opened. The baby was a boy and she was allowed to keep him with her for eighteen months, but then he was taken away from her. He was given to a couple for adoption, but after five years the couple split up. The wife became depressive and finally committed suicide, so the boy ended up in a care home. Someone in the care home traced Ekaterina and let her know, and this gave her something to live for. Her early release half-way through her sentence was refused as punishment for her "lack of cooperation", and for other conflicts she had with the prison authorities (she would not admit her guilt but insisted she had acted in self-defence, which was seen as a lack of remorse — she also had several fights in prison, which she again claimed were in self-defence.) She was only let out after eleven years.

She tried to find her son, but the children's home he had been sent to had been closed down six months before and the children transferred elsewhere. After knocking at many bureaucratic doors, she was told her son had been moved to a care home in Birmingham, and was given the address. But when she went to the home to see him, the director told her the boy had run away ten days before. She demanded to know the circumstances and was told he had run away while on an outing with a benefactor of the home, who often took the children out on excursions. She asked for the name of the benefactor and was at last, with much reluctance, told it was Mr Cyril Jones, the local Member of Parliament. Ekaterina tried to telephone Mr Jones but was unable to speak to him. She went to his house in Birmingham and three times to his flat in London, but could never find him in. Ekaterina wondered if Camilla could help her to talk to Jones and get some idea of what might have happened to her son. She was afraid he had been abducted by a paedophile ring, because he would not have run away knowing his mother was due to be released, and she was sure he was a timid boy, not at all wild or turbulent.

Camilla was alarmed by this story because of the rumours that had circulated some years before about Cyril Jones's paedophile tendencies. He was a larger-than-life figure in more ways than one. He was incredibly fat, weighing a hundred and eighty kilos, and he had a no-nonsense manner and a boisterous sense of humour that made him popular among ordinary voters. He was born in a Birmingham slum and grew up in poverty, not knowing his father. He moneyed his working-class background and ready tongue into a political career, first as a Labour councillor, then switching to the Liberals when they became a viable force. He came out as gay as soon as it was not only legal but politically trendy to do so, and lived with his mother till she died. This apparent filial piety, as well as his down-to-earth, forthright manner, endeared him to the locals and ensured his election to parliament for the recently formed Liberal Democrat Party. In the meantime he founded the youth charity, Other Relations, to help children in care, and was a great visitor of children's homes. He was given an OBE by the Queen for his services to youth after his second term in parliament. It was at the moment of the award that rumours surfaced about his odd behaviour with boys. It was alleged that he had spanked boys in care homes on their bare bottoms. A number of his parliamentary colleagues sprang to his defence. A Senior Politician laughed off the spanking story as something harmless — "no worse than what went on in my day in every boarding school in the country!" This dismissal of the accusation was almost like a signal to the authorities. All inquiries into paedophile allegations against Cyril Jones were from then on mysteriously dropped. It was as if the OBE and the public defence of him by a Senior Politician had sealed his respectability forever and made him untouchable.

Camilla promised Ekaterina that she would do what she could to help her find her son. Ekaterina had nowhere to live after coming out of prison with almost no money. She was staying in doss-houses and squats of fortune. She didn't dare ask for state help because she was afraid she might be deported from the country, unless she could prove she was living with her British-born son again, even though she couldn't find him and the authorities were doing nothing to help her do so. Camilla found her a place to stay in a shelter for battered women, whose director she knew. Ekaterina could be of use to them as an interpreter for immigrant women, since she spoke Ukrainian, Russian and Polish, and had earned a degree in psychology from the Open University while in prison.

A few days after meeting her, Camilla went on impulse to an art exhibition showing an installation called *Boy in Formaldehyde*. When she read about it, it struck her as something so revolting that she instinctively linked it with child abuse and went along to check it out. She was disturbed by what she saw. The figure of a boy swimming in a glass tank of what was said to be formaldehyde looked uncannily real. Of course the other visitors to the gallery joked about it and assured one another it couldn't possibly be an actual dead boy. She took photos of it from all angles. Because she was shocked that any artist could create something in such bad taste she put some of the photos on her website, with a long diatribe about the trivialization of violence to children, and how shocking this piece of pseudo-art was. This was paedophile art, she claimed, and on the macabre level of a snuff movie. The next day Ekaterina came to see her in a terrible state. She had gone on Camilla's website at the battered women's shelter and seen the photos. She claimed the boy looked like her son. Camilla showed her the other photos she had taken. One in particular revealed a mole on the boy's arm which Ekaterina swore was a birthmark she had seen on her baby. Her son had also sent her a photo of himself a year before and the resemblance was striking, even if the face of the boy in the installation was partly hidden by the green-tinted diving mask.

"Are you going to go to the police?" asked Romain, disturbed by this story.

"I want to," said Camilla hesitantly, "but I'm not sure that's the best option. You see, this is supposedly a work of art, so they'll have lawyers arguing it can't be destroyed to see if the body is a real body or not. They'll solemnly declare it isn't and demand to know what evidence there is to the contrary. That might put Ekaterina in danger. Above all they might just whisk it away and make it disappear into some private collection. And the police would be too bloody slow and hampered by rules to stop them doing it."

"So, what's the alternative?"

"I need to have more evidence first to force the police to act — to seize this work and examine it. I want to find out more about the artist who made this monstrosity, what sort of person he is, and who his friends and acquaintances are. I also want to look at the other end, how the boy disappeared, who saw him last. If it was Cyril Jones, I want to track down any contacts between Jones and this artist."

"But that's police work you're wanting to do," objected Romain, frowning.

"But I don't trust the police to do it without giving the game away. There's a long history of Cyril Jones being protected by the police or people higher up. Someone in the police may warn him or even block the investigation. I want to dig so far into this that they won't be able to cover it up again." Her face showed grim determination. "This is investigative journalist's work. But I'm just a bit scared, that's all. I'm worried these people might be violent."

"So, that's where I come in — with my aikido?" Romain mused, with a half smile. She evidently wanted something more from him than mere advice. "Look, what you need by the sound of it is somebody who walks around with a pistol under his jacket, not a guy who can throw people on the ground."

"Then that would mean leaving it to the police. Even private detectives can't carry guns here." She looked at him with a slight air of reproach. "All I need is someone to watch my back and stop me being beaten up. I don't think guns or murder would ever come into it."

"If they've killed somebody, it's always worth killing again to cover it up. As well be hanged for a sheep as a lamb, isn't that the expression?" He was pleased that he had come out with an English proverb at the appropriate moment. "In French we say: *Qui vole un oeuf, vole un boeuf.* Anyone who steals an egg will steal a —."

He couldn't think of the word.

"A beef, a big bull castrated at birth. An oxen — an ox!" he cried triumphantly. He thought she might appreciate getting a few crumbs of a French lesson after all, but it didn't seem to have worked. She looked at him blankly. "It rhymes in French," he explained lamely. *"Qui vole un oeuf, vole un boeuf."* A look of impatience crossed her face.

"So you won't help me?" she said, with marked disappointment in her voice.

He perceived in this tone and attitude the eternal threat on the part of the attractive female not just to withdraw her affection or friendship but in addition to cancel all possibility, however remote, that there might one day, perhaps in some future life, on another planet, be something romantic between them. Even if this remote possibility had never been frankly dangled in front of him as a carrot, its abrupt and definitive withdrawal was being used quite clearly as a rather nasty stick.

"I didn't say that," he said hastily, clinging to the departing train of the romantic possibility. "I just need to know what you have in mind."

She stared at him severely, daring him to be insincere in his holding out of hope.

"I want to go back to the gallery and ask a few more questions, and then I want to pay a visit to that artist. And to the care home the boy was in. I want you to come with me. Moral support. A man's presence. That's all. For the moment."

His gaze fell on her hand, a rather pretty hand, which had formed a tight little fist on the table, betraying a certain tension. He had an odd feeling this decision might be a turning-point in his life. He could not refuse, but he was still wary about what he was letting himself in for.

"In that case, I think I could probably give my provisional accord to accompany you on that kind of limited mission," he said judiciously, stroking his chin slowly with a finger and thumb, in a parody of a politician making a commitment with extreme caution to bomb an underdeveloped country, while explicitly ruling out mission creep and ground forces. He was not sure this attempt at deadpan comedy had worked or even been noticed. It was part of the French male's self-deprecating humour to pretend to be more cowardly than he really was, but he wondered if the exquisite modesty of this would be appreciated by an Englishwoman, or if he was merely cutting a rather sorry figure in her eyes.

"Of course, I wouldn't want to talk you into doing something you don't really want to do," she said, with a hint of mockery that revealed a certain pique. "If you think it might be dangerous. I realize it is a bit of a cheek on my part asking you, but I just thought you might enjoy the adventure. And it would get you out to do something in the real world, saving widows and orphans, instead of sitting like a potato in front of a computer all day. But if you're not all that keen, please don't let me pressure you."

This had a slightly barbed tone that made it sound more like a threat to withdraw the request than an assurance of his liberty to refuse it.

"I don't feel pressured in the least, let me assure you. And I'm actually far keener than I might appear." He decided to counter her mockery with his own irony. "I didn't want to make any unseemly Latin displays of enthusiasm but I was indeed attracted to the idea of saving widows and orphans. I have so few opportunities on an average day. My only worry is that I'll become so absorbed by this adventure that I'll neglect my writing activities entirely."

"But it'll give you something to write about," she countered archly. "Writers should get out more. If you spend your life sitting writing, all you can write about is spending your life sitting writing."

"I had noticed a certain circularity creeping into my inspiration," he conceded. "You've explained it very succinctly. I think it's one of the weaknesses of many modern novelists. Not enough time out in the world. They sit in their monkish cells scribbling about sitting in their monkish cells scribbling. All of modernism and postmodernism has the disease. Painters no longer paint the world. They paint the act of painting. Composers seem to be hearing sound for the first time and wondering how hideous it can be made to be. It's a kind of return to origins, which is always circular. Art has disappeared up its own backside."

"Well, I'm glad that's settled," she said. She seemed slightly confused by the aesthetic and philosophical dimensions this had taken on.

"So, what are we going to do first?" He decided to put on a show of the eagerness which he had apparently been found wanting in until now, and which seemed to be *de rigueur* when embarking on adventures of this kind. "The gallery? I want to see this horrible thing."

"Yes, the gallery," she said brightly, as if only now grasping that he was in fact on board.

"When?"

"What are you doing now?"

"Nothing. I've reserved these two hours for you. The French lesson, the yoga."

"So, let's talk French on the way there."

"And we'll do yoga on the way back?" He stood up. "In the Tube? Do we take the Tube? I want to do yoga on the Tube. Perhaps they will give us money."

She smiled broadly at last and then laughed outright at him and touched his arm in a gesture that would have been a playful punch if she had not lost the habit of familiarity. He felt his shares had suddenly risen and the day ahead looked full of promise.

3

In the Underground as they sat side by side he said to her in French:

"What are we trying to find out by this visit? You've already photographed this thing. The next step surely is to take this woman, Ekaterina, to see it."

"No, she'll make too much of a fuss, I'm sure, and they may panic and take it away. We want to find out more about the artist, discreetly. I want to meet him, and find out where he lives so we can watch him."

"He's not likely to be there, is he? And will they give out his address?"

"I don't know. It depends. If we show real interest. Do you think I should pose as a journalist and ask to interview him? I mean, I am a journalist. Sort of. I could ask about the materials he used, and so on."

"If he has something to hide, will he be willing to talk about it? It's better to pretend to be a buyer. Then his greed may take over." An idea struck him. "Do you think I should pose as a buyer? Or maybe say I have a cousin who could be interested in buying it, a cousin with a château in France?"

"Yes, that might work," she said, suddenly interested.

"I should have dressed better, maybe in a suit."

"No, you look fine, the bohemian look, this is a relaxed milieu."

"Maybe I should have a business card made: International Dealer in Art Works."

"No, that would look pretentious and therefore phoney. The real thing never looks it."

"Anyway, I could be the poor cousin, trying to make a buck as an intermediary for my rich cousin, the moneyed branch of the family."

"Exactly."

"By the way, I think we should use *tu* with each other. It'll sound more natural, if we are partners, in any sense of the word."

"All right. Where is this château, in case he asks?"

"In the Bordeaux region. Near St Emilion. The castle dates from the fifteenth century, though most of it is sixteenth. It's been in the Lagarde family since the late seventeenth, when the previous owners, who were Protestant, fled to Geneva after the Revocation of the Edict of Nantes. Montesquieu stayed there. In earlier times Montaigne visited — he lived just a few kilometres away. They will have heard of Montaigne and Montesquieu, no?"

"They are names to conjure with, even in England — or at least to drop at dinner parties."

"My cousin became interested in collecting art to attract visitors so they would buy his wine. You see, his vineyard doesn't produce a *Premier Grand Cru Classé*, just a *Grand Cru Classé*, one of over sixty in the region of St Emilion. But if the wine isn't all that exceptional the castle certainly is, and people love to visit it. He uses it for entertaining. It has a ballroom the size of a tennis court. In fact it used to be a tennis court. For real tennis. The indoor version. The Prince of Condé played there. The first castle on the spot was built by Englishmen, during the time Aquitaine belonged to the English crown. In fact Eleanor of Aquitaine and Henry the Second of England slept there, but that was in the old castle, destroyed by the Black Prince in the Hundred Years' War."

"Is any of this true?" she asked in amazement.

"What do you mean? The castle is imaginary. So of course it is true."

"And what's his name, this cousin?"

"Henri de Lagarde, Comte de Mayne. There's some obscure connection with the Duc de Maine, illegitimate son of Louis the Fourteenth, but I've never been able to follow what it is. The name Mayne is found all over the St Emilion region."

She laughed in delight.

"But where does all this stuff come from? Are you making it up as you go along?"

"I lived in Bordeaux for two years. I visited a lot of vineyards. And I was fascinated by the history of the region."

"And how much of this is factual?"

"Who cares? Will they have an encyclopaedia to check? Even looking up Wikipedia on a smartphone will take them too long. History is just a good story well told. Whatever sticks in the mind becomes the truth. That's how Hollywood rewrites the past."

They got out at the Aldgate East Underground station. When they emerged she led the way along the street, pausing to look for street signs, as she couldn't quite remember the way. It was a fine spring day and summer was already in the air.

"One of the appalling failings of many European cities," he pontificated, like an Enlightenment philosopher out for a walk, "is the lack of signs with street names. In some cities you can walk three blocks before you can see what street you're on. In a car it's impossible. Three-quarters of urban accidents are caused by drivers looking for street names."

"Is that true?"

"Of course not. It's a statistic. You invent them. They are figures of speech."

"Nowadays it matters less, people have satellite navigators."

"The other one quarter are caused by people looking at their satellite navigators. They could reduce accidents and revive growth and employment all over Europe with a huge project to put up street signs every thirty metres."

"Come on, not a single local worker would be employed. They'd import half a million immigrants to do it at half the wage. Then they'd all stay on and go on the dole and demand housing subsidies. It would bankrupt the country." She waved her hand at their surroundings as she set a brisk pace up the street. "You should be looking at all this. It's fascinating. It's the East End. Do you know it? It was traditionally working class. Slums. Brothels. Gangs of cutthroats. Then waves of immigrants arrived. Russian Jews. Now Asians. And now from being a colourful slum it's suddenly become trendy, arty, and cool — in short, yuppy territory. Full of new, cutting edge art galleries. Up there is the old Spitalfields Market."

"So it's like the new Camden Town?"

"No," she said scornfully, "Camden Town is old counter-culture, third-hand biker jackets, vegan restaurants and tattoo shops — you ought to know, you live above one. This is arty cool, not hippie cool. You have to get your cools right."

She turned abruptly down a side street, and then another, and finally they came to the elegant, wrought-iron sign of the Grafton Gallery. They stopped. Beyond the paintings in the window they could see a crowd of people inside. She glanced at Romain with a flicker of nerves, wondering if he was really up for this.

He smiled at her coolly and said with bravado: "I'm sure this will be just cousin Henri's cup of tea." He pushed the door open.

They walked into a large white room with a dozen or more people in it. A balding man sat at a desk near the front and raised one eyebrow in their direction. They nodded as though they were habitués. There was a collection of pictures on two walls. Closer inspection revealed they were a series of photographs of young men's buttocks, with close-ups of their genitalia in various states. Some of these anatomical parts looked very small as if they might belong to children. This was apparently Bendigo's earlier work which had made his sulphurous reputation as an artist on the edge. In the middle of the room, on a three foot-high white base, stood the large glass tank which housed his new work.

It had a small sign below it: "Full Fathom Five, or Boy in Formaldehyde". Romain puzzled over the first title, till Camilla explained the reference to Shakespeare's play, *The Tempest*. She pointed out that in the play it was not the boy but his father who was thought to have drowned.

"That could be a clue," said Romain, without quite knowing why.

It was certainly a striking image, the young underwater swimmer heading upward at a shallow angle towards the surface. It looked to Romain disturbingly like a real body. The boy's skin was white and his hair was dark brown, so it seemed quite plausible that this was the offspring of a blonde Slavic mother and a Middle Eastern father. The other people gathered around it seemed unsure what to make of it and commented to each other in low murmurs. One young man in punk clothes with a ring through one eyebrow stamped mischievously on the wooden floor near the tank to make the water ripple slightly, causing the body to waver a tiny bit. There were grim smiles at the macabre effect, but also frowns, and he didn't repeat his prank. Romain took out his smartphone and took a few photos. The body looked frail and pathetic — not a water-sprite, he thought, but a child in danger of drowning. He peered at the texture of the skin. It seemed to his eye to have one or two tiny hairs on the lower left calf and on the right forearm as if they had been missed in some depilation process. He pointed them out to Camilla in French. She did not understand *poils* so he showed her the back of his hand and discreetly pulled at the little hairs on it.

"Remarkable realism," he murmured, smiling for the benefit of the other patrons.

Nobody else offered a word of conversation and they all seemed rather subdued. Feeling emboldened, Romain murmured to Camilla in French: "Shall we try to buy it for my cousin?" He jerked his head towards the balding man at the desk.

She nodded. He led the way across the expanse of polished wooden floor towards the desk. The man was in his fifties, with aquiline features and a high forehead sloping back towards a bald dome, bordered by a ruff of curly grey hair. He was reading some sort of catalogue and glanced up questioningly as they approached.

"Good afternoon, sir," said Romain, exaggerating his French accent very slightly.

"Good afternoon, can I help you?"

"We were wondering if this installation is for sale."

"Ah. At some stage it certainly will be, but we haven't yet —." The man seemed rather embarrassed, even amused. "Of course, the price will be rather high."

"Yes, I couldn't afford it myself, I'm sure," laughed Romain. "But I have a cousin, the Comte de Mayne, who is an art collector. I know his tastes very well. I don't think price will be an issue for him."

"Well, I could definitely talk to the artist and see what he says."

"Could we have his co-ordinates? His phone number, how to contact him."

"His contact details? I'm afraid I don't have Mr Bendigo's permission to give them out. It might be better if you would leave your phone number, which I could then transmit to him."

"Certainly. I don't have a card, but do you have a pen?"

"Of course."

The man handed him the pen lying on his desk, and indicated a sheet of paper. There was already one name and phone number on it, so he quickly turned it over. Romain wrote his name, adding an aristocratic "de" before the surname, and his mobile phone number. As the man studied these details, Romain suddenly felt inspired to go further in his little imposture.

"Would you be so kind as to tell the artist that if this work is not for sale, or has already been sold, my cousin might be interested in commissioning a similar one? Perhaps with one or two modifications. I'm not sure he would appreciate the diving mask. And he would prefer a boy a year or two older, with rather longer, flowing hair, maybe blond hair. And the swimming costume, it is perhaps a little superfluous, a little British in its ... how shall we say... modesty? My cousin is a believer in naturism, and like that the boy would seem more like a — how do you say, *lutin*? Elf! Yes, an elf. Like our petrol company!" He laughed quietly at his own joke.

"Yes, well that is very interesting," said the balding man, his eyes widening, it was not clear whether in interest or alarm. "Very interesting, indeed! I shall transmit what you have said to the artist, and I am sure he will be in touch. If he is interested."

"Good. My cousin is a great admirer of British art. He acquired two Hirsts and a Koons some years ago. He likes to discover artists who are about to become ... unaffordable."

"And your cousin's name again?" He had been scribbling notes and lifted the pen briefly as though about to jot it down.

"Ah, if you don't mind, I prefer to be discreet," said Romain coyly. "I will provide his name and title when I know the artist is interested in selling. I am sure you will appreciate the reasons. We don't want names bandied about to inflate interest — and prices."

"Of course," said the man, biting his lip. He was clearly racking his brain trying to remember the name Romain had already let drop.

"Thank you for transmitting my message. I will be in London for another five days at that number — after that I shall be travelling and it may be more difficult to arrange a meeting."

He held out his hand to the balding man and shook hands with all the vigour the French put into this ceremony. Camilla felt she should do the same, and the man half rose and even gave a slight bow over her hand as if he assumed she was French as well.

They walked out with a suitable swagger in their stride. Romain opened the door for her with a Gallic flourish. They strolled along the street back the way they had come. Only when they were round the first corner did Camilla double up laughing and punch him on the chest in admiration.

"You were incredible! You're a natural! You should have been an actor!"

"Or a spy," he said coolly. "I suspect I missed my calling as a secret agent. If only I had lived during the war, or even the Cold War. Alas, it is the epoch that makes the man."

"Do you think he'll contact you?"

"There is a very good chance. He would be a fool not to if he wants to make any money. These artists spend their lives exhibiting things and apart from a few lucky ones, whose personal lunacy happens to correspond to the fashionable madness of the times, most of them sell only a few works for peanuts. Like us writers."

"Do you think he'll bite at the idea of commissioning a second one?"

"Why not? How many fish and animals has Hirst put in formaldehyde? Artists today like to have a signature work which they keep repeating, reproducing, in endless copies and variations so people remember who they are. And also so they can sell some to private buyers while having others in museums. It's like a brand. It goes right through Modernism. Think of Rothko. Always two big sheets of colour, one above the other. And he made dozens upon dozens of variations by changing the colours. Or Giacometti: rough-cast stick-figures that are ludicrously thin. Again, dozens of them, almost identical. You see an absurd stick-figure, you know it's a Giacometti. Bendigo will be the artist of boys in formaldehyde. Paedophile art, as you called it. He has already specialized in juvenile pricks and arses. This is really his line."

"And he won't be suspicious?"

"Why would he be suspicious that someone else shares his own tastes? He will think it's normal, because he thinks he is normal. That's the thing about perverts. They all think they are normal."

They walked on towards the Tube station.

4

Ekaterina found the battered women's shelter a rather depressing place. It was full of women having crises, crying, talking endlessly or sitting in deep depression, nursing their bruises. It reminded her too much of prison. Her interpreting skills were not needed that afternoon (the Polish woman had left and the Russian-speaking Latvian had talked herself out that morning) so she told the Irishwoman who ran the place, Maeve, she was going out for a walk. The battered women's shelter was in Bayswater, just off Queensway, next to a rather tired Greek restaurant called the Elysium. It was only a few minutes' walk from Kensington Gardens, which is where she now headed.

She walked through this park nearly every day in order to go anywhere and she always enjoyed it. She was used to walking everywhere as Maeve couldn't afford to pay her — she only gave her a bed and meals (and the odd ten-pound note as pocket money, twice so far) in exchange for what was seen as volunteer work. This meant she couldn't afford the buses or the Underground, which now had a system where you could no longer pay for just one journey — you had to have a day pass which cost five pounds. Her last ten pound note hadn't gone very far (shampoo, soap, deodorant and knickers) and she had only fifty pence left in her pocket. But she was a good walker and could walk for hours, so she felt all of central London was within her reach. She loved walking. She felt she could never have enough of seeing new sights and scenery, after the long immobilization and theft of her life. It was as if the perpetual motion of her body could make up for the frozen years and the lost time. All she needed to keep walking all afternoon was free water and a free toilet, and both of these were available in the many museums that had free admission. She knew where they all were.

She made a beeline across the park for the Victoria and Albert, one of her favourites. She remembered it from the many hours she had spent there as a penniless illegal immigrant of twenty, taking advantage of free museums to give herself an education in art and history. The man she had met on the Slavic Romance site, who had paid for her flight to London and her visa, had taken her there on one of their first outings. He was a kind man who respected her scrupulously, but he was fifty-two and she was twenty, and he was not a fascinating adventurer with an exciting life who might have made her forget the age gap but a lonely, sad insurance agent, living in a small terraced house in Dulwich. Later on, fellow prisoners told her she should have married him and then divorced him after she got her papers, but that was not something she could do. So instead she left him an apologetic note and disappeared from his house while he was at work. She rented a bed in a cheap hostel and found work as a cleaner within a few days. Then after three months, just when her life seemed to be settling into a routine, it turned into a nightmare of rape and murder. How she regretted her insurance agent during those eleven years behind bars! He had even come to visit her a few times, alerted by the reports of the case in the newspapers. But after a while he told her sadly that he didn't have enough good years left to wait for her, and he stopped coming.

As she crossed the park she breathed in the mild spring air with childlike pleasure and admired the bright green of the grass and the leaves, which looked so young and fresh. It was a sunny day and the birds were singing gaily as if glad to be alive. It made her feel her youth was not yet over and life still held possibilities for her, in spite of the way it had gone so far. She walked quickly, not pausing to examine any of the statues or monuments in the park, as she knew them by heart. She avoided looking at the Peter Pan statue because it reminded her of her son and made her sad. She glanced in bafflement at the ugly sculpture on the other side of the pond, a huge arch that was crippled and bent like an old man, and looked like the thing you put on an ox to pull a cart. Then she went past three old arches in the distance, temples built for a queen, said the signs, but she thought they looked like dog kennels. Next came the Serpentine art gallery, which she steered clear of, because it was always filled with hideous, stupid pieces of modern art which depressed her. At the very end she came to the Albert Memorial. The gold statue was impressive, under what looked like the porch of an old church, and it had lots of statues around it of people she didn't know, but the whole thing looked elegant and solemn as if it expressed deep emotions. She glanced at it with a slight feeling of nostalgia for the past and recalled the heartbreak of the old widowed queen. Then she walked out the gate and down Exhibition Road.

When she went into the imposing, venerable edifice of the Victoria and Albert Museum she felt like a little girl visiting an enchanted castle. Everything was old and beautiful and rare, and yet she was allowed to see it all — and all for free and for as long as she wanted. She had two favourite places she always went to, but she went towards them slowly, looking at everything else on the way, like a child saving an ice cream for as long as possible. One was the Cast Courts, where there were replicas of famous statues like Michelangelo's David and the most impressive columns she had ever seen — Trajan's column from Rome, cut in halves to fit it in under the roof. She visited that first, and stood below gazing up at it in wonder that people so long ago had built something so huge and magnificent. Then she admired the famous Michelangelo statues and the fabulous golden doors from Florence, covered with fine sculptures of biblical stories, which she tried to guess. She couldn't imagine paradise having more beautiful doors. She dreamed of going to Italy and seeing the originals of all the works on display here. Perhaps one day she would. After she had walked around for a while admiring everything, she made her way to her second favourite place.

This was the mediaeval section, where there were religious statues of Christ and the Virgin. She walked among them respectfully as if she was in church. Then she found what she was looking for. It was a statue of Mary carrying her baby. But unlike the ones next to it where the baby was sitting on the palm of her hand in a way no woman could possibly hold a baby (only a man could, as a woman's arm was not strong enough), this one was holding her baby on her hip. She looked like a peasant girl in her teens and her body was curved like a bow as she thrust out her hip to the side and balanced the baby on it, exactly the way any real girl does. She looked kind and open and good-natured, and Ekaterina had always liked her. She even thought she resembled her a bit. The inscription said the statue was Norman, and she liked to think this Virgin was a Norman girl. She knew the Normans were descended from Vikings, like the Ukrainians, who traced their ancestors back to Rurik, the Swedish Viking who founded Novgorod, and his son Oleg, who founded Kiev as the first capital of Russia. She felt this gave her something in common with this girl. Perhaps this Norman Virgin would look kindly on another girl of Viking descent and help her find her baby, who had been taken away from her. She would know how it felt to lose a child. Ekaterina prayed to her for a moment and asked for her help, as if she was in church, and then she made the sign of the cross and turned away. She was sure this Norman Virgin would do her best to help her, if her son was still alive.

The shadow of what might have happened to Viktor fell over her again. She tried to forget it by walking through the Chinese and Indian sections, but even these exotic statues couldn't distract her. When she came out (after a stop in the toilet for some water) she thought of visiting the Grafton Gallery and confronting the horror that she had nightmares about — her son in a tank of formaldehyde. But she didn't have the courage to do it alone. She knew she would break down or make a scene and begin shouting. She might get arrested and sent back to prison. Anyway it was in the East End, too far away even for her to walk, and she had no money for a bus. Instead she walked down Brompton Road and Sloane Avenue towards that other place that obsessed her. Pimlico, where Cyril Jones had his flat. She had a small creased map in her pocket but she didn't need to consult it as she knew the way from having walked it several times already. It was a pleasant walk through the prosperous streets of Chelsea, and after that she came to the Thames and walked along Grosvenor Road.

The weather was warm for May and there was less wind than usual along the river bank. Seagulls were swooping over the river and made it feel like summer. Pimlico, she thought, was an odd combination of large, ugly blocks of flats in hideous brown brick and long rows of pillared white stucco houses of three or four storeys in a much grander style. Wilmot Street, where Cyril Jones had his flat, was built in the latter style. The houses were even more imposing than those on the elegant St George's Square, which she had to go through to get to it. She walked slowly along the street till she came to Jones's house and stared up at it. She stood to one side of the pillar-flanked entrance just in case his huge figure emerged from it. She supposed he went to the House of Commons by chauffeur-driven car, since he was certainly too fat to walk there. What hours he kept she had no idea. How often did members of parliament go to the House and at what times? She couldn't imagine it was a nine-to-five job. More like two-to-six, she thought, with a few hours propping up bars afterwards. She made a mental note to look up the daily timetable of parliamentary sessions on the internet.

She wondered next where his car was kept. There were no cars parked on the street. The row of white stucco houses was unbroken, and there were no vehicle entrances leading below ground. So perhaps the chauffeur brought the car around from a garage on another street, and Jones had to come out the front door to get in. There was a chance then that she would see him coming out or going in. She wondered what she would do if she saw him. Should she accost him, demand to speak to him, even make a scandal in the street to draw attention to her story? Perhaps that was the best thing to do in England. Nothing was done unless the press got hold of an affair and blew it up.

She had walked about forty metres past the house and had just turned round to stroll back towards it again, wondering if she should ring the bell, when a car came along the street and stopped in front of it. She quickened her pace so as to get a look at the occupants. A man got out of the back door, as if it were a taxi, though it wasn't, and he was followed by a boy of about fourteen. The man held his arm firmly and led him up the five steps to the porch of Jones's building, with its white neo-classical pillars. The car pulled away again and drove past her. She walked quickly towards the two figures standing at the top of the steps in front of the door, evidently waiting for it to open.

"Excuse me," she called out. "Do you know Mr Cyril Jones?"

The man turned and glared at her. He was nearing forty, good-looking in a hard, somewhat thuggish way, with black hair swept up in a retro Elvis style. He was well-built and fit-looking, and wore a black leather jacket and jeans with a large metal belt buckle.

"Never heard of him. Who wants to know?"

"Yes, you have," said the boy unexpectedly. He spoke slowly as if slightly dazed. "That's the man we're going to see."

"Keep your trap shut!" snapped the man and tugged the boy's arm viciously.

"Ow!" said the boy. "You're hurting!" He was a very good-looking boy with longish blond hair and he sounded vaguely foreign. He reminded Ekaterina of the boy in *Death in Venice*, which her insurance agent had taken her to see at the National Film Theatre.

"I've told you not to talk to strangers," the man growled.

Some instinct made her talk to the boy in Ukrainian, asking if he spoke it, and then in Polish. He answered the Polish question with a yes. She told him in Polish, the language of her mother:

"This is a very bad man. You are going to be raped and then killed. Run away! Now!"

"Stop jabbering at the boy and get lost, you witch!" said the man menacingly.

Suddenly the door opened. A huge fat man stood there. She had never seen Cyril Jones in the flesh but she had seen photos of him in the papers and knew this was him.

"Run!" she yelled at the boy in Polish. At the same time she rushed up the steps and poked the thuggish man in the face with her fingers extended, aiming at his eyes. It hurt her fingers, but it hurt him more and he flinched and raised a hand to one eye.

"Fuck! She's blinded me, the bitch!"

The boy managed to squirm loose and he ran past her down the steps and headed down the street.

"After him!" bellowed Cyril Jones.

The man in the leather jacket shoved her aside and dashed after the boy. The boy was running unsteadily, as if not in his right state of mind, and his pursuer caught him fifty metres down the street. Meanwhile Cyril Jones stepped out the door and seized Ekaterina by the wrist. His grip was as strong as that of a gorilla.

"Who are you, you bitch?"

"Where is Viktor, where is my son, Viktor? What have you done with him?" she screamed in his face, and tried to jab him in the eyes as well. It was a tactic eleven years in a prison full of drug dealers and violent psychopaths had taught her — how to use her long arms, strong from playing volleyball, to make up for her slender build. Cyril Jones fended off her jabs, using his huge bulk to keep his face out of reach, and he held tight to her right wrist with his other hand. She could only jab with her left arm, which was not her best. She tried to kick him in the knee, but it had no effect as she was wearing soft trainers.

The other man came back with the boy, twisting his arm and cuffing him into submission. Ekaterina, furious that he had caught the boy, tried to fly at him again, but Cyril Jones dragged her back.

"You're a madwoman! Get lost!" he yelled. He shoved her violently away from him and let her go so that she stumbled down the steps and fell hard on the pavement, hurting her knees and the palms of her hands. As she was getting to her feet again, she saw the two men and the boy disappear quickly inside the door. It slammed shut in her face as she rushed back up the steps. She hammered on it in fury with her fist. It was locked. There were no names by the bells but only five flat numbers. She rang all of them in turn. At last, after two minutes, a man's voice came over the intercom speaker above the buttons, asking: "Who is it?"

"Please call the police!" she cried urgently. "A boy has just been taken into this building by Cyril Jones, and he is in danger. The man is a paedophile. Please open the door or call the police."

There was silence. She rang again. After a while the same voice answered in a bored tone: "Please go away. This is nothing to do with me."

She tried ringing other bells for five minutes and then gave up and walked away. She didn't have a mobile phone to call the police. She wondered which way to go to find a telephone box. Her legs were shaking. She walked along the street, then into another street and found nothing. Then she thought she should go to the police station. She looked at her map. She knew that the main police station, New Scotland Yard, was somewhere near Victoria Station. She found it on the map and set off towards it. On the way she finally saw a phone box, but now that she had decided to go to the police station she kept to that plan. She felt she had to explain things at length, including what she knew about Cyril Jones and the disappearance of her son, before the police would believe that he was a paedophile and the blond boy was in danger. If she just phoned the emergency number they would ask what crime she had actually seen. They were unlikely to act on her mere suspicions.

Then as she kept on walking towards the police station she began to have second thoughts and wondered if phoning would have been better. The closer she got to it the more nervous she became. In spite of this, she pushed herself to walk faster, thinking every minute must count. At last she came in sight of it. It was a huge building of metal and glass, but none of the glass was transparent. On the lowest row of windows there were some policemen's faces on a big advertising display recruiting for the police. She couldn't see any door. She walked to the left down a side street to see if there was an entrance there but there was only a huge fence with bars like steel girders protecting the front of the building near the famous revolving sign. Behind this massive fence, at some distance, she could see a policeman standing guard. Next to the iron fence there was another low building with blue panels. Again it had no visible doors. No one went in or out. The whole place looked like a fortress. Worse, it looked like a prison. A dull fear began to take hold of her.

She had not seen a prison since her release and this rising surge of terror took her by surprise. All at once she knew she couldn't go in there. She was terrified she would never come out again. The sense of helplessness came back to her like a state of possession.

She was a jailbird. A convicted murderer. Out on parole. What if they somehow interpreted her complaint as a breach of her parole terms, a false accusation against a respected member of parliament, and sent her back to prison? She knew the consequences of making an accusation against a prison officer: the memory still haunted her sleep. Maybe she was even on a list for deportation and would be arrested at once. How would she then contact Camilla? She knew how completely they could stop you communicating with the outside world. Once they had you in their power, you had no rights, you disappeared into a black hole. She had no faith in their police or their courts. They had imprisoned her for eleven years for defending herself. They considered her a hardened criminal because she refused to admit her guilt. The helplessness and the terror came back to her in waves that washed over her. She was not a human being! She was a convicted murderer! An illegal immigrant! She had no rights! She turned and walked back to the end of the street on shaking legs, afraid she was being watched by the guard behind the fence or by hidden cameras. On the corner of the street she found a tiny park, just a patch of dirt with a few benches under some trees. She sat down on a bench. Her legs felt weak. She thought of the blond boy and what they were probably doing to him.

"I'm sorry," she said to him. "I'm really sorry, but I can't." She put her hands over her face and began to cry quietly, ashamed of her own cowardice and of her betrayal of the blond boy. What had she become? Was this all she was? She had survived so much and she thought she had become strong enough to face anything. Now she understood that this terror of being locked up again would never leave her. She sat trembling as if she had a fever.

She noticed vaguely that one or two people were passing by and she felt they were staring at her. One old man cut through the little park and passed close behind her bench, limping very slowly with a walking-stick. She stopped crying and recovered her composure. When she got up she noticed there was a pound coin on the bench beside her. She picked it up in surprise, looking around for someone who might have dropped it. There was nobody in sight. Now she could phone Camilla.

First she needed to change her one pound and fifty pence coins into smaller coins, as a call was sixty pence. It took her some time to find a shop, to get some small change and then to find a phone box. It was just before six when she called Camilla.

5

Camilla was sitting in Romain's flat having a cup of tea. They were talking about creating a website for the imaginary castle in Bordeaux. Ekaterina was upset and slightly incoherent and Camilla asked her to talk more slowly and calmly. She looked at her watch. According to Ekaterina's story it was an hour since the boy had been taken into Cyril Jones' flat. Was it too late to get the police to investigate it? How could she persuade them to?

She tried to calm Ekaterina and assured her she would do something. She told her to call her again in exactly twenty minutes. Then she searched quickly on her smartphone and dialled the Paedophile Unit of the Metropolitan Police. There was a recorded message. The Unit closed at six o'clock. She glanced at her watch. It was five past. It was Friday, so it would reopen on Monday morning. The message told her to call an emergency number for urgent cases and to report crimes. She decided to try it. As she had feared, the woman at the other end asked her a series of standard questions and then told her she had no grounds for making an emergency call. The matter should be taken up with the Paedophile Unit on Monday morning. She swallowed her anger and explained slowly and calmly all over again.

"Look, a man long suspected of being a paedophile has just had a young Polish boy of fourteen delivered to his flat by another man. The boy tried to run away and was brought back by force. A reliable witness saw it. Can you send someone to investigate and ask what he is doing with this boy?"

"We can't do that, Madam, it could be a member of his family. Even his own child."

"The man is gay. He has no children."

"We cannot discriminate on the grounds of sexual orientation, Madam. That is not grounds for suspecting he is a paedophile."

"I'm not saying it is. I'm saying: he has no children, so what is he doing with a fourteen- year old boy?"

"It could be a nephew. Do you know the age of the boy for certain, Madam?"

"Look, my friend judged he's about fourteen."

"That's a judgment, Madam. He might well be sixteen, in which case a relationship is perfectly legal."

"But isn't it your job to find out? Listen, I'm an investigator into paedophilia, and I know this man has been the object of paedophile allegations for a long time."

"Has he ever been convicted of this kind of offence, Madam?"

"I don't know."

"Can you spell his name so I can check the Sex Offenders' Register?"

Camilla spelled his name and added: "But he probably won't be on it. There's always a first time."

"I'm afraid we can't intervene if he's not on the Register." There was a pause. "No, he's not, Madam. We do have to be careful not to make false accusations against innocent members of the public."

Camilla found herself trembling with fury.

"Listen, right now a boy is being raped by a paedophile, thanks to you. Are you willing to have that on your conscience? Do you have any children?"

"Madam, I should warn you that abusing members of the police is an offence."

"I am not abusing you. Someone is abusing that boy, and you could stop it and are refusing to do so."

"Madam, the guidelines tell us clearly what kinds of situations we can intervene in and when we can't. If you have concerns about any individual, please take them up with the Paedophile Unit."

"I would like to but they are closed for the weekend. Do you think paedophiles only rape from Monday to Friday, you stupid woman? This is an opportunity to catch the man red-handed and get a conviction. And save a boy's life! Doesn't that mean anything to you?"

"You are becoming abusive, Madam, and I am going to end this call. I'm afraid we can't help you." The line went dead.

Romain and Camilla looked at each other. She was fighting back tears.

"Shall we go there?" said Romain. He put an arm round her. "At least we can see if he brings him out again."

They waited anxiously for Ekaterina to call back. At last she did. Camilla told her they were coming to Jones' flat and to meet her outside it.

It took an eternity to get there in the rush hour with a change at Euston, and then they had to walk ten minutes from Pimlico Tube station. They found the address in Wilmot

Street Ekaterina had given them, but there was no sign of her yet. They walked up the steps and stood in front of the door, trying to look in through the narrow glass panel beside it. They could see a hallway and a lift door. A minute or two later they saw a movement inside. They stopped peering in and stepped back. A middle-aged woman came out the front door.

"Oh, hello," said Camilla on the spur of the moment. "I've just moved in here and I seem to have forgotten my front door key. Would you mind letting us in?"

Her private school accent and well-bred manner did the trick and the other woman smiled and held the door open for her. They walked into the hallway. They looked at the mail boxes and found Cyril Jones's. It indicated the third floor. They summoned the lift and found it already there. They waited for Ekaterina. If there was any trouble and the police were called her testimony would be important. Camilla went to the glass panel beside the door and looked out through it, and a minute later saw Ekaterina arrive. Camilla opened the door and let her in.

They went up in the lift to the third floor. There was only one door, and it had the name Jones on a card beside it. Camilla pushed the button and a buzzer sounded. Romain took off his jacket in case things became physical. He and Ekaterina stood to one side so as to be out of the line of sight of the spy-hole in the door. Only Camilla was visible. They waited tensely. Nobody answered. They rang again. There was no sound from inside. Then they knocked. Either he had gone out or he was keeping quiet and had no intention of opening to anyone. Camilla felt sick as she imagined what might be happening to a boy inside the flat even as they waited.

"Why don't we make a scene and get the police to come?" said Romain.

Camilla nodded. He pounded on the door with his fist.

"Open up! Police!" he shouted. "Paedophile Squad! Come out, Jones, you paedophile pervert!"

Still nothing. Then he kicked the door several times, but it was solid and he had no effect on it other than to scuff the paint. He took out a credit card and tried to slide it in the lock but the doorframe had an overlapping panel to make this impossible. Nobody in the flats below reacted to all the noise. The building remained deathly quiet.

At last they gave up and went down in the lift again. Once outside on the street they looked vaguely about them as if in the hope of seeing Jones's car arrive.

"If this is a paedophile ring, the pimp may have taken the boy to see Jones, who may then have taken him to see someone else," said Romain. "A pervert VIP. A lord or high court judge or cabinet minister. Or even to a perverts' party of some kind."

They strolled back and forth for a few minutes, staring up at the windows of the fourth storey but the curtains were drawn and there was no movement. They debated whether they should wait longer. Dusk was beginning to fall and they saw that no light appeared in Jones's windows, unlike some of the flats in the next building. They decided to call it a day. Romain suggested going to a pub to eat. He wanted to make sure Ekaterina got a square meal. They found one with a reasonably priced fish menu on a board outside, which she seemed to like. Over dinner they discussed what to do next.

"The first priority," said Camilla, "is to go to the children's home in Birmingham and see what we can find out about Viktor's disappearance. We'll go there tomorrow, shall we?"

The others agreed.

"If that's Jones's constituency, does he go back there on weekends?" asked Romain.

"He might do. To hold what they call a surgery with his constituents. We can find out on his website."

There was free wifi in the pub so she checked on her smartphone. Sure enough he had a surgery scheduled at the Liberal Democrats' office in Yardley, Birmingham the next day.

"We should go there and see him," she said. "It would be good to confront him before we go to the police on Monday."

"If he sees me," said Ekaterina, "he'll recognize me and he may say something that gives him away. If your phone can film him...."

"It certainly can," said Camilla. "I'll have it ready."

Later in the meal the conversation went back to the phone call Camilla had made to the police, and the lack of an adequate response.

"It's as if she didn't want to know," said Camilla. "She accused me of prejudice because I thought a middle-aged gay man having a fourteen year-old boy taken to see him by another man looked suspicious."

"It's now politically incorrect to find anything suspicious," said Romain.

"You can just imagine how it must have been in Rotherham and Rochdale and all those other places." She turned to Ekaterina and explained. "In case you missed it, these are scandals that have been all over the papers, where hundreds of thirteen year-old white girls were drugged, raped and passed around as sex slaves by Pakistani gangs all over England. It's gone on for years and the police totally ignored it, despite being told dozens of times. You can imagine how those conversations went." She put on the voice of a naive, middle-aged caller. "Officer, I'd like to report something a bit odd. Some Pakistani men in their thirties are picking up young white girls outside their school and taking them for rides in their cars."

Romain quickly chimed in and played the policeman.

"Madam, are you against interracial relationships? Are you a racist?"

"But some of these girls look very young, officer. They look about thirteen."

"Well, that's the way it is now, Madam, they start younger and younger. What are we supposed to do about it? Stop every interracial couple on the street and ask how old the girl is? How do we know they're even sleeping together? There's no law against them going out."

"But don't you think it's a bit odd, officer? I mean, *very* young white girls and Pakistani men who are often much older?"

"Would you be asking this question if they were white men, Madam? Clearly not. This is now a diverse society, and we can't find something suspicious just because of the racial diversity of the people involved."

"That's it," said Camilla, throwing up her hands as though the point had been made. "How do you stop the sexual enslavement of young girls if people's reports of strange or unusual relationships are dismissed as bigotry?"

"Well, it's now forbidden to see any relationship as strange or unusual," said Romain.

"Exactly, and anyone who reports something is seen as denouncing people on the basis of wicked stereotypes and prejudices. Even by the police. That's what lay behind Rotherham."

"As if it would matter anyway if someone got questioned about a relationship that turned out to be totally innocent!" said Romain. "Normal people wouldn't care. What's far more important is that we can only detect the most appalling evil and cruelty that is happening behind closed doors by reading the tiny signs it leaves on the surface of everyday life. Things that look bizarre, out of place, not quite normal. And checking them out."

"Like a fourteen year-old Polish boy with a homosexual politician," put in Ekaterina.

"I can't believe that woman actually suggested he might be sixteen — that it might be his legal lover," said Camilla. "She was trying to explain it and justify it. As if that wouldn't be disgusting anyway."

"Careful!" said Romain with a grin. "You could get arrested for that."

After dinner, they took the tube together as far as Oxford Circus, where the girls got out and took the Central Line to Queensway while Romain continued north. The battered women's shelter was at the beginning of Moscow Road, on the way to Camilla's flat in Bark Place, so she saw Ekaterina home and went in to talk to Maeve. The Irishwoman was an old friend of hers, as she had worked there years before. Camilla brought her up to date on Ekaterina's search for her son. It was as well to have as many allies as possible, and to let them know what was going on, just in case. She explained to Maeve where they were going the next day, and arranged to come by and collect Ekaterina in the morning.

The next day the two women met Romain at Marylebone Station. Camilla had bought cheap tickets online for the 8.15 train, with a return at 17.52. They managed to get seats facing each other and began to eat the cherries Camilla had brought with her. They watched the grimy buildings filing past the windows until they gradually gave way to the green countryside basking in the spring sunshine. Ekaterina gazed at the changing landscape with fascination. They discussed what questions they would ask the manager of the children's home and how they would threaten to go to the police if he refused to talk to them. An hour and three quarters later they pulled into Birmingham New Street Station.

When they found their way out of the futuristic new station building, which was still unfinished, Camilla consulted the small map she had printed off the Internet and led the way to a bus stop. There they waited ten minutes and got on a bus heading for Solihull. They got off at Acocks Green village and from there Ekaterina remembered the way and led them the two hundred metres to Gaveston House Children's Home. It was a large, three-storey, red-brick gabled house with a wall in front of it enclosing a scruffy lawn. A path led to an old-fashioned gabled porch over a green front door, flanked by bay windows with yellowing gauze curtains. They rang the bell. The door was opened by a slim young man with fair curly hair, dressed in a baggy pullover and jeans. Ekaterina recognized him from her last visit.

"Good morning," said Camilla brightly. "I was wondering if we could talk to the manager of this home. It's about the disappearance of this lady's son about a month ago. I'm a journalist specialized in child abuse and abductions and I'd like to talk to someone who can tell us about what might have happened to the boy."

"Oh. The director's not here right now. It's Saturday. But he might call in later." As he spoke, the young man glanced at Ekaterina and recognized her. He blushed and became a little flustered. "Oh, hello, you came here a couple of weeks ago, didn't you?"

"Yes," said Ekaterina. "I spoke to the director, but I saw you for a moment."

"Yeah, I remember you. Let's see, your son's name is ... Viktor, right?"

"That's it. Viktor Lysenko." Ekaterina was pleased that he had remembered.

"Yes, I remember little Viktor. Dreadful business, that. My name's Kayley, by the way."

He stepped forward and held out his hand to shake hands with her. She was not expecting it and hesitated for a split second. Then she grasped his hand and shook it warmly.

"Ekaterina," she said. In order to make up for her initial hesitation she held onto his hand for a second or two longer than usual, and when they finally let go they both blushed slightly. His grey eyes looked into hers as if he wanted to express his sympathy but they also looked a little shy as if was unsure of himself. He spoke quickly and nervously, his words tumbling over one another in his hurry to express himself.

"I didn't have a chance to talk to you last time. I just want to say how awful I feel about what happened. For your son to go missing like that is just appalling! I wasn't on duty that day so I don't know much about it and nobody has explained anything. I'm also new here, so I didn't know Viktor very well, but I can get you someone to talk to who knows more about what happened than I do. I really hope we can find Viktor but I'm afraid as far as I know nobody has heard anything since."

He shook hands with the others and invited them all inside. He led the way into an entrance hall, along a short corridor and into a large, dark-panelled room. It was dominated by a long, massive wooden table with old-fashioned, brown upholstered chairs along either side. Ekaterina looked around the room. There were heavy dark beams across the ceiling and a huge fireplace at the far end with crossed swords above it. It made her think of a room in an old manor house in a black and white murder film. She wondered how her son had felt living in this gloomy place for the last six months before he disappeared.

Three boys were lounging about, one of them bouncing a ball, and Kayley asked them politely to leave. He invited his guests to sit down and they sat on a long couch with a wooden frame along the left wall. Then he went away down the corridor again. One of the boys who had gone out slipped back into the room. He was a tall, brown-skinned, mixed-race boy of about fifteen, and he was the one with the ball. It was the kind of ball used for handball and he bounced it automatically as he talked.

"You someone's family?" he asked carelessly, not directing his question at anyone.

"Yes. A boy called Viktor Lysenko," said Camilla. "This is his mother. Do you know him?"

"Yeah. Saw him around. He's not here any more."

"Do you know what happened to him?"

"Dunno. Didn't come back." He kept bouncing the ball, not looking at them.

"From what? From where?"

"Dunno."

"Did he go somewhere with someone?"

"Yeah. Think so." He bounced the ball again.

"Do you know who this person was?"

"Yeah. Big shot. Old Fat Guts. Cyril, his name is. Weighs a ton."

"Does this person come here often?"

"Yeah. Likes to come and see the boys. Especially the young ones." He gave a knowing leer and looked at them quickly.

"Why does he come and see boys here? Is he someone's father?"

"Nah. Not him. Poofter, ain't he?"

"You mean he's homosexual? How do you know that?"

"Only takes the boys, don't he? Never the girls." He laughed unpleasantly and bounced the ball again.

"Has he ever done anything to any of the boys that you know of?"

"What do you mean?"

"Does he molest them?"

"What's that mean?"

"Does he ever touch them in ways he shouldn't?"

"Dunno. Could do. Lots of talk, ain't there?"

"Have you ever spoken to him?"

"Nah. I'm too old for him. He likes 'em really young, does Cyril."

At that moment steps could be heard walking back along the corridor.

"Do you know who Viktor's best friend is?" asked Ekaterina.

"Yeah. He's called Eric," the boy said quickly.

Kayley walked back in, followed by another man. The boy with the ball looked guilty and slid sideways out of the room.

"This is my colleague, Brian. He's the one who knew Viktor the best and knows what happened the day he disappeared. He might be able to help you."

The newcomer shook hands with them. He was a burly man in his late thirties, with somewhat coarse features and hair that was receding on all fronts. Ekaterina took an instant dislike to him, just as she had taken an instant liking to Kayley, who was slim with fine features. She studied Kayley again as he stood there, looking ill at ease, as if hesitating about whether to stay. She liked his face and his blond curls and the warm, earnest way he had talked to her, as if he really cared about Viktor. Even his nervousness with her seemed to her rather amusing. He reminded her of someone, but she couldn't think who. All she could think of was the cat she had had as a child, Mishi. But why should he remind her of her cat? She wondered if he was as old as her. He looked a bit younger. Brian sat down at the table and turned his chair to face the three of them sitting on the couch.

"Kayley, do you mind keeping an eye on the boys in the games room?" he said, a little brusquely. Kayley nodded, not looking pleased. He glanced at Ekaterina and went out again.

Ekaterina stared at Brian. She resented him for telling Kayley to leave the room when she wanted to talk to him further. Something about Brian gave her an unpleasant feeling, as if something was crawling over her skin. A suspicion began to form in her mind, without any reason, that this ogre might well be a paedophile who had abused her son. If Viktor had been kidnapped by a paedophile ring, they must have accomplices in the home. Despite her study of psychology, Ekaterina retained a rather simple understanding of paedophiles. She thought they were most likely to be men who did not have much chance with women. This man was not only ugly but built like a bear and rather surly-looking. Since she couldn't imagine him having any success with pretty girls, she thought it was not entirely implausible that he might fall back on a pretty child in his care instead. Her child.

"Could you tell us what happened when Viktor, this lady's son, disappeared?" asked Camilla.

"Yes. Well, nobody quite knows because he was...." Brian hesitated, "not here at the time." He spoke in a rough, mumbling voice with a strong local accent, which Ekaterina found it hard to understand. It sounded different from Kayley's accent, which was clearer and more pleasant to her ear as if he was much better educated.

"Not here at the home?" Camilla pressed him.

"No, he'd gone out."

"Alone or in company?"

"In company. He'd gone on an outing. An excursion with a visitor." He cleared his throat and began to talk more loudly and confidently. "We have volunteers who are interested in helping the kids, taking them places, giving them the sort of outings we can't really organize for them. They're a decent lot in this town. Very caring. Very supportive. Not like down south. People care less down there."

"And who was this visitor?"

"One of our most regular. A real benefactor of the home." He sounded deeply respectful. "The Member of Parliament for Yardley, Cyril Jones."

"And Viktor never came back from his excursion with this person?"

"Well, Mr Jones says he just disappeared from his house. He'd taken the boys in to watch some videos, he told us. Documentary films about the war, about the rebuilding afterwards, the poverty, so he said. He's always been interested in educating the kids, you know. Giving them a sense of history, local history. He's got a great collection of old films, apparently."

"So what happened?"

"Well, Viktor asked to go to the bathroom and then it seems he just disappeared from the house." He sounded baffled. "There were no locked doors or anything so he just walked out, so Mr Jones said. Ran away. We get the odd case like that once or twice a year. Boys get fed up with the home. Want to live on the street to see how it is. Or they have some mad idea of going to look for relatives that have abandoned them. A long lost father, maybe. It's very sad. They usually come back after a few days. When they get hungry."

"And did you call the police?"

"Well, we did after a day or so. We usually give them that long to see if they come back."

"You mean you didn't give the alarm at once? Who took that decision?"

"Well, I suppose it was the director, I can't recall exactly." He shifted uncomfortably.

"So, how did you hear about this disappearance?" pursued Camilla. She had an air, thought Ekaterina, of a prosecuting lawyer who knew her job. "Did Cyril Jones come back to the home and announce the disappearance to the director?"

"No, not immediately, he didn't — only the next day."

"So, is that when you found out?"

"No, the driver told us the same day. You see, he always took the boys in his big flash car, with a driver, and the driver came back and reported one had run off."

"What do you mean — one? How many boys were there?" Camilla pounced like a cat.

"There were two of them." His face gave a nervous twitch. "Just the two, that's right. The driver brought the other boy back and announced Viktor had run off."

"And did this other boy give an account of what happened?"

"No. He didn't see anything. Didn't know anything either."

"What was this other boy's name?"

"Let's see. Who was it? Gosh. I'm afraid I can't remember." He frowned with the mental effort and then shrugged. "The kids come and go, you know, it must be nearly a month ago."

"You mean there is no sort of log-book noting which children have been taken out by which visitors?" Camilla sounded incredulous.

"Oh, we're not that formal here."

"Have you ever heard of child abuse — paedophilia?" Camilla said sternly.

"Yes, of course." He looked shocked. "We don't have anything like that going on here."

"But you seem to take very little care about the people from outside who have access to your children. Do you know the name of Viktor's best friend?"

"Ah, that I couldn't tell you, I'm afraid." He looked sly. "We don't get that close to the kids. We're not allowed to, for the reasons you've just mentioned."

"Would he be called Eric, by any chance?"

"I've no idea."

"Is there a boy here called Eric?"

He scratched his head. "Yes, there is, actually."

"Of the same age?"

"Yes, about that. Maybe a year or two older."

"Were they together on that outing with Cyril Jones?"

"I've no idea, but I suppose it's possible."

"Can we see Eric?"

"I don't know whether he's here or has —"

"It's Saturday. There's no school on Saturday."

"Yes, but there's sports, various sporting activities, I believe he's playing football somewhere. He does play for a club sometimes, as a substitute. Now, where was it they were playing today?" He gazed at the ceiling as if trying to remember. "Perhaps if you were to come back later, they're usually back here in the late afternoon."

"If we come back it will be with the police," said Camilla firmly. "Now would you kindly go and get Eric or find out where he is so we can go and talk to him? We've come all the way from London, and this lady is Viktor's mother. She has the right to talk to the boy who last saw her son before he disappeared, don't you agree?"

"Oh, of course, absolutely. I'll go and see where Eric might be."

He went out of the room, looking rather chastened and a bit rattled.

"That's the way," Ekaterina said admiringly. "We're getting somewhere at last. But he's hiding something."

"That's for sure," said Romain. "He looks as guilty as hell. And getting a bit panicky, if you ask me."

They waited. Several minutes went by. Finally Brian came back, looking a bit calmer.

"It's just as I thought. Eric is playing football today at a ground called Oaklands Recreation Ground. It's not all that far away, you can take a bus. I have the address here." He handed Camilla a piece of notepaper. "His team is called Arden Forest U12."

"What time did the match begin?" asked Camilla.

Brian looked at his watch.

"It started twenty minutes ago. So you should have time to make it."

"All right. Could you give us the number of a taxi firm?"

He reeled off a number, and she keyed it into her smartphone and ordered a taxi.

"By the way," she said when she ended the call, "I believe Cyril Jones is up here for a surgery with his constituents today. You don't expect him to drop in here later on, do you?"

"No. Why should he?" He looked surprised.

"I understand he comes in here quite regularly."

"No, not that often." He seemed defensive and slightly ruffled.

"Do you know him well?"

"Only through his charity work with the boys."

"How long has he been coming to this home?"

"Oh, hard to say. Five or six years, I'm not sure."

"Have any boys ever disappeared before in his company?"

"I've certainly never heard of it."

"Are you aware of the paedophile allegations that have been made against him?"

She kept her tone neutral but studied him carefully.

"Oh, that was years ago and I'm sure it was just vile gossip." Brian sounded indignant, but looked a bit uncomfortable. "Of course, he's gay. Some people quite shamefully tried to lump the two things together. It's pure homophobia. They should be prosecuted for slander and hate crime. There's absolutely no connection between being gay and being a paedophile. It's sheer bigotry to pretend there is. Fortunately, that kind of slander is heard less often now. The law is being applied a bit more rigorously against it."

"Have any cases of child abuse ever been uncovered here?"

"Not in the seven years I've been here."

"Do you have an anti-child abuse programme — asking the children to report any abuse of this kind? Are they given the opportunity?"

"They certainly know they can talk to us about anything at all. That goes without saying."

"Experts on the subject believe it never goes without saying. Children must be asked specifically on a regular basis, if anything of this kind is ever to be brought to light."

"We don't want to give them ideas or they'll start inventing all kinds of nonsense," said Brian defensively. "Some of these children are very emotionally disturbed. And vulnerable."

"Exactly. That's why they need to be encouraged to speak out."

There was the faint sound of a horn from the direction of the front door.

"I think that's your taxi," said Brian.

They walked along the corridor. In the entrance hall the boy with the ball was still bouncing it. He gave them a piercing look as though trying to figure out how much they had found out. Ekaterina had a feeling they ought to talk to the boy and try to learn more from him, but Camilla was in a hurry to make it to the football ground. She opened the door. A black taxi was waiting outside the gate. She led the way out.

After the door closed behind them, Brian walked up to the boy with the ball and grabbed his ear and twisted it.

"Any more crap out of you and we'll feed you into the meat grinder," he said. "One hand at a time. Keep your fucking mouth shut."

Then he went upstairs to the dormitories. He found the boy skulking as usual on a bed, playing some weird game of his own with tiny bits of paper. Nobody else was around.

"Eric," he said. "There's some good news. I've just had a call from the Arden Forest Under 12s football coach. The game over at Oaklands Recreation Ground against Marston Green — it's the final game of the season — the team needs you. Two boys called in sick and another one sprained his ankle after ten minutes. They've got no one on the bench if there's any more problems. You've got to get over there. It's your big chance to play in the team at last. Get ready, I've got to take you over there by car immediately."

"I've got no gear," the boy said sullenly.

"It doesn't matter. You can wear someone else's. They've got everything there. They just need you, as you are. It's your big day, hurry, we don't want to be too late."

Eric began to get ready in slow motion and at last was heading downstairs with Brian. They passed two other boys, who exchanged a few words with Eric. They went out the back door, down the path and out the gate into the lane where Brian's car was parked. They got in.

After a few minutes' driving, they got onto the ring road. Eric, who was looking moodily out the window, said: "This isn't the right way."

"Of course it is. What do you know?"

"You're heading south instead of north."

"We'll get there, it's a different route."

After a few minutes they turned off into a side road. The road was empty except for a big black car parked a hundred metres along it. Brian drove up behind it and stopped.

"I'm lost, I'll ask directions," he said. He flashed his lights.

A man got out of the black car and came towards them. Eric had time to see the car was a Bentley and fear flooded through him. A man with a face he knew opened the passenger door and pulled him out by the arm and half-dragged, half-carried him whimpering and kicking towards the Bentley. He opened the rear door and shoved him inside and slammed it shut. Eric scrabbled desperately to find the handle to open the door again. A man sitting beside him on the rear seat, an enormous whale of a man, reached a powerful arm across and seized him by the neck. The boy turned and looked at the face and his blood ran cold.

"Hello, Eric. Remember me? We had such fun together, didn't we?" The enormous face grinned and its triple chins wobbled in mirth. "And we're going to have fun again."

6

The taxi stopped at the entrance to the Oaklands Recreation Ground, and Camilla, Romain and Ekaterina got out and began walking, looking for the right football game. Romain was reminded of his own Saturdays playing football as a kid. There was the same smell of grass and mud, the same sporadic, rowdy excitement among spectators on the sidelines. They walked past two games before they came to one that looked like an under-12s game. Camilla asked some spectators who was playing and was told it was Marston Green against Arden Forest. Then she asked who the coach of Arden Forest was and went over to him.

"I'm looking for a boy called Eric, from Gaveston House Care Home in Acocks Green," she said. "Is he playing?"

"Eric who?" The coach was middle-aged and overweight, with a red blotchy face.

"I don't know his other name. Are there any Erics in the team?"

"Are you the police?" the man asked suspiciously.

"No, but I'm an investigator. Of child abuse. We want to talk to Eric."

"What makes you think he's playing here?"

"They told us at the children's home."

"Black boy, is he?"

"No, he's white."

He nodded towards the teams on the field. Half the players in one team were black.

"Take a look. There's only five white boys in the team and none of them is called Eric. Someone has put you wrong."

"They told me at Gaveston House Children's Home — that's where Eric lives."

The man stared at her and then frowned.

"Wait a minute, I think I know who you mean. There was an Eric who wanted to play for the team at the start of the season. Boy with fair hair. He came to a few practices but he didn't have the skills. Too slightly built. Not as strong as the other boys. So I told him we'd maybe call on him later if we ever needed him. But so far we haven't."

"All right. Thank you." She turned to the others. "Let's get out of here."

They walked away from the football field, uncertain what to do next.

"That bastard, Brian, lied to us," she said. "To get us out of the way."

"He doesn't want us to talk to Eric," said Ekaterina. "He's probably back at the care home, but now they've had time to move him."

"It's been more than twenty minutes," said Camilla, looking at her watch.

"We could rush back in case," said Romain.

"I'm sure that bastard will have taken him away, or made a phone call and got someone to come and pick him up," said Camilla. "Look, according to my little map the Liberal Democrats' office is not far from here. That's where Cyril Jones is giving a surgery today, according to his website. It's on Coventry Road. Number 1772. Let's go there and talk to him, and record how he reacts when he sees Ekaterina."

They looked at the map she had printed off the internet. Coventry Road ran past one end of the recreation ground. They asked a football mum which way it was and headed over there at a fast walk.

"At least we have one more name to give to the Paedophile Unit for investigation," said Romain. "That guy Brian. He's clearly in this up to his neck."

They got to the road and found a bus stop. An old black woman waiting there told them which direction to take the bus in. The bus came five minutes later and they asked the driver which stop it was. After a few minutes he called back to them and told them they were there. They found the Liberal Democrat Party office between a fishing tackle shop and an Indian takeaway.

They went in. A small crowd of mostly elderly people were clustered around a desk. An Asian girl of about twenty was addressing them in a posh, rather bossy voice.

"I'm afraid Mr Jones has been called away to London on urgent business. He won't be able to see you, but I'll take down all the details of the problem or question you might have, all right?"

There were murmurs of frustration and discontent.

"But he was here just a while ago! I saw him, only half an hour ago!" said one old woman in a loud, querulous voice.

"Yes, he got a phone call about half an hour ago and had to leave urgently. I'm really sorry, and so is he."

"These MPs, are they at our service or not?" muttered the old woman, making her way out slowly through the crowd leaning heavily on a walking stick.

Camilla turned to the others and shrugged. They walked out.

"So, do we go back and confront Brian?" said Romain.

"We should have a go. And at least get his last name, so we can tell the police," said Ekaterina.

They agreed it was important. They took a taxi back to Gaveston House. Kayley answered the door again.

"Is the director there yet by any chance?" asked Camilla.

"No. I don't think he'll be in today after all."

"Could you tell us his name?"

"Edward Marlowe."

She wrote it down in a little notebook with a stub of a pencil.

"What about Brian, is he still there?"

"No, Brian has taken the rest of the day off. He went out somewhere and then he called a few minutes ago to say he wasn't feeling very well. So he won't be back till tomorrow. Can I give him a message?"

"We'd like to write to him directly with a question or two. What's his last name?"

"Spenser."

"And do you have an email address at the home, or perhaps a card?"

"Yes, of course." The young man went inside and came back out with a business card.

"And what was your name again?" said Camilla, glancing at the card.

"Kayley Burke. I'll write it if you like." He wrote his name on the back of the card and handed it to her. She asked him to add his phone number. As he wrote it down she said casually:

"Do you know a boy called Eric, who was the best friend of Viktor?"

"Eric?" He stared at her. "Yeah, there is a boy called Eric."

"Do you know his other name?"

"Page. Or is it Cage? I can look him up. Why don't you come back in for a minute?"

They walked into the entrance hall again. He went along the corridor into an office and came back with a large tattered book. He laid it on a small round table in the hall and thumbed through it.

"We have actually got all this on computer now but I can't get into it without the secretary. Yes, here we are. Eric Page. Orphan, his mother overdosed."

"No other relatives at all?"

"Doesn't say. Father not mentioned. Taken into care at five. Apparently a couple of foster families tried him. Didn't seem to work. So he came back here. He's a rather withdrawn boy. Not easy to talk to. Especially lately. Here's a photo of him."

They crowded round the little table to see it. The photo showed a boy with a pale, slightly freckled face, mistrustful brown eyes and untidy fair hair sticking up in spikes.

"Is Eric here at the moment? We'd like to talk to him about Viktor and what happened the day he disappeared."

"I'll go and see if he's here. A lot of the kids are out today."

He went away up the corridor and came back a few minutes later.

"The other boys say that Eric left half an hour ago to go to a football match with Brian."

"Do they really believe that?" said Camilla. "You see, Brian sent us to a football match at Oaklands Recreation Ground so we could see Eric and talk to him. But Eric wasn't playing in that game and was never in the team, according to the coach."

Kayley looked puzzled.

"That's really strange. Two boys say they ran into Eric on his way out the back door with Brian and he said he was going to play in a game at Oaklands."

Camilla studied him as if trying to figure out what he knew.

"How long have you been working here, if you don't mind my asking?"

"About two months. Before that I was in a children's home up in Leeds."

"Have you ever suspected there might be a paedophile ring operating here?"

Kayley Burke turned pale.

"No. Why do you ask?"

"You see, when we talked to Brian about Viktor, we asked if we could talk to Eric, his best friend, according to another boy here. Do you know if they were together on that outing with Cyril Jones, the member of parliament?"

"No idea. I wasn't on duty that day. And nobody has told me anything about it."

"Well, Brian deliberately sent us on a wild goose chase to a football game to talk to Eric and meanwhile he seems to have taken him away. Not to a football match. Somewhere else. And half an hour ago, Cyril Jones cut short his Saturday surgery with his constituents and went somewhere in a hurry after getting a phone call. Cyril Jones being the person from whose house Viktor disappeared. Do you see how all those pieces fit together?"

"It's very strange. I don't know what to make of it." He looked bewildered and alarmed.

"If you suspect there might be paedophile activities at this home, if you even suspect it and do nothing to report your suspicions, you could be seen as an accomplice. You know that, don't you?" Camilla looked at him searchingly.

"Yes, that's all very well, but if one has no evidence, nothing concrete...." he said defensively. "One can't go around accusing people.... without proof."

"There might not be proof, but there's certainly circumstantial evidence now. There have been paedophile allegations against Cyril Jones in the past. And now this disappearance of Viktor's friend, Eric, as soon as we asked to talk to him about Viktor, looks very strange. Don't you think it's time you went to the police? Do you trust your director, Edward Marlowe?"

"I've got no reason not to, but he isn't the most open person in the world."

"Why don't you talk to him? Demand that he hold Brian to account for taking Eric away. We're building a case against Brian as well as against Cyril Jones. We're taking it to the Metropolitan Police Paedophile Unit on Monday. You'd be well advised to get your complaint in to the police before you get arrested with the whole bunch of them. Unless you want your career in social work to come to an end."

Kayley nodded glumly, looking worried.

"Here's my card," said Camilla. "I have a website about child abuse. If you have any more information, even a suspicion, please let us know. Kids' lives may be in danger."

Kayley took the card from her and studied it. Romain thought Camilla had been rather hard on him and Ekaterina apparently felt the same. She went up to Kayley and spoke to him as if she was trying to smooth things over.

"Of course, we don't think for a moment you're involved in any of this, but it's really important to me if you could help me find my son." She appealed to him with all the feeling she could put into her voice. "I'm sure you understand what it must be like to lose a child. Do you have any children?"

"No," he said. "Not yet."

"And do you want them? And does your wife want them?"

"I haven't got a wife. I'm single," he said awkwardly.

"But I am sure you want them. Don't you?" The intimacy of the question had the kind of personal intrusiveness that only a foreigner could get away with in England, thought Romain.

"Of course. When I find the right woman." Kayley attempted a light-hearted grin, but it was a rather weak one in the face of her earnest expression.

"My son was taken away from me when he was eighteen months old. He was so small, to be without his mother. I need to find him again." Ekaterina's brilliant green eyes gazed into his. They had a glint of tears in them. "And now that his best friend has just disappeared too, we're sure that Viktor didn't run away. Something horrible may have happened to him."

"I'm really sorry. I can only imagine what you're feeling." Kayley seemed sincerely upset at the sight of her distress. "It's just awful what you're going through. And I feel somehow responsible. I was working here, and I saw nothing of what happened to Viktor." He glanced behind him and lowered his voice. "It seems clear from what you've told me that some of the people here were involved in this. It's a strange place, the whole atmosphere. I don't know any of the other staff members very well."

"I know you're on our side," said Ekaterina with feeling, as if to reassure him. She put her hand on his arm, which was crossed in front of him as he held Camilla's card in both hands. "I trust you. I know you'll help me if you can."

"I will. I — I'll certainly do all I can," he stammered. He was looking into her eyes from inches away as though hypnotized by their brilliance and the intensity of her gaze.

"I don't have a phone number but you can contact me through Camilla. If you find out anything."

"Of course." He nodded. He seemed to want to say something more but was unable to.

"Good bye," she said, and offered him her hand as though it was a flower. Once again they shook hands for so long it seemed neither wanted to let go, and both of them blushed a little before they managed to. Then Kayley shook hands with the others, mutely, as if he couldn't think of anything to say.

Romain observed the little scene with a writer's eye as if he was witnessing the beginning of a story. He noticed that Kayley followed them to the door and stood gazing after Ekaterina as they walked down the path. When they reached the street, Romain caught her turning quickly to look back.

7

Cyril Jones contemplated the scrawny-looking boy sitting beside him on the car seat, petrified with fear, as the Bentley headed smoothly for the motorway.

"What makes me attracted to these little runts?" he asked himself. "It can't be beauty. There's nothing much voluptuous about these bodies. What the hell is it? Why would I rather have this than Kate Moss or even her boyfriend, whatever his name is? It's got to be the fear itself. The fact that he's a trembling little wretch, totally in my power. Kate Moss or her boyfriend would be looking at me snidely, judging my body, judging my performance. This little shit doesn't judge. He's terrified of me. I guess that's what people like me need. Someone who can't judge. Who can't criticize. Who can't say no. Who believes everything you tell him. Who thinks what you're doing to him must be normal, because you're the adult — you know the world and he doesn't. So you can impose any outlandish shit on him as normal and he accepts it. It's as if you're creating your own world and he's part of it. He's a blank slate for you to write on. He's an innocent, just asking to be corrupted! And you're the one who has the power to do it."

He seized on this idea with relish.

"You're destroying innocence! Desecrating it! The thing the world holds most sacred — in its twisted, hypocritical way! It's as if you're striking a blow against the whole human race, against life itself, against the entire universe and whatever warped God created it! It's fucked up already so let's fuck it up some more! Let's fuck their children! Why not? Nothing is sacred! No one is innocent! Fuck the world!"

He recalled the last time he had taken Eric out, along with his little friend, the late-lamented Viktor. He remembered every detail as if it was stamped on his brain. He had told the care home director he was taking them to see a film, and his pal Brian that he was taking them to watch videos at his home. Historical videos about the war and its aftermath. Brian, he was sure, was not fooled. Cyril had taken the boys into his house and up to an upstairs lounge and had sat them on the sofa beside him in front of the big screen and the DVD player. He asked if they wanted to see history or sex, and when they giggled, he showed them some porn, both gay and straight, a kind of mixed orgy. They were fascinated! They couldn't take their eyes off it. Then he told them the correct way to watch this stuff was with their trousers down and playing with themselves. He showed them how and they followed suit on his orders.

"You're getting something very rare, my lads," he assured them. "Something no teacher is going to give you. Instruction about sex, the most important and most fun thing you'll ever do. And who the hell teaches you how to actually go about it or gets you started? Nobody! So I'm going to, as a special favour to you two, because I like you. This is a manly thing and it's time you became men. I want you to forget about shame and moral crap and just take your dick and twist it and turn it and beat it like a piece of meat till it gives you real pleasure. It's good for you, don't believe any of the crap the fucked-up priests and parsons tell you. We're living in a time of freedom when people can do what they like, and still the puritan, mealy-mouthed, uptight, impotent mob will tell you it's bad for you and if you do it your knob will drop off! Well, it won't, and I'm here to prove it to you. Your knob won't drop off from wanking it a bit. You're just giving it a bit of exercise, and your cock needs exercise every day like a dog does. In fact, treat it like a dog, give it a stroke and a pat every time you can and make it rear up and beg for more! That's the way! Now I want to give yours a stroke and a pat too, so come over here."

The boys reluctantly moved a bit closer, Eric with slightly more confidence.

"That's it, Eric, you've done this before with me, haven't you, lad, you know the ropes, you give mine a stroke and I give yours a stroke. Good! Now, little Viktor, the same thing, take my cock in your hand, it won't bite, and I'm going to take yours. Now, you see that, yours likes it, doesn't it? And mine does too. That's the proof there can't be any harm in it. To think there are people who would leave you poor kids ignorant of this beautiful and healthy sensation, out of vile moral bigotry, it's a crying shame! I'm giving you the most important lesson you'll ever have in your entire education, and the one you will never forget. Practical lessons, that's what you need! They talk of sex education and they don't even let you touch the bloody thing or take it out and look at it, and show everyone else! Why ever not? Because there is still all this shame attached to it! Sex education lessons ought to be given with the whole class naked! Encouraging the kids to play with each other! What is there to be ashamed of? It's part of our bodies and a beautiful part! Now, I'll show you how beautiful these parts are, they can even be sucked and licked. Did you know that, Viktor? Now Eric, let's have yours first. That's it, you like that, don't you? What a wonderful little tiddler it is, like a little eel. And now I want you to do the same for me. Always give and take, that's the rule. That's right, give it a good suck, lad, you won't hurt it. It can take a lot of that. Yes, harder still, suck on it really hard! And look at the difference you're making, see how it appreciates it! Now, little Viktor, you too, give us yours to nibble on. Just a gentle suck, there we go, and yours likes it, doesn't it? What are the tears for, what's this? Now, just take mine in your mouth and do the same. What do you mean, shaking your head? What's the matter? Do you think it's dirty? Look at this cock, freshly washed before I came to pick you boys up, nothing dirty about it, now take it in your mouth like a man! What do you mean no? Are you defying me? Do you want me to put you over my knee?" He flew into a rage, or at least pretended to. "All right, that's it, lad, I'm not going to have any of this bigoted, homophobic nonsense, take your jeans off this minute."

Cyril pulled off Viktor's jeans and underpants roughly, and tore off all his other clothes and his shoes in a sort of frenzy that terrified the boy.

"I want you naked as a worm! Right, over my knee you go, lad!" He swept him up and put him over his elephantine knee and began to slap his bare bottom as hard as he could. Viktor yelled in pain and began bawling.

"There, did you like that?" snapped Cyril, setting him on his feet again. "No? Are you going to behave in a civil manner then? Any time you say no, you'll get another one of those! Now, take my cock in your mouth, you ungrateful little wretch! Suck on it, I say, suck!"

Viktor sucked, but clearly with extreme ill-will. He was making faces as if it disgusted him. This homophobic prejudice enraged Cyril (even at that age they've been brainwashed by the homophobic Christian bigots!) But he kept control of himself and pretended to be calm again as he tried to reason with him.

"I can see you've got a lot to learn, lad, about respect for the body. You're a little puritan, aren't you? You've been brainwashed by the priests to hate bodies, and above all male bodies. Homophobia, it's called. It's a disease, lad. There's even a law against it. You can go to jail for thinking cock-sucking is wrong. Did you know that? It's called bigotry and hate crime. Was your mother some superstitious Christian? How dare she bring you up in these backward, medieval superstitions in this day and age! They should lock up Christians as lunatics! I want you to repeat after me: God is a piece of shit!"

Viktor looked at him in terror and shook his head.

"Go on, say it! God is a piece of shit! He's an invention, like Santa Claus."

Viktor still refused to say the blasphemous words.

"Then say this: cocks are made for sucking!" The boy merely sobbed miserably. Cyril glared at him. "No, you won't say that either, you homophobic little bigot! Do you realize anyone repelled by sex between males secretly wants it? It's been proved scientifically. All psychologists agree. Repulsion for gay sex is secret attraction to it. All homophobes are gay! You're in the closet, that's your problem, and I'm going to get you out. You need to confront your own secret desires. You're secretly gagging to be screwed up the backside, aren't you, and I think this is the moment to liberate you. What do you think, Eric?"

Eric was looking on, at a loss. Cyril focused his attention back on him.

"I think it's time, Eric, you moved to the active phase of your sex education. You've already been fucked up the arse several times by me and some of my friends I've taken you to see. Now it's time you learned to do the fucking. I want you to fuck Viktor up the arse."

Eric looked uncertain at this, and Cyril pulled him over by his cock.

"Look, it's ready for it, Eric, it's dying to get into something. Surely you know the basic principle? This time you're going to be the top, not the bottom. Now, Viktor climb up on the sofa and kneel down. Knees apart. Lean forward. Back horizontal. Not that way! With your backside facing out, how are we going to get at it otherwise?"

He arranged Viktor on the sofa so that he was kneeling with his hands holding the back of it. He tried to coax Eric to shove his cock into his arsehole. Eric was very uncooperative.

"Right, I'm going to have to show you. Now, the best thing is to grease the little hole with something for a start, I just happen to have a little bit of Vaseline on me, and it does ease the pain a bit, especially the first time." He took a tube of Vaseline out of his pocket and unscrewed the cap. "This will help to soothe you, Viktor, after the little spanking you forced me to give you." He put some Vaseline on his index finger and shoved the finger into Viktor's anus. The boy whimpered and began to cry.

"I don't want to!" he blubbered. "Please let me go home!"

"Let you go home! In the middle of the lesson?" Cyril sounded scandalized. "What kind of teacher would I be if I let you leave in the middle of a lesson? I'm your personal sex trainer, you little brat, and you're going to learn your lesson. And you'll thank me afterwards for the best day's education you've ever had. Now, Eric I want you to put some Vaseline on the end of my prick by way of preparation."

Eric was not terribly enthusiastic but he complied.

"Right, now, you see what you've done, you've got it in tip top shape, all ready to go. Now, Viktor, you're about to be liberated from the closet. This will hurt a little. Feel free to scream, it excites me!"

He seized the hips and thighs of the boy kneeling on the sofa, pulled his backside towards him and put his own knees on the sofa edge to get into position behind him. The Vaseline was obviously not going to be enough to facilitate entry, a lot of brute force would be needed. Pulling the buttocks apart with his thumbs, he thrust his organ at full tilt into the tiny pinched hole. He pulled the boy's hips towards him as he launched all his vast weight forward and shoved with all his might into the tiny narrow passage. Viktor screamed like a stuck pig, a scream not of terror but of agony. He hit High C, as Cyril liked to call it.

"That's it, High C, you little bastard!" he yelled in triumph, as he felt himself piercing the first centimetre of flesh, felt the flesh tearing and the blood flowing around his organ, lubricating it in a delicious hot wash. Viktor's blood did the trick and enabled him to force it further and further inside, and he was sinking into the boy's innards, tearing his insides, and the blood was gushing more freely, giving him a wonderful sense of liberation. He felt as if his awkward, elephantine body had become a juggernaut, an all-powerful weapon concentrated on this one point, a huge, irresistible drill going into soft slushy flesh. He felt himself harden even more with the sheer exhilaration of it as he thrust into the boy so violently his head hit the wall on the other side of the sofa. He continued to shove vigorously and he heard the knocking of the boy's head against the wall like a drumbeat as he thrust and thrust, further and further in, till he felt orgasm building up. The screaming had now stopped. This felt terribly good and somehow the knocking of the boy's head on the wall was an extra excitement, a barbaric accompaniment like a native tom-tom in some savage dance — it was a wonderful dull thumping and the boy's body felt more and more limp in his hands as if he was giving himself passively to the orgiastic experience. He came at last with a tremendous shudder, into what was now like a ragdoll in his hands, its head crushed against the wall for the climax, and then lolling as if it could no longer take any more.

"He must have passed out," a vague thought crossed his mind, as he flung the ragdoll down on the sofa and extricated himself carefully from the bloody hole, which had given him one of the most exciting experiences he could remember.

"Oh dear, he's fainted," he said sarcastically to Eric. "He must have enjoyed it too much." He reached forward and pulled Viktor's head up off the sofa by a hank of its thick, dark brown hair. His fingers felt a sticky, hot mess.

"He may need to rest for a bit," he said quickly. "I don't think he'll be able to go back with you to the home. I'll send him on later, when he fully recovers."

He noticed for the first time a smear of what looked like tomato sauce on the wall behind the sofa, a little distance above the back of it. His fingers were the same colour. He felt a vague disquiet.

"Is he all right?" asked Eric stupidly, with his yobbish mouth hanging half open.

"Of course, he is," said Cyril roughly. "You don't imagine the boy's dead or something, do you? He's fine. He's broken his duck and he's out of the closet. Now, let's forget about him, we'll wait for him to wake up again. I've been neglecting you, we can't let you go without your dose, can we?"

He pulled him over and began wanking him with his bloody hand, working him up into an excited state again. When the boy got near his climax, Cyril suddenly said:

"Right, squirt all over your friend, on his legs and backside, so you can tell him tomorrow: I sprayed all over you as well. It'll teach him a lesson for passing out in the middle of things. Go on, you little sissy, what are you waiting for?"

He shoved Eric against the sofa and directed his ejaculation onto Viktor's thighs. He rubbed some of it up onto his bleeding backside. Eric was suddenly in tears.

"Now, put your trousers on. Stop blubbing! And just remember what you did to him. Something to be proud of, lad! You sprayed all over him, the little faggot! Don't forget it! Now, let's get ready, the driver will be waiting downstairs."

He pulled up and fastened his own trousers as the boy did the same, and then hustled him out the door with his hand squeezing the back of his scrawny neck. As they went down the stairs he primed him.

"What you're going to tell them is that Viktor ran away while he was in this house, he asked to go to the toilet, and after that we couldn't find him. That'll give us time to take him to the hospital if he needs it and get him all fixed up. Then when he comes back nobody needs to know anything. Is that clear? And just remember, it's your spunk that's all over him, so you'll get the blame if ever anything goes wrong and the police get involved. Just keep in mind, no one is going to believe a lying little orphan brat, they certainly won't take his word against a Member of Parliament for the Liberal Democrat Party, given an OBE by the Queen for services to youth, so just tell them the story I told you, all right? And none of this sex stuff ever happened between us because they're puritanical, gormless morons and wouldn't understand what real men get up to, have you got that? And don't forget you've done this three times with me already, besides two of my friends you've given a piece of arse to, you wouldn't want that to come out, would you? You'll be called poofter for the rest of your life. They'll spit on you like dirt. No girl will ever look at you. You won't even get a job. They may even lock you up forever or cut your balls off for being a pervert. So keep it to yourself."

They got downstairs to the heavy oak door and he guided Eric by the neck down the steps. He shoved him into the back seat of the waiting Bentley and then shook Jameson's shoulder through the driver's window, as he was just waking up after a nap.

"The other little bastard ran away. You didn't see him come out, did you?"

"No, guv, no way. Must have dozed off."

"He may have gone out the other door. The police will find him. Anyway, take this one back to the home and if they ask about the other one, say he ran away. Asked to go to the toilet and disappeared. No point in calling the police for now, it's just another problem kid on the lam, he'll be back when he's hungry, or when some copper picks him up. And after that you can take the evening off."

Jameson nodded and started the car engine. The ageing Bentley pulled away and Cyril waved to Eric sitting in the back looking scared and pale. Of course, he always looked pale — why did these little bastards never get any sun? He should have been born in Morocco, that's where the street boys had copper-coloured, flawless skin and it was like going into a ripe peach. He had been there on holiday once with Rigdon, who was a professor at the Social Services Institute — he had written the definitive book about care homes for boys and knew every male brothel in the Mediterranean. That had been some trip! On some days they had had three boys apiece. Some of them as young as eight. God, they were tight! His organ still kept the memory after all these years. Come to that, this little bastard upstairs was not much more than that, he supposed, maybe ten. The bleeding arse was a bit of a problem but he could take him to Matthew and get that fixed up a bit — but if he was dead that would be damned complicated. That head wound had felt serious.

He climbed slowly up the stairs again. No point in rushing things with his weight problem, didn't want to snuff it from a heart attack too soon, just when he was onto such a bloody good vein of juvenile arse for years to come. These children's homes, God, they were like free brothels for the likes of him! Not a hint of suspicion from the managers when he came by at all hours to take boys out for a drive. Why would they suspect the local Member of Parliament? Of course, they could be doing the same thing, just quietly. Burrowing away every night after lights out. Perhaps they recognized a fellow-aficionado and put out the welcome mat so he wouldn't cramp their style in return. It was true, in his position he could recommend them for extra grants and so on. Make sure they passed inspections, and no questions were asked, no boys interviewed. What had become lucrative for him were the favours he could do other cat-flap burglars, as he called them. He could rent the boys out for at least a hundred a go, sometimes double. In these days of tight controls over MPs' expense accounts, that was not to be sneezed at. He had acquired a surprisingly large circle of prominent, successful acquaintances who shared his hobby. Judges, senior civil servants, politicians, bishops, lords. They were a select but steady market, utterly dependent on one of the few trustworthy sources of juvenile arse. That's why he didn't want any scandal over this unfortunate incident. It would ruin the whole lucrative business.

In the upstairs lounge the boy was still lying as he had left him. He leaned over him. He felt his jugular vein, put his hand on his heart. No trace of a beat. He held his wrist and searched for a pulse. Not a whisper of one. He turned the boy's head sideways and opened the eyelids. Whites of eyes. Not a flicker of movement. "Damn!" he said. He felt the wound on the front hairline. It was a nasty gash. And another on the temple, a big lump that had burst. But it was only blood, damn it all! Only a cut and some lumpish bruising. What had happened? Why was he dead? The boy was a bloody nuisance even now. A useless, snivelling little prick who couldn't even suck a dick! And now he had to dispose of his useless body.

There really were some superfluous people on the planet, he thought to himself. Hitler and Stalin had been right to get rid of a few million. This little shit, born in some dank council house of some pale, overweight, slatternly mother, who sat all day in a torn dressing gown, reading the newspaper something had come wrapped in over cups of stewed tea, the father long since vanished, wandering from one bleak, boarded-up town to another, one dole centre to another, leaving a trail of brats in his wake, and at one point some bright spark of a social worker had decided that the slatternly mother was "not coping." Perhaps she had taken to drink or drugs, or was sending him off to school with no breakfast, or with a few more bruises than the others. So the order went out to confiscate the child and stick him in a home. Home! That was a great laugh. Care home! Right! Care home. In the care of squads of dismal, balding, solitary buggers who had gone in for juvenile care homes as the one place they might possibly get their ends away into pre-pubertal backsides. These places were full of opportunities for it. These unruly boys needed twenty-four hour supervision. People sleeping on the premises in shifts. Doing the rounds of the dormitories to check there was no masturbation or buggery going on. What an opportunity! Boy having a nightmare, take him out to be comforted. Now, this won't hurt, it'll make a man of you, and it's our secret! He had often wondered if he could take them into his confidence, the care home workers — probably half of them were doing it. The only trouble was, he couldn't tell which half. Brian was a good egg and a fellow aficionado. But who knew about the others? All it took was one sanctimonious bastard, holier than thou. Even the ones he'd spotted as poofters were not necessarily into this and might not approve. It was a special taste — that of the ancient Greeks, the Romans. A superior, classical taste. Not given to everyone.

He had never been able to understand most poofters. How anyone can do it with an adult man he couldn't comprehend. The Greeks and Romans had stopped shafting boys when they got a beard, at around sixteen or seventeen. He saw modern fairies as delayed adolescents who had gone past their sell-by date. Mutton pretending to be lamb. Of course once it became accepted he had "come out" and claimed to be gay. It was simpler. It explained the lifelong bachelorhood, the sordid rumours. It gave him instant friends and allies. It also gave him protection. There was a whole caste of public school poofters in Westminster, stretching right across all parties, who stuck together and protected their own against bigotry, persecution, and "homophobia". And this protection seemed to be extended, almost without question, to those who did it with young boys. A lot of these people couldn't see the difference. Their own initiation into buggery had taken place at boarding school where their partners were by definition young boys. The active partner tended to be adolescent, but the passive partner, the young catamite adored for his rosy cheeks and plump buttocks, might be as young as eleven. Or even nine, in those schools that still taught all age groups in one place. So the average upper-class poof had been a paedo at school. He had probably done the odd pre-adolescent just for practice. He had certainly done somebody under sixteen — the legal definition of paedo. (When fagging still existed — small boys acting as personal servants to the sixth formers — it was pretty much institutionalized: "When you've finished my bed, young Fotheringay, here's something to suck on.") So a public school poof could hardly turn up his nose if some of his peers had kept up the boy habit, out of nostalgia, so to speak. For many politicians, any attack on paedos was a stalking horse for homophobic attacks on gay men, now regarded as the most normal men on earth — and not only normal but martyrs to centuries of persecution, and admirably courageous for coming out with it and telling the world about their habits. So the rumours of this one or that one with a penchant for boys were treated with contempt as vile homophobic calumnies against a perfectly healthy, normal, same-sex orientation, as respectable as that of Plato or Michelangelo.

He remembered when rumours about his own habits had come out in the press — notably gossip about him spanking boys on their bare bottoms in care homes. A Senior Politician had intervened in memorable fashion: "As far as I know he hasn't done anything that wasn't common practice in my day in every boarding school in the country. Spanking boys on their bare bottoms? Par for the course!" And with a tolerant, broad-minded laugh, the Senior Politician had dismissed the whole thing. That had been the end of that. From then on every inquiry into Cyril's activities had been smothered from above. MI5 and Special Branch had even confiscated police files of complaints and allegations against him. He was to be protected from vicious homophobic attacks because he was a Member of Parliament (and in later years a Member of the Privy Council.) He could sit on Defence or Foreign Affairs parliamentary committees privy to state secrets and be the target of blackmail by foreign agents. It was essential to protect him. Besides, if anything really unpleasant came out then his protectors would be investigated too, so they had a vested interest in covering for him to the very end.

He looked at the useless lump of pale boyhood on the sofa. Pity he hadn't confined himself to spanking.

"I suppose I could preserve it in formaldehyde and take it out and fuck it every now and again," he thought cynically. Then an idea struck him. "I wonder if one could pass it off as a modern art installation? Like that Damien Hirst's stuff — the shark in formaldehyde, the sheep in formaldehyde."

He wondered seriously if he could sell the body to Hirst to be used for an installation. He had put half a cow in formaldehyde, hadn't he? That had caused a stir. What about half a boy? Hirst might be looking for the next step in sensationalism. Hadn't there been rumours he had already used human body parts? But it might be difficult even for him to pass off an entire boy — or even half a one, he thought despondently. Busybodies would want to know where he'd got it. Though they hadn't worried about the shark or the cow. But a boy might be a step too far. For the moment. Would Hirst be interested in holding onto it in a freezer until times became more liberal? Surely, if things kept progressing, there would one day be dead boys preserved in formaldehyde in public art galleries? Why not get a stock of material in to be ready for that great moment — the ultimate blow struck against stuffy, bigoted, spineless bourgeois morality?

But no, he was dreaming. He almost certainly wouldn't be able to flog it to an artist. He considered briefly the various ways of disposing of a body. You couldn't just abandon it in a wood. Not with his sperm inside. It had to disappear. Bury it in the garden? Too damn strenuous for someone of his girth. Besides, there were the neighbours. Cut it up and put it in bin bags? Bit messy. Burn it on the fire? Smell and smoke getting out would be the problem. Or get someone or something to eat it? A large dog or two? What about a boa constrictor? He rather fancied watching a boy disappear inside a boa constrictor. Would have to be a damn big one, though. Or else he'd have to cut him in bits and feed the animal a limb at a time. How easy would it be to get hold of a large boa constrictor? Probably not very easy. There'd be health and safety regulations. You might even need some sort of permit. No, there must be people, for God's sake, who would eat a boy! Cannibals! There must be associations of them out there. Secret societies that would pay good money for a fresh boy. To be roasted on a spit amid a riotous pagan celebration. A Witches' Sabbath! Naked dancing in the moonlight! Copulation with masked strangers! There'd be the problem of transporting him. But groups like that probably had vehicles fitted out for the purpose, maybe even refrigerated vans. The difficulty was to contact them. They would keep a low profile.

He wondered if his mate Wayne would have any entrée into those circles. Wayne knew a lot of kinky people. He was a supplier of boys, and he disposed of the ones that had gone past their use-by date by transporting them to the boy brothels of Amsterdam where they would be sold out the back door to all sorts of oddballs. Not just common or garden paedos but sadists, fetishists, torturers, human sacrificers, Satanists and the like. Surely there would be the odd cannibal among that lot whom he'd be able to contact. Someone who would be quite happy to receive a fresh boy already dead. That was of course the problem. Most of these people would probably want to do their own slaughtering. But surely there must be some whose interests were more culinary than sadistic. Gourmets of human flesh. Partial to a slice of roast rump of boy with mint sauce.

He decided he had better put the boy in the freezer till he found a solution. A frozen carcase would be as good as a fresh one, surely. It worked with lamb from New Zealand. Tasted just as good. He picked the boy up and carried him from the room. He was surprisingly light. But it's true his legs and arms were rather thin. Hadn't been eating his spinach, obviously. He put a cushion under the bleeding backside to keep the blood off his clothes, and tried to keep the bloody head from nodding against him. He'd have to wash all the cushion covers afterwards. Or even buy new ones. He went down the stairs carefully. Be a bastard to fall over and have to call an ambulance with a dead boy at the bottom of the stairs. But he got him down to the utilities room, where the freezer was standing beside the washing machine. He rested the boy on the washing machine and opened the lid of the freezer. It was almost empty, apart from a stack of TV dinners dating from God knows when. The body slid in quite easily, doubling up nicely to fit snugly into the space. Room for a few legs of lamb on top of him, come to that. He looked remarkably like meat down there in the icy depths alongside the TV dinners. Pale. The white skin reminded him of a frozen turkey. He wondered how long he could keep him there. Perhaps there was no real hurry about moving him. Who would come looking here? He could take his time tracking down some cannibals, and move him only when he was sure they were reliable.

He telephoned Wayne in London and asked in code if he had any use for a bit of cold lamb. To his surprise, Wayne expressed great interest. He had had an inquiry from an artist. Damien Hirst? Cyril joked. No, not him but an imitator, on the way up, still needing to shock and scandalize, said Wayne. He was an occasional customer for young rent boys, so he could be trusted. Wayne wanted to know the age and condition. When

Cyril reassured him on those points, Wayne promised to come up immediately and transport the body down to London in his van. They agreed on a price.

And so Viktor's body was taken off his hands remarkably quickly and easily, and at a nice little profit. Wayne travelled with a portable freezer plugged into the cigarette lighter, so the body did not deteriorate at all in transit. And the artist, whose name Cyril was not told (but later found out), received the goods in excellent condition. Which was essential for the aesthetic quality of the art installation to be constructed.

Afterwards Cyril was surprised how little interest anyone took in the whole affair. He went to the children's home the day after it happened and explained the circumstances, elaborating on what his driver had already told them. It didn't seem to faze anyone. They apparently lost a couple of boys a year from each home. Runaways. They assumed they were living on the street or had been taken in like stray cats into various kinds of relationship. The police didn't even interview him when they were eventually informed of another runaway. It wasn't thought relevant whose house he had run away from. This was assumed to be a shiftless, feckless population of semi-feral juveniles who could only be expected to light out on their own occasionally in quest of adventure.

So it was not going to be difficult for them to explain the sudden disappearance of Eric. Another runaway. He knew he had no choice when Brian told him on the phone about a bunch of people, including Viktor's mother, fresh out of prison, asking questions about Viktor and wanting to interview Eric. They might even be the same people he had seen hanging around his flat in Pimlico, including that hysterical blonde woman, probably the mother. He had to get Eric out of the way immediately, just in case he blabbed the whole thing. He had no sooner got Brian's call at his surgery than he called Wayne, who proved helpful again. He offered to take Eric off his hands and told him to bring him straight down to London. Cyril wasted no time in calling Brian back and fixing a rendezvous for delivery of the boy.

Cyril assumed Wayne would use Eric as a rent boy, but he knew there were also other possibilities, particularly if the boy became difficult or dangerous — if he tried to escape or contact the police. Wayne had told him of his connections with the internet porn trade, and the network of film-makers for the dark internet. These included makers not only of hard-core porn but also of snuff movies. According to Wayne, this market was expanding fast. There were also people who wanted to buy a child sex-slave for long-term use, or people who liked to organize live shows to entertain friends, where some of the young performers, after a thorough going over, were sacrificed in ancient rituals. And these too could be filmed for the dark internet, to generate another layer of income from royalties for downloading.

Cyril contemplated the multiple ways a simple ware like a boy could be exploited for profit. It gave him a quiet, dreamy optimism about the future of the country. This place had enormous potential. With the extraordinary number of kinky people produced by a repressed, puritanical culture, with a tradition of single-sex schools, suddenly liberated to accept as normal all the outlandish erotic practices of the Roman Empire at its most decadent, the market was limitless. An entire generation of boys could be brought up to believe that buggery was normal. From the age of five they could be taught it at school, given their control of education. What a future of sensual bliss lay ahead! England, the paedophile paradise! They would soon make Bangkok and Manila look tame and even repressed. And all done with such discretion, such sublime hypocrisy, with not a vulgar ripple on the surface of the most morally staid society! Filled with high-sounding talk about love and the freedom to love in any way one might feel the urge to! Tolerance! Human rights! Equality!

He reached across and seized the boy by his thigh. Might as well start on him now and warm him up in time for the evening's entertainments. There would probably be a welcoming party for him if he knew Wayne. He would bring in several connoisseurs to try out the new piece of flesh. He ought to get in first before the boy's arse was banged out of shape. He rubbed Eric's thigh slowly, ogling him with an exaggerated expression of lust. The boy shrank into the corner of the car seat, closed his eyes and seemed to go limp as if he had given up hope.

8

When Camilla, Romain and Ekaterina got back to London, they had dinner in a Greek restaurant off Queensway near where the girls lived, and once again discussed their plans. They decided there was not much they could do on Sunday, except watch Cyril Jones's flat for any movement. They would have to wait till Monday before going to the Paedophile Unit of the Metropolitan Police to tell them what they had found out. They agreed to meet for brunch the next morning in Pimlico and then do a bit of spying on the politician's flat.

Camilla and Ekaterina were depressed that they had failed to find Eric, and worried that Cyril Jones might be planning to do away with him to silence a witness. Even a few glasses of wine did not cheer them up. It was midnight when they left the restaurant. The girls had only a few metres to walk but Romain accompanied them out of courtesy. He was curious to see what a battered women's shelter looked like, but all he saw as they said good night to Ekaterina was a dark, rather dilapidated old building where even the hall light didn't work.

The Boy in Formaldehyde

When he walked Camilla to the door of the house where her bedsit was located, he thought he would see if she might like to be kissed. He moved his head forward tentatively, but instead she gave him a quick kiss on each cheek in the French manner, as if she had misread his move, and said: "Thanks for walking me home." He said good night as if nothing had happened and walked away towards the Tube station.

On Sunday morning at eleven they met at Pimlico Underground station and walked to Cyril Jones's house. They rang the bell to flat four. There was no answer. They stood on the edge of the pavement and looked up at the fourth storey windows. They were curtained. There was no movement. After a while they went to a restaurant for brunch and came back afterwards for another spell of surveillance. Ekaterina thought she saw someone behind the curtain for a moment. But there was nothing more, and nobody answered when they rang the bell again. They waited and watched a bit longer. When they finally got bored they went for a walk along the river, the part of the embankment called Millbank.

"The trouble with detective work is that it's so bloody long and boring," said Camilla. "They don't show you that in the films."

They walked as far as the Tate Britain Gallery and decided to go in and look around, to try and take their minds off Cyril Jones and Eric for a while.

They went up the wide steps and through the imposing neo-classical entrance, and soon found themselves in some rooms full of modernist installations. They included some of Damien Hirst's works — a white display cabinet full of old shells, and a set of shelves with little bottles on them, supposed to represent a pharmacy. These were alleged to be profound comments on the scientific world. Someone else had attempted a sculpture, some skeletal bits of metal furniture painted red. Then there were the usual blank white paintings, at least a dozen by different artists. One or two had little reliefs of smaller white squares by way of variation (perhaps just to prove they hadn't bought the canvas already whitewashed in a shop.) There was a blank grey painting with four little square holes in it, which was entitled *Painting with Four Square Holes.*

"Are these people mentally handicapped?" asked Ekaterina curiously.

"I think you will find the mentally handicapped have a lot more imagination," replied Romain.

An installation called *Empty Room with the Lights going on and off* took the prize for sheer... well... emptiness, and it had indeed been awarded the Turner Prize. They walked about amid this junk in disbelief, with a growing feeling of depression.

"I wonder how long it will be before the *Boy in Formaldehyde* is exhibited here?" said Ekaterina bitterly.

"Yes, and perhaps a second one, with Eric in it," added Camilla. "They love series, don't they? Look at all those blank white paintings. I wonder what each one cost the museum — and the taxpayer, through state subsidies."

"Incredible how they get away with it, isn't it?" said Romain. "These things wouldn't have taken ten minutes to paint. And the ugliness, the emptiness, the repetitiveness of it all! This is the expression of shallow, ignorant minds, which have never been taught any skill, which have never been through the long, hard apprenticeship of learning a difficult, complex art, like painting portraits or landscapes — the only path to any form of wisdom." He looked around almost in wonder at so much imbecility. "You know, if you took all these blank canvases and vacuous installations and threw them on a rubbish tip full of miscellaneous junk and then asked people to go and find the works of art among the junk, they wouldn't bring back a single one of them. Yet if you did the same with the works in the Uffizi Gallery, most of which are hundreds of years old, ordinary people would find the lot in fifteen minutes. And the charlatans who run these places wouldn't even consider that an indictment."

They walked into another room and saw some Victorian pictures by John Everett Millais. The contrast provided by a painter who could actually paint was startling. It was like coming upon professional adult work after being in a kindergarten looking at the efforts of four-year olds. They admired a painting of three girls playing cards, which was set in an idyllic garden but was full of hints of love rivalries between friends, with all their jealousies and adolescent heartbreaks. It magically captured the atmosphere of an age, a bit like a Chekhov play, and was overshadowed by the same sadness — the sense both of time and youth fleeing and of a world ending. After a while they made their way to the Turner collection, and marvelled at pure genius. His landscapes and paintings of Venice and Carthage were of a visionary luminosity, the light almost supernatural. They stopped in front of one called *Regulus*, with a sunrise over Carthage of blinding intensity.

"You know who Regulus was?" Romain threw out by way of conversation.

"No, who was he?" asked Ekaterina.

"A Roman general captured by the Carthaginians and sent back to negotiate with Rome on their behalf. He gave them his word he would return. He persuaded the Roman Senate not to accept the enemy's terms, and then he returned to Carthage to face his punishment. They cut off his eyelids and staked him out to face the sunrise, which would of course blind him. In the painting we see that blinding sunrise as he would have seen it, the last thing he would ever see. The sun as a source of terror and torture."

"Good God!" said Ekaterina, impressed. "And it does look blinding."

"I didn't know you were such an expert on art," said Camilla, half teasingly.

"I used to take my students to the Louvre," he said. "I was able to justify it as French literature or philosophy, since I taught both. They were kids from the bad part of town, but they liked it. I used paintings to hang ideas on. Every painting can inspire a lecture."

"Oh, let's have a lecture then," said Camilla mischievously.

"Yes, we want a lecture!" cried Ekaterina, waving her fists like an excited child.

"All right," said Romain, slightly embarrassed to be put on the spot. He thought for a moment. "I'll give you one on Modernism. I did it once with a final year class. They were a bit shocked by my views, if I remember. I used an Impressionist painting to hang it on, but let's look at some late paintings of Turner."

He led them to two of Turner's late seascapes: *Snowstorm: Steamer off a Harbour's Mouth* and *Yacht Approaching the Coast*, and then to the apocalyptic *Shade and Darkness: the Evening of the Deluge*. They all featured dramatic clouds whirling in tormented and threatening vortexes, merging with a tumultuous sea.

"Strange how almost abstract his late paintings are, aren't they?" said Romain. "The things in them are so indistinct in this swirl of misty colour."

"Yes, you can see how his late work led on to Impressionism," agreed Camilla. "And even Abstraction."

"Exactly. And yet the important thing is that it is never entirely abstract. There is still this vivid expression of the physical world, of nature, which inspires a deep emotional response. That is what gives the pictures drama." He gestured at one of the paintings. "We see a boat outside a harbour in a storm, and we feel fear for the lives of the crew, a sense of helplessness before nature's terrifying power. All of that would be lost as soon as you crossed the line to a mere abstract pattern of colour — no boat, no storm, no sea, just a swirl of colour representing nothing real — it would be totally emptied of any emotional content whatsoever. To me that was the great wrong turning of modernist art, the shift to abstraction, the elimination of human emotion. Painters like Mondrian or Van Doesburg or movements like the Bauhaus were deliberately impersonal, machine-like, mathematical. They tried to eliminate every emotion, every personal feeling, everything human, everything natural, and to replace it with abstract, geometrical forms, utterly impersonal and machine-like."

He paused to see if they were following. He was satisfied he hadn't yet lost them.

"You have to understand this was not any sort of protest against the modern machine age, as we might imagine today — they worshipped the machine age! All their manifestos proclaim it. They hated nature! They hated personal feelings as mere slush! This was a declaration of war on human emotions! It was unprecedented in the history of Western art. It went against every artist's instincts in every age up until that time. It was so unnatural you could almost compare it with eliminating every personal emotion from sex — which is the essence of pornography or perversion. The abstract artist purges art of any personal or emotional element, just as pornography purges sex of any personal or emotional element. To me both are signs of sickness, and it is the sickness of the over-masculinized mind of the twentieth century — the century of world wars and militarism and mass murder on an industrial scale. All of that required the elimination of all emotions, a total lack of empathy, an ability to shoot a child in the back of the head or burn thousands of children alive by dropping incendiary bombs on cities, and see it as merely an abstract, ideological act of annihilation of an enemy. And that is something that psychologists are beginning to see is specifically a characteristic of the ultra-masculine mind. There is a Cambridge psychology professor named Cohen who claims that the male mind tends to be wired for systemizing, and the female mind for empathy. He says that at its extreme the masculine mind is autistic, incapable of empathy — the mind of a psychopath. If this is true, it is clear that our civilization for the last hundred years has been pushed in an extreme masculine direction. You can see this over-masculinization, this suppression of emotional empathy, not just in the trenches or the death camps or the carpet-bombing of cities but in every aspect of the twentieth century. The treatment of sex in literature moved from the realm of romance, a feminine, emotional thing, to the realm of pornography, a male, objectifying thing. Art moved from the depiction of people or the beauty of nature to the depiction of mere abstract forms, often geometrical or machine-like, the very image of the ultra-masculine mind. The machine was the god of Futurism, the first wave of Modernist art. Then Cubism reduced human bodies to machines. And it is when we reduce the human body to a machine in real life that we have pornography, and beyond pornography, perversion, rape and sexual slavery. In short, to me Modernist art is a perversion. It dehumanizes in the same way pornography dehumanizes. It's the reduction of human experience to an abstraction, a pattern of forms devoid of emotion. It's a perversion, like rape, like child abuse, like pornography, like mass murder."

He stopped, and waited for their reaction.

"Wow!" said Camilla, with a laugh. "That must have shocked your students!"

"They included quite a few budding drug dealers, thugs, pimps and prostitutes, so they could handle the shock. But I did adapt it a bit for your sake."

"You're right," said Ekaterina soberly. "And the greatest example of this art you're talking about is a boy in formaldehyde, a human being reduced to an object, to be used in a so-called work of art as he can be used in a work of pornography or an act of rape."

"Exactly," said Romain. She had summed up everything.

"I'm not entirely sure about this idea of masculine and feminine minds, and the masculine mind as tending to the psychopathic, but I agree we have moved away from human emotions in every domain," conceded Camilla. "The economic system, for example, is now a machine with its own dynamic, which steamrolls over any human feelings, just like the hideous urban architecture it has produced. The new capitalism exalts the financial machine, the market and its algorithms, over the needs and feelings of people."

"Just like communism in a different way," said Romain. "The historical process of industrialization requires this many deaths, so what? They are simply numbers."

"Tell me about it," said Ekaterina. "We Ukrainians lost six million peasants to Stalin's collectivization of farming. Deliberately starved to death or shot for trying to escape."

"The twentieth century was a sick period and it produced sick art," said Romain. "None of this modernist art protested against the new fascist machine world. It glorified it as wonderfully modern. Malevich, the Soviet inventor of the blank white painting, saw the airplane dropping bombs as the highpoint of art. Destruction was his god. Civilization had to be swept away as bourgeois dross. Humanity had to start all over again from zero. A blank slate, like his blank paintings. Destruction and the machine: that is modernism. To me the last normal, healthy artists were the Impressionists, clinging to life and nature and beauty against the coming horrors of the industrial machine age."

"But there were some protests," objected Camilla. "Picasso's *Guernica* is a protest against a mechanized war."

"Only superficially," said Romain. "It was largely a continuation of the distortion and mutilation of human bodies he was engaged in from Cubism on. He did more to deform and dismember the human body into hideous, grotesque fragments than anyone else — and that was nothing to do with a protest against war, just his twisted vision. He was a misanthropist, a misogynist and a clown. He just happened to be very good at drawing and did lots of it."

"I'm glad you allow him that!" laughed Camilla. "So who were the greats of the twentieth century, according to you?"

"Edward Hopper. Pietro Annigoni. The early Anselm Kiefer. Rodin, Mestrovic. Just like Rachmaninoff in music, they kept on with serious art in the face of the total collapse and surrender to charlatanism of the corrupt Modernist art establishment."

"There won't be too many who will agree with you in that analysis."

"Not in this generation. They've been brainwashed by the Modernist sect. But the revolution is beginning. Go to the European Modern Art Museum in Barcelona, the MEAM. There you see the new figurative artists in revolt against abstract-conceptual crap. In thirty years they will have changed perceptions. People will understand that Modernism was a cult of vandalism, an extremist movement that destroyed the tradition of art instead of renewing it. It was the artistic equivalent of fascism and communism, an attempt to return to a year zero and annihilate a thousand years of humanist civilization. Only those who resisted this nihilism were great artists. You can take any art form."

He paused as though waiting for suggestions or inspiration. Then he chose one.

"Take music. Take Debussy or Ravel. They experimented with a sort of abstraction, with breaking down the traditional scale, just as Turner or Monet flirted with abstraction. But like these painters they didn't go all the way — they stayed rooted in the expression of human emotions, in melodies that convey emotion. When later composers crossed the line into modernist, serial or atonal music, there was no longer any emotion, just a confusion of hideous, grating sounds, like madness. Human emotions are lucid, flowing, coherent, they have shape and development, they are narratives — all of that has gone from twentieth-century avant garde music. That's why popular music — jazz, rock, pop, or film music — has now taken centre stage, and academic music has become an irrelevant farce, culminating in the supreme idiocy of John Cage's *Four Minutes of Silence*. The equivalent of the blank canvas. The very definition of charlatanism. The refusal to create and the pretence that that is creation. Just because I, the spoilt brat artist, say so. Or like Marcel Duchamp declaring any piece of rubbish found in a junkyard — a urinal, a shovel — to be a work of art. But only because he says so. Someone else's urinal or shovel is not a work of art. That is the artist as conman, setting himself up as a medieval alchemist, able to transform a worthless piece of junk into a million dollar art-work by signing his name on it. Art as voodoo, or four generations of gullible zombies in thrall to a gang of conmen. Modern art is a new superstition as empty as medieval witchcraft. And when people wake up, modern art prices, believe me, are going to collapse. I only wish it would happen now while we can still put on trial the museum directors that have wasted public money on this garbage."

Romain had got carried away by his argument and had made it more passionately than he had intended, because of his rage at the modernist rubbish they had just seen and its destruction of the great tradition of art that had produced Turner. No London art school taught its students any longer how to draw, paint or sculpt. Instead, they taught them how to come up with silly pranks — like a room with the lights going on and off, or tearing up bits of paper and putting them in an envelope — a sort of Zen for idiots. This state-sponsored charlatanism, which kept the real, talented artists poor and unrecognized, was one of those forms of contemporary intellectual madness that drove him to fury whenever he thought of it. He had to walk away a few steps and look at some more Turners to calm down.

He was a little worried that Camilla did not share his views and he might have alienated her by his extremism. He knew that trendy English intellectuals always equated any attack on modernist art with ignorance and philistinism. It was the story of the emperor's clothes: they all had to keep up the pretence of seeing something in this garbage, for fear of being thought uneducated. When asked what they saw in it they would fall back on clichés ("it makes us think, it challenges our prejudices about art!") or else aggressiveness ("what allows you to say there's nothing in it? Who are you to judge?") He hoped they would not get to that point, as this really was a make-or-break issue for him in any relationship. Anyone so gullible and shallow as to accept Duchamp's urinal or Ryman's blank white canvas as a work of art could not be intelligent in any domain. They would be suckers for all the pseudo-intellectual crap of an age where organized artistic and academic fraud had become a trillion-dollar industry. He was silently praying that Camilla would not turn out to be a shallow, trendy, modernist-groupie fool, when she sidled up to him as he stood in front of another Turner and said:

"I see the point you're making. It was good for artists to get close to a point of rupture with representation of the real world, but not to go all the way. To flirt with the collapse of all traditions of figurative art or melody, but not to actually go over the edge."

"That's exactly it," he said, relieved. "We love Turner and Monet and Debussy because they pull back from the abyss of abstraction, after getting very close. They dance on the edge of the cliff. And that was really the high point of Western art. Artists should have continued dancing on the edge of the abyss. Instead of that they jumped. Art is now in the abyss."

Ekaterina drew them back to the subject of Cyril Jones, and they decided to leave the museum and take a walk past his flat again. They rang the bell and then looked up at the windows. Had the position of the curtains changed slightly? They could not agree on it. They walked up and down for a while longer, staring upwards. Camilla thought she saw someone behind the curtains, just for a moment. They waited and watched. Then Ekaterina claimed she saw a small dark object between the curtains. A camera, a phone? They stared intently. Nothing more happened. They didn't know what to do. Then Romain proposed having a pizza, and offered to pay for everyone. He was worried that Ekaterina might have no money to eat properly, and that Camilla might be a bit short as well. They found a pizzeria and had a meal and a glass of house wine. Then they walked to the Underground and agreed on a time to meet the next morning. At Oxford Circus they separated as usual, as the girls got out and took the Central Line to Queensway.

Ekaterina was in a talkative mood. After a while she asked how long Camilla had known Romain. She was surprised to learn they were only student and teacher and had never actually gone out together.

"He likes you," she said.

"Why do you say that?" Camilla sounded sceptical.

"I just know. He was trying to impress you today with all his talk about art. Also to find out what you think. Do you like him?"

"As a friend, yes. I've never really thought about him in any other way."

"Why not? He's interesting, kind, and good-looking. And an intellectual, like you."

Camilla did not encourage the conversation. But she found that Ekaterina, once her Slavic reserve was broken, was not one to tolerate barriers to communication. Camilla's bedsit was just along the street from the battered women's shelter, and since Ekaterina was facing a boring hour or two in a depressing place before bedtime, Camilla invited her to come up for a cup of tea. When they got into the bedsit and Camilla put the kettle on, Ekaterina settled down for what she thought would be a long, heart-to-heart conversation.

"Why are you interested in paedophilia?" she asked. "Why the website? Were you a victim of that?"

"In a way, I suppose I was." Camilla sat down in the armchair opposite her.

"Was it someone close to you?"

Camilla looked at her as if debating inwardly how much to tell her.

"My step-father. The man my mother married when we came here from Serbia."

"You are a Serb?" Ekaterina was astonished. "I thought you were English."

"I went to school here from the age of thirteen. So I don't have an accent. And my name — well, Camilla is also a Slavic name, but I was named after a Hungarian actress my mother admired."

"And your step-father — did your mother know about it?"

"In the end. It was very complicated." She looked away for several seconds as though lost in thought or unsure about what to say. "You see, I was in love with him. So I went along with it and kept it secret. But she eventually found out and told the police."

"And where is your mother now?"

Camilla shrugged.

"She has no more to do with me. She went back to Serbia and married again, a year after my step-father died."

Ekaterina hesitated, squirming with curiosity. Then she asked: "How did he die?"

Camilla looked at the floor. Then she spoke in a dead voice.

"I'm not sure. He was found dead in prison. Apparently hanged."

Ekaterina stared at her. She said slowly: "And why was he in prison?"

Camilla made two attempts before she could answer, as if her lips would not move as she wanted them to.

"Because of what he did with me."

"And you loved him?"

Camilla nodded this time, unable to speak. Ekaterina felt almost as distraught as Camilla looked.

"You poor thing! That must have been hell!"

"Nothing like what you went through." Her voice was unsteady, and then she got it under control. "You spent years locked up for defending yourself."

"But now I am free. I'm not sure you are."

Ekaterina wanted to give her a hug and reached out a hand and placed it on her shoulder. But Camilla did not lean forward into her arms as she expected, but instead merely put a hand on her outstretched arm and rubbed it slowly. It was an awkward moment, and after a minute Ekaterina took her arm away. She knew that some English people were not very comfortable with physical contact, and Camilla seemed to her to be thoroughly English. Ekaterina looked at her sadly, at a loss to express her sympathy.

Camilla gave her a tight smile and patted her arm as if to reassure her.

"I'll go and make the tea. And then we'll talk about you and what you're going to do with your life now."

9

Wayne sat in his Soho flat half-heartedly playing a video game in front of the big window that looked out at the city skyline. He was expecting delivery of a boy and wondering vaguely what he would look like. His mobile phone burst into the crazy first bars of AC/DC's *Highway to Hell*. Cyril's voice was more relaxed after the panic he had exuded earlier.

"That piece of lamb. I've got it on board. I can deliver it in about an hour and a half."

"Fine. See you then."

He ended the call. They had to watch how they used the phone and internet these days. Never knew who was listening in. Cyril was clearly relieved to be getting this boy off his hands. Wayne was getting him at a bargain price, and he would be a good little earner in one way or another. It was becoming a very profitable relationship.

He had been lucky with Cyril. The fat man's recent offer of a dead boy had come just after the surprising inquiry about one from that sicko young artist. Wayne was able to match supply and demand with perfect timing and at a very good profit. He was fairly sure he could place this new live boy quite easily, and in the meantime he could be rented out. There wouldn't be any problem if it was necessary to dispose of him for good. Young rent boys had a short shelf-life anyhow. After they lost their bloom, after a few hundred customers, they were shipped by special courier to Amsterdam to a boy brothel and then finished their days in internet porn, and finally in a snuff movie. If they had to be got rid of faster, there would be sadists, Satanists, human sacrificers, cannibals, all sorts of weirdos who would pay for the privilege. It was never hard to make them disappear.

He had never indulged in that sort of thing himself. He saw the weirdos, however useful, as sick. You couldn't judge them, of course; they were probably born like it. Wayne considered himself completely normal, apart from being queer. (He despised the word "gay" as a limp-wristed, sissy word, used by lisping fairies.) He didn't even see himself as a paedo. He was queer with a young tooth, as he put it. Fourteen and fifteen-year olds. Thirteen even. Twelve was the extreme lower limit. They had to be adolescent. Pre-pubertals were not for him. Not that he had much of a moral objection. It was purely a question of taste. Anyone going for genuine children, ten or below, had to be slightly kinky. They wanted total power. And of course he understood that, he wanted total power as well over the fourteen-year-olds — he loved to make them cry, scream, beg him to stop. But there was a certain satisfaction in dominating them because you already saw the beginnings of male strength and potency — you were humiliating and turning inside out a young buck, a potential stud and future rival. Someone who reminded you of the handsome young jocks you had known at school, those who were already taking out the pretty girls and showing off their success to the less confident. Those were the good-looking boys you really wanted to see on the floor blubbing as you screwed them up the arse. But he saw that as normal pleasure in power and domination. To do it to a kid who was a feeble, pre-pubescent little runt was just not satisfying. Who were you taking revenge on? What satisfaction was there in wrestling down a boy who had no muscles to put up a fight? He just couldn't see the point. Paedos who went for ten-year olds or even five-year-olds were going for something so weak that domination lost all sense. You might as well beat up a baby. It looked to him as if they really hated kids. But why? Was it their own weakness as children that they hated? Was it a form of self-hatred? Were they taking revenge on the innocence and naivety that had once been theirs?

He often wondered if scientists would ever understand paedophilia. Would it be regarded one day as simply a different sexual orientation, like homosexuality? But homosexuality had been explained biologically. It was all to do with hormones at the foetal stage. He had made a study of this. It was the aspect of his self-education he was most proud of, as it enabled him to understand himself. He had gone a few years before to the free lectures of a kinky professor called Rigdon, who had the reputation of being both a queer and a paedo and was a cult figure in those circles. (Later he became Wayne's client for the odd boy or two and they got to know each other slightly.) According to Rigdon, foetuses are not sexed in one shot at conception but progressively as they grow. A male foetus is directed to follow the male blueprint rather than the female blueprint (which is the default form) by the male hormone produced by its testes. But if the mother's body contains a chemical like dioxin which blocks the male hormone for a certain period, then during that period the foetus will follow the female blueprint instead. If this happens when a part of the brain called the hypothalamus is being formed, which contains the mating-centre, then the foetus will keep on with a female mating-centre — that is, an attraction to males. That's all homosexuality is: a male with a female mating-centre in his brain. Or vice versa, as lesbians have simply had an abnormal dose of male hormone at the foetal stage, which has switched their mating-centre to the male version.

Wayne had been led to follow Rigdon's free public lectures when he had a boyfriend who was transsexual (the only real boyfriend he had ever had.) He wanted to understand what made this boy think he was really a girl. Rigdon explained that there is also a gender-centre in the hypothalamus of the brain which determines what sex you think you are. If that thing doesn't get masculinized because of dioxin or other chemicals blocking the male hormone, then the gender-centre stays female instead of switching to male. The guy then thinks he's a girl, even though he has a boy's body. But ending up with the wrong gender-centre is rare — it occurs only in one in perhaps twenty thousand. Ending up with the wrong mating-centre is a lot more frequent: it occurs in one in twenty or thirty, depending which statistics you believe. The link between homosexuality and hormones had been discovered early, according to Rigdon, by observing animals. Even in the eighteenth century British farmers had noticed that some cows were lesbian and tried to mount other cows: they called them freemartins. They also noticed they were always cows which had a male twin. In the early twentieth century they discovered why. The calf foetus in the womb is inside a sheath, but often the sheaths of twins get stuck together. The male hormone being produced by the male twin can then pass to the female twin, causing her to be partly masculinized as well. That made her lesbian and sterile. That's how they discovered that the wrong sex hormones at the foetal stage cause homosexual behaviour in later life.

But to explain homosexuals and transsexuals in terms of sex hormones is fairly logical. But hormones can't possibly account for paedophilia. There is no hormone that makes you attracted to children. So, is it something you're born with? Or is it caused by things that happen to you in life? If so, what sort of things? What is it that made a Cyril Jones?

In the lectures Wayne followed in order to understand the riddle of his transsexual boyfriend, he learned a lot about his own sexual urges. Rigdon explained why there were butch homosexuals like Wayne, who only played the active, penetrating role. It was because in their case only the mating-centre in the hypothalamus of the brain got feminized, and no other aspect of the personality, so they had normal, masculine characters. By contrast, when the male hormone gets blocked by some chemical throughout the development of the foetus, then most of the personality follows the female blueprint, and you get an effeminate, sissy queer. Rigdon pointed out that butch queers were the only kind accepted among free men in Ancient Greece and Rome, where to be penetrated was a shameful thing. Only slaves were sodomized, usually by force. Wayne began to understand why he despised his effeminate, passive partners: it was as if he felt they were his slaves. And it was because he despised them that he had sadistic urges towards them. But this contempt didn't stop his sexual attraction to them — that was the paradox. He was attracted to boys who looked like girls while at the same time he despised them for it. Except in the case of the trannie, Lazlo, who pushed the buttons of desire far more strongly than those of contempt. Lazlo looked like a beautiful girl. He usually dressed as one. He acted like one. He liked to be treated as one. But he wasn't one. He had the body of a boy.

For Wayne that was perfect. To the point that he almost felt towards him that peculiar emotion others called love.

And then Lazlo ruined it by wanting to have a sex change. Wayne tried to stop him. He knew it would destroy everything he felt for him. But Lazlo wanted to be "normal", he said. They quarrelled violently. Wayne remembered one of the last things Lazlo said to him: "Do you think I want to spend my life with freaks like you?" After the operation everything was over. Wayne felt nothing for him. What did he want with a girl? If he wanted a girl he could have had hundreds. What he wanted was one of those extraordinary creatures who were exactly in-between, so that he could hardly tell which sex he was looking at. Where he looked at a girl and saw a boy and vice versa. Lazlo did it to him to perfection. He pushed all those buttons of sexual confusion. That was the essence of sexual fascination for Wayne. Not to know which sex he was screwing. It was as if the object of his desire must remain a mystery, forever out of focus behind a veil. And when Lazlo became a girl he was just another piece of meat of a kind that held no interest for him.

After his sex-change Lazlo married a straight man and began camping the role of wife. They even adopted little African children. Wayne never forgave him. He had destroyed that perfect in-between state that made him a dream partner for butch homosexuals. Wayne knew his own tastes were far from unusual. The gay districts of every big city in the world were full of drag queens, transvestites, and transsexuals in various stages of transition. They knew what butch queers wanted: men who resembled women — the in-between sex. But why did they want that? That was the mystery. Some of them perhaps wanted to pretend they were having a woman when they were really having a man. Or they wanted to feel the delicious ambiguity, the sense of the forbidden that comes from sliding from one sex to the other. Or they wanted to relive the moment of revelation when they first realized which sex they wanted. Whatever the cause, butch queers of the kind Wayne belonged to needed, in order to satisfy their ambiguous desires, a class of beings who were permanently trapped in gender ambiguity — who were lost in a no man's land between the sexes.

He had often wondered where this strange need came from. Perhaps butch queers like himself were in some sense bisexual. He knew that in Ancient Greece and Rome most butch queers had also shagged women. He had no desire to do so, so why was this feminine aspect in his partners so necessary? Rigdon had suggested that the butch queer's masculine personality was often in conflict with his sexual orientation, which made him self-hating and violent. This was perhaps because his discovery of his sexuality came much later when he had already adopted a strong heterosexual sense of identity. It was more of a shock for him than for the sissy queer, who usually knew from early childhood that he was different. The butch queer might have been a tough playground bully and suddenly he discovers to his horror in adolescence that his interest is in boys, not girls. This discovery is a shock because it goes against his whole self-image and sense of male identity. He has been socially conditioned to pursue girls and suddenly his balls are rebelling. Part of him wants to go with that social conditioning. He may resist his homosexual urges and try hard to make it with girls. He may even marry and then sneak off to public toilets to bugger strangers. In rare cases he may even try to repress his own impulses and join the religious moralists in violently denouncing homosexuality, as one or two fundamentalist preachers in America have done, before being caught in the act — not so much hypocrites as victims of an urge they have fought against in vain. But most often the butch homosexual ends up trying to have the best of both worlds. He goes for boys that remind him of girls, so as to satisfy both his sexual urges and his social conditioning. In short, he adapts his homosexual impulses to fit his heterosexual personality. The result is often an attraction to men who look like women, dress like women, play the role of women, or are even changing into women — provided they are not women. So he lives in a permanent world of gender blurring, where he does not have to decide whether his urges are homo or hetero, where he can use a woman's face to arouse desire but a man's arse to satisfy it. And because his partner is really a male, who triggers an instinct of aggression, he can give vent to all his pent-up violence and self-hatred, and shag as brutally as he wants. And many sissies, paradoxically, like exactly that kind of brutal treatment. The sissies' male aspect, however suppressed, makes them enjoy violence, and they may identify with the violence done to them as an expression of their own aggression. They may even take pride in the fact that they can endure a degree of sexual violence no woman would ever be able to stand.

It is this conjunction of sex and aggression that Wayne was addicted to. He wanted to screw hard, rough, and without any tenderness or affection whatsoever. To him sex was an affair of aggression, not love. It was like a boxing work-out where you try to take your sparring partner's head off. And he was always surprised to find how many sissy queers, with all the appearance of delicacy and sensitivity, wanted that rough treatment as well. Was it masochism, he asked himself? Was it self-contempt, a craving for punishment that made the sissy homosexual want to be brutalized? In any case this tendency was quite widespread in the milieu, and had its own name — a liking for "rough trade". He had encountered sissy partners who yelled for more: "Harder, rougher, rape me to death!" After a few years he found it disturbing and rather off-putting. He wanted to be the one imposing the brutality, not just supplying it on demand. That is why he began to prefer the boys younger and younger (and preferably heterosexual, to start with.) They were more naive, and more shocked by his violence, which was the reaction he sought. He didn't want jaded partners who took his most brutal moves in their stride and yelled for more. He wanted someone who was devastated by his brutality, who was shocked, reduced to tears, as a girl might be, so he could roughly comfort, or coldly humiliate. In short, he wanted to be the one inflicting life's cruelty on the other, making him feel it for the first time. He wanted to violate innocence and naivety and see it in tears, and then choose what degree of comfort he offered. He did not want someone to get up and say: "Well, you didn't make me bleed much or hurt much — that was pretty average." It was this need that gradually made him shift from jaded drag queens to the very young, the naive, the easily shocked, the heterosexual.

He supposed, in a way, that paedophiles might have something of the same need, but just pushed it further along. They wanted to see children cry. He was content to see fourteen-year-old boys cry. There wasn't really that much difference, he admitted. All butch homosexuals have something in them of the paedophile, because anyone who wants a boy who looks like a girl is inevitably attracted to the very young, since they look the most girlish. Despite the shrill gay propaganda that paedos and homos are totally different, it was in fact hard to draw the line between them. What would you call that American football coach who shagged his fourteen and fifteen-year-old players in the shower? Was he a paedophile? Or was he just a butch homosexual who liked them young? Where was the borderline between paedo and queer? It couldn't be just the legal age of consent, which in Europe varied from thirteen to seventeen, and until recently eighteen or twenty-one. How could that change the nature of the impulse? You don't have one sexual urge when shagging a fifteen year-old and a different urge the next week when he turns sixteen, or when you cross a border into a country where it is legal at fifteen. It's all the same urge. To him the only real dividing-line was puberty. Pre-pubertal targets means paedo. Post-pubertal but under-age means queer with young tastes. That was the definition Wayne preferred. He saw himself as a queer with young tastes, not a paedo.

The doorbell rang. He got up and looked through the spy-hole in the door. Then he opened it. A man stood there with a boy of about fifteen with longish dark hair. Wayne noted with pleasure he was good-looking. They had obviously cleaned him up and washed the street smell off him. He handed the man the envelope in his back pocket, and took the boy by the shoulder as the man shoved him forward. He stepped back in and drew the boy into the flat. He had the door closed and locked again before the boy could even consider flight or yelling. He shook his limp hand.

"My name's Wayne. What's yours?"

"Alex." The voice was neutral, not sullen, not friendly. Worried perhaps. He was waiting. Bewildered. Trembling slightly. He looked around, took in the spacious apartment, the view of the city skyline through the big windows, the white leather furniture.

Wayne looked at him with satisfaction. He would just have time for this before Cyril got here with the next one. Things were shaping up into a decent Saturday evening.

"You're a pretty boy, Alex. Ever been fucked before?"

"No." Sullen this time.

"I'll show you how it's done. You're going to need to know, where you're going, and it's better if I'm the one who breaks you in. Have you had a shower?"

"Yeah. They gave me one."

"Had some food?"

The boy nodded.

"Good. Then come over here on the sofa. I'd like to kiss you. Ever been kissed?"

"No. I don't kiss men. I don't like this. What's going to happen?" His accent sounded vaguely middle class. He was beginning to panic. He ducked away from Wayne's outstretched arm.

"Nothing. You're just going to be taught the facts of life. And if you fight me, I'll hurt you. Got it?" He moved slowly, very calmly towards the boy.

"What are you going to do to me?" Really scared now. Backing away.

"I'm going to turn you into a faggot. A raving queen. In a week you'll be gagging for it. Then I'm going to sell you to friends. They'll take care of you." His voice was silky smooth. "You're going to be rental property. You might even be filmed. You'll be on the internet. Not your face, of course. Just your arse."

He paused, trying to gauge the boy's reaction. Would he break down and blubber straight away? The soft brown eyes were clouded, struggling to take this in. He thought he would offer him some comfort.

"You'll earn a living. Of sorts. You won't have to sleep on the street anymore. You'll have a bed. You'll have food. And you'll have sex. What more could a young boy want?"

"Sex?" the boy said uncertainly. "You mean with a girl?"

He must be really stupid, thought Wayne. His voice hardened somewhat to show his irritation.

"No, not with a girl, you twat. You're going to be the girl. I'm going to turn you inside out."

10

On Monday morning Camilla, Romain and Ekaterina went to New Scotland Yard and asked to talk to the Paedophile Unit. Ekaterina was nervous going into the building and didn't dare look at anyone for the first five minutes. Camilla did the talking because she sounded English and had her paedophile victims' website as a reference. They were sent to a higher floor and finally shown into a room with a table and chairs. A few minutes later a plump, fair-haired woman in her forties came in. She introduced herself as Detective Inspector Stubbings and sat down across the table from them. With their consent, she recorded the interview.

Camilla began the story with the Boy in Formaldehyde, and Ekaterina's recognition of the boy as her missing son, Viktor. She gave a brief account of Ekaterina's time in prison, and how Viktor disappeared from a children's home in Birmingham while on an outing with Cyril Jones. Then she recounted their visit to the children's home and how one of the staff, Brian Spenser, lied to them to stop them talking to a boy called Eric Page, who had apparently been with Viktor at Cyril Jones' house when he disappeared. Brian was later seen by other boys leaving the home with Eric. At the same moment Cyril Jones interrupted his constituency surgery and went somewhere in a hurry. Camilla concluded Eric had been spirited away so they couldn't talk to him about Viktor's disappearance. She mentioned Ekaterina's visit to Cyril Jones's flat and how a Polish boy of fourteen had been taken to see him, and had tried to run away. She had called the emergency number to ask the police to intervene, but they had refused.

Detective Inspector Stubbings looked intrigued and then increasingly worried. But at the end she looked slightly embarrassed.

"I'm glad you've come and told us all this, we will investigate it all fully. However, I should warn you it may be difficult for us to act decisively at this stage."

"My son is in a tank of chemicals, on show in a gallery, and you cannot act?" asked Ekaterina, both sad and incredulous.

"The problem is to know whether it is your son, or even a real body," said the inspector.

"But surely the only way to find out is to examine the installation," said Camilla.

"That will mean confiscating it and dismantling it. There will have to be a court order. It is private property, and a work of art, probably insured for a certain sum, and so on. It will certainly get into the media and cause a scandal. Interfering with artistic freedom, witch-hunt for paedophiles, and so on. It could make us look ridiculous or lead to a court case. That decision will have to be made by someone higher up. And we don't want to scare them into moving it somewhere else and hiding it."

"And what about the disappearance, probably abduction, of Eric, Viktor's friend, and the only witness to what happened to him — surely you can demand that the children's home tell you where the boy has gone?"

Detective Inspector Stubbings looked a little uncomfortable.

"There we'd have to have somebody with a legitimate interest in the boy, a relative, for example, asking about him, to launch an inquiry."

"But surely you can do it in the context of an inquiry into the disappearance of Viktor, which his mother here is demanding?"

"We can certainly launch an investigation into Viktor's disappearance, that is no problem at all," she conceded, as if to reassure them. "And we can demand to see Eric as a key witness, and we'll then inquire into where he has gone. This will all have to be done in liaison with the force in Birmingham. We'll also interview Cyril Jones."

"I suppose you're aware Cyril Jones seems to have benefited from a certain amount of protection in the past," said Camilla pointedly. "As a Member of Parliament."

"I can assure you we are not influenced in our inquiries by the position people occupy," Stubbings said firmly, looking at her directly. "Nobody is above the law. Now, apart from Brian Spenser, were there any other social workers you spoke to?"

"We spoke to one called Kayley Burke," said Camilla.

"But he seemed entirely innocent," Ekaterina put in quickly, "and did all he could to help us."

"What about the director of the home?"

"We didn't see him."

"But I don't think Kayley trusts him," said Ekaterina. "He gave that impression."

"It's not clear whether the director, Edward Marlowe, is part of the paedophile ring or not," said Camilla. "But Brian Spenser is."

"I'm not sure we really have enough evidence at this stage to assume the existence of such a ring," said the inspector, smiling sympathetically but a little embarrassed. "We mustn't get ahead of ourselves."

"But what else would explain the disappearance of these two boys and the deliberate attempts to cover it up and stop us talking to one of them?" demanded Camilla.

"Of course that may be the conclusion we eventually reach. But we must let the evidence take us there step by step, not make assumptions in advance, which may prevent us following up other leads." The inspector smiled kindly and patiently, as though explaining an esoteric science to the uninitiated. "Police methods are rather pedestrian, rather methodical and painstaking, a bit like scientific research, but we get there in the end."

"Let's hope there'll be somebody left alive when you finally do," said Camilla with a tight smile.

Detective Inspector Stubbings looked at her with deliberate calm, as though her training was holding down an instinctive reaction of irritation.

"What I mean is, don't expect the immediate arrest of the people you suspect, or the immediate confiscation of this work of art with the boy in it, but we will be investigating behind the scenes even if it's less spectacular than you might have hoped."

"But what if there's a real emergency, like there was when Ekaterina saw a boy being taken into Cyril Jones's flat? Can we call you and get some immediate response?"

"Yes. Here's my card and I promise we'll respond at once if there's an emergency where lives are at risk, or children are in immediate danger. I can be reached on my mobile 24/7. And I'll make sure the appropriate units are mobilized to intervene."

She handed Camilla a card. She seemed to realize they were disappointed things were not going to happen as fast as they had expected, and tried to cheer them up.

"Now, I can't emphasize enough how valuable your information is, but you must be patient till our work bears fruit. And don't take things into your own hands. These people could be dangerous and you might compromise our work."

She gave them a maternal smile and indicated the interview was over.

The three left the police station in a mood of despondency.

"Well, that's the police," said Romain, when they were outside. "They're the same everywhere. Bureaucrats."

The two women were angrier and more disillusioned.

"They don't care," said Ekaterina bitterly, gazing down the street at the trees where she had sat three days before. "My son can stay in his tank as far as they are concerned."

"They're cowards using their own stupid rules as an excuse for doing nothing," said Camilla. "They should take that installation apart and then search Cyril Jones's flat for the DNA of boys he's had in there. They're just scared of making waves. Or else he's above the law, whatever she says."

11

Ekaterina had to go back to the battered women's shelter to help Maeve talk to a Lithuanian woman who had come in the night before. Romain and Camilla took her to St James' Park Underground station, where she could get on the Circle Line direct to Bayswater, since she still had a few problems navigating the Tube system. Camilla then suggested going to a café but Romain said he was feeling a bit out of sorts after the interview with Stubbings (he had also got up earlier than usual after writing till late) and thought an hour of yoga might be what he needed. He proposed going back to his place for the French and yoga lessons they had missed on Friday. Camilla agreed.

Romain suggested taking the number 24 bus to Camden Town so they could see the streets of London from the top deck like tourists, by way of a distraction. As they sat side by side on the front seat looking at the moving panorama of famous buildings and animated crowds, he felt for a moment like a sightseer open to the impressions of the world. The sun was pouring down on them from the side window on the right and as they passed Westminster Abbey Camilla took off her jacket and sat in a T-shirt that didn't quite meet her jeans. He was conscious of her slim body next to him, and he felt an urge to put his arm round her or take her hand. He felt a hollow in his stomach like hunger and realized he was miserable. The time he spent with Camilla without any physical contact or progress in their relationship was beginning to get him down. With any other girl he would have just taken her hand to see how she reacted, but he couldn't with her because too much was already at stake if she rejected him. He knew any seduction had to come through talking, through a meeting of minds and souls. He hoped they would talk seriously in his flat and get off the subject of the paedophile ring and also get beyond the teasing, ironical banter that had become their way of relating. He wanted to get behind the defences she seemed to put up, and see what it was that made them necessary. He suspected it was neither shyness nor aloofness, but some kind of alienation from the world caused by something in her past. He wanted to know what underlay this state of mind, to see if it was something that he himself might recognize.

Meanwhile they continued talking about the matter at hand and what to do next. They agreed things could not be left to Inspector Stubbings, and they had to keep on with their own investigation, and especially try and get to know Bendigo. They talked about setting up the website for the fictive castle in Bordeaux. They discussed what sort of photos they needed to steal from other websites. And if they got to meet Bendigo, what kind of incriminating things they would try and get him to say, which could be recorded on a smartphone. As they walked into Romain's flat, Camilla suggested they should enlist Kayley to spy on Brian and find out all he could about his movements and contacts.

"We should get Ekaterina to ask him," she said with a smile, throwing her jacket on the sofa. "I think she fancies him."

"Yes, I noticed there was a little spark between them." Romain began filling the kettle for a cup of tea in the kitchen alcove. "You gave him a hard time there at the end and she came galloping to his rescue and turned on all the Slavic charm."

"Do you think he feels the same way about her?"

"I imagine so. She looks like a top model; why wouldn't he fancy her too?"

"Well, you never know." She shrugged. "He might be gay, for one thing."

"I doubt it. When she started gazing into his soul, he couldn't string three words together. His brain was short-circuited by those green laser eyes of hers."

He felt the irony that they could talk about others' mutual attraction but not their own. He plugged in the kettle and got out two mugs and tea-bags. She sat down on the little sofa.

"It would be nice if they got together, wouldn't it?" she said. "She deserves a bit of joy in her life. After the hell she's been through. And Kayley seems quite a gentle, sensitive person, don't you think? Just what she needs."

He sat down in the armchair opposite her.

"Is that what made you think he might be gay?" He grinned teasingly. "Men can't win, can they?" He found the English obsession with speculating about people's sexual orientation childish, but he also wanted to stay on the subject of sex in its less conventional forms for a reason. She had hinted that her interest in paedophilia was motivated by an experience in her own childhood, and he wanted to lead her on to talk about it.

"That's unfair." She sounded a bit hurt and embarrassed, as though he had accused her of a prejudice in judging someone. "You must admit, he's got such a boyish-looking face, it's almost girlish-looking, his features are so fine."

"That doesn't mean anything," he said dismissively. "Most of the poets and artists in history were a bit girlish-looking but the vast majority weren't gay." He saw a chance for a bit of humour. "Milton at Cambridge was nicknamed the Lady of Christ's College. Yet he married three times — and his third wife was less than half his age. A trophy wife, they'd call her today. Even if he couldn't see the trophy by then, poor bastard." He was indebted for these titbits to his English professor at university, a hard-drinking Australian with a taste for ribald literary gossip. She laughed obligingly.

"All I meant was: in England you can no longer assume a man is attracted to even the most beautiful woman, because so many men are gay. I think it's something in the water."

"It's a bit the same in parts of Paris. But it's true it's a lot more obvious here. What is it? Boarding school culture? Single sex schools? What do you think?"

"I really think it's a change in society," she said seriously. "I think men and women here are mutating — the women becoming more masculine in character because of feminism, and the men becoming more feminine and wimpish as they get hen-pecked and walked on by aggressive, domineering women. And this new war between the sexes is leading to a gay epidemic on both sides. It's a historic change."

"It's true that the characters of the sexes and the relations between them change subtly in every decade," he said thoughtfully, feeling another bout of lecturing coming on. "And men's characters have mutated radically in every century for the past three or four. In the eighteenth century upper-class men dressed in silk cloaks in colours like red or gold, they wore pink stockings, high heels, and huge blond wigs, and in their novels they were always kissing everyone or bursting into tears. In the nineteenth century men dressed entirely in black, tears were forbidden, and they didn't even kiss their own children. In the period of the world wars they became shaven-headed Marines and SS thugs who didn't blench when somebody beside them had his head blown off. And then in the sixties they revolted against war and went back to long hair, beads, flowers, free love and writing soppy love songs. Right now I think they're a bit undecided which way to go. And the gay sect is definitely in the driving seat."

"But why did this gay cult suddenly become so dominant, do you think?" She sounded mystified. "The idea of two men getting married and calling each other husband is frankly hilarious but nobody dares to laugh. And is it an increase in numbers or just an increase in noise?"

"Well, as you said, the feminist movement put an end to the flower power honeymoon between the sexes by declaring war on men. When sexual liberation keeps barrelling ahead, with sexual images as urban wallpaper, and 24-hour porn on your smartphone, but girls are brainwashed to see men as the enemy, as a horde of rapists, wife-beaters, and oppressors, then logically you get a homosexual cult in both sexes."

"So, you agree it's all down to feminism?"

"Pretty much so. I think feminism, with its preaching against motherhood and marriage and its demonization of men, actually aims at creating a homosexual world, with artificial reproduction. The gay sect is just carrying out their agenda. While selling itself as a trendy, touchy-feely extension of the pop culture, the fashion world and sexual liberation."

"So where will it end? Does this gay cult go on spreading till it takes over?"

"It's a suicide cult, so it will end in death. The result of both feminism and the gay cult will be white demographic collapse and an Afro-Asian majority, dominated by Muslims, within fifty years. Then both these suicide cults will be wiped out by Sharia law. They'll be hanging gays in Hyde Park before the century is out. The West will die but we'll lose feminism and faggotry in the process. There's always a silver lining."

"That's a rather bleak view." She stared at him uncertainly. "Are you serious?"

"What do you think? I taught in immigrant ghettos in France where gays would go at their peril and lesbians got gang-raped, along with white girls. And yet the feminist-pinko-gay left were in total denial it was happening, accused anyone who mentioned it of being a Nazi, and screamed for more immigration. What does that tell you about the future of Europe?"

The kettle signalled by a whistle that it had boiled. He got up and poured water onto the tea-bags in the mugs.

"Sometimes I do get the impression Western society has a death-wish," she said gloomily. "And its wish is going to be granted. If only we could start again somewhere else, maybe on a remote Pacific island, where people still have natural instincts, and without all this baggage from the past." She sounded wistful and melancholy. He came back and sat down. "Speaking of which, why did you leave your Pacific island and come here to Europe?"

"The lure of a complex, doomed and dying civilization." He grinned sardonically. "I wouldn't miss the death of the West for the world."

"No, seriously, what was wrong with New Caledonia? It sounds like paradise."

"Too far away. Completely out of the loop. Too wild and untouched by man."

"And why is that bad — untouched by man?" Her curiosity seemed to be aroused. He saw it as a challenge to keep it that way.

"No haunted castles. No medieval cities with winding cobbled streets and mysterious ladies on balconies, while the notes of a Chopin nocturne drift from an open window. Impressive landscape, but without any soul. Without any history — at least that I could relate to. I always felt I was in the wrong place on the planet when I was a kid. All the best stories happened in Europe. The place of my ancestors."

"So you'd never go back and live there?" She studied him, as if imagining his childhood on a Pacific island for the first time. "Do you ever go back and see your family?"

"I go back to visit my mother when I can afford it. My father's dead now."

"I'm sorry. Were you close?"

"Not really. We got along but we were very different."

"What was he like?"

He thought for a moment as he called up an image in his mind.

"He looked like a Breton sailor, with curly hair, piercing blue eyes and a weather-beaten face. He was a great sportsman, a football player, a champion wind-surfer. He then set up a business running charter surfing boats for tourists. He was outgoing, sociable, he got on with everyone including the Kanaks. He got into local politics. He completely overshadowed my mother, who was from an old cattle-ranching family, originally from Alsace, and a lot more reserved. My older brother took after him. He became a kite-surfing champion and then set up a diving school." He stood up again and moved to the kitchen alcove. "You take milk, don't you?"

"Yes, please. So, what sort of boy were you, growing up?"

He removed the tea-bags from the mugs and added milk. He was pleased to see she was now in full interrogation mode and was trying to find out about him seriously for the first time since they had met. He was keen to keep this conversation going so that he could get her to talk about herself in the same way.

"I had a fairly normal boyhood. Swimming. Surfing. Fishing. But I never became a great sportsman, apart from the aikido. I was more of an introvert, a dreamer, a secret scribbler. My mind was always somewhere else in the pages of Dumas and Hugo."

He put the mugs of tea on a small coffee table, and then brought a sugar bowl. She took her mug on her lap. He sat down again and served himself two spoons of sugar.

"So how did your family react to this strange bird in their nest?"

He smiled fleetingly, amused at the memory, now so far away.

"In their eyes, I was a slight disappointment, in spite of my success at school and university. To them I could never be half the man my father was."

"That sounds like a bit of a burden to carry."

"That was just the mentality of that milieu and way of life. But my father did his best to communicate with me, to try and figure me out, even though his own education was limited, he hated school." He looked vaguely out the window at the sky above the brick wall. "I remember he once came across me reading Cicero. He asked me what I saw in it. I told him Cicero was a Roman lawyer and philosopher. He said he knew that but why was he worth reading now? I tried to explain. I said that Cicero believed in a universal moral law, true for all ages and places, which every human being could intuit, whatever his culture or the laws of his country. My father asked: and was he right? I said it was a fine idea but I thought that Cicero was wrong, that there is no universal morality. His society accepted slavery, torture and paedophilia, and he probably did too. My father concluded: in that case, why read him? I couldn't actually answer that. Something about the history of ideas that I couldn't explain, that even false ideas pose insoluble problems — because in some sense they're true." He looked at her with a slightly puzzled grin. "I didn't fit into that world. I had to go somewhere that understood the world of ideas. The life of the mind — that of the writer. The world of words."

"And did you find all that?"

"In a sense, but it was not what I thought it would be."

"In what way?"

He sipped his tea, ill at ease. He was now getting to the heart of his real feelings, and he was afraid of how she might judge them, as well as afraid of seeming self-absorbed.

"Writing is a solitary business. The life you live outwardly is just a show. The real life is in your mind. The relationship you want with the world is through your writing. But if you can't get published and nobody reads your stuff, that relationship is missing. You remain cut off; you have no existence in the outside world. Except for your day-job, which is just a game. The essential you, the writer, is like a ghost. You can't evolve artistically because in the real world you don't exist. And you finally lose sight of what you wanted to say, as your own alienation from the world begins to dominate and even distort your way of thinking."

She studied him thoughtfully for a few seconds.

"I read your book," she said awkwardly. "It was well written, as far as I could judge in French, but I felt you were writing about what really meant not very much to you. It was well observed, but you felt very little about it, as if you were at a distance from it, or as if you were holding everything back."

He smiled slightly, a little sardonically.

"The trouble is if we wrote today what we really feel strongly about, it would be a diatribe that could never be published, and if it was, it would get us arrested."

She stared at him, as if unsure what he meant by this.

"You mean because of the *pensée unique* we live under, the political correctness? The intellectual dogmas that can't be questioned?"

"Exactly."

She was silent for a moment, gathering her own thoughts. When she spoke again it was with a slightly nervous, self-conscious air.

"I can relate to that. I was born on the wrong side of history."

"Europeans have been taught they were all born on the wrong side of history, and it's time to die out. But I take it you mean because you were born in Serbia — or rather, Yugoslavia?"

"How did you know?" she asked in astonishment.

"A little bird told me this morning, while we were waiting for you to top up her Oyster card. She asked me if I knew. I was surprised. You really sound English."

"I came here at the age of thirteen. Now I am English."

"With an impeccable public school accent. The dulcet tones of Oxford."

She shrugged.

"That's where I went. As Shaw pointed out, it's the accent that makes an Englishwoman of the educated classes. Not origin, not pedigree, not wealth, not even a university degree. Just the accent. You can get it at thirteen. If you go to the right school."

He felt a slight nervous excitement at how quickly they had got onto her personal history. Now he was eager to know all about her, and began to prod her to recount her past, but carefully, tactfully, for fear she would clam up and go back into her shell.

"So, if I calculate right, you left Serbia round about the time of the war?"

"Just after. When Belgrade was a smoking ruin thanks to NATO's bombs. My mother and I saw no point in staying."

"And your father?"

"My father had been killed a few years before in Bosnia."

"I'm sorry. So he was a Bosnian Serb?"

"No. He was in the Yugoslav Army. He was stationed there and when Bosnia declared independence he stayed on as a volunteer to help train the Bosnian Serb rebels."

"Fighting for Milosevic. And Mladic." His gentle irony was not so much a provocation as an invitation for her to say more. He saw her flush slightly and knew he had touched a nerve.

"Fighting for his country and for those who wanted to stay part of it, who didn't want to be part of a breakaway state ruled by the descendants of their oppressors, the lackeys of the Turkish Empire, who had treated them as serfs until the twentieth century — and be forced to accept their version of history, while being separated from their own people and their own identity forever." She paused. "In the eyes of the West, Bosnians only had the right to feel like Bosnians, the wonderful multi-cultural Western ideal, with its moderate Muslim majority, an artificial identity invented by the Austrian Empire to counter the movements to join Serbia and Croatia. Those Bosnians who actually felt like Serbs or Croats or Yugoslavs were seen by Western media and politicians as evil nationalists who had chosen an evil identity."

"So, he was part of the fiendish plot to create a greater Serbia," he prompted, hoping she would perceive his irony.

"Exactly, the fiendish plot to have a country for our own people like all the other ethnic groups were getting. We demanded the same right of self-determination for the

Serb regions of the breakaway states as they were getting, and NATO refused to let us have it because we were cast as the villains of the conflict. They still have troops there to stop us having it." Her voice had risen slightly. She paused and looked down at her hands. "When they found his body, they wouldn't let my mother see it. It had been too badly mutilated. By torture."

"I'm sorry," he said. "I'm really sorry." He reached out and put his hand on hers.

"I don't know why I'm telling you all this." She shook her head as if to get rid of an image inside it. Her voice was unsteady. "I didn't mean to go into all this stuff from the past. It makes my blood boil still but it must sound like really obscure history to you."

For a second he was afraid she was going to end the conversation. He took his hand off hers and sat back.

"No, it isn't," he said quickly. "I was a student then, I followed events closely. And above all what happened afterwards." He wanted her to see what he knew about the subject to encourage her to go on. "Because the Bosnian Serbs committed massacres in Bosnia, and NATO did nothing to stop them, NATO then decided to make war on Serbia over Kosovo. Even though the Serbs had agreed to all their demands, except the final, deliberately unacceptable demand that NATO troops be allowed to occupy all of Serbia."

"You're better informed than most people," she said, surprised. "The Rambouillet Agreement was even called by Kissinger a document no sovereign country could have signed. It was just a pretext for aggression."

"Amazing what a repeat it was of the First World War, when Serbia was also given an ultimatum that would have meant the end of its sovereignty as a nation. For the second time in history Serbs had to refuse an unacceptable ultimatum and face a war of aggression."

"And it's only because the Russians were in a position of weakness this time that it didn't lead to the Third World War, the same as it led to the First."

"The West would have got exactly what it deserved if the Russians had launched Armageddon," he said soberly. "For the regime of lies we live under. I really do believe that in democracies people are responsible for the lies they swallow from their government and the media, and from intellectuals wanting to strike a heroic pose, as we had in France, with that insufferable Bernard-Henri Levy."

She looked down suddenly and he saw she had tears in her eyes.

"Did I say something wrong?" he said anxiously.

"No. You just reminded me of someone. So much." She shook her head and wiped her eyes.

"Tell me about what happened. I mean, how you survived and how you got out afterwards."

He longed to know everything about her, as if he had a feeling her story was going to be part of his own. She looked at him for a moment, and then over the next few minutes her gaze wandered vaguely around the little flat and out the window as she recalled the past.

"My grandmother had a small guest-house, like a bed-and-breakfast, in Belgrade. After my father was killed, we lived there. My mother was the receptionist, even though she had a degree in literature and wanted to write. A young Englishman was staying there. He was a sort of writer, or freelance journalist, but not a very successful one. He had been travelling through the country, trying to sell articles to papers in Britain, when the bombing started. He was trapped there. The other guests all got out of Belgrade. He stayed on and wrote about it all in a journal he kept. He hoped to publish it later, but nobody wanted it. It was telling the wrong side's story. He became close to my mother. And to me. I adored him. My father was a vague memory by then, just an ache where something was missing — the shoulders I used to ride on, the stubbly chin. This foreigner was so funny but also warm and kind. I had started learning English at school and I loved talking to him. He and my mother began sleeping together. Under the bombs."

"Pretty grim circumstances to start a romance."

"It was partly because she was terrified that she wanted to come into his bed. Those cowards always bombed at night. I came into his bed a few times too. All three of us, but it was a big bed and on the ground floor, where it seemed safest. My grandmother had gone to her sister's in the country and there was no one else there. He was the only man in the house and we ran to him for protection by instinct. When it was all over and they had destroyed our beautiful Belgrade and killed two thousand civilians, he insisted that we come with him to England. My mother hesitated, because these were the people who had bombed us. But I begged her to. The fact is I was in love with Brendan myself."

"Brendan?"

"That was his name. His mother was Irish. So he got us out. He had money for plane tickets. Via Moscow. And my mother married him. Again, at my insistence. I was deliriously happy at first. It was like a honeymoon for me too."

"And then? Didn't it last?"

"Things happened." She went silent and looked down at her hands.

"What sort of things?"

"You know my website. You know what I told you the other day."

"You didn't tell much. What happened?" he coaxed, his curiosity piqued by her reluctance.

"I don't know. Gradually a child's love became an adolescent's love. I was thirteen when we met. By the time I really knew I was in love with him, I was fourteen. I suppose you could say I seduced him. And by letting me do it, he seduced me."

He stared at her. He was slightly shocked.

"And who do you blame now: him or yourself?"

"I made all the play," she said quietly. "He didn't know how to say no. He thought I was traumatized by war. He didn't dare say no. He loved me too much. I used to play on it. I claimed I could still hear the bombs. I wanted to come into his bed. This was when my mother was away, because she went back to Serbia often to see her mother and I couldn't go because of school. I told him I saw horrors when I closed my eyes. We had seen dead bodies in the street. People blown to pieces. I said I saw them still in my dreams. He cradled me in his arms. It was paradise. And then I wanted more. He looked like a rock star. He had long, curly, golden-blond hair and blue eyes. So blue. I loved him. He played the guitar and sang for me. I had fantasies of my mother dying and me becoming his girlfriend. And then she became jealous. When she came back after a week or a fortnight away in Serbia, we had such a feeling of complicity between us she could sense it, sense that she was excluded. I spoke English far better than her, and I understood all his jokes, his wit, his crazy humour. She never got half of it. I was bright at school, he was the one who helped me with my homework. I also read the stuff he wrote and couldn't publish because it was too pro-Serb. I loved it. He also wrote other stuff, poems, plays, philosophy. I read it all. I encouraged him, even though he couldn't get published. I thought he was a genius. My mother resented how close we were. They had married in a rush for the sake of the residence permit and then found they were very different. She was down-to-earth and pragmatic, organized, a bit bossy. She was two years older than him. He was a dreamer, an eternal child. They began having rows. He was less successful than she had hoped. She had to go to work in a supermarket. Then she began to talk of going back. She was trying to be a journalist as well. She wrote articles for Belgrade newspapers and got them published. She talked of moving back and becoming a journalist there, and maybe getting into politics, helping the country rebuild. I was terrified. If she went back she would take me too. I would lose England, my school, Brendan, everything I loved. There was no question he would move to Serbia. He had a job at *The Guardian*, and even if it wasn't very secure or well-paid, he still believed in his future here. He thought he would succeed as a writer. He was trying to get a play produced about the war. The crazy idea came to me that he had to become my lover. Only if he loved me as a girlfriend would he fight to hold on to me and keep me with him." She stared out the window.

And then my mother started going on longer trips to Serbia as my grandmother got ill. I started sleeping in his bed on a regular basis. The first few times I came into his bed in the middle of the night and pretended I had had a nightmare and begged to sleep there. He never refused, he didn't know how. And then he just accepted it as a matter of course. One morning I remember we woke up side by side and grinned at each other and he said: "Well, Mrs Brendan, whose turn is it to make the coffee?" And I knew at that moment I loved him not as a daughter but as a lover, and I saw how it would be between us when my mother had abandoned us and I had persuaded him to keep me as his girlfriend, and then later when I was old enough as his wife — I knew he was the man who could make me happy forever.

But nothing happened immediately, in fact not for ages. I just got the habit that whenever my mother was away I would sleep in his bed for company, and he never touched me except to kiss me good night. He assumed I just wanted to be there for a sense of safety and he saw nothing else in it. And then one night I did have a nightmare and I woke up beside him crying. And he woke up too and put the bedside lamp on and asked me what the matter was.

"I had a horrible dream," I said, still sobbing, "that my mother divorced you and she took me away and I wanted to stay with you and I couldn't and the judge made me go and live with her in Serbia, and she was horrible to me, she beat me and called me names. You won't ever let her take me away from you, will you, even if she divorces you? It's you I love. I want to be with you, not her."

He stroked my hair and tried to calm me.

"Sweetheart, that is not going to happen, there's not going to be a divorce, you are not going to be taken away, I'll make sure you can always live with me, all right?"

"Do you swear it?" I was desperate. "You'll never leave me?"

"I swear it, darling."

"Oh, Brendan, but you know it may happen, she's going to do it, she's going to divorce you, I can see it coming, please, promise me, if she takes me away that if I run away and come back to you, you'll take me in?"

"Of course, I will, sweetheart. Can you imagine me turning you away?"

"But it may take me time to run away and come back here. Maybe years, till I'm old enough to travel alone. Promise you'll keep up contact and you won't marry again, you'll wait for me." And then I added, as if I was spilling the most important secret of my life: "Because you know when I'm old enough I want to marry you."

My voice had gone high-pitched and tearful and the words came out of me like a yelp of pain. He stared at me in shock. Then he said tenderly:

"Camilla, darling, by the time you are old enough for that a lot of things will have happened in your life. You may have met a boy your age you'll have fallen in love with, you may no longer be thinking about marrying your step-father, that's a little girl thing and you'll grow out of it."

"No, I won't. Do you mean that's all it is to you? A little girl thing?" I was angry and hurt and tears began coming again.

"Who knows what the future will bring?" He tried to reassure me. "Maybe it's true that when you are old enough you will still love me and me you. In that case we'll do what we want to do. But we can't make those plans yet. They're dreams, sweetheart. You're still a child."

"I'm not a child," I said resentfully. "I'm fourteen years old. I have periods, I can get pregnant. And I've got breasts. Feel them."

I grabbed his hand and planted it on my breast. He left it there casually, and then he took it away very slowly as if afraid I would be hurt by any sign of rejection.

"There's a difference between being a woman physically and being one in your head, darling. You're still a child in your head. It's not bad being a child. That's why I adore you. It doesn't mean we can't be close and understand each other. You're far more intelligent than your mother. And you understand a lot more. But we relate as father and daughter. It can only be that way till you're much older and then you can decide if you want to change that relationship into something else. But if you do, remember it'll be a huge risk. Because father and daughter generally lasts a lot longer than lovers do. It's something stable that lasts a lifetime. Sex complicates everything, and makes it unstable."

"I don't know about sex yet and it's unfair because you know about it and I don't. I wish you would show me."

"I can't do that, Camilla, and you know it." He sounded serious and was rather curt.

"Only a little bit, just a bit at a time, I don't expect everything at once, just a little hint of what it's like."

"You already know the best part of what it's like. Lying next to each other and hearing each other breathing and feeling each other's warmth and feeling perfectly happy. That's really the best part, and we have that already without the complicated bit."

"No, what you're talking about is love," I said scornfully. "I know about that already. I've known about that ever since I first saw you. It's the sex I don't know about."

"But you can't learn it from me, sweetheart. That would make a relationship too confused, too full of opposite things. We can't be both father and daughter and lovers, it doesn't work that way."

"I don't expect to be lovers. I just want a little bit of tenderness, of love, that's all."

"But I hold you in my arms, sweetheart. That's enough. What else do you want us to do?"

It was an appeal to reason. But something irrational possessed me and drove me onward.

"I want you to caress me."

"Where?"

"You know where. Some of the other girls have got boyfriends who stroke their breasts. No one has ever touched mine."

"Then you'll have to look harder for a boyfriend. Isn't there someone you like?"

"I can't talk about that with you!" I said angrily. "And they are stupid and childish and clumsy! It's you I want as my boyfriend, and stop trying to pretend you don't know it. I want you to caress me there."

"I can't do that. It wouldn't be right."

"Of course you can. You just did. A moment ago. And I didn't bite, did I?"

He was silent for a moment, as though thinking about how to answer.

"You'll see, it's no big deal, sweetheart. It's not as important as you think."

"Then if it's not important, why won't you do it? You're mean. You don't love me at all." I turned away from him sulkily. I knew he would be too weak to handle my sulks.

He sighed and after a minute he said: "All right."

I turned back and kissed him at once as a reward. Then he put his hand on one of my breasts and began to stroke it gently. It felt like an electric current was going through me. I lay and breathed more and more quickly, and finally I was panting. He stopped.

"No!" I said, and grabbed his hand and made him keep going. It was so good I thought I would die. I pressed his hand against me and I began to moan very softly. Then I turned to him and pulled his face towards me and kissed him on the mouth for a long time. It was him who finally broke off and pulled away.

"That's enough for the moment," he said, sounding a bit afraid.

"Brendan, darling, that was so good," I whispered. "I'll always be so grateful you did that. I know now how good it must be."

"I don't think we'd better do it any more," he said and turned over.

I thought to myself: "We'll see!" but I didn't say it. I thought I had him now. Once I had got him to do it the first time, I was sure he would do it again whenever I asked. And I was right. Within a short time, whenever my mother was away and we slept together, he did the same thing: he stroked my breasts for several minutes till I began to moan and wriggle and thresh about, and then he would stop and we would kiss for a long time and then go to sleep. And after a few months, I took the next step. While we were kissing, I reached out a hand and slid it across his belly.

"No!" he yelled, and grabbed my hand. "Camilla, we can't do that!"

"I know you want to," I whispered intensely. "I know you're not making love to my mother any more. You must be feeling so frustrated. I'm the one who excites you now. I want you to know, whenever you feel you want to, I can do it. I know how. I've seen it on the internet. You have to understand. Young girls of my generation are not what you think. We're not afraid to make love. Lots of the girls at school do it. I can give you everything you need. Just as you are giving me so much pleasure, I can give it to you."

"Darling, you're a child, that doesn't change with generations."

"Yes, it does. Generations are different. In the Middle Ages, princesses often married at fourteen. And had babies. I could do that too. I'd love you to make love to me. But I'm not asking for it. I know you're an old Puritan. I just want to help you relax and feel good while you're with me. So that you'll know how much I love you. It's not really sex. It's just being good to each other."

He held my head against his as if he was in despair. I could tell how afraid he was of going down a path that was dark and forbidden and dangerous, and I knew I had the power to make him go down it. I knew he loved me and could not resist or disobey me. He was too afraid of losing my love. And I loved him so much I wanted him to be mine completely.

And within a few days everything happened that I was determined would happen. We began making love. Not all the way. I never lost my virginity. He refused to do that. But we did everything else. I found a way of making him give in to me. I lay on top of him and moved on him and he had a choice: either throw me off violently or else submit to what was happening. And since he couldn't be violent to me, he had to submit. And I made him understand that submission to my will was happiness, that I knew best for both of us. And I had such a sense of power as well as pleasure. I had started horse-riding and he was like a horse I controlled with caresses and sweet words. And the first time he made me come I felt a triumph and a fulfilment and a peace I had never felt before.

Years afterwards I asked myself what made him give in to me. Was he so much in love with me? Was I so fascinating to him, with my combination of innocence and diabolical determination to make him bend to my will? Or was he a man without any real moral sense, just a wish to feel comfortable and loved, by taking the path of least resistance? I'm sure he would have preferred to limit things to just kisses and hugs, but he didn't know how to impose limits, because he was afraid of losing me. He depended on me for love and I gave him love so deep and intense that he was addicted to it, he couldn't live without it. It was never sex he was addicted to with me, no, it was my love, my whispering in his ear, my arms around him and my lips against his cheek. It was for the sake of that that he gave me the sexual pleasure I craved and demanded. And later they turned it all on its head and pretended that he only wanted sex with me and used my love to manipulate me. It was just the opposite. I was in control, and I used him as I wanted, but I knew he would be happy submitting to my will for the rest of his life. I knew I had found the man for whom I was the unique object of love and that it gave me infinite power over him. And the fact he was eighteen years older than me made me all the more confident that he would be mine forever, because his looks were beginning to fade as mine were still getting better, and my power over him could only become stronger and stronger.

Sometimes he would have a crisis of conscience and tell me we couldn't do it any more, it was wrong. I at once began to sulk and threatened to stop loving him, and he soon gave in to me again.

I remember saying to him once: "It's too late now, why stop? You're guilty now, you're a criminal, you can't change that, so why not enjoy it and make me happy? Why stop when it's too late? You can't remove the guilt by stopping now. So why not love me as I want? As I deserve, after all I've been through? Dozens of princesses and queens loved at my age. Read your history! Read *Romeo and Juliet*! I'm your Juliet! But I'm not thirteen like her, I'm fourteen, nearly fifteen, and I love you!" And his rebellion soon came to an end.

Romain studied her uneasily, and said: "Were you really as formidable and domineering as you're pretending now?"

"I don't know. That's what I can't really know now." She laid her head against the back of the sofa and stared at the ceiling. "That's how I saw myself. As the dominant one. Was it all an adolescent delusion? Was he really the manipulator all the time? Can you be a passive manipulator? A passive seducer? I think most women would say yes, because that is how most women seduce. By letting the man make the running and think he is the dominant one, while they control him with the flutter of an eyelash. Of course that's the theory the prosecutor put forward — the diabolical manipulator, the insidious seducer. But I knew it was all bullshit."

She raised her head from the sofa back and looked at him steadily.

"The idea that an adult always knows what he's doing, and an adolescent only thinks she does is just a cliché, it's pious nonsense. It's a Victorian, angelic view of girlhood. The innocent, pure maiden, who has no desires, no passions, no will of her own, who can't be held responsible for anything she does! It's just condescending crap! Making out adolescents are helpless children. In reality, he was the one who was naive and confused, not me. The few times he tried to assert authority over me as a parent and told me we couldn't go on, I flew into a rage, I cursed him and even hit him till I saw fear in his eyes, fear that he had lost my love. And then when I went back to him in tears and begged forgiveness, he was so glad he couldn't refuse me anything."

She seemed to contemplate the turbulent, passionate teenager she had been as though that girl was someone she had once known, far removed from her.

"How did it end?"

"I was fool enough to write poems about him. When I was fifteen and a half, I took one to school by mistake in my homework. It fell on the floor. A girl I disliked got hold of it and read some of it to her friends and made fun of it. They began to jeer at me. I was furious. I fought with her to get the poem back. The teacher intervened and took the poem, which had been torn in half. She told me to see her after class. She demanded to know who the man in the poem was. I said he was an invention. She didn't believe me. The girl I hated began talking about Brendan and me on an internet chat room everyone used. The girls had seen him pick me up from school a few times and they all drooled over him, so they guessed the truth straight away. What she said was all over the school in days. My teacher called my mother and asked to see her. She showed her the poem and my mother didn't take long to figure things out. I wasn't fool enough to put a name but I mentioned his blue eyes and golden hair. That was enough for her. She had a showdown with Brendan. He denied everything but she saw through him. She went to the police and denounced him. I'm sure she wanted to divorce him and go back to Serbia. She knew it would be difficult to get me away from him and force me to come with her, and she saw this as the solution. The police interrogated him for days. They questioned me too, but mostly him. We both denied everything. They searched our house and found other poems of mine I had hidden. They took away his computer and restored things he had deleted — love poems he had written about me and a short story he had started about a man having an affair with a young girl. The fact he had deleted them was seen as proof of guilt.

"He was put on trial. He denied that we had ever done anything but kiss. The doctor testified I was still a virgin. But the judge considered kissing on the mouth a sexual act with a child, even if we had done nothing else, which he doubted. When I saw how it was going I begged the judge not to send Brendan to prison, I told him I loved him, that it was me who was to blame, I burst into tears in court. When the verdict was read I became hysterical. I screamed and hit my mother. The judge told me I was a sick little girl and he knew who was to blame. He called Brendan a cynical, manipulative paedophile and gave him five years.

"He lasted a year. The other prisoners were allowed to beat him up regularly. The guards put the worst ones into his cell so they could. They even raped him. His lawyer told me that years later; he showed me the autopsy report. They thought he hadn't received a long enough sentence and they were going to make him pay. Finally they killed him. He was found hanged but covered in bruises. Suicide, they said. I never saw his body. I wasn't allowed to see him at all after the trial, or have any contact with him. I'm sure he wrote to me, but his letters were confiscated and destroyed, the same as mine were."

"And your mother in all this?"

"My mother was so disgusted with me after I refused to denounce him as a paedophile that she wanted to send me away. I hated her. We hardly spoke. I refused to go to Serbia with her. I said she would have to drag me to the plane in a straitjacket. She talked of putting me in care or sending me to a reform school. Or even a psychiatric hospital. I was having panic attacks, fits of shaking, for weeks after the trial. Then a Catholic boarding school in Suffolk heard about my case through Brendan's mother and offered me a scholarship. My mother hoped it would be like a reform school but it was a posh place, full of girls from old, Catholic, upper-class families and daughters of European diplomats and Russian oligarchs. I was there all year round except for the holidays, mostly at Brendan's mother's place in Ireland. My mother went back to Serbia and remarried there. She didn't want to know me. When I finished boarding school I got a place at Oxford and a scholarship. Brendan's mother helped me while she was still alive. I studied History and English. I wrote a novel about my affair with Brendan but no publisher or agent wanted it."

"And then?" It seemed she was about to end her story but he wanted to hear more.

"I wanted to become a journalist but I couldn't find a job. I worked briefly at a publishers and did a number of other things. I became a freelance journalist, sold a few articles, and started my own blog. I began working for associations helping victims of domestic violence, sexual trafficking and so on. I became interested in paedophilia, helping victims, and those wrongly accused of it. My own experience had left me such a wreck I wanted to understand it through the experience of others, to get another perspective on it."

"And did you? Get a different perspective?"

"No. My view of what had happened didn't change." Her face seemed frozen as she gazed at nothing. "Most other cases were so different from mine. I saw everything. Men that were manipulative, cynical, sadistic. Who ruined girls' lives. Or the opposite, the fifteen year old groupie who gives a blow job to a rock singer or footballer, the holy grail among her friends, and then takes him to court because her friends called her a liar and she wants him to go to jail for it to prove to them she succeeded, even if that will destroy his family and leave his own children fatherless. Once or twice I heard of romantic affairs, real love affairs, that led on to marriage when the girl was old enough, when they kept it secret or her parents were tolerant enough to understand. How I envied those ones! But in most romantic affairs the boyfriend was just arrested and jailed on a ludicrous charge of child abuse or statutory rape and the girl went mad with grief. Often the boyfriend was jailed for longer than the sleazy Muslim gangs who drugged thirteen-year old girls and passed them round like cigarettes or men who raped little boys. The judges punish the romantic affairs the most viciously because they're jealous. But in all the affairs I got to know about, none of them was quite like mine — a man who loved me so much he couldn't say no to me, and whom I could twist round my little finger. I felt I was one of a kind and nobody else had ever behaved like me. It made me feel more and more like a pervert. A teenage vamp who had seduced a gentle, romantic poet and dreamer who adored her — and got him killed by a pack of animals."

Romain did not know what to say. She was so bitter any question seemed trivial, but he forced himself to find one so as to make her go on talking.

"Did they ever give you any sort of counselling or psychological support?"

"Yes, if you can call it that," she said with a sneer. "Before the trial they sent me these people. They were vile apparatchiks who were out to destroy me. They tried to convince me I was a victim of a cynical predator, that it was impossible for a thirty-three year old man to feel real love for a fifteen-year old girl, and abnormal for her to love him! They just wanted to trap me into saying something they could use as evidence against Brendan. I refused to go on seeing them."

"And how do you feel about all of it now — the relationship you had with him?"

She looked at him with burning eyes.

"It was the greatest experience of my life. I've never known so much love, before or since. It was paradise. I don't feel any revulsion now for anything we did. That's often a sign people mention: revulsion for what happened. I never felt it. It's only when I have sex with other men that I feel revulsion." She stopped and looked down and shook her head. "In fact, it's not only revulsion. At times it's more like panic. I still get these horrible panic attacks where I can't stop shaking."

"So, it's affected your relationships pretty badly?"

"How wouldn't it?" she said bitterly. "I'd been told the great love of my life was a perversion, that I was either a sick little pervert or the victim of a pervert or both. So everything was confused. I trusted no one, not even myself. I was twenty-one before I dared to make love again, and then it was with my tutor at Oxford. I suppose it had the same sort of secret, forbidden aspect, even though he was only nine years older than me. But physically it left me cold. And emotionally it was screwed up. Everything seemed ambiguous. I never knew who felt what, who was using who. I asked the questions for all relationships that I didn't ask for that first one. I went from being the most naive, trusting, spontaneous girl on earth to the most cynical, cold and closed one. As a young girl I had set out deliberately to seduce a man I loved, and he had ended up beaten to death in a cell. I could only see all seduction as treacherous, all attempts to attract as insidious, all love as a perversion or a kind of madness. I analyse everything. I can't be spontaneous. I can't let myself go. I don't want to do anything that is going to leave me full of pain and guilt and bitterness. The result is I feel nothing for anyone. Nothing."

"You just need time."

"I've had thirteen years."

"No, I mean, you need time for a relationship to develop slowly, for you to develop trust in the other person, to get to know his feelings and yours. You're not someone who should rush things. That won't work for you."

"I know. I found that out the hard way."

"Do you know what I think?" He looked at her seriously. "You need to start with a relationship of the kind you say he would have preferred with you. Just kisses and hugs and nothing else. Only when you're really sure of your feelings and his should you go any further."

"Do you know many men who just want kisses and hugs?" She looked amused for the first time since she had begun telling her story.

"I'm sure there are some who would be happy with that till you were ready for more."

"Really? You're sure of that?" she teased. "Some? How many?"

"Oh, I couldn't say how many." He looked coyly at the ceiling.

"Do you know even one?" she asked, with sudden intensity.

"Yes. I know one," he said. He met her intense gaze, willing her to understand at last.

"I'm hungry," she said abruptly. "Are we going to eat here?"

He cooked an omelette and they quarrelled good-humouredly over how to do it, what to put in it and whether to fold it or turn it over. They washed it down with a glass of wine. After they had eaten he suggested they might do some yoga.

"After a meal? I don't have the energy," she said.

"So, what shall we do?" He was sitting beside her on the sofa.

"What about my therapy?" she suggested in a small voice, looking sideways at him.

"What therapy?" he said, mystified.

"You've forgotten already." She sounded disappointed.

"Therapy?" he repeated, at a loss. "You mean for your accent?"

"There's no therapy for that. Except to be born again. I mean my other therapy. For my other problem."

"What other problem?" A vague idea was forming in his mind but he didn't dare allow it to come to the surface.

"Think! Think!" She became comically hectoring. "Girl seduces stepfather. Becomes totally frigid. What does she need?"

"Hugs and kisses," he said humbly. His heart was now beating furiously.

"Exactly. Where are they?"

"What, you mean, right now?"

"Right now," she said peremptorily.

"I can see what he was up against," he muttered in French.

She demanded a translation. He offered: "I said how much I envied your step-father."

"Why? Because he had me at fourteen? Are you saying I'm past it? You'd have preferred me at that age?" She had adopted a teasing, slightly bossy humour, as if the gloom of her memories had vanished.

"I'd prefer you at any age," he said. "Fourteen, forty. And anything in between." He leaned towards her and smothered any reply by kissing her on the lips. She put her arms round his neck and their kiss grew more passionate. Then gradually she went limp in his arms and caressed his head slowly as he kissed her face and neck.

"Is it working?" he whispered.

"I think so. But it's too soon to know. I need a much longer session. Much longer."

After a few minutes things grew more intense and she was pushing her tongue into his mouth and playing with his. They were embracing tightly and their bodies felt hot against each other, as if bursting to get out of their clothes. He was beginning to think things were going to take their natural course sooner rather than later, when suddenly he felt her go stiff in his arms and she began trembling like a day-old kitten. She broke off and pushed him away and he saw that she was in tears. She covered her face.

"I can't do this!" she sobbed. "I'm sorry! I can't do it. I thought I could."

He looked at her in consternation. She was staring between her fingers as if at an image that terrified her.

"What is it?" he asked.

"I don't know," she said.

"Yes, you do. Close your eyes and tell me what you see."

She closed her eyes. Tears welled out between the lids.

"I see his face," she said, in a strangled voice. "His face in the courtroom as they led him away for the last time. It was trying to tell me something and it was so full of despair."

"And what did you feel?"

"I felt terror. I knew they were going to kill him. That I would never see him again. And I knew it was my fault." She buried her face in her hands, sobbing. "I killed him! I killed him! My only love! How could I have been so stupid!"

She was in a rage against herself. He held one of her hands. It was shaking. She held onto his tightly and the tears gushed over both their hands as she sobbed. He hugged her close as she went on shaking and he began to talk quietly in her ear.

"It's not your fault! Your love didn't kill him! Your poem didn't kill him! Those narrow-minded bigots killed him by locking him up for something that wasn't wrong. And letting the scum of the earth murder him. You are allowed to love someone else now. You don't have to be afraid that if you make love it will end in death. They made that connection in your mind. You have to break it! They poisoned the whole idea of love for you. Don't let them. Fight them! It's your memory of what you did with him that is the truth, not their interpretation of it. They were hate-filled bigots and puritans. Enemies of love. They didn't know you. They didn't know him. They didn't know what feelings you had for each other. And they didn't want to know. They just looked at ages, abstract numbers on paper, and said: this is a crime! He is guilty! And they murdered him. Don't let their lies destroy what you had together. You know how it felt for you. That's what you have to think about. Not what happened to him in that cell. Your love didn't kill him. Love doesn't kill. It's the breath of life. You gave him life, not death. You can't blame yourself for the evil of others."

She gradually stopped crying. He gave her a paper tissue. After she wiped her tears, she put her arms round his neck and held him tight. She was not trembling so much now but he could still feel her heart thumping against his chest.

"Keep talking! You're like a priest. You know I converted at the convent? I don't go any more. But you're my priest. My therapist. You'll help me over this if anyone will."

"Of course I will. And when we're through this together, we'll be shagging like rabbits." He whispered in her ear. "It's all being done for one purpose. To get in your pants. You realize that, don't you?"

"Of course." She giggled with a half-sob.

"And you accept how wonderfully good and innocent that motive is? The love of a man and a woman for each other is the one miracle that keeps all of life going. Without it the world ends. They tried to destroy that miracle for you. But we won't let them. We'll get it back! We're going to do everything slowly, step by step, and any time you feel panic we'll stop and go back a step. Do you understand?"

"Yes, doctor." She kissed him again and after a while she clung to him more tightly and her kisses grew more passionate. It was him who finally broke away.

"You're not shaking? You're not panicking?"

"No, I'm not. I feel calm, I feel good." Her shaking had stopped.

"What do you see now?"

She closed her eyes and thought for a moment.

"I don't see his face any more. I see yours. But above all I hear your voice. Echoing in my head. It's so like his, apart from the accent. It's so warm and tender. It's like a caress not of my body but of my mind."

"That's just what it's meant to be." He kissed her cheek.

"I'm totally screwed up, aren't I?" she said anxiously, after a moment. "Do you think you'll be able to handle someone this screwed up? This wrecked? For very long?"

"Try me. I'll take you in any condition you're delivered in. And if it takes me a hundred years I'll make you as good as new again."

She held him round the neck and relaxed against him and closed her eyes. After a minute or two he thought she had gone to sleep. Then she began to murmur in his ear in a voice that sounded as if it came from her dreams.

"You seem to understand so well what I need. But I'm not sure I understand it myself. I think what I need is to relive what I did with him, only this time with you. To be the one that makes the play, to seduce you slowly, step by step. But to be told at every moment that it's good, it's not evil, it won't lead to your death. That I'm not a sinner who has to be punished by seeing her lover in hell."

She buried her face in the hollow of his shoulder and he could feel there were one or two tears loose again. He stroked her hair softly and willed her to forget all the pain and guilt and torment and bitterness that was in her. He tried to find words to calm and comfort her.

"Hell is to suffer alone. So now you're out of it. And I'll make you feel we're both in paradise, every moment we're in each other's arms."

She drew a deep breath.

"Then, please, caress my breasts gently, for a long time."

He went on stroking her hair. Then he said softly: "Think back half your lifetime, and imagine you're fourteen again."

He moved back from her and lifted up her T-shirt. She was not wearing a bra and her breasts were small like those of an adolescent. She had tiny, exquisite pink nipples which he couldn't resist kissing. Then he began to caress her breasts slowly and lightly as if he was tracing spiders' webs all over them, and as if he knew it was the first time she had ever felt it.

12

In Gaveston House Children's Home Kayley Burke was sitting thinking about what he should do. He had spoken again to the two boys who had seen Brian taking Eric out the back door on Saturday. They repeated their story that Eric had said they were going to a football game and he was going to play. It seemed clear that Brian had got Eric out of the way so Ekaterina and her friends couldn't question him about Viktor. Now on Monday Eric still hadn't come back. He thought of Ekaterina and the expression in her eyes as she asked him for help in finding answers about her son. He had to do something. He thought of going straight to the police, but decided he had better see his director, Edward Marlowe, first. He didn't particularly like him, but he thought it was common courtesy to tell him before he went to the police, and also to inform him of his suspicions of Brian. He remembered Camilla's words: if you don't report suspicions of paedophile abuse, you may be seen as an accomplice.

He went downstairs to Edward Marlowe's office and knocked. Marlowe opened the door. He was in his late forties, a well-groomed public school man, now putting on a little weight. He was a stylish dresser, and he wore a flamboyant tie and a Bordeaux-coloured waistcoat in a milieu whose uniform was the baggy, roll-neck pullover. Even though he seemed in a relaxed mood, his manner was cool. Looking past him at the mirrored cabinet-door behind his desk, Kayley glimpsed a reflection of Brian sitting in an armchair out of sight behind the door. There was a decanter of sherry on Marlowe's desk. He knew he had to be careful.

"I wondered if I could have a word with you some time in private," he said.

"Oh? In private?" queried Marlowe with a frown, as if this was somewhat irregular.

"Yes. Of course, if you're busy I can come back later, any time that suits you."

"Well, shall we say, in half an hour?"

Kayley nodded and went back up to the small upstairs staff-room. He was somewhat disturbed by the presence of Brian in Marlowe's office. Still, he reflected, Brian had been at the home for years and they probably had a regular drink together to talk about rugby, an interest they shared. It didn't necessarily mean any complicity of Marlowe in paedophile activity. He tried to put it out of his mind. This was downtime while they waited for the children to come home from school. He went on the internet on the staff-room computer and did a search on Cyril Jones. Two of the entries referred to newspaper articles where there was a mention of the paedophile rumours about him and how other MPs had come to his defence.

When Kayley went down half an hour later, Brian passed him in the hall, with a hard stare and a slight smirk on his face. Marlowe ushered him into his office and gestured towards a chair. He made no offer of a glass of sherry, but asked him what this was about.

"It's about Eric Page. He disappeared on Saturday. And he hasn't come back. I was wondering if you've alerted the police."

"That's all taken care of," said Marlowe, staring at him through narrowed eyes. "What is your involvement in this?"

"I was the one who talked to the three people from London who came here on Saturday, including the mother of Viktor, the boy who disappeared a month ago. She's desperate to find her son. She wanted to talk to Eric, who was apparently with Viktor when he disappeared. And somebody prevented them from seeing Eric by first of all lying about where he was to send them away, and then taking Eric somewhere else. Don't you think that's odd?"

"Odd?" Marlowe stared blankly. "What do you mean — odd?"

"Well, for want of a better word, suspect."

"Suspect? Has a crime been committed?"

"The disappearance of two boys, one in the company of a man who has been accused in the past of paedophile acts, yes, that does suggest a crime may have been committed." Kayley spoke firmly, but without any aggressiveness. He found Marlowe's obtuseness not merely irritating but incomprehensible. Even slightly sinister.

"You're not by any chance insinuating that this children's home, under my management, has been guilty of complicity in some sort of paedophile activity?" Marlowe's expression was an odd combination of contempt, pity and a sort of incredulous outrage.

"The children's home, no. But some of the people working here, who knows?"

"And who do you suspect, among your colleagues, then?" The question dripped with sarcasm. "Is this general sordid innuendo to be given more precision?"

"Yes. Viktor's mother and her friends claim that Brian told them Eric was playing football at Oaklands Recreation Ground, when he wasn't. And two boys claim they later saw Brian take Eric out the back door and out the back gate, to where his car is usually parked, and that Eric told them he was going to play football."

"That's amazing! Truly amazing! In terms of sheer cheek at any rate." Marlowe stared at him in disbelief.

"I beg your pardon?"

"Brian has just told me almost the exact same thing about you. That he and some of the boys saw you taking Eric away to your car parked out the back, and that you had your arm round his shoulders. What have you got to say about that?"

"That's a complete lie!" Kayley felt his face flush. He was not prepared for this kind of slanderous counter-attack. "I never left the home all day Saturday, and I was here when the three people from London came back here looking for Eric. At that moment Brian and Eric were both gone. I looked for them, and the boys told me Brian had taken Eric away."

"Yes, well you can explain all that to the police. I decided to call them to get to the bottom of this. I've already done so. If there is any investigation into alleged paedophile activity going on here, I think it needs to start with you. Many people here noticed you were rather too close to Eric."

"Too close to Eric?" He was astounded. He heard his voice take on a shrill note. "Other people ignored him or treated him like a leper, and he's a very withdrawn, deeply disturbed boy. I tried to bring him out of himself."

"Yes, I'm sure you did," he said sarcastically.

"What's that supposed to mean?"

"I'll let you figure it out."

The doorbell rang.

"That may be the police now," said Marlowe. "Will you wait in the hall while I talk to them first? Then they'll want to talk to you, I imagine."

Kayley walked out and sat in an armchair in the lobby, and watched as Marlowe opened the door. Two men in plain clothes stood there, one of them casually holding up an open wallet showing an identity card and badge. Marlowe ushered them in. They glanced at Kayley coldly as they passed him and went into Marlowe's office.

He sat and waited, puzzled by Marlowe's sudden hostility towards him. What was behind it? Was he after all an accomplice of Brian in a paedophile ring? He recalled that Marlowe had at first seemed very friendly to him when he applied for the job. Even over-friendly. Then his attitude had gradually cooled, as if he was disappointed Kayley had not turned out to be what he had expected. He wondered if Marlowe might have thought initially that he was gay. He suspected Marlowe was, along with one or two other staff members, and snippets of conversation he had overheard tended to confirm it. Was Marlowe's obvious hostility towards him the spitefulness of a would-be seducer whose hopes had been dashed?

After ten minutes the policemen came out of Marlowe's office. Kayley stood up as they approached him and stopped in front of him.

"Kayley Burke?" said one.

"Yes. I suppose you would like to hear my side of this," he said nervously, but with a vague hope that he would soon put this right.

"We'd like to do that down at the station, if you don't mind," said one of them. He was solidly built with a battered-looking face and a potato-shaped nose. The other was tall and thin and had a narrow, hatchet face and thin lips. They looked at him coolly and shrewdly.

"Are you arresting me?" he said, astonished. "I'm the one who raised the alarm about the disappearance of this boy and demanded that the director call the police."

"We're drawing no conclusions for the moment." The thickset one's tone was even. "But we'd like to talk to you at the station, in the capacity of a witness, so we can record your statement. Of course, if you refuse, that might change our view, and we could then consider you as a suspect and interview you under caution in that capacity."

The policemen looked unruffled, as if they didn't care which alternative he chose. Kayley bowed his head and walked ahead of them outside to the waiting police car. As he got in some of the children arrived back from school and stood staring.

Once inside the police station they sat him in a room at a table with a tape-recorder on it and began questioning him. About how long he had been working there, where he had worked before, his qualifications, etc. Then the potato-nosed one, who was taking the lead, said:

"So, Kayley — by the way, that's an interesting name. My daughter's got a friend called Kayley. She's a girl. So how did you get a girl's name? Was your mother expecting a girl?"

"It's a name she liked. She doesn't believe in sexism."

"Doesn't believe in sexism," he repeated slowly, with irony. "So she thought you were a girl. Did she bring you up as a girl to match the name?"

"Kayley is a name for both boys and girls."

"Sounds like a girl's name to me. So I bet you got bullied at school. They called you a girl, right?"

He blushed. There had been some bullying.

"Most people got used to the name. There was some teasing."

"Some teasing? I bet it screwed you up, didn't it?" Potato Nose leered with false sympathy. "You got a girlfriend?"

"Not right now, no."

"Ever had one?"

"Yes. I had one in Leeds before I left. We broke up a month ago."

"Why did you break up?"

There were reasons why Kayley preferred not to answer this question. He had first met the girl when she was fifteen and a resident of the care home in Leeds. He was falsely accused by another girl of having a relationship with her, though he was cleared of it by an internal inquiry. She left the home but came back into his life when she was twenty. She threw herself at him and ended up moving in with him. The care home director in Leeds felt this relationship was improper, given their history when she was a juvenile in his care, and pressured him either to break up with the girl or to resign to avoid a scandal. That was why he had moved to this care home in Birmingham, losing the girlfriend in the process. Not perhaps the best story to tell them in the circumstances.

"I think that's rather a personal question. Let's say, we were too different."

"Refuses to answer," Potato Nose noted, as if talking to the recorder. "Ever had a boyfriend?"

"No."

"Ever had sex with a man?" He had an expression that again verged on a leer.

"No."

"What about with a boy? Someone under age?"

"No, of course not." Kayley was indignant.

"Why, of course not?"

"Because it's against the law for one thing."

"Is that the only thing stopping you?"

"Of course not. It's also totally immoral."

"You haven't said: I wouldn't want to do it," said Potato Nose with an insinuating smirk.

"That as well."

"Oh, now you think of it?" He grinned triumphantly. "Ever heard of any paedophile activity going on in this home?"

"Not till the visitors from London on Saturday warned me about it."

"And how did you react to that?"

"I began to look more closely at what might be going on."

"And did you discover anything?"

"The behaviour of one of my colleagues, Brian Spenser, seemed odd. The visitors from London included the mother of a boy called Viktor, who disappeared a month ago on an outing with Cyril Jones. They asked to talk to his best friend, Eric Page, who was apparently with him at the time. Brian lied about where Eric was, claiming that he was playing football at Oaklands Recreation Ground. After the visitors left to go there, two boys saw Brian take Eric out the back door to where his car is usually parked. That was the last anyone saw of Eric. There are now two boys that have disappeared from this care home — Viktor, who was last seen by Eric, and now Eric."

"And they have both disappeared in the past month. Right?"

"About that, yes."

"How long have you been working here, Kayley?"

"I told you, two months."

"There weren't any disappearances before that?"

"I don't know. You'd have to ask the director."

"We have. He said there weren't any. Only since you came here have these things been happening."

"That's ridiculous!" He felt his face getting hot. "Are you accusing me of this? Just because of the short time I've been here?"

"Not only." Potato Nose leaned forward, staring at him with slightly bulbous eyes. "You've got form on this, haven't you? Your director contacted your last employer in Leeds, in the Fairview Children's Home. It seems you were in trouble for a relationship with a fifteen-year old girl there."

"I was found innocent of any misconduct by an inquiry."

"Insufficient evidence is what we were told. And you then began sleeping with the same girl later on. That does seem like evidence, doesn't it? So, it's not your first time, is it?" He stared at Kayley morosely, his insinuations feeding his own growing hostility. "You think you can get away with this, don't you? Just move from one children's home to another and do it again." His voice was low and menacing, full of pent-up aggression.

"I have never done anything to any child, I have always —."

"Shut up!" The words were like a slap. Then he resumed his calm, insinuating tone. "Everything adds up. You see, we think you correspond to what is known as a paedophile personality type."

"What on earth are you talking about?"

"These things have been studied." He smirked slightly with a knowing air. "The average paedophile is a rather shy young man of a wimpish sort, a bit of a sissy but not obviously so, a sort of gay type but not completely gay, who is a bit shy with girls, and a bit shy with men, who turns to children because they're the only people that don't make him feel shy or inadequate. He's really good with kids, relates to them easily, charms them." He paused and sat back. "Your director thinks you're really good with kids and relate to them easily."

"It's part of my job, for God's sake! I've got to establish a rapport with them."

"Establish what?" Potato Nose cocked his head as if he hadn't heard.

"A rapport."

"Rapport? That's a French word, isn't it? It means relations, doesn't it?" He turned to his colleague for confirmation. The man with the hatchet face confirmed it with a nod.

"It does indeed. It usually means sexual relations."

"It simply means a good relationship," said Kayley indignantly.

"So you want a good relationship with these boys, do you, Kayley?" said Potato Nose. "Who do you think you have the best relationship with among them?"

"I don't think it's any business of yours to talk of my work with the children in this care home. It's confidential."

"Refuses to answer. Getting very touchy. Doesn't want to talk about his relations with the boys."

"I object to this entire line of questioning. You're treating me as a suspect, and I want to see a lawyer."

"That's been noted. Pausing interview here for a break at four twenty-one."

Potato Nose stopped the recorder. Then he stared at him silently for a long minute across the table.

"Do you think you're calling the shots here, Kayley?" He leaned forward. "Listen, son, we could put you in the cooler right now. And it won't just be in a police cell. No, it'll be in a proper prison. And because of the usual overcrowding it'll have all sorts of prisoners in it, including those doing quite long sentences for quite ugly things. If we let them know you're a nonce, a man who screws around with kids, what do you think will happen to you?"

Kayley stared back, feeling his face draining of blood and his cheeks going cold. The other noted his reaction with satisfaction.

"I'd think about that. Now we'd like you to start talking to us seriously. When did this start? When did you start interfering with boys? Names. Dates. Incidentally, was it usually with boys? Was it only the one girl you did it with or were there others?"

"There were never any others, there weren't any at all," he said emphatically.

"Only the one then?"

"I have never interfered with any child."

"Keep on with that story and we'll put you in a cell with a big brutal bastard who likes men. You know what that'll feel like?" He leaned forward, grinning. "Just like those children felt when you molested them."

"I have never molested anyone." His voice rose. He was beginning to feel he was in the power of madmen.

"Keep stalling. You'll talk in the end. You'll confess. They all do. Just depends what sort of state they are in when they get there." Potato Nose looked quietly confident and superior.

"Look, the person you should be interrogating is Brian Spenser." He felt he was sounding desperate, flailing about him. "Those visitors from London, including Viktor's mother, told me Brian lied to them about Eric's whereabouts, pretended he was playing football, so as to prevent them talking to him. Why would he do that if he wasn't hiding something? The boys told me they then saw Brian leaving the home with Eric."

"Apparently other boys saw *you* leaving with Eric."

"That's a lie! Get them all together and ask them."

"You think they'll defend you? That you're their favourite? What have you done to be their favourite?" He let the insinuation sink in, leering all the while. "Or maybe you think they're afraid of you?"

"I'm confident the children will tell the truth."

"Look, you don't seem to realize we're on to you. The game is up. We've got you and we'll keep up the pressure till we make you crack. So why don't you make it easy for yourself? Tell us now what we want to know."

"I don't understand. I've told you already all I know."

"You haven't given us the dates of when you started abusing children."

"I have never abused children, so how can I give you the dates?" He felt he was talking to mental defectives and his voice rose even more in frustration.

"Are you shouting at me? Do you know where you are and what trouble you're in? We might have to bring in somebody to make you behave a little more politely."

"I didn't mean to shout but you're being completely irrational. Why won't you believe me?"

He sounded desperate and heard the panic in his own voice. The other leaned forward again.

"Because we know you're guilty. You've got guilt written all over you. You're a paedophile personality type with form, and since you arrived here boys have started disappearing. What do you do with them?"

He stared at them in a state of mental numbness. He began to understand these people were not just incredibly dumb and obstinate in their error. They were evil. They were deliberately trying to frame him. He began to feel frightened.

"Could I ask you to turn the tape recorder back on? You're now treating me as a suspect. You're supposed to record interviews with suspects."

"Are you telling us our job?" The tone was quiet and menacing.

The Boy in Formaldehyde

"Yes. I demand a lawyer and I demand that you turn on the tape recorder." He looked him in the eyes without blinking. He thought it was time he stood up to them.

"I think we need some help to make you understand who you are and what sort of position you're in." He spoke softly. Then he reached behind him and flicked a switch on the wall and spoke into a small intercom speaker beside it. "Can we have Dan in here?" He flicked the switch back again.

The door opened and a big man in uniform walked in.

"Dan, this gentleman needs to become acquainted with the telephone directory. He's suffering from memory loss."

The man walked out again. Potato Nose gave a slight grin of anticipation.

"This will really help you remember things. It's a bit like shock treatment, only the old-fashioned way."

The big man came back in with a thick telephone directory, walked up to Kayley and hit him over the head with it. Kayley saw stars and felt he had been hammered into his chair. He rocked violently from the impact and his head was spinning as if he had just got off the most tortuous ride in a funfair. He had a sensation of sickness in the pit of his stomach and a deep fear about the possibility of brain damage if they repeated this.

"That's illegal," he heard himself say, as if he was speaking down a long tunnel.

"Do it again. He didn't understand," came the faraway voice of Potato Nose.

The policeman called Dan advanced to hit him again, and this time Kayley put his arms up and protected his head, cowering away from him. Dan put the directory on the table, took his wrists and pulled them up, raising him from his chair. Then he punched him in the solar plexus and, as he doubled up gasping, the telephone book came down again on the back of his head. This time he fell to the floor and stayed there.

After what seemed like several minutes of swirling blackness, light reappeared. The room began to steady. Two thick-soled black shoes came around the table, squeaking slightly, and stood next to him. He expected a kick in the face.

"Get up, you paedophile bastard, or we'll really start to work on you. We can do anything we like to you. Have you got that?"

"I demand a lawyer. And a doctor." His voice was shaky. It seemed far away. He got slowly to his feet, holding his head. There was a ringing sound and something was wrong with his eyes.

"And what else? A fucking call-girl? Oh no, I forgot, you prefer little boys. What do you do to them, eh? Rape them? Force them to suck you off? What's your thing?" His voice was now filled with hatred of a jeering, contemptuous kind.

Kayley said nothing. The uniformed policeman had gone. The telephone book was on the table. He slowly straightened up and tried to look Potato Nose in the eye as he stood close to him. His vision was extremely blurred with little exploding stars blinding him but he could feel the other's eyes boring into him with pure hatred from inches away. As he reached full height Potato Nose suddenly punched him, this time in the groin, and he doubled up in agony. Then the telephone book came down on his head again. Kayley staggered and collapsed over the table, holding on to a chair back to stop himself from falling to the floor.

"You're forcing me to get my hands dirty," the rasping voice came at him as if down a long tunnel. "I hate doing this and I'm going to make you pay for making me!"

"You seem to be under the illusion," came the other voice, even further away, "that the law is going to protect you from this sort of interrogation. It's not, you know. We have a lot of discretion to use all sorts of enhanced interrogation techniques, pioneered by our colleagues in Northern Ireland before we passed them to the CIA, on certain kinds of criminals who are a threat to the most vulnerable members of society and deserve no particular favours."

Kayley found himself hyperventilating from blind panic and the mental confusion of concussion.

"I am a social worker," he gasped. "I have never hurt anybody. You have no evidence against me!"

"No evidence!" repeated Potato Nose in astonishment. "That's what you're counting on, is it? Listen, matey, you're going to provide the evidence! Your confession is going to convict you. We don't need anything else. Now, if you want to have a brain in your head that functions for the rest of your life, you'd better start providing us with the evidence we need. Start talking, paedo scum!"

The telephone book came down on his head again. Again he saw stars. He reeled and clutched the chair back. He didn't know where he was any longer. He seemed to be falling through space but he never landed anywhere. He just kept spinning. A voice began to talk to him inside his head, like a public address system echoing in a huge cavern. It was his own voice, calm and rational.

"You can't let them ruin your brain. Brain damage is irreversible. No amount of compensation will ever give you back your brain. You've got to stop them doing this now. You can't take one more blow to the head or you'll never be able to think, to read, to write, to remember, to talk properly, to work again. You'll be a vegetable. Instant Alzheimer's. Better to give them what they want and sort it out afterwards. You can always retract it. When you get in front of a proper judge. They won't let this stand. But you have to stop it now."

"All right," he heard himself say. "What do you want?"

"We want you to tell us everything," said the voice in his ear coming from far away.

"I can't remember," he stammered, holding his hands to his head to stop the spinning. "I can't think. You write what you want me to confess and I'll sign it. I'll sign anything you want." He thought vaguely they might write stuff nobody sane would believe.

"Where do you think you are, paedo scum? Some kind of dictatorship?" The voice was a snarl. "Russia? China? Saudi Arabia? We don't dictate, even to worms like you. That's not our way of doing things. You're going to do all the work. Now, sit down and tell us what you did, and we'll decide if it's acceptable. By the way, you're now under caution. Anything you say may be used against you in court, and you have the right to remain silent, though that also may be held against you as an indication of guilt. You are suspected of committing paedophile offences on children in your care. So let's begin. When did you start?"

After forty minutes during which his head was full of stars exploding like sky rockets and a dull buzz grew louder inside it, he had stammered out a version they found acceptable, with a certain amount of guidance on their part. He confessed to beginning to molest boys shortly after his arrival at the home. He did it with half a dozen boys. Viktor was among his first victims. He had raped him the day before he went out with Cyril Jones. That had obviously driven the boy to take the opportunity to run away from the home. Eric was his most recent victim. On Saturday he had taken him out to a wood to rape him, and while they were there the boy had run away. He did it because he had a compulsion which he couldn't control.

The hatchet-faced one typed his statement into his laptop as Kayley spoke, adding a few corrections of his own, and printed it on a printer in the corner of the room. They handed him the text. They turned on the recorder again, read him his rights and recorded him reading his confession aloud. He struggled to make out the words through his blurred vision. At the end they asked him politely to sign it, and he did. Then they turned off the recorder.

"That wasn't so bad, was it?" said Potato Nose with a smarmy, sadistic smile.

"Now, can I go?" he asked.

"Go?" Potato Nose looked at him in astonishment, his smile broadening. "Go where? You're not going anywhere, lad. Your place is here with us from now on. You'll be sleeping tonight in a remand prison. Tomorrow we show the judge this, you'll get three months remanded in custody, renewable if necessary, while we prepare the prosecution. And then you'll be tried and sent down for maybe ten years. Minimum. Or thirty if the court thinks you murdered the boys." He held up the paper Kayley had signed. "This confession is a one-way ticket to hell. There's no wriggling out of it. You're ours, now, boy. We've got you, you little paedo bastard, and we won't let you go. The other prisoners will love you, Kayley. They'll love you to death. We'll find a way of keeping you even after the ten years is up. If you survive that long. Too dangerous to let out. You'll die in our care, lad. Your life is over."

Kayley put his head in his hands, with his elbows on the table. His head was now aching violently. His vision was still blurred and full of flashes like a firework display. He wondered if a retina was detaching. That meant permanent loss of sight. He felt tears coursing down his cheeks. In the distance, he heard Potato Nose commenting quietly to his colleague.

"They always end up this way. Cry babies. They really are spineless scum."

"Of course everybody cracks in the end if you keep at them long enough," the other voice commented judiciously.

"But this one was remarkably quick. Just four taps with the phone book and he signs away his life. That must be a record. Congratulations, chief."

"How long did it take the Aye-ties to beat a confession out of that American bitch, Amanda what's her name? Eighteen hours?"

"Yeah, but they only slapped her head. And kept her from pissing. Didn't use the phone book. It's the shock that scares the hell out of them. Then the headache. Make their own bodies hurt them. Really saves time. Now we can go home early."

13

On Tuesday Romain had to teach a student for two hours in the morning (a real paying one, an executive moving to a Paris office.) He invited Camilla to come for lunch afterwards. After their emotional rollercoaster of the day before, he felt oddly nervous waiting for her. Would they still feel the same closeness and express it? Or would she feel embarrassed by what had happened, even mortified by what she had exposed of herself, and try to go back into her shell by denying it all? After all they had not slept together to cement the relationship so it seemed a bit more nebulous and deniable than it would have been otherwise. As he let her in and they exchanged kisses on the cheek, he found it hard to read the expression in her eyes, other than a hint of nervousness like his own. Was this a new day for her and had yesterday already become a dream or an illusion? She made no move to fall into his arms, but seemed to hang back, so he took his cue from her. Given her complicated attitude to sex, and the problems they had talked about, he thought it was best if he erred on the side of distance. He would wait for her to make the moves. Besides, the thought of kissing her and being pushed away was more than he could bear. He proposed to prepare lunch together, and launched into a comic speech in praise of *spaghetti alle vongole*. He thought cooking would give them something practical to do as if they were a couple and also keep them in close physical contact in the tiny kitchen alcove. They were soon engaged in good-humoured squabbling over how to cook the meal. After they had eaten, they sat on the sofa and finished their glass of wine. He was casting around for something to talk about when she got in first.

"Where did you learn these Italian recipes? Have you lived there?"

It was the kind of conversation they might have had a month earlier and he had a sinking feeling of going backwards in the relationship, as if he had to start all over again. He had a gloomy sense that nothing in a relationship is ever acquired; it must be recreated every day.

"No, but I've been there several times. I like Italy." He decided to go on chatting to ease the slight tension. "They have their own zany way of revolting against the crassness of modern life. In the north they have a movement called Slow Food. It means taking time to eat, hours and hours, even longer than the French do, and eating only fresh, local food. It's a revolt against American fast food. The idea is to savour every mouthful. To live in the present moment. And the concept is spreading to other things. Slow cities, slow living, slow travel, even slow education."

"It needs to be extended to everything," she said. "Even love. I believe in slow love."

"Why not? Slow love-making? For hours on end? I'll drink to that." He grinned and raised his wine glass to her.

He felt relieved she had brought the conversation back to the essential so quickly. It was like a coded message.

"Not only. Taking time before you make love." She smiled coyly. "Taking time for what used to be called courtship."

"That's a word you don't often hear these days." He slipped into the same tone of gentle irony she was using. He now saw their conversation as an old-fashioned dance where they held each other at arm's length, but it was not devoid of an element of a tease.

"I know. It's like something our grandparents did. It's because there are no taboos any longer, no moral rules against making love at once. So people feel almost obliged to do it as soon as they feel any attraction. To hold off is seen as uncool." She sipped her wine and thought for a bit. "Yet when we see a romantic film, we don't want the lovers to jump into bed in the first scene, we want them to wait for the right moment, to make it more intense. Why don't we live real love like in a film?" She sounded wistful, as if nostalgic for another age. "Isn't that better than being consumed in minutes like an ice cream, and then feeling vaguely dissatisfied because it was all so quick and easy, and all that remains is repetition?"

"So you think fifties' puritan morality had its advantages — in making people take their time before leaping into bed? The postponement of gratification?" He was toying with the idea as something fanciful and quaintly archaic. Of course he had advised her to take things slowly in just this way but he hadn't quite expected her to take his advice so literally and above all to apply it to him.

"In a way. Sex is at its most intense when it's forbidden. When you have to overcome a moral prohibition under the impetus of passion. Once you remove the forbidden aspect from normal sex, then people look for it in the abnormal. So they need adultery or perversion to feel any excitement. Like the Romans at their most decadent."

"So, you believe true love is born of frustration, of desire for the forbidden or the unattainable, and in the days of instant gratification it will soon cease to exist?" He had a fleeting vision of himself as a troubadour discoursing on love at the court of Eleanor of Aquitaine. He wondered if the troubadours had taken their own words seriously.

"Exactly." She gazed into his eyes as though searching their depths, he was not quite sure for what. "But that doesn't mean desire for the unattainable can't be stimulated by a little instant gratification along the way. Hugs and kisses, for example."

"Is that a hint we are due for another session?" This sounded more promising.

"I suppose you could interpret it that way if you really wanted to," she said coyly, laying her head on the back of the sofa as if in invitation. He was just leaning in to kiss her when his phone rang on the little coffee table in front of them. Glaring at it resentfully, he picked it up.

"Is that Romain de Lagarde?" came a voice. Romain admitted it was.

"This is Piers Bendigo."

"Ah, Mr Bendigo, so glad you called," said Romain, staring wide-eyed at Camilla to indicate the importance of the call.

"I understand you are interested in buying my *Full Fathom Five*?"

"Yes, the *Boy in Formaldehyde*. Though I'm actually acting for my cousin."

"Oh, it's your cousin." The voice sounded disappointed.

"Yes. My cousin has a castle in the Bordeaux region, and he has a collection of contemporary art on display for visitors."

"And has he told you he is interested in this work?"

"Of course. I telephoned him after I saw it and told him about it. I sent him some photos from my iPhone. He's very interested."

"I see. Could I have your cousin's name?"

"He prefers not to disclose it for the moment." He had visions of an internet search coming up blank. "Not until we meet and talk about the price. I can tell you that he is a count and his château is near St Emilion. It's both a castle and a vineyard. It has been in our family since the seventeenth century. I act as his agent. He prefers to stay in the background for now. But once the sale is ready to conclude he may come over to see the work and meet you."

"I see." There was a pause. "So, could you and I arrange to meet sometime?"

"Certainly. I am at your entire disposition."

"Good. Would you happen to be free right now?"

"Right now? Why not?" He looked at Camilla and made a face.

"So, here's the address." Bendigo gave an address in Shoreditch, which Romain scribbled on an old envelope Camilla had grabbed from the other table. "How long will it take you?"

"I'm not sure. Shall we say, half an hour to an hour?"

"That'll be fine. I'll be expecting you." The call ended.

Romain raised a fist in triumph and then kissed and hugged Camilla ecstatically.

"The bastard has taken the bait!" Then he pulled back and stared at her. "What were we doing when he called?"

"I've forgotten," she said, kissing him lightly. She insisted on coming with him. She set up her smartphone recording app to record everything at the touch of a button and placed the phone carefully in her handbag, facing a perforated section of the leather. They took the Underground to Old Street station and then walked through the scruffy, seedy streets to the address. It looked like a converted warehouse and the building next to it was covered with elaborate graffiti, including an enormous lizard. The door was not locked. Inside there was a hallway, half of which had been painted red. There was a lift as large as a small garage and Camilla turned on her phone's recording app as they went up to the first floor. There were two doors several metres apart and both had Bendigo's name on a grubby card. They rang the bell beside one. The other door opened and a man of about their own age stood there. He was wearing paint-spattered, purple overalls, which made his pudgy body look like that of an oversized toddler in rompers. They advanced to meet him and shook hands with him. Camilla noticed there was some paint on his fingers but it was fortunately dry.

"I'm at work on some pitch paintings," Bendigo announced by way of explanation.

"Interesting. I wonder if we could see them," said Romain.

The other looked at him in shrewd appraisal and then gestured for them to enter. He closed the door behind them before he answered.

"I'll show you." He led the way along a short corridor into a huge atelier, with a high roof with skylights in it. It was divided into separate spaces by shoulder-high partitions. In the first space a large canvas was spread on the floor, with lead weights on each corner. It was a splodge of various colours and a small paint can lay on its side in the middle with yellow paint still oozing out of it.

"The idea is you pitch opened paint cans and see what happens," said Bendigo. "Then you either leave it in its primal state or you modify it using various objects."

He picked up a small can of paint, prised the lid off with a teaspoon and pitched it into the middle of the canvas. Green paint splashed out into the general mess. He stepped around the canvas and stirred the can and the paint about with a dirty, stained child's cricket bat, spreading the paint in meandering lines over the surface. He stopped to study the effect.

"I'm hesitating between Miro, Kandinsky and Jackson Pollock. It's a question of how much cricket bat to use — a little or an enormous amount. And how fast to stir. Slowly or in a frenzy." He seemed to expect them to comment.

"The element of chance," murmured Romain. "The key to all original creation."

"Exactly. Sometimes I throw the cat in the middle of it. He produces some spectacular effects. Of course, the whole thing is the work of the subconscious."

"Really? You mean the cat's subconscious?" queried Camilla.

"No. Mine. Mine works through him," said Bendigo irritably. "Or through the cricket bat. As the case may be."

He led them back along the corridor into an untidy living room filled with a clutter of objects, including a fish tank with a naked doll floating in it, pieces of old armour and bits of machinery. He gestured towards a sofa. When they were seated, he handed them bottles of beer from a crate on the floor. He opened his bottle and sat down in a big armchair, which had a loose canvas cover on it to protect it from the paint on his clothes. There were no glasses and he did not hand them the bottle opener but tossed it onto the coffee table between them.

A tabby cat stalked into the room, mewed in disapproval and then turned and stalked out again. There was a streak of red paint on its erect, quivering tail, and its fur looked a ruffled mess as if it had been scrubbed. It smelled strongly of turpentine.

"I feel the time is right for this Boy of mine," Bendigo declared, swigging his beer. "Timing is of the essence in art, but I also have to get the marketing right and see whether this is the right sale to make."

"So, price is not the main concern for you?" suggested Romain, reaching for the bottle opener on the coffee table and opening Camilla's beer and then his own.

"If the price is right, that's one aspect, but the publicity surrounding the sale is another thing to get right. You see, art today is mainly marketing. The creation is the easy bit, as you just saw. For anyone with talent, that is."

"And what are your criteria for a good sale?" Romain took a pull on his beer.

"It has to be a buyer one can be proud to have among the owners of one's works," said Bendigo, reflecting. "A buyer adds value, if you will. He is part of one's CV, one's calling card. Part of one's image as an artist. You can't imagine how Hirst benefited from having Saatchi as a regular buyer. It was like a guarantee of his importance."

"I think you'll find my cousin will be a buyer who will give your work considerable exposure on the Continent that will not do it any harm."

"What kind of collector is your cousin?"

Bendigo put his designer trainers comfortably on his fake antique coffee table and lay back and sucked on his beer. With his short plump body he reminded Camilla of an oversized baby with its bottle. Only the black, three-day stubble on his pasty jowls spoiled the effect.

"He follows his own personal taste," said Romain. "But he has an eye for the next wave. He was onto Hirst and Koons before their prices really took off. His collection is on display in his château, which is visited by thousands every year, so your work will not be hidden away in a vault. It'll be seen by a great number of people of taste and class. There's enormous rivalry among the major wine-producing châteaux of the Bordeaux region to draw visitors. Some of them have brought in famous architects to redesign their wineries in avant garde styles. My cousin prefers to rely on his art collection, which people visit before settling in to taste the wine. And of course there's the castle itself, which dates from the fifteenth century but has a much later, finer interior. He likes to give parties there, which often feature in the magazines about the rich and famous. He's a socialite, but a rather unconventional one."

"What sort of parties does he give?" asked Bendigo, licking beer froth off his lips.

"The last one I went to had a mythological theme. Young men and women in mythological costumes, gods and goddesses — not overdressed, shall we say — and things ended up in the Trevi Fountain, or the replica of it which he has in his garden. The evening was warm and many of the guests stripped off to be in the fountain with gods and goddesses."

"Sounds rather decadent — but in quite a postmodernist way," pronounced Bendigo. "The Trevi Fountain, references to Fellini. The cliché as a form of originality. Second degree. Like Campbell's soup. Marilyn's face. A cliché image, if copied enough times, becomes kitsch, and once the kitsch is seen as ironical, it becomes postmodernist. That is Koons's whole approach, of course."

"Exactly. Decadent but in a very postmodernist way is how I would describe my cousin. When you're from an old, distinguished family, for some it can be a constraint but for others it is a liberation — they feel free to be whatever they want. The count — my cousin — is not a dull, boring type.

He will confer upon your work some of his own flair and class. In fact, he has asked me if it might be possible to commission another work of this type from you with some modifications, in line with his own tastes."

"What do you mean — modifications?" Bendigo was alert, slightly suspicious.

"He would prefer the boy not to wear a diving mask, and to have much longer hair, flowing freely, perhaps even blond hair. And also the swimming costume, it is rather English, shall we say, in its modesty — my cousin believes in naturism. Why not a naked boy, a more natural, more elemental creature, more like a young Greek god. And perhaps also two or three years older, an adolescent Dionysus."

Bendigo looked thoughtful.

"I'll have to see what the technical possibilities are."

"Of course, I have no idea how you have made this figure — if this is synthetic material — or a real body — a found body in the manner of Duchamp."

"Duchamp?" Bendigo looked at him blankly.

"Marcel Duchamp and his found objects, which he picked up from junk yards and displayed as works of art — you remember, the urinal, the snow shovel, the bicycle wheel, and so on?"

"Oh, yes, of course, Duchamp," said Bendigo hastily, rather embarrassed that his knowledge of art might be in doubt. In fact, he was quite a fan of Duchamp's work, but he had pronounced the name mentally as Dutch-Amp. He was wondering who this Dishong was.

"My cousin was curious to know if this was a 'found body', so to speak, from a morgue or graveyard or other source — of course, it is not essential for him to know — if these are secrets of fabrication, he will respect your discretion — but he was thinking in these terms — if there was a possibility of you making another one, perhaps it would be a question of how easy it would be to obtain a body corresponding to certain specifications — age, beauty, hair colour, etc. He was curious to know how easy these bodies are to come by. Is there a supply of them? Is anyone else working along the same lines?"

"Anyone else? You mean another artist?" Bendigo looked alarmed, even horrified. "Of course not! This is an absolutely original idea, and it is *my* idea! I hope he's not thinking for one moment of commissioning a work of this kind from another artist — that would be utterly unacceptable! I'm sure there must be plagiarism laws even in France that would forbid it!"

"But of course!" cried Romain, trying hastily to reassure him. "That's why my cousin is so eager to obtain this work from you! He has total respect for the originality of the artist! A mere imitation has no value at all! It's the first artist who thought of something who gives it value, authenticity. If somebody else found an old urinal like Duchamp's and displayed it as a work of art, it would have no value whatsoever, even though Duchamp's urinal is worth millions! The same with his snow shovel — anyone else's snow shovel would be utterly worthless, even if they found an identical one of the same brand as Duchamp's. *His* shovel is the only one that has value because *he* was the one who thought of it first! He had the *concept*, as they say. The same with Hirst's shark in formaldehyde. If someone else puts a dolphin or a cod or a tuna fish in formaldehyde, it will have no value whatsoever. But if Hirst chooses to put a cod in formaldehyde it will be worth millions, because it will be one more of a series by an artist already established as a brilliant creative figure and the originator of that concept." Romain stretched his arm dramatically towards him. "Now, you, in taking the unprecedented step of placing a human being in formaldehyde, have broken new ground, which wouldn't be broken even by a swordfish or a walrus or even a hippopotamus in formaldehyde — they would be seen as mere imitations of Hirst. Yours is a new concept, you have taken it a stage further, a quantum leap!"

"Precisely! One has to know in art which crucial step creates a new original concept and what merely repeats what has gone before!" Bendigo came to life and became passionate on the subject. Here was a client who seemed to understand! "Hirst's shark in formaldehyde was a revolutionary idea — if you exclude the displays in natural history museums — but the boy in formaldehyde is a further revolutionary step which is just as original! As you said, a quantum leap! I have made a crucial new contribution to the history of art, and this concept is now mine — I alone can exploit it! Everyone else who tries to do the same, to put human beings in formaldehyde, becomes merely an imitator of me without my talent. There is such a thing as the unofficial patenting of an artistic idea, and that idea is then authentic only for that artist. The work has value only with his signature upon it, and all such works by other artists are worthless imitations! I alone can put a boy in formaldehyde and be original no matter how many times I do it! No one else can!"

"Exactly!" Romain matched his enthusiasm. "That's why I think it's essential to patent this idea as yours beyond any doubt, by converting the single work into a series, by making a second one as soon as possible. Then it becomes your trademark, your concept, it becomes yours alone to exploit. That's why my cousin would be interested in commissioning a slightly older boy, with the changes we discussed."

"The idea is an interesting one," said Bendigo slowly. "I'll have to think about it."

They pulled on their beers and looked at each other for half a minute, their burst of energy and passion having run out of steam as they reached agreement.

"I have just a suggestion," Romain began again hesitantly. "I hope you will not be offended by it, but it is an idea, in terms of the supply of material for such works." He stopped, as if thinking about how to proceed, and then appeared to change his mind. "No, perhaps I shouldn't. It might not be thought to be entirely.... how shall we say.... ethical?" He glanced questioningly at Camilla, as if silently consulting her.

"Why not let him be the judge of that?" said Camilla on cue.

"Yes, tell me, tell me! I'm open to suggestions, it can't do any harm." Bendigo's curiosity was aroused.

"It is, of course, the raw material that poses the problem," said Romain, stroking his chin meditatively. "But do you know there is one place in Europe at the moment that has an almost unlimited supply of material for this kind of work?"

"Really?" Bendigo sounded intrigued.

"That place is an island off the coast of Sicily closest to Africa. Lampedusa. Every day their morgue is overflowing with bodies drowned trying to make it from Africa. Most are in perfect condition, and not all of them are black, some are quite white. Syrians, for example. Some Syrians even have grey or green eyes, did you know? A throwback to the Crusaders, so they say. A lot of intermarriage. They can't keep track of all these bodies, some of them are not even registered. There's a black market operating from the morgue which my cousin has heard of — it's controlled by the Sicilian mafia, and it would be child's play to obtain a body of any colour, sex and age you might like, for a very reasonable price. They could be delivered from Lampedusa by yacht to the coast of France, and from there by refrigerated truck to my cousin's château in the Bordeaux region. Quite simply and directly. You'd be able to work on the spot in his château. The tank of formaldehyde and everything you need could be delivered there, and you could produce your work of art at minimum cost, very quickly, which would leave a huge margin of profit. You could even produce several at once."

"I see, like a sort of production line!" Bendigo's eyes were lighting up. "Like Andy Warhol's Factory! One could, in fact, have several works produced at the same time and sell them to different buyers. Your cousin, of course, and then a buyer in New York, and perhaps one or two institutional buyers, among the more forward-looking European museums, the Guggenheim in Bilbao, the Pompidou, or the Tate Modern. One needs to place works strategically, in various locations worldwide, where they are seen by a certain number of visitors and art critics, increasing recognition and demand for purchases by other museums. And one could vary the race of the figures on display — Africans, Afghans, Syrians." He began to be carried away by the vision. "It could be a kind of United Nations of drowning figures, a great collective image of the human race, all of them struggling from the depths towards the surface, towards air and life! An epic series! One might even call an African figure simply: *Lampedusa: a Plea to the Conscience of Humanity*."

"Brilliant!" said Romain, almost breathless at this idea. "Absolutely brilliant!"

"Or even, more simply: *Indifference. The Mediterranean Claims One More.*"

"Slightly more understated. Better, perhaps."

"Definitely better," chimed in Camilla.

"And there would be the hidden irony, known only to the few, that these figures actually came from there. That they are what they pretend to be. A kind of double bluff!" Bendigo looked inspired. "A perfect, strategic positioning at the forefront of politically engaged art, humanitarian art, if that's the way things are moving. Art in support of human rights. We artists are so often accused of frivolity and irrelevance. This would be placing art at the centre of the human conscience. One could be at the cutting edge of a new humanist art — but totally avant-garde, postmodernist, provocative! So, you can tell your cousin that I would be very interested in this proposition and we should discuss it in more detail. Of course, when we get to the question of price for this work, we'll have to bring my agent into the conversation. He is far better attuned to what the market can bear at this point, though I suppose your cousin has no particular maximum in mind at this stage."

"He told me that for this work he would be willing to go as far as a high six figures. For the slightly older boy he wants to commission, he might be persuaded to go as high as seven."

"We are talking pounds, of course."

"No. Euros, but the difference is not huge these days."

"I shall pass that on to my agent."

"Good. And remember this will only be the beginning of a much more fruitful collaboration. And as your reputation grows, as you extend the series and these works are placed strategically, the prices will soar."

"True." Bendigo looked transported by the thought. "I am much obliged for your visit."

"The pleasure is all mine."

Camilla, who had been treated by both of them like a piece of furniture, now stood up with Romain and shook hands with Bendigo as they took their leave.

"Haven't I seen you somewhere?" he asked her curiously.

"I don't think so," she replied. "Unless it was at an exhibition. But I did do some modelling when I was younger, magazines and so on, and it does catch up with me sometimes. People think I look familiar."

"That's probably it. And your name? I didn't quite catch it."

"Melissa Brandt." They had agreed on a pseudonym for her.

They went out. They were both silent as they walked away. Only when they were out of sight of Bendigo's building did she say:

"He said enough to hang him! Let's hope my phone has got it all nice and clear."

"The media will love that recording!"

"The police may be interested in it too."

After they left, Bendigo stared for a moment at the wall and then got up and switched on his computer on a small table in a corner of the room. He called up a website and looked at the photos of his *Boy in Formaldehyde* and then at the tirade of abuse written about it. Paedophile art! A slow anger began to creep over him. If it was her, then he had been an enormous, unbelievable fool! Nervously, he clicked back onto the home page about the author of the site. There was a small photo of her and he made it bigger. To his surprise it looked nothing like the girl he had just met. She had the same brown hair and brown eyes — that was all. He could have sworn he remembered seeing a different photo there, the face of this girl, Melissa. Had the photos been swapped? He stared in bafflement. Then he shook his head. He was being paranoid again. This was clearly not the same girl. Why should it be her?

He picked up his phone and dialled his agent to tell him the good news. They agreed to meet to talk about the price which this French count might be induced to pay.

14

Camilla went back home in the late afternoon as she had to teach a yoga class in Notting Hill Gate. When she got back she transferred the recording on her smartphone to her computer, listening again to the incriminating things Bendigo had been led on to say. Then she noticed there was a message on her voicemail and was surprised to find it was from Kayley. He said he had been arrested and charged with the rape of Eric and Viktor — on the testimony of his director and Brian Spenser, after he had insisted they should report Eric's disappearance. He asked if she could help with his defence by testifying it was Brian, not him, who had prevented them from seeing Eric and then left the home with him. She at once called Romain and Ekaterina to discuss what to do. They agreed she should call Inspector Stubbings, and that they would all go back to Birmingham the next day and talk to the police there. They would put a statement on record accusing Brian and exonerating Kayley. Ekaterina in particular was upset that an innocent man was in prison, and she feared for his safety.

Camilla telephoned Inspector Stubbings and let her know what had happened. Stubbings promised to do what she could to get Kayley released. The next day Camilla, Ekaterina and Romain travelled to Birmingham by train and went to the main police station to make statements about the case. They made a formal request for an investigation into the disappearance of both Viktor and Eric, and accused Brian Spenser of lying to them about where Eric was so as to stop them talking to him. They spoke briefly to the chief inspector in charge of the case. They told him they were present when Kayley learned from other boys that Eric had been taken away from the home by Brian.

The chief inspector, a man with heavy features and a bulbous nose, replied that they were pursuing an investigation based on diverse pieces of evidence which could not be disclosed, and Kayley would have to answer the charges against him. He seemed utterly impervious to anything they had to say. They then asked if they could visit Kayley in prison and were told they would have to apply to the prison authorities. He offered them no help in going about this. Ekaterina was determined that she at any rate was going to visit him. She used Camilla's phone to call the prison and asked about visiting hours. She was asked what relation she was to Kayley and she replied at once she was his fiancée. She was told she could come the next Saturday morning at eleven, but should be there twenty minutes early. She suggested to the others it would be better if she went alone and pretended to be Kayley's girlfriend. She said it might help to convince other prisoners he was not a paedophile, which might save him from being attacked.

That afternoon when they got back to London she used Camilla's computer to write Kayley a letter and said she was coming to see him. After all, she wrote, I am your fiancée and you have a right to see me. She assured him they would soon prove his innocence and the guilt of those at the care home who had framed him. She signed the letter "with love" and enclosed a photo of herself that she asked Camilla to take with her smartphone and print on normal paper. She assumed the letter would be opened by the prison officials. She hoped it would change their attitude to Kayley, sow doubt in their minds as to whether he was a paedophile, and get him better treatment. She was terrified he would be beaten up by other prisoners or that some vindictive guard would spit in his food every day, or even put him in a cell with a homosexual rapist. All the horrors she had known for eleven years came back to her. The relentless, petty cruelty of human beings in a position of power over others was a nightmare that still haunted her. It had pushed her to the brink of suicide several times. If there is one place, she thought, that might convince somebody that life is not worth living and human nature is beyond redemption, it is a prison. She was filled with an irrational fear that Kayley might kill himself, and she felt her mission in life was to save him.

She had just finished the letter and was going out to post it when Camilla said she was going to the supermarket to buy some food for dinner. It was the day of the week when the tenants of the three bedsits in the house cooked dinner together and ate with the landlady.

"Why don't you join us?" she suggested. "One of the other girls is Ukrainian. I'm sure you'll like them."

Ekaterina accepted. They went out to the supermarket together. There was a Tesco's round the corner in Queensway and just up the street from it was the post office. Ekaterina went and bought stamps (Camilla had given her the money) and posted the letter. Then she joined Camilla in the supermarket. Ekaterina was embarrassed she had no money to contribute for the food. Camilla assured her it didn't matter — she could make dinner for all of them when she found a paying job. As they walked around the supermarket Camilla explained a bit about the house she lived in.

"My landlady, Mrs Konstantinou, is a Greek Cypriot. She had to flee Cyprus when the Turks invaded and took her house. She came to London in the seventies with her husband and sons and they finally managed to buy that house in Bark Place. Now she's seventy-eight and her husband's dead. Her three sons all live outside London. So she turned three of her spare bedrooms into bedsits. But she's special. She only takes girls as tenants, and they have to be from countries that use the Cyrillic alphabet."

"So that would include me."

"Yes, the other two girls are Russian and Ukrainian. I was OK as a Serb. The Russian girl has a steady boyfriend so if she ever leaves to live with him, you can take her place. The rent is only half what most people charge. And the old girl is very flexible if you have problems. In exchange we take turns helping her with her shopping and walking her to church on Sunday. There's a Greek Orthodox church a short walk along Moscow Road. But she likes to have an arm to lean on in church as well so we stay with her and walk her back afterwards."

"That sounds pretty easy. Who does her cleaning?"

"We do, partly. She lets us cook in her kitchen every Wednesday and have dinner all together in her big dining-room. Provided we give the kitchen and dining-room a thorough clean afterwards."

"Do you think she'd like someone to clean the rest of her place? I need work."

"I'll have a word with her about it."

"The thing is I'd like to buy some make-up." Ekaterina seemed embarrassed. "I want to look good when I go to see Kayley. Do you think I could ask Maeve for some money?"

"She may not have any. Her centre's always struggling to stay open." Camilla thought for a moment. "I'll tell you what — talk to the other girls about make-up and stuff tonight. They're much flashier dressers than I am. I'm sure they have oodles of stuff they can lend you, not just make-up but clothes. And I'm paying for your ticket to Birmingham, don't worry. And I'll give you some money to get around there and buy some lunch."

"You're really kind."

"Come on, we're all in this together! We all want to help Kayley out of this mess. We're just sending you to represent us." She grinned mischievously. "Because we have the impression he'll be happier to see you than the rest of us."

Ekaterina blushed but looked quietly pleased. They carried the groceries back to Bark Place. Ekaterina joked about the name and asked if it had noisy dogs.

"No, but it's funny you say that," said Camilla. "Do you know what I call this place in my mind? Bark Mews. You get it? When I came to London as a kid and learned that word, I wanted to find a Kitty Mews or a Lion Mews or a Dog Mews. But I never did. The next street along is a mews. So I just call this street Bark Mews."

They went into the landlady's ground floor flat, which was unlocked, called out to her, and began preparing dinner in the kitchen. Mrs Konstantinou limped out of her bedroom with her walking-stick and Camilla introduced Ekaterina. They chatted.

"And where are you from in Ukraine?"

"Lviv. I was born in a village near it."

"It used to be called Lvov," she pointed out doubtfully.

"I called it that growing up. We spoke Russian at home because my father was from Kharkov."

"So, you're not one of these nationalists," Mrs Konstantinou said approvingly.

The other two girls arrived home from work and came into the landlady's kitchen too, and Camilla introduced them to Ekaterina. Alena was Ukrainian from Donetsk, and Olga was Russian from Novgorod. When they heard Ekaterina was from Lviv, the western hotbed of the nationalists, they exchanged glances. As they helped to peel the vegetables, they sounded her out tactfully for her views on the Ukrainian civil war, by making a few jokes.

"So you are from Lviv?" said Alena, who was lively and high-spirited. "You don't want to bomb Donetsk, I hope?" She laughed carelessly. "Not the opera house, anyway. We still keep performing operas, you know, even under the shelling. My mother goes all the time. They've made it free, since no one has any money. The singers and musicians sing and play for free every night to keep our spirits up. There's standing room only. Donetsk opera house never stopped performing even during Hitler's invasion. It's funny how mining people love opera, but the city was founded by a Welshman, so maybe that explains it."

"I think this war is stupid," said Ekaterina. "My father is from Kharkov so we always spoke Russian at home. He never liked the nationalists who made him feel he didn't belong in Lviv because he couldn't speak Ukrainian properly."

"So you don't support the Kiev government?"

"Not in making war on the Donbass. If they want their own state, or to join Russia, that's their choice."

"And you don't think Putin is just trying to grab territory?" said Olga slyly.

"Why would he want it? Russia is big enough. As for Crimea, that was always theirs. It was a stupid mistake for Khrushchev to transfer it to us. Sevastopol is a symbol of Russia. Potemkin built it. Tolstoy fought to defend it."

"Against the English, the French and the Turks," added Olga, who was serious and thoughtful. "Always the same enemies. I suspect the West planned this whole crisis just to take Sevastopol, like in 1855 and 1942."

"Do you think so?" asked Ekaterina, surprised. "Why?"

"Because it's the home of the Black Sea Fleet. They thought if they put a pro-Western government in Kiev, up to its neck in debt, they could pressure them to cancel the lease of Sevastopol to Russia, and deprive Russia's navy of its greatest port. Without firing a shot. Then Kiev would be pressured to lease Sevastopol to the US Navy and turn the Black Sea into an American lake. But Putin read their game too well and moved too quickly by taking back Crimea and making Sevastopol Russian again, as it's been for two hundred years. That's why they're so furious. Their nasty plan failed." She smiled. "And Putin was only giving Crimeans what they wanted. Their parliament voted to separate from Ukraine in 1992 but Kiev stopped them holding a referendum. They've been kept in Ukraine against their will ever since."

"Who would have believed a year ago all this would happen to us?" said Alena, almost in wonder. "That we would be torn apart like Yugoslavia? There was no reason for it. But it's true the region around Lviv has nothing to do with Russian history. They never spoke Russian. The rest of Ukraine was part of Russia for three hundred years and all the educated people spoke Russian. But the two western provinces, Volhynia and Galicia, were part of Poland, then the Austrian Empire, and then Poland again until 1939. That's where the extreme nationalists began. Then when the Nazis occupied the area, the Ukrainian nationalist movement of Stepan Bandera began to kill all the Polish people in those provinces so they could be annexed by Ukraine after the war. They killed thousands of Poles and Jews, and joined the Nazis to fight the Red Army. But the Nazis lost the war, so those provinces ended up part of Soviet Ukraine instead of a nationalist Ukraine. So a lot of those Ukrainian Nazis had to flee from the Red Army and go to America, where they've been spewing out their hatred of Russia ever since. Those are the people now in power in Kiev."

"My mother's family were part of all that," blurted out Ekaterina, blushing, her voice unsteady. She was speaking of family secrets that she had never talked about to anyone. "She was Polish. Her parents were among the few who survived when the Bandera nationalist gangs began murdering Poles. Her aunt and uncle lived in another village. The nationalists arrived one day in 1943 and ordered her uncle to kill his Polish wife with a hammer. When he refused, they burned her alive and then killed him with a hammer." Before she got to the end of the sentence, her voice went high-pitched and then she choked up. She wiped away her tears and plunged ahead, determined to finish. "The Ukrainian nationalists murdered a hundred thousand Poles. In addition to the Jews. And now they want to start on the Russian-speakers — like my father, who's now old and sick. And his wife can't walk any more. And I'm not there to help him and protect him from the fascist thugs in the streets. What if they won't serve him in the shops any more? How will he eat?" She choked on her tears again. "In Lviv they have a statue of the Nazi, Bandera. They still see him as a hero. And in Kiev too."

Alena, who was standing next to her, put her arms round her and hugged her.

"My family is in Donetsk, it's a lot worse. The fascist battalions shell the city every day. When Lviv declared independence from Yanukovych's government, did he send in the army? No. Yet when Donetsk and Lugansk declared independence from the new government, they sent in tanks and planes to bomb us. Why? How can the world accept this? The fascist battalions are blockading our cities. My family are starving. The other eastern Ukrainians try to send us food but their trucks are stopped by the Kiev fascists. And these are the people the West is supporting!" said Alena indignantly. "A regime that sends tanks and planes to bomb our cities and kill thousands of our people! Do they think we will accept their government after that? We will never forgive them! They are trying to starve the Donbass, they've stopped food getting in, medicine, water, they've stopped paying pensions, they've stopped people getting any money from their own bank accounts. So what choice do we have but to rely on Russia? They're the only ones feeding us! Without Russian aid my family would be dead! If we didn't have the border with Russia, the Kiev fascists would starve us to death. In Odessa they just burned forty people alive for demonstrating against them! I would rather die than live under those mass-murderers again! We should join Russia instead!" She was becoming as emotional as Ekaterina and wiped away tears angrily with her sleeve. But when Olga put an arm round her she insisted: "It's only the onions!"

"It's because the Kiev government is obeying the orders of Washington," said Olga, trying to be more analytical, "and America wants an excuse for a new Cold War against Russia and more military bases and missiles in Europe. What they want is to separate Europe from Russia forever, to make us enemies, because they were scared we were getting too close. They want to destroy all the trade between us so they can impose their trade treaty on Europe and their corporations can rule the world."

"And Russia is being forced into an alliance with China, instead of the one it wanted, with Europe," said Alena. "And English newspapers are keeping up this hate-propaganda against Russia. Why? A million Ukrainian refugees have fled to Russia! Half my mother's friends. Why would they do that if Russia is invading us? Why does the West keep up this lie? Russia is defending us — against the fascists in Kiev who want to murder us to impose their peasant language on a people who have spoken Russian for three hundred years! The same length of time the Irish and Scots and Welsh have spoken English! Would those nations accept it if a fanatical nationalist government wanted to ban English? Even if English was forced upon them centuries ago, it's now *their* language! Just as Russian is now *our* language! And Russian literature is *our* literature! And the NATO puppet fascists in Kiev want to stop our kids being able to read it! So they can make us hate Russia! They have stopped Russian being an official language. They keep closing schools which teach in Russian. Soon our kids won't be able to read Pushkin or Tolstoy, except in translation. It's the assassination of a culture so we will be cut off from Russian books, so the Americans can control our minds! In Kiev they pretend they are fighting against Soviet tyranny, two decades after it ended. But the Soviet Union was the tyrant! Not Pushkin! Not Tolstoy! Not the Russian language. If the West Ukrainians, who have never spoken Russian in their history because they were part of Poland, don't like speaking Russian, they can speak Ukrainian as they always have! While we speak Russian as we always have! Like the Swiss with their three languages. And if they won't let Russian be an official language, we will leave and rejoin Russia."

She had grown emotional by the end of her speech and she was embarrassed by her tears. The others applauded. But she hadn't finished. She wanted to say one more thing.

"The Kiev fascists pretend we were a colony, conquered by the Russians. We were never conquered by Russia! Not like Scotland and Wales and Ireland were conquered by England. We were the centre of the first Russian state from the ninth century till the Mongols destroyed it four hundred years later and nearly exterminated us. Then we agreed to join Russia again in the seventeenth century to defend us from the Catholic Poles, who were invading the whole country after taking the western provinces already, and the Tatars of Crimea in the south who were selling us as slaves to the Turks. Of course later on there were tensions and revolts and repression like all over Europe as nationalism grew everywhere. And then came the revolution and civil war and the Stalinist terror and the famines, which the whole USSR suffered from, not only us. But the Russians today are as glad to be rid of all that as we are. Right now it's corruption that holds us back and prevents reform, not Russian influence. We have always been a free people, the Cossacks, and the fascists want to rewrite our history in a version dictated by the CIA to make us enemies of Russia and a pawn of NATO!"

The others cheered again and Olga hugged her. They both shouted "Cossacks!" with their fists in the air, and then they burst out laughing. Suddenly they began dancing in a ring like Cossacks and Ekaterina joined in, and everyone began clapping in time and cheering, even though Alena had been in tears only a few minutes before.

The political talk continued after they sat down to dinner. Mrs Konstantinou turned the conversation to the West's betrayal of Cyprus.

"Where were the sanctions against the Turks after their invasion?" she demanded. "The West wants to ruin Russia for giving a bit of help to their brothers in eastern Ukraine, yet the Turks openly invaded and occupied a third of our country for forty years and were not punished at all — not even expelled from NATO for their aggression. What sort of double standard is that? The West has been engaged for centuries in a war against the Orthodox world. Look what they are doing to Greece, to Russia, to Ukraine, after what they did to Serbia! Instead they favour the Muslims. They supported the Turks against the Russians for centuries, despite the Turkish oppression and enslavement of all the Christian Slavic peoples. Then they allowed the Turks to massacre and drive out a million Greeks, then they let the Turks invade Cyprus, and then they supported the Bosniaks and the Kosovars against the Serbs. The West have betrayed their own civilization! They'll get what they deserve when there is Muslim rule in Britain and France, and that is not many decades away. Then they'll regret their endless, stupid treason against their own culture and religion!"

She shook her head in disgust. She had been a teacher in Cyprus and felt a mission to educate the world about the appalling injustice done to her country.

"Western politicians keep talking of the annexation of Crimea as the first change of borders by force in Europe since 1945," said Olga. "Have they forgotten Cyprus? Have they forgotten Yugoslavia, which they tore apart? Why don't they count?"

"Because those border changes were imposed by the West," said Camilla. "The West recognized every separatist state in Yugoslavia immediately and started arming them. They armed and trained the Croats to ethnically cleanse over a million Serbs from their territory. If the Russians bombed

Kiev tomorrow, they would be doing exactly the same as NATO did when they bombed Belgrade to make us accept the loss of Kosovo, which they tore away from us. And Kosovo is now a gangster-ruled failed state whose people are fleeing in droves."

"Like Iraq! Like Libya! NATO creates failed states wherever it goes," said Olga.

"And NATO still has troops in Kosovo just to stop the Serb part in the north from breaking away and rejoining Serbia," Camilla went on. "And they have troops in Bosnia to stop the Republika Srpska declaring independence and then voting to rejoin Serbia as well. Everyone has the right to self-determination except the Serbs!" She was becoming passionate in her turn.

"Or the people of Donbass," added Alena. "In short, anyone friendly to Russia!"

"Anyone of Orthodox faith!" exclaimed Mrs Konstantinou.

"And yet we are Europeans!" cried Olga. "Why do they hate us? What would European culture be without Tolstoy, Dostoyevsky, Chekhov, Tchaikovsky, Rachmaninoff?"

"Or Gogol, a Russian-speaking Ukrainian," added Ekaterina, "or Pushkin, who lived in Odessa and wrote poems about it, so is a little bit Ukrainian too."

"And the Americans and the Kiev fascists want to stop our children being able to read Pushkin!" cried Alena in disgust. "So they can make them hate Russia! The Americans are trying to change our identity and culture and language so they can control us! They are killing our souls! They are worse than Stalin or Hitler!"

Olga held up her glass of wine.

"Let's drink to Pushkin!"

They drank to Pushkin, and then to Tolstoy, the defender of Sevastopol, and then to Gogol, the Russian Ukrainian.

Mrs Konstantinou proposed Kazantzakis. Then they drank to the glories of Greece: Homer, Aeschylus, Sophocles, Plato, Aristotle.

"And they are bankrupting Greece!" Olga exclaimed. "They will destroy the cradle of our civilization for a few filthy euros!"

"And they'll start the Third World War and destroy the human race because they won't accept that the people of Donbass speak Russian and the people of Crimea *are* Russian!" cried Alena at the top of her voice.

Their heads were beginning to turn with the wine and the talk was becoming more and more animated. Then Camilla raised the subject of Ekaterina going to see a boy in prison who had been wrongfully arrested. The other girls wanted to know what for, and so the story came out of Ekaterina's son and the paedophile ring they suspected of his disappearance. Ekaterina explained how the framing of Kayley as a paedophile by the gang could put his life in danger in prison. When they found out that Ekaterina wanted to look good when she went to visit him and had no money for make-up, Olga and Alena at once offered to lend her some. They took her into their rooms between dessert and coffee to find things she might like to wear. Olga was exactly her size and they brought her out again wearing a tight black sweater that showed her curves, a short, tight, black skirt, black stockings and high heels. Her face was made up expertly by Alena, who worked in a beauty salon, her second profession after that of history teacher. The three of them were now chatting in Russian and switched back reluctantly to English for the sake of the others.

"Black looks good on you with your blonde hair," pronounced Olga, and Camilla agreed that Ekaterina looked stunning.

"Are these shoes all right?" asked Ekaterina anxiously. "I didn't want the very high heels because I can't walk in them and I don't want to look much taller than him, he's only about my height."

"They look good," said Camilla. "I can't walk in the very high ones either."

"So tell us about this boy. What's he like?" asked Alena.

"He's very good-looking," said Ekaterina, blushing. "But above all he is nice, and has a warm personality, and has a very good heart, I am sure. He is a bit shy."

"Camilla, what do you think of him?" asked Olga.

"When she says shy, he isn't shy with others, it's only when she speaks to him. Then he blushes and stammers and can't get his words out properly," she laughed.

"That's a good sign!" cried Alena. "He's in love with you!"

"But is he as good-looking as she says?" Olga asked Camilla.

"I think he's very attractive but I also think she's looking with the eyes of love."

"She can't judge because she is always thinking of someone else we know," said Ekaterina slyly to cover her own blushes. "She has eyes only for him! A Frenchman with a lot of charm who is funny and knows everything and talks all the time."

They all laughed. Olga told Ekaterina she could keep the clothes till after her trip to the prison, and Alena told her to come and wake her up on Saturday morning and she would put on her make-up again.

"It doesn't matter how early it is. I can go back to sleep afterwards."

Later, when Ekaterina said good-night and went back to her battered women's shelter, she was happy that she had found some more real friends. It had been a strange experience to chat in Russian again and be with people who talked so passionately, laughed with such abandon, and cried so readily on each other's shoulders. She realized how much she missed her mother-tongue, the language of Pushkin, and the company of those who shared it. Making new friends made her feel her life was getting better and better, like a story that was moving towards a happy ending, after the horrible chapters she hoped she had now left behind. She could imagine a future, with friends, a job, a place to live, and above all a life shared with Kayley. She found it hard to explain why she was so sure that someone she had spoken to for only a few minutes was going to be the man of her life. She just knew when she looked into his eyes that he could understand her, as if they had always known each other. And the fact that he was now in prison and beginning to go through what she had been through seemed like an omen, and made her see him almost as a lost brother. She had to stop him going through it, to save his life, or at least to give him courage and something to live for.

But of course it was not that that had attracted her to him in the first place, because that spell had been cast before he got arrested. As she climbed into bed in the dark dormitory, she remembered exactly why she had recognized him as the man of her dreams. It was because of a prince on a white horse that she had seen all through her childhood and had spent hours gazing at in reverie, while her cat, Mishi, purred in her arms — the prince on the marvellous painted Easter egg that had sat for years in her mother's glass cabinet, beside the Matryoshka dolls. The first time she saw Kayley, the image of that prince had come into her mind, like a sign.

15

Kayley's arrival at the prison was like the beginning of a nightmare that he was trapped inside, unable to wake up. The check-in was a process of dehumanization in which he was stripped of everything he possessed as though he was entering a strict monastic order for life. It would not have surprised him if they had shaved his head. The prison clothes were hideous and made him feel vulnerable, as if he was in pyjamas. His smartphone was taken away from him but he was allowed to copy down the telephone numbers he wished to call onto a form and keep a copy. He was given a bag of toiletries along with telephone credits for £2 and a pin number but no explanation was given as to how it worked. They let him keep his Swatch. He was given a perfunctory medical examination during which he told the doctor he had been beaten with a telephone directory. He asked for a brain scan and an eye examination. The doctor made no reply, though he shone a light in his eyes and examined them briefly. His vision, to his relief, seemed to have become almost normal again. The flashes had gone, though he still had a headache and a ringing in his ears. He was placed in a cell with another prisoner, a man called George, who was not hostile but was not inclined to talk. He did explain about the telephone credits and how he would have to wait till they let him out of the cell the next day to use the phone down the corridor. Kayley went over the telephone numbers he had copied, and realized there was nobody he wanted to call. His mother not, his ex-girlfriend, Zoe, not, his best friend in Leeds who had emigrated to Canada not (too expensive and needlessly worrying, since he couldn't visit.) He didn't have Val's parents' number in his smartphone. That left Camilla, whose number he had copied down from her card before it was taken away. He decided he would call her.

The next day he was transported straight after breakfast to a courthouse and seen briefly before the bail hearing by a lawyer who had been assigned to him. He told the lawyer the confession was beaten out of him and he wished to retract it. When he was taken before the judge, the lawyer mentioned this claim in an offhand manner. The judge raised his eyebrows and looked at Kayley pointedly and then consulted the papers in front of him. He asked him why he had given such a detailed account of his abuse of boys at the home if it was all false. Kayley told him it was because he was ordered to do so after a beating with a telephone book, which left him badly concussed with a severe headache and blurred vision, and the details were dictated to him. He said he made the confession to avoid further beating and irreversible brain damage. The prosecuting lawyer smirked at this and shook his head. The judge cited the report of the doctor who had examined him and found no visible injuries. His lawyer asked for his release on bail and the prosecutor argued that, given the number and seriousness of the offences he had confessed to, he constituted a danger to the public. He certainly could not return to work in the children's home: he was a manifest risk to children. There was a brief exchange between lawyers and then the judge remanded him in custody for three months. Suddenly it was all over before Kayley had the presence of mind to insist on being heard again. He had assumed he would be questioned further on the evidence against him and would be able to explain his case at more length. Now it was too late. He was hustled out as if any further attempt to speak would be seen as an act of insubordination.

When he was driven back to the prison he was taken into a big room with other prisoners and given an hour's induction lecture to explain certain prison procedures. There were a dozen other new arrivals, including some transferred from other prisons. At the end he was called up the front by a prison official and told that given the nature of his offence he would normally be sent to the Vulnerable Prisoners wing but that it was full at the moment and he would have to stay in a normal wing but would be in a single cell. Other prisoners overheard this. He did not really understand its significance. He was led to his new cell, which was very small but had its own toilet, shower and tiny washbasin at the far end. At noon his cell was unlocked and he was told to go and get his lunch at a servery down the corridor. As he walked back with his tray, carrying a soup, a plate of stew and a roll of bread, there were men moving in both directions and a little congestion in the corridor. Suddenly he was leg-tripped and fell flat on his face. His face landed in the stew and a passing foot kicked him in the side of the head. As he was getting up someone stood on his foot, and an elbow hit him in the face. His head hit the wall. When he turned he saw only men's backs. He got up and limped to his cell. He had only the roll of bread to eat. He felt his face was swollen. He called the guard and asked for some medical treatment. After a visit to the infirmary where they put on a sticking plaster and a sort of spray, he was taken back to his cell. This time shouts of abuse came from some of the cells he passed. He felt fear come over him, like a cold shower down his back.

At four his cell was opened to go to the exercise yard. He was issued with a cigarette at the door of the yard. Since he didn't smoke, he offered it to the next prisoner. He got a cold stare in return. In the yard, where most people were not doing any exercise, but sitting or standing around smoking and talking, those close to him turned their backs and those further away stared with open hostility. Somebody muttered as a group of men passed him: "Stay in your cell, paedo, nobody wants you here." At the end of the break as he walked into the corridor again with the others, there was a shove from behind and his face smashed into the wall. Someone trod on his ankle for good measure. Back in his cell he called the guard again. He was escorted, limping because of the ankle, to the infirmary again. He asked the nurse who put a plaster on his bleeding eyebrow and strapped his ankle what he should do. She said he could always stay in his cell and get his meals delivered to it. He was sent to an official to make this request. It was noted coldly without any expression of sympathy. On the way back to his cell, under escort, he passed the phone, which for the first time did not have a queue in front of it, and asked if he could use it. The guard stopped and showed him how to use his pin number. He called Camilla's number. There was no answer but he left a message explaining the situation and asking if she would help him by testifying in his favour. His credit ran out before he finished the call, since he was calling a mobile phone.

He did not get any dinner that night. The next day his meals were delivered to his cell, but the hot meals were almost cold. He was now confined to his cell permanently. He did not go to the showers, but washed at the cold tap and tiny wash basin beside the metal toilet bowl. None of the guards treated him with any sympathy. He was seen as getting his due. He was a nonce, the lowest of the low.

As he sat in his cell, he contemplated a future where he would be treated like this for ten years. He almost assumed he would be convicted at his trial, given his treatment so far. Even if he paid for a proper lawyer, it would probably make little difference. They would regard his confession as damning evidence and any retraction as a lie, because what suited them was to have a conviction, not the truth. No doubt they had targets for numbers of convictions to be achieved, and these were more important to them than any notion of justice to an individual. This way of thinking suddenly seemed quite normal, as if it was obviously how the system worked. It was the new reality he had to adapt to in order to keep his sanity. What astonished him was how quickly he had been robbed of his personality and had become simply a creature that conformed to a role imposed upon him. He was no longer a human being with free will. He was a robot that stood up when told to, walked when told to, spoke when told to and kept silent when told to. It would be like this for ten years. He would be an empty shell. He thought he probably wouldn't make it. Opportunities to commit suicide would certainly arise and there was not much point in not taking one. What was there to fight for? If human beings were like this, able to condemn, imprison and brutalize someone without a shred of evidence, he didn't really see the point of living among them after he was released, if he ever was. Why live through ten years of hell for the prospect of living afterwards in the company of human beings that were capable of this?

As his general pessimism grew and the prospect of happiness ever in the future seemed more and more remote, suicide began to seem like a goal, a thing he should look out for the chance to pull off. The idea that he needed to clear his name seemed less and less important. What did it matter what people like that thought of him? Who did he know whose opinion of him he really cared about? Zoe had forgotten him, he had broken off all relations with his mother, his best mate from university now in Canada was gone from his life for good. He couldn't care less what anyone thought of him at this children's home. He had made no friends there among the other social workers, whom he found strange, suspicious and cliquey. The children who liked him would know he was innocent anyway. The rest of the world didn't matter.

The three people from London were the only normal adults he had seen lately. The blonde girl, Ekaterina, was something special, from the realm of dreams, but now it was as if she had sailed away to another continent. He had left the message with Camilla without much hope, like a message in a bottle. He didn't imagine there was much they could do, unless they brought down the whole paedophile ring, which was unlikely.

As he sat in his cell, with no newspapers or books (he didn't feel up to limping to the library for the moment, apparently they came round the cells once a week and he was waiting for that), only a tiny television set fixed high up on the wall above the door with the controls out of reach (there was no remote) which came on automatically and inaudibly in the evening for two hours, and cold meals shoved through the trap in the door, he began to think over his life. There was nothing else to do but go over it like a film, and he began to think it through from beginning to end, almost as if he was planning to write his life story. It was the only narrative he had access to, and he thought it was a good chance to examine it and try to see if it made any sense — if there was anything in it he could look back on with pleasure or with pride. He was looking at his past to see if it held any promise that there was a future worth living for.

16

Kayley was an only child. His mother Doreen, a feminist who had graduated in the early seventies, was a university lecturer in sociology, specializing in gender studies, and had given birth to her only child when she was already thirty-four. With the mature convictions of a veteran militant, she was determined to bring him up in a non-sexist manner — or even, in so far as possible, in a "non-gendered" manner. She was determined to let him decide even whether he was a boy or a girl or something else, without imposing some patriarchal binary stereotype of gender upon him. She chose a name which could be for either sex, dressed him in an artful combination of pink and blue, and bought him dolls as well as cars for Christmas and birthdays. If he showed any interest in the dolls (he was vaguely curious about them) she hastened to buy him accessories and clothes for them. When he was four she bought him a Barbie doll, along with Barbie's boyfriend, Ken. He staged little dramas between the two, in which he acted out the conflicts his child's mind imagined to be typical of the adult world, before he put them in a car to drive away and have an accident with a bulldozer. One day in the kindergarten he joined the girls as they played with their Barbie dolls and expressed interest in what they were doing. The other boys looked on in stupefaction. When he confessed he had a Barbie doll at home, one boy asked: "Is it your sister's?" Kayley replied that he didn't have a sister, it was his own, and they stared at him in disbelief. "You play with dolls?" asked one. Someone began to laugh. Though they didn't yet know what names to call this behaviour, they considered it odd in the extreme. He learned from this incident that this aspect of his upbringing was unusual, and he began to exercise a certain independence of judgment about the activities that his mother encouraged him to engage in.

His father, Eddy, a veteran of the sixties' counter-culture, who had had a brief flowering as a guitarist in a third-rate rock group before withering into a failed song-writer, backing player for aspiring singers, and occasional composer of advertising ditties, was happy to let his wife decide most matters concerning the upbringing of their son. He was seven years older than her and instinctively felt she knew more about children than he did. Even though he did the lion's share of the parenting tasks because he was more often at home, he bowed to her superior wisdom as both mother and sociologist. He was mildly surprised to find Kayley being given dolls, but he humoured Doreen's conviction that this was essential in order to prevent him growing up with sexist prejudices, and above all to avoid the trauma of sensing homophobic disapproval of his effeminate behaviour. While Eddy found little evidence of effeminate behaviour in his son apart from the doll business, he treated with respect his wife's female intuition that their son was very probably a budding homosexual. They must hence prepare him carefully for his future lifestyle by showing complete support for it and praising every behavioural trait that pointed in that direction.

Doreen was the one who dictated how Kayley's hair was to be cut, and her decision was to leave it long. This was initially in order to give him a non-gendered choice, and then, when he showed signs of preferring it short, to discourage this manifestation of sexist conformism. She impressed upon him that as a superior individual with intellectual and artistic parents he owed it to himself to show his own artistic inclinations by adopting the hairstyle of most of the great rock stars of the age. This was a choice his father could hardly object to, since he still had shoulder-length hair himself as he neared fifty. When Kayley complained that other children often mistook him for a girl and made fun of him, his mother had a heart-to-heart talk with him. Holding back tears, she explained that this might be the first sign of the sort of prejudice that he would have to get used to in life, and it was better to start early. He was somewhat mystified by this prognostication of a lifetime of persecution for him, and even more so by his mother's tearful embrace of him as if she was suffering already in anticipation. She was, however, adamant that he must continue to wear his blond curls down over his shoulders, as this was something that would prepare him for the future he faced.

One day when he was nine he finally rebelled against this penitential regime. The other boys were ragging him about his hair, and he said petulantly: "I wish I could cut it off!" One of his friends took him at his word, and after school produced a pair of scissors he had stolen from the sewing class, which in that school was compulsory for all the boys while the girls could choose between woodwork and metalwork classes.

"Hey, Kayley, if you want to cut it, here you go!" he said jokingly, holding them out.

Kayley felt he could no longer back out of it. A girl in his class, Jemima, whom he was secretly in love with, had a small mirror and stood in front of him holding it up for him to see. With sudden determination, he began to lop off the longest, curliest locks.

"Are you sure you want to, Kayley?" cried Jemima, seized with last-minute qualms, since his long blond curls were the secret envy and admiration of many of the girls in his class, even though they made a show of laughing at them. He hacked away with perseverance at his hair and made such a mess of it that his best friend, Frank, intervened.

"Here, you're botching it, let me do it," he said. Frank evened up the botched haircut, and Kayley at the end had a head a bit like a football, with the back and sides cut fairly short, but the top still full of hair, as Frank didn't know how to layer it. They all pronounced it an improvement, and slapped him on the back with encouragement as he set off for home to face his mother. Jemima gathered up the fallen curls and put them in a plastic bag, and kept them as a souvenir to allay a slight feeling of guilt, as well as to keep some part of Kayley under her pillow.

As Kayley walked in the door, his mother, who had finished work early that day, looked round at him happily from the computer screen and then her smile froze. Her expression changed to horror as if he had come in mutilated and on crutches. She ran to him and hugged him in her arms. She squeezed him for at least a minute, humming and cooing to comfort him as she covered him with kisses.

"You poor darling!" she cried. "You poor darling! It's started already! Who did it to you, what are their names?"

Eddy wandered in from the side patio to see what the fuss was about, hiding the joint in his hand, as he didn't like to smoke in front of his son.

"Look what they've done to him!" she cried, stepping back to show him Kayley's rounded head. "Those homophobic bastards, they've started bullying him already! I told you they would! You wouldn't believe me — look what they've done!" She turned and hugged her son. "Darling, we're going to get them for this — who did it? We'll make them pay!"

"What happened, Kayley?" asked Eddy.

"I wanted to cut it," said Kayley, "so someone got some scissors. And Frank did most of it, because I couldn't do it properly."

"Frank did this!" cried his mother. "Frank, you mean Frank who came to play the other day? What's his name? Evans, Frank Evans. I'll talk to his mother, I'll call her this minute. Who else did it? Who else was there?"

"All of them were there, all my friends, most of the class came and watched," said Kayley, rather proudly, "and Jemima held up the mirror." He was still confused about why this should have caused such a sensation.

"Jemima! I know Jemima's mother, I'll soon see to that little bully!" Doreen was in a rage as she strode to the telephone on the small table and pulled the directory out of the drawer beneath it.

"Just a moment!" cried Eddy. "Who are you going to call? Listen to what the boy is saying!"

"What more do you need to hear?" yelled Doreen in fury. "This was a homophobic mob attack! You're not going to deny it! Look at the state of the boy's hair! This is what they did to women in France after the war! All those they accused of sleeping with Germans! Shaved their hair off! It's mob rule! Homophobic mob rule! They did it because he's gay!"

"What are you talking about, woman? They don't know what gay is!" said Eddy, desperately appealing to reason. "They're nine years old!"

"Of course they know!" she said witheringly. "They hear it from their parents and older brothers. They read it on the internet. They all know! And they've started bullying him! You remember the last time he went to the hairdresser, he made a fuss and wanted it cut short. Who gave him that idea? They've bullied him!"

"No, mum, I asked for it, I did it," pleaded Kayley. "Don't get them into trouble, don't get Frank into trouble, he's my best friend. And Jemima is too!"

"Stop trying to defend them! You don't have to be afraid of them!" shouted his mother. "They're going to be expelled from the school and you'll never see them again! I'm going to take this to the governors, and to the police if need be! You're going to be all right, my boy!" She stooped and hugged him to her. "What you are is all right! It's normal! It's them that are abnormal!"

Kayley broke out of her arms and stared at her in shock and incomprehension.

"What does she mean, Dad — what I am is all right?" he said miserably, on the verge of tears. "What am I?"

"This is ridiculous, Doreen," said Eddy quietly, taking another pull on his joint. "Look what you're doing to the boy!"

"Kayley," said his mother earnestly, as she stooped down again to his level. She was a tall woman and he was rather small for his age. "We didn't want to tell you about this until much later, but it may be you'll have to face up to it now. You see, darling, you might be what is known as gay."

"Gay!" cried Kayley in horror.

"Doreen, this is ridiculous!" repeated Eddy, at a loss. He dreaded having to explain this whole subject to his son.

"But gay's something stupid!" said Kayley.

"There, you see, look how they've been brainwashed!" cried Doreen. "It's shameful! Shameful! This kind of homophobia is rampant! Even in nine-year olds! Those teachers should be sacked! They haven't done their job! They should be guiding children even at five or six to understand and be tolerant of different sexual orientations! They've received guidelines! Instructions from the Department of Education. He should be reading stories about same-sex couples! Even at the kindergarten level! And he's not! Have I seen a single book of his with a same-sex marriage in it? Does he get given stories of children with two fathers or two mothers? No, he doesn't! He's never been given one! I had to buy him one myself! And this is supposed to be a progressive school! With a feminist principal! And what's the result? They think gay means stupid!"

"No, it means weird," said Kayley. "Something weird and not right. I'm not weird."

"Exactly, darling, you're not. That's why they're monsters for filling your head with this nonsense. You're perfectly normal. It's normal to be gay! We're glad you're gay!" She stooped down to hug him again, growing more impassioned. "Mummy and Daddy are happy that you're gay! Be happy as well! What you are is wonderful! I've dreamed of having a gay son all my life! I've dreamed of helping him to dress up for his first party, his first date. Of organizing his wedding! Two smart, handsome young men in morning coats! Every mother's dream! And we'll be able to, my boy! You're making my dreams come true!" She kissed his cheek passionately.

"Doreen, we don't have any idea —" began Eddy feebly.

"Then how the hell do you explain this?" bellowed Doreen, pointing at his hair. "They know! They can sense it! They know he's gay! That's why they did it! Bullies always know!"

"That's crap!" said Eddy. "God, when I was travelling around with long hair in the sixties, people in backward countries often thought I was gay. It didn't mean I was."

"These kids are not backward! They're the internet generation! They're up with every trend! And they can sniff it out a mile away! They know he's gay even if you don't!"

"Look, you dress him half like a girl, you give him dolls, you make him wear his hair long, and then you feel indignant when people think he looks girlish...." began Eddy.

"How the hell can you talk? Look at your hair, look at the length of it!" she yelled.

"Exactly, but I grew my hair long by choice, at the age of twenty-three, in the sixties — I was rebelling against stereotypes of masculinity which went too far in the twentieth century and led to world wars and mass murder!" He was becoming desperate in his effort to get through to her. "He's not old enough to rebel, he knows nothing about stereotypes! Let him wear his hair the way he wants to — the way the other boys do!"

"He wants to have long hair like you!" shouted Doreen. "Are you going to deprive him of that because of a bunch of homophobes?"

"Look, Kayley, did you cut your hair yourself, yes or no?" Eddy was trying to make some sense out of this fog of emotional hysteria. He wanted some clarity once and for all, and his own stoned state was not making it any easier.

"Don't answer him, Kayley, it's a trap!" yelled his mother frantically. "He's trying to get you to justify this attack on you! He's trying to get you to deny it! Don't enter into denial!"

"I don't know what to answer!" wailed Kayley, looking from one to the other. "It's not fair!" He began to cry.

"There, you see what you're doing to him!" snapped Doreen. "The boy is on the verge of a nervous breakdown! Because you refuse to recognize he's a victim of homophobia!"

"He's not a victim of anything except you, you silly woman! You're mad! He wanted to cut his own hair and they helped him! Because you wouldn't let him! Because you want him to be gay!"

"Look, Eddy, if you don't support me in this, our marriage is finished and I'm taking Kayley!" She was standing with hands on hips, her head thrust forward, her body quivering with rage. "I'm not going to have him brought up by a homophobe! And don't forget who pays the mortgage. Your gay son has been the victim of a homophobic attack and I'm demanding your support! Is that too much to ask? Now, I'm calling the school principal."

She went to the phone, pulled out a list of numbers from the drawer and dialled. Her voice became unctuous.

"Is that Ms Simmonds? This is Kayley's mother, Doreen Burke. I'm afraid I must come and see you about Kayley. He's been the victim of a homophobic gang attack. They've hacked his hair off." She listened for a moment. "So, tomorrow morning, at nine-thirty? He'll have to be taken out of class. All right then. See you tomorrow."

She put the phone down and glared at Eddy.

"Are you coming with me?"

"Of course I'm not coming. I have nothing to do with this. It's madness, what you're doing. You're ruining the boy's life, his standing with all his friends." He was indignant, but his tone was subdued, as if he had been cowed by the threat she had just made.

"Those are friends he doesn't need!" she declared imperiously and stalked out of the room.

Eddy looked at Kayley, but the boy ran crying to his bedroom.

The next morning Doreen went in to see the principal, Ms Simmonds. Kayley was sent for in his classroom and escorted by a secretary to the principal's office. Ms Simmonds took one look at him as he walked in and drew in her breath sharply.

"Kayley, come and sit down. Are you feeling all right?"

He nodded, and sat on the chair beside his mother.

"Now, can you tell us, is it true that Frank Evans and Jemima Lennox cut your hair yesterday?"

"Yes, they helped."

"They helped? You mean others took part? Could you tell us who else was there?"

"They were all there. There was Bill and Steve and Richie and I don't know who else. They all thought it was a good idea."

Ms Simmonds scribbled these names down.

"So they encouraged Frank and Jemima?"

"Everyone gave advice and tried to help."

"And how do you feel about it now?"

He looked shamefaced, and glanced at his mother.

"It doesn't look good, does it?" he ventured quietly.

"So, you feel embarrassed and uncomfortable? Ashamed even?" Ms Simmonds was eager to help him find his words.

He nodded glumly. She wrote the three words down.

"Is this an experience you would like to see repeated?"

He thought of his mother's hysteria, the rows at home, and shook his head.

"So, this is something you feel very negative about now?"

"Negative?"

"Bad. You feel bad about it?"

"Yes, I feel bad about it. I didn't mean to...." He tailed off.

"Don't worry," said Ms Simmonds grimly, writing again. "We understand this is not something you meant to do. It was done to you. Against your will. But justice will be done." She smiled briefly. "That's all, you may go back to class."

"Bye, Mum," he murmured and left the room.

That afternoon the five culprits whose names had been mentioned were given letters by the principal to take home to their parents. The letters informed them that the children were going to be suspended for a day for taking part in a homophobic gang attack and the parents were being summoned to come and see the principal. A meeting would later be organized for all parents to be addressed by militants from gay organizations on the combat against homophobia, biphobia, and transphobia. The parents of the five offenders would be obliged to attend on pain of having a further suspension for their child.

Over the next week Kayley's world crumbled about his ears. His classmates crowded around him at the break the day after their suspension, demanding answers.

"How could you, Kayley, how could you?" Frank in particular felt the betrayal. "I did it for you, I helped you! How could you snitch like that? And lie?"

Kayley was in tears.

"It wasn't me, it was my mother!" he howled. "I didn't want to get anyone into trouble!"

"But you gave her everyone's name!" cried Jemima. "How could you give her our names?"

"I don't know. She got them out of me!" snivelled Kayley.

"And Mum wants to know," added Jemima, holding up the letter from the principal, "what the hell is transphobia?"

"I don't know either," he said, wiping his nose on his sleeve miserably.

After that he was left alone, an outcast in the playground, pitied but despised, like a prisoner who has collaborated with the guards, with the enemy, and betrayed his fellow prisoners, even if it was under torture. He did not have a friend left in the school.

After a week his grades had plummeted, he was not eating, and he seemed depressed. He finally refused to get up and claimed to be ill. Worried, Doreen sent him to the doctor and then to a psychiatrist. After one session, the psychiatrist advised a change of schools.

"You mean the homophobic bullying is continuing?" asked Doreen, worried.

"I'm afraid he is a pariah at his school. Call it homophobia or whatever you like, but he is not popular, has no friends any more, and hates school. He needs a new start."

"I think he needs more than that. He needs someone to talk to him about his homosexuality. To get over his shame and self-hatred."

"I have already raised the subject with him. He has no idea what homosexuality is, and I have not the slightest indication that that is his problem."

"The very fact he doesn't know what it is, that's his problem," she said tightly.

Eddy was in favour of the change of schools, and so was Kayley. But Doreen insisted that he should go and see a homosexual therapist who specialized in breaking the news to confused boys about what their real sexual orientation was and explaining it to them. He was a small bald man with a head like an egg. He spent an hour telling Kayley about the various forms of sexual intercourse, showing him explicit photographs, and the various kinds of love relationship. Then he told him kindly but bluntly:

"You see, Kayley, you're gay. Take it from me, I can tell. I've seen hundreds like you, I only have to talk to a boy for five minutes and I can tell. You're gay and you'll never be happy until you accept it and begin living the gay lifestyle positively. You should find yourself a boyfriend. Isn't there another boy you like?"

Kayley left his office in a state of confusion but above all of fury and humiliation. How dare this man tell him what he was! How dare he claim to know him after a few minutes' conversation! When he got home Eddy tried to talk to him about the interview.

"He thinks I'm gay," said Kayley, and began to cry with shame and frustration. "What the hell does he know?"

"Did he explain what it means?"

"It's a boy who wants to screw with other boys. It's disgusting! He's a disgusting man!"

Doreen overheard the conversation as she came into the room. She walked quickly across to the sofa and slapped Kayley's face, lightly but firmly, as current progressive guidelines still permitted for egregious offences, such as sexism or homophobia.

"Don't you ever let me hear you spewing homophobic abuse again! It is *not* disgusting! It is normal for a large part of humanity, and it is probably normal for you! So get used to it!"

"Doreen! That's uncalled for! The boy's been hurt and traumatized by what this gay militant bully has been telling him. He's trying to dictate to him what he is!"

"And you're trying to lock him into denial! This man is trying to liberate him, to free him from his prejudices and you are trying to reinforce them!" She glared at him as if he was the ideological enemy. "And I will not have him saying that homosexuality is disgusting! That is homophobia, and it's against the law! He can even be expelled from school for it and we can be prosecuted!"

"Of course he thinks it's disgusting!" said Eddy indignantly. "He's heterosexual, that's why! That's what heterosexual means to a child — to find homosexuality disgusting. It's a normal reaction to hearing something as weird as that described!"

"Being gay is *not* weird and homophobia is *not* normal!" shouted Doreen.

"What about a gay person who finds heterosexual intercourse disgusting? Is that a crime too?" Eddy was trembling with anger. "The right to feel disgust for others' sexual practices is also a human right! Repulsion is a right! Disgust is a right! We don't have to like everything!"

"You're not going to justify homophobia to your son!" she yelled.

"And you're not going to force him to be gay just to satisfy your weird hang-ups! What are you going to do next — have him seduced by some pervert?"

"They are not perverts!" she shouted. "When are you going to adapt to the age we live in, you spaced-out, flower-power leftover! Look at that boy! That boy is gay! Open your eyes!"

They glared at each other, realizing that something was permanently broken between them and they really could not stand each other any longer.

To Kayley's relief, Doreen finally agreed to let him change schools. A new life opened up for him. He found new friends. He played football. His grades improved again. He got money from his father to go to the hairdresser regularly and got his hair cut to an average length for boys of his age. Life became enjoyable and entered a period of stability for over two years. Doreen and Eddy kept out of each other's way as much as possible and organized their practical family life with a minimum of friction. Theirs became a marriage of convenience —the outer framework of a relationship, without a relationship inside it. Then Doreen became involved with a militant group at her university promoting LGBT rights. She explained to Kayley over dinner one evening what Lesbian, Gay, Bisexual and Transgender rights means. When Kayley asked what exactly the group was trying to achieve, she gave some examples. One of their goals was the removal of urinals from all schools so that transgender pupils (of whom there were known to be two in the city) did not feel embarrassed about being the only boys to go into a cubicle to pee, thus showing they were different. Urinals were also discriminatory in giving boys an unfair advantage in being able to pee faster than girls.

"The urinal is a symbol of male privilege and domination. It's the first encounter girls have with their institutionalized inferiority to boys. Being excluded from using something that boys alone have the right to use — that is incredibly damaging to girls' self-esteem. It may be the root cause of gender inequality, of why the world is still dominated by men."

"So, everyone in this group hates boys, then, do they?" asked Eddy carelessly, serving himself some organic dandelion salad, which appeared to be the main course (Doreen had taken a rare turn at preparing dinner.)

"We do not hate boys!" snapped Doreen. "We want boys to behave themselves. And to accept that they have no privileges because they are boys. If they have to sit down to pee the same as girls do, they will perhaps feel they are not so different from girls. It will change their construction of their own gender and bring the two genders closer together. That is essential for more equality — for more women in the sciences and in politics. And let's not forget boys grow up to be men, and men make up one hundred per cent of all rapists! We have to stop this behaviour early. We want boys to be gentle, kind and sensitive."

"So, you want them to be like girls?" suggested Eddy.

"More like girls, yes."

"So, you want them all to be gay? You don't want them screwing girls, ever, do you?"

"We certainly don't want them raping girls, and that is what screwing is for most of them. At least if they're gay, they won't be predators."

"Not towards girls, you mean. Only towards other boys."

"There is no such thing as a gay predator!" she declared crushingly. "Same-sex relationships are by definition between equals!"

"So male rape doesn't exist, according to you?"

"Of course it exists! Male rape of women and girls! That's the only kind that exists. Anything else is just a figment of your stupid, ignorant homophobia, and I won't tolerate it in this house!"

Eddy shook his head and said nothing more on the subject, so as not to provoke another crisis. Over the next months Doreen went regularly to her LGBT meetings. When he referred to this group, Kayley had trouble remembering the letters in the right order. Eddy suggested he should think of the word "Legbite" as a memory aid. Kayley thought this was funny and they got into the habit of referring to her group jokingly between them as her Legbite group. They amused themselves thinking up variations: Lesbian Gender-Bending Twats was their most imaginative, but it was Legbite which stuck for its quirky catchiness. One evening when Doreen was going out, Kayley asked her unthinkingly if it was for her

Legbite meeting. She demanded an explanation. He blushed and said it was just a joke.

"A joke between you and Eddy?" she said. He turned pale and his lips began to quiver. She stormed into Eddy's music room where he was composing on his computer.

"So, it's my Legbite meeting, is it? How dare you make a mockery of my human rights work! How dare you teach our son to make fun of me! How dare you make homophobic jokes to him! When you know he's going to have to deal with this himself when he finally realizes what he is! You're a monster! This has gone far enough! I'm not going to have you screwing up his mind, you pathetic homophobe! It's time to put an end to this charade of a failed marriage! I'm getting him away from you!"

Eddy tried to placate her in vain. There followed many months of legal wrangling and then a court case. When the divorce judge, a feminist, heard of Eddy's mocking use of the word "Legbite" to refer to Doreen's LGBT group, she shook her head in tight-lipped shock at this blatant piece of homophobia, biphobia and transphobia. It was difficult, she said, to imagine a more horrific expression of bigotry and intolerance. It was frightening to think of any child being indoctrinated with this hate cult, let alone a gay one. She accepted all Doreen's arguments. Eddy was clearly a drug-taking, workshy, shiftless homophobe who was trying to bully his gay son into denying his sexuality. Kayley was in court but was not questioned or heard by the judge, who considered Doreen a progressive and understanding mother. She took one look at Kayley's slight build, cute face, shy, gentle manner and curly blond hair and concluded that Doreen was right. He was obviously gay. Eddy was ordered to leave the house, which was awarded wholly to Doreen, who had paid most of the mortgage for the past few years anyway. Doreen was given sole custody of Kayley, and since Eddy was a drug-taking homophobe, he was denied all visiting rights, and strictly forbidden to see or contact his son again. However, he still had to pay Doreen child support from his meagre and irregular musician's income.

Kayley was now left alone with his mother. He was twelve. He knew that his mother was the worst enemy he had, that she had worked tirelessly to ruin his life, and now he was condemned to live totally in her power, forbidden to see his father ever again. The fact that Eddy was the one who had cooked his meals, dressed him, helped him with his homework, played with him and looked after him all his life, and was the only person he had ever loved, weighed little against the crime of homophobic blasphemy of which he stood convicted. In the eyes of the court a blasphemer, a user of forbidden words, clearly deserved to be deprived of contact with his son forever.

Kayley had to fake affection for this woman who now controlled his life. She watched his every gesture like a spy to try to gauge his real feelings for her. He became an actor in his everyday life. He mistrusted the men friends she occasionally brought home, who were mostly Legbite types whom he found sinister. He secretly feared one of them would rape him with her complicity, in order to turn him into what she wanted him to be. He was relieved that none of the men became her boyfriend or stayed overnight. In fact, it was one of the women in the group who often spent the night there. This woman tried to befriend Kayley but he detested her cloying character and she soon became his enemy, making catty remarks about him whenever she could. She seemed to be constantly in the house and spied on him as well. Kayley lived for two years without a single human being he could confide in.

He tried from the start to find out where his father was living. He knew it must be in a run-down part of town and he began going for walks on weekends in poorer neighbourhoods in the hope of catching sight of him. He knew he wasn't allowed to speak to him as that could get him sent to prison, but he thought it would be nice just to see him and exchange a look that would make clear they still cared for each other and hadn't forgotten the years they had spent together. But he was never lucky enough to see him. After a year he looked in the new telephone directory for his number but his name wasn't in there. He just assumed Eddy couldn't afford a telephone. He had never had a mobile phone as he wasn't into consumer gadgets, and if he had one now Kayley didn't know how he could find his number.

During those two years his life at school went downhill again. It was now a new school, a large comprehensive secondary school, and he had not had time to make real friends before his home life fell apart. He became withdrawn and prickly to approach. He was usually alone at break. He spent time in the library, reading novels and books on psychology. The others saw him as a nerd. The girls shunned him. The worst moment came when he was fourteen when the school, in imitation of certain American high schools, organized a Gay Rights Day to celebrate "National Coming Out Day". It was seen as part of the school's sex education programme. Militants from gay organizations addressed every class and urged students who were secretly gay to "come out" and admit it. Several pupils came forward, like converts at a revivalist rally, and made tearful announcements to their class. They were applauded in a way that was palpably fake. As their classmates acclaimed these public confessions, they exchanged knowing grins and winks. They began to have bets on who would be next. Boys who looked a bit girlish or were not good at sport came under pressure to confess and "come out". At lunchtime a small group gathered around Kayley and began taunting him.

"I reckon Kayley's gay. He's always alone. And in the library! That's like being in the closet! He's never kissed a girl. Why don't you come out, Kayley?"

"Yes, come on, come out, Kayley, you'll feel better for it if you just admit it! Why hide it? Are you ashamed of it?"

"Nobody minds, Kayley, just be up front and admit what you are! Be proud of it!"

Under their snickering pretence of tolerance was a profound, jeering contempt. They had mastered the language of political correctness as a new and insidious form of bullying.

Kayley replied with a string of expletives, and walked away. They followed him with their taunts. One boy got too close behind him and flicked his hair with his hand in a gesture of contempt. Kayley turned and punched him in the face. At once there was a fight. Kayley was smaller and got the worst of it. But he was so blind with rage he refused to give in and after several minutes he was bruised and battered, with a bleeding nose and a face that was starting to swell. A teacher intervened. He was taken to the infirmary and then sent home.

Doreen arrived home five hours later, took one look at him and went into hysterics. He refused to say anything except that he had been in a fight. The next day she called the school. She accused the headmaster of allowing a homophobic attack on her child — on the very day dedicated to gay rights! She refused to allow Kayley to go to school. He went to the doctor's instead. The next day he insisted on going in to school and the principal sent for him to come to his office. He apologized solemnly for allowing this homophobic incident, and pleaded with Kayley to believe that he was serious in trying to root out anti-gay prejudice.

"I'm not gay," said Kayley curtly.

"I beg your pardon?" The principal looked confused. "But your mother —"

"My mother is a mental case. A hysterical feminist nutcase."

"Then what was this about?"

"I punched someone because he called me gay."

The principal stared at him.

"Now, Kayley, you must understand there is no point in entering into denial and self-hatred, your mother seems to think —"

"Fuck my mother! She's a fucked-up, lesbian fag-hag!"

The principal looked as if he had been hit. He stiffened.

"I don't like your attitude, young man, or your language! You are rude, aggressive and foul-mouthed. I'm not surprised somebody gave you a good correction! I hope this has taught you a lesson."

Kayley stared at him sullenly. Somehow in his battered state he felt invulnerable. He could take it.

"Can I go now?"

The principal glared at him and then nodded grimly. Kayley got up and slouched out.

When he went back to the classroom the others watched him slyly. At break he sat at his desk pretending to write something when the others went out. He did not want to go outside with them. He noticed a girl lingering at the back of the room. When everyone else had gone, she came over to him. It was Val, a slim, pretty girl with long red hair.

"Your face must be hurting, Kayley," she said shyly. "You need some cream on it. I've got some here. It's stuff I use if I get sunburnt, because of my fair skin."

She held out a tube of ointment, put some on her finger and began applying it to his bruised face. He accepted her ministrations, at first with a show of indifference, and then with a growing sense of excitement. He felt his heart beating faster as she leaned close to him and her pale blue eyes flickered onto his as she concentrated on his swollen cheeks and eye-lids.

"You know, a few years ago I got bullied because of my red hair," she said.

"That's crazy!" he answered, astonished that a girl so pretty and popular could have been bullied. "It's beautiful!"

"Not everyone thought so."

She put some cream on his swollen lips, and her long slim finger moved slowly back and forth across them, like a caress.

"I bet it must hurt to kiss," she said.

"I don't know," he replied. "I've never done it."

"Want to try?" She glanced at the door, then took his face carefully in her hands and kissed him gently on the lips. "Did it hurt?"

"No. It was nice," he muttered, his lips trembling.

"Want some more?"

He nodded, not trusting himself to speak. And so he had his first snogging session. Neither of them wanted to stop. They were still at it at the end of break when the others came back in. They looked on in astonishment.

"Hey, who's the fag-hag?" joked a boy named Slater. Several others laughed.

"What did you say, Slater?" The rough, deep voice had an aggressive edge to it. They looked around. The biggest boy in the class, Wronski, a wrestler with massive shoulders, had taken Slater by the collar. "I think you're going to apologize to Val. And to Kayley."

"Yeah, sure, Wronski. I apologize, guys. It was just a joke. I didn't mean it."

"No, you didn't, did you?" Wronski was going to rub it in. He shoved him so hard he stumbled backwards across the room and fell over a chair. "I think Kayley's taken enough shit. Don't you all agree?"

There was a chorus of agreement. They all sat down. Wronski had made it clear whose side he was on. Kayley would be part of the gang from then on. And Val would be his first girlfriend.

Of course he knew he couldn't bring her home. Or admit to his mother who he was spending all his time with. His mother was shocked and furious when she saw him kissing Val on the street a few weeks later. She began making snide remarks about people not being able to run away from themselves forever.

"You can hide in the closet but it won't change who you are," she sneered.

But he ignored her now and her remarks passed over him almost without effect. He knew his mother was a twisted person, someone wrestling with deep sexual hang-ups of her own. Whatever obscure suffering she had endured had turned her into an intolerant, spiteful bully, who was furious that he wasn't what she wanted him to be. And he had found a good person, a girl full of spontaneous kindness towards any human being or animal that she thought was being badly treated. Those were the two main kinds of people in the world, he decided. Those in whom suffering breeds compassion and those in whom it breeds malice. There were no other springs of human behaviour.

It was Val who persuaded him to talk to her favourite teacher, her French teacher, Christine, about his father. She knew how much Kayley wanted to see him. Christine listened to him and promised to talk to the social services. She finally got through on the phone to the woman responsible for his case. When she asked for a meeting to discuss a possible lifting of the court order forbidding Kayley any contact with his father, the social worker replied that the order had been carefully considered, and it was utterly unthinkable to re-establish contact with a drug-taking, homophobic father, who would be a disastrous influence on a vulnerable gay child. Christine informed her that Kayley was not gay and now had a girlfriend, the best student in her class. The social worker told her in no uncertain terms that she had no right to interfere, that Kayley was evidently under homophobic pressure to deny his sexual orientation, and if Christine didn't stay out of his life she would get a court order to stop her too having any contact with Kayley, as well as the so-called girlfriend. She said that her mission in life was to protect vulnerable gay children from the pernicious influence of bigoted homophobes trying to "convert" them to heterosexual "normality", and she would have no hesitation in reporting Christine to the police for harassment of a vulnerable child if this continued. Christine tried to remain calm and reasonable, and proposed a meeting to discuss this in the presence of Kayley and his girlfriend, so the social services could hear Kayley's point of view. The social worker replied that she did not intend to facilitate a plot to put a gay child back under the influence of a homophobic father. She added that if Christine persisted she would report Eddy to the judge for having put her up to this, which could make him guilty of conspiracy to breach a court order, an offence punishable by a prison term. Christine's own job as a teacher would also be in jeopardy. On that note the woman hung up.

Kayley was disappointed and depressed by this outcome. Val, on the other hand, was furious. She became determined to get back in touch with Eddy. She pressed Kayley for the names of Eddy's friends, but he could only remember first names. Then she got Kayley to hunt for all the clues he could find at home. Eddy had given him one of the records his group had made years ago and Kayley wrote down all the names of the fellow musicians and producers that were on the sleeve. Val was into computers and she put the names into the search engine AltaVista, which had just started up. The name of the group's singer came up. He had gone on to a long career with other bands and had a website. It had an email address and she wrote to him asking if he had had any contact lately with his old lead guitarist, Eddy Burke. She explained how his son wanted to get in touch with him following a divorce. The singer was sympathetic. He emailed back that he had just been through a divorce himself, and had not only lost his house and most of his earnings but had also been denied access to his children by the anti-father brigade that ruled English courts. He hadn't heard from Eddy for many years but he gave her a list of all their fellow band-members and mutual friends from that time and all the telephone numbers he still had, in case one of them was still in contact with Eddy. Val was now on a mission and she began ringing them all. Many had moved or couldn't be reached, but the second to last one on the list came up trumps. He was still working as a bass guitarist in the area and he had heard that Eddy had played backing to a rising local female singer at a gig just a few months before. The singer had a website with a phone number. Val called her and after her convoluted explanations seemed to be met with some suspicion, she put Kayley on the phone. Kayley's shaky voice saying: "Can I have my dad's phone number or where he lives?" convinced her. She gave him Eddy's mobile phone number. And she added: "He talked about you. He misses you."

They decided to go to a telephone box, instead of using Val's parents' phone. That way the call couldn't be traced if

Eddy was arrested and they examined his phone. Eddy broke down and cried when he heard Kayley's voice, and that set Kayley off too. Val spent the phone call hugging him tight, with tears streaming down her face as well. They got Eddy's address and Val gave Eddy her parents' address and phone number, but she said he should only call her from a phone box. They agreed to meet in a park the following Sunday. Val suggested they should all wear dark glasses and hooded jackets in case they were seen by the social services. She said they had to act like spies or Eddy would be in trouble.

They met that Sunday on a park bench and it was another emotional moment. Eddy was looking thin and not in the best of health. He had had a heart attack a few months before and was taking pills to lower his blood pressure. He was living in a bedsit and still trying to obtain some kind of income support but the bureaucracy was proving complicated. He complained that he was only getting a fraction of the amount he was entitled to because his situation as a self-employed musician playing the occasional gig, with an income that varied each month, was not a clear case for the bureaucrats to comprehend. This made the child support he had to pay Doreen also greater than it should have been, as it was based on his income when he was earning a lot more. There was no hope of getting that amount reduced unless he hired an expensive lawyer to make submissions to a judge, who might then convene a special court in which Doreen would also have the right to argue against him. All legal costs of both parties would be at his charge with no guarantee of success in reducing his payments. It was safer to keep paying. The same applied to any attempt to get the ban on contact with his son lifted. He couldn't afford the whole legal process required, especially as the social services would oppose his request and they had unlimited funds to fight the case. They decided therefore to keep seeing each other in a clandestine manner each Sunday.

The next Sunday Eddy brought his guitar to the park as he wanted to play them a song he had written. It was a sad song about passing time and it had Val in tears. Eddy hugged her and said to Kayley: "This is your lifesaver, never let her go." His playing drew a small group of children around them and one or two adults who watched from a polite distance. This made Val nervous and she persuaded the others to move. They decided to take the risk of going back to Eddy's bedsit. With their hoods and dark glasses they thought they should be safe from spying eyes. Eddy made them a cup of tea and was proud to play host to them in his modest room. It was a ground floor room with a separate entrance, so they decided to come there the next week, as it was perhaps less conspicuous than meeting in the park.

From then on Kayley went every weekend to visit Eddy either at his bedsit or at some other meeting place, sometimes with Val and sometimes alone, always wearing a hood and dark glasses. He and Eddy went a couple of times to amateur football matches which were free to watch, and once to a shooting gallery in a funfair. Eddy began teaching Kayley the guitar again. They kept up this clandestine contact for six months. They were surprised by their luck, as they had thought the social services would keep a closer watch. Perhaps they had given up watching after the first year. Then one day Kayley went to his father's place at the usual time but there was no answer when he rang the bell. He was suddenly afraid. He didn't know what to do. If Eddy was ill or injured inside, if he had had a heart attack, he had to get help. But if he did so Eddy would be arrested for breaking the ban on contact. He went to a phone box and rang Eddy's mobile phone to see if he had simply gone out and forgotten their rendezvous. There was no answer. He then rang Val to ask what to do.

Val offered to phone the police and say she was a guitar pupil of Eddy's and had gone there for a lesson and he hadn't answered the door. Kayley admired her quick thinking. She called the police, told them that story and asked them to go and check on Eddy. After making her wait a few minutes, the policewoman on the end of the line said it was all right, Eddy had been arrested that morning and was being held in custody. When she asked why, she was told that that was confidential information. The policewoman then asked her to identify herself and Val hung up. She kicked herself that she had used her parents' telephone instead of going out to a phone box, but she had been afraid Eddy might be in urgent need of help.

Val and Kayley then went to the police station and asked to see Eddy. Val repeated her story that she was a guitar pupil of Eddy's, and said Kayley had recommended his father as a teacher but had had no contact with him. They wanted to know why Eddy had been arrested. They were told it was for breaking the court order banning contact with his son. They had been photographed together. The police refused to allow them to see Eddy because of the court order, and demanded that Kayley let them take a DNA swab from his mouth. Val was against it until they could consult a lawyer, but the police threatened to arrest her for obstructing the course of justice by lying to them about being Eddy's pupil. They said they would question Eddy and if he didn't confirm her story she would be arrested for making a false statement and obstructing a police investigation. Only if Kayley co-operated would they drop charges against her. Kayley then agreed to the DNA swab and to be fingerprinted.

The police soon found Kayley's DNA and fingerprints in Eddy's bedsit. A trial date was set, and the judge sentenced

Eddy to six months in prison for repeatedly breaking the court order banning contact with his son. The social workers testified to the damage this may have done Kayley. Doreen testified to his growing indifference and even hostility towards her, a clear sign of this damage. Both the social workers and Doreen expressed grim satisfaction as the sentence was read. Eddy collapsed and was carried out of the courtroom. The judge repeated the justification given for the banning order — the need to protect vulnerable gay children from homophobic parents. At that point Val began kissing Kayley in open court. They were ordered to stop by the judge and seized and pulled apart by police officers.

"There's your gay child, you morons!" yelled Val in fury. "He makes love to me twice a week!"

They were both fined for contempt of court and the judge declared that Eddy should be made to serve the full six months, for trying to pervert the course of justice by organizing this disturbance at his own trial. The no-contact order was prolonged indefinitely and Kayley was expressly forbidden to visit his father in prison or hospital or communicate with him in any way. Kayley was ordered to report to the social services and attend a six-month course in Homophobic Awareness to protect him from attempts to convert him to heterosexuality. The social services argued that Val should also be forbidden contact with him as a dangerous homophobic influence, as her mother was a member of an evangelical church. However, the judge decided that might be a step too far. He would leave it to the social services to monitor the situation and get back to him if they found evidence that Val was attempting to pressure a vulnerable gay person to deny or change his sexuality. This would justify a court order banning her from contact with Kayley as well.

Doreen pretended to be shocked at Val's announcement in court that she and Kayley had sex regularly. She saw this relationship as merely grooming, sexual abuse and rape of a minor by a predatory girl of more advanced sexual development. A few weeks later she announced to Kayley they were moving in September to London, where she had been offered an associate professorship at Emmeline Pankhurst College (part of the former Croydon Polytechnic.) This meant it would be almost impossible for Kayley to go on seeing Val. He refused to go. He told his mother he was going to live with Val, whose parents were willing for him to move in and share her bedroom. Doreen answered that was out of the question and he was going to accompany her or she would get a court order forcing him to do so. She took a trip to London to find a flat to rent (she did not intend to sell their house but to rent it out), then got movers in to pack up their stuff and take it south. They were to follow by train, as she had sold her car. On the day they were due to leave Kayley refused to go with her to the station and ran away. He didn't go to Val's but went for a walk in a large park on the outskirts of town. That evening, thinking that Doreen had left on the train, he made his way to Val's place. His mother, however, had not left but had gone to the police. They were waiting for him as he approached Val's house and arrested him. They told him he would be held overnight and taken to the train station the next morning and put on the train with his mother. If he got off it again he would be arrested and sent to a juvenile prison.

The next day Kayley was put on the train to London. He waited till they were half-way there, then he got off the train and hitch-hiked back. This time he went straight to Val's place and stayed with her in her bedroom. She was excited by the whole adventure and they made plans for him to hide from the police. When the police came early the next morning looking for him, Val's little dog gave the alarm. Kayley ran out the back door and hid in the garden shed inside a big tool cupboard, against which Val piled old lawnmowers and wheelbarrows. Val's parents played the role of indignant householders outraged at this police intrusion. After a cursory search (including a glance in the garden shed) the policemen went away again.

Val and her mother, who had attended Eddy's trial, began to feel concerned about Eddy's health in prison and were determined to visit him. They applied to the prison but were told that Eddy had been transferred to the hospital as he had had another heart attack. They went to see him there, and the police guard allowed them five minutes with him. In fact Eddy had had a stroke and was now half paralysed and could hardly talk. "They wouldn't get me any more of my pills!" was all he could stammer to them.

Val's mother then asked the police whether Kayley could be allowed to visit his father, who might well die at any time. The police replied it was up to the social services and the judge. Val's mother phoned the social services and asked if Kayley could see his father before he died. The social services accused her of sheltering the runaway and committing a crime. She said that Kayley was willing to make a deal with them: he would go back to stay with his mother in London if he was allowed to visit his dying father. After some discussion at the other end of the line, the woman at the social services agreed. They said a car would come and pick up Kayley at her place the next day.

The car that arrived at their house was a police car. Val and her mother were a little suspicious and questioned the policemen in the car. The sergeant assured them that Kayley would be taken to the hospital to visit his father. Kayley got in. The car drove away. It took him not to the hospital but to a juvenile prison.

"You thought you were going to get away from us, lad, didn't you?" jeered the sergeant, leaning over the back of the front seat. "You're going to learn to do what you're told. You're going to be taught who has the power here. And it certainly isn't you."

Kayley was locked in a cell. He began a hunger strike. After a few days he was force-fed and when he resisted violently the doctors concluded he was a paranoid schizophrenic who needed hospitalization. He was sent to a high security psychiatric hospital and kept sedated and in a straitjacket for weeks. He was given injections that gave him violent headaches and made him vomit all day. Val and her mother were not allowed to visit him. But Doreen came to see him and suggested to the doctors that electric shock treatment might be the answer. They replied that this was no longer allowed, but that certain pills and injections could have almost the same effect. She told them that all of his problems came from his refusal to accept that he was gay. The psychiatrists found this a fascinating case. With her permission they decided to experiment not only with the pills and injections to induce a state of shock, but also with a course of female hormones to reduce his aggressiveness and increase his feminization. This would lead him, they reasoned, to accept his sexuality better. When he began to develop breasts from the hormone treatment he again went on hunger strike. Once more he was force-fed. The psychiatrist in charge tried to reason with him.

"You're not going to win. We've determined scientifically that you're gay. Your finger measurements, your anal-genital distance, penile reaction tests, everything confirms it. The very fact you're denying this so violently is further proof of it. Homophobia is nearly always a sign of repressed homosexuality. You're suffering from a mental disorder as irrational as rejecting one's left-handedness. We think as many as a quarter of males in this country may be homosexuals in denial, and we're determined to find methods to make them accept their true orientation. Now you will either comply, accept what you are and agree to go back and live with your mother and do what you're told, or you'll die. Make your mind up."

But Val had not given up. Kayley smuggled a letter out to her through the parents of a fellow patient. She wrote to newspapers about his case and told them he was being force-fed with female hormones because his mother wanted him to be a girl. Though the letters were not published, as they were judged by the editors to be transphobic, one was passed to an eminent psychologist who wrote a column for one of the papers. He took an interest in the case and demanded the right to see Kayley. A group from Val's mother's church also tried to visit him in the psychiatric hospital and demonstrated outside when they were refused permission to see him. They carried banners calling him a hostage to the totalitarian gay culture, and were all arrested and charged with hate crimes. The doctors at the hospital all agreed that militant homophobes should be given no access to their patient, and this included Val, the pseudo-girlfriend, and her mother.

When the eminent psychologist finally got to see Kayley, he pronounced that there was no reason at all for him to be kept in a high security psychiatric hospital. He claimed that Kayley was the victim of a conspiracy by an ideological clique determined to make him conform to their notion of what he was. He demanded publicly that the boy should be freed. He managed to get an article published in the local paper with the headline: "Forced to be Gay." It caused a scandal and he was accused by gay rights campaigners of vile homophobia.

The newspaper was threatened with a boycott and prosecution for hate crime and was forced to sack the psychologist from his column and to print an apology to the gay community, and an eight-page supplement about the heroic struggle of homosexuals against persecution throughout the ages. But the psychologist's article was seen by a veteran campaigner against abuse by the social services who wrote for *The Daily Telegraph*. He recounted Kayley's story in his next round-up of the latest examples of child abuse and sequestration of children by the social services. He mentioned that the boy's father had died without ever being allowed to see his son again. This caused an outcry among conservatives and led to demands for an inquiry by a panel of outside experts. The experts finally saw Kayley and after talking to him decided he should be released and allowed to stop taking the pills they were forcing him to take. When he came out, he was taken in by Val's family again. They welcomed him as a returning hero.

The two shared Val's bedroom and the parents treated Kayley like a son. Doreen applied to the judge to get him taken away from an immoral situation where she claimed he was being made to have sexual intercourse even though he was a minor. She found out somehow that Val had turned sixteen, while Kayley was still fifteen. That constituted statutory rape of Kayley by Val, she argued, with the complicity of her parents. The judge issued a court order forbidding Kayley to go on living with Val and compelling him to go back and live with his mother, or else he would be put in care. If Val's parents continued to put him up they would face a jail sentence for contempt of court. But this time a well-known lawyer who had heard about his case offered to defend him for free. He appealed against the court order and it was suspended till an appeals court could decide. By then Kayley had turned sixteen and the appeals court finally overturned the order.

He was now able to work, and he began to do a few evenings in a fast food restaurant to earn some money so he could pay Val's parents some board. He continued at school and despite his part-time work and the time lost in hospital he did well. A couple of years later he got high enough grades in his A-levels to get a place at Leeds University. He got a grant and moved there to study psychology. Val got a place at Cambridge but they saw each other when they could and spent holidays together. They went to France during their first summer holiday and travelled around the country camping. Val loved France and especially Avignon. The highpoint of their trip was going to the theatre festival there and seeing theatre groups from all over the country performing everything from Molière to bawdy medieval farce in the streets and squares of the old city. On the night of Bastille Day they watched the dancers in eighteenth-century costumes dancing on the famous ruined bridge, after the fireworks over the River Rhone, while the crowd on the riverbank softly sang the old song: *Sur le pont d'Avignon on y danse tout en rond.* It was a magical moment. Since Val was studying French she decided she wanted to go and live there for the Year Abroad that was part of her degree.

Once back at Cambridge she applied and got accepted for an assistantship at Avignon University, which would involve giving English conversation classes to French students. A year later she moved with great excitement to the old papal city. She came back to spend Christmas with Kayley and her family and then left again. Kayley had just booked a cheap flight to go and see her for the Easter holiday when her father called him and gave him the news. Val's body had been found half-naked in the bushes beside a dirt path used by joggers along the bank of the River Rhone near the ruined bridge. Three North African youths, part of the large immigrant population of the town, had been arrested and charged with rape and murder. Kayley sat in his room and stared at the wall. Val's sister came to Leeds and found him still sitting there the next day.

For months after her body was flown back for the funeral, Kayley lived in a kind of trance. He spent the days and nights writing poems about Val. He could not comprehend how anyone could do that to her. Val of the delicate, pale skin, the smile like a Leonardo angel, the flaming hair of a princess from the *Nibelungenlied*, Val of the quick wit and the lightning brain, the pale blue eyes that were always the first to cloud over with sympathy for anyone who was hurt or sad, or to blaze with anger at any injustice done to someone else. He tried to imagine the minds of the men who could hold that beautiful, fragile being down and rape her, then beat her head against the stony ground until she was dead. His imagination failed him.

He went to the trial and watched the three young North Africans, two of them born in France and only nineteen years old, sitting surly, indifferent or defiant, as the evidence was presented. They made no denial. They had killed her, one said, because she had resisted rape, which was her natural fate as an infidel. He got thirty years, the others twenty-two, but they would be eligible for parole much sooner. Kayley had fantasies of coming back then and waiting for them with a gun. Even before the trial he spent months doing research on the North Africans of France. On populist websites he read articles claiming that seventy per cent of prisoners in French prisons were Muslims, and the vast majority of rapes committed by strangers were by North Africans. For them, said the populist commentators, white girls were whores, infidels and slaves, whom they had the right to rape. Kayley sank into a state of mental torpor where he spent hours reading the websites of extreme right-wing groups in France, Britain, and even Sweden, which now had one of the highest rates of rape on earth, thanks to its huge immigrant population.

The organized efforts of the left, the government and the media in all these countries to conceal and lie about what was happening was a shocking form of complicity. Anyone who tried to publish the facts was vilified as a racist, and threatened with prosecution for inciting racial hatred. The girl victims had no voice, as the feminist movement blamed all rapes on the inherent violence of all men, and denied that any specific culture was responsible. Best-selling Swedish novelists won plaudits for demonizing the neo-Nazis, while working-class Swedish girls in immigrant areas were dyeing their hair black and wearing headscarves to guard against rape. And things were only going to get worse. The websites predicted that with present immigration and fertility rates, France, Britain and Sweden would have Afro-Asian majorities by 2070 and Islamist governments by 2080. Once Muslims became the dominant political force, the polarization of communities would fuel extremism on both sides and Sharia law would be imposed out of historic revenge. Kayley felt a burning rage against the political elites that were letting this happen. The most civilized countries on earth would become Third World cultures, where Western freedoms would no longer exist, where young women would never again be able to go out alone at night or go jogging along a riverbank at sunset. Were the politicians blind or deliberately committing treason against their own civilization? Did they imagine there would be no violent revolt sooner or later — by at least part of the white population — against this destruction of the Western way of life? Since this was happening everywhere from Scandinavia to Greece, the whole of Europe would be plunged into chaos, violence and civil war in his own lifetime. And once it began, it would never end, because there would be no solution.

One night, as he lay in the grip of this tormented vision of the future, he seemed to hear Val's voice in his head telling him not to go down that path. "It leads nowhere," she said, "only to hatred and violence. Try to make the world better, not worse. Try to stop conflict, not cause more of it. You can't reverse the course of history by yourself. If our nation or race has decided to commit suicide, there is nothing you can do to stop it. Most white women no longer want more than one child, and a quarter of them want none. Feminism has given them other ideas, and there is no going back to the past. That means we will be replaced by other races who still have the love of family and motherhood that we have lost. Accept what the future brings, even if it means our race and culture will disappear. Those who are taking over our country are also human beings, with their own values, which are just as worthy of respect as ours. It is racism to believe our culture is superior to theirs. Try to make all human beings happier, not incite some to hate others or try to keep them out of our country."

He remembered how quick Val had always been to denounce any form of racism or bigotry, and he felt ashamed. Gradually her gentle philosophy of universal love won the day over his violent, hate-filled reactions, and he decided to try to become what she would have wanted him to be.

He had failed his exams four months after Val was murdered because of his state of mind. The following year he decided to switch from psychology, which seemed to him more and more academic and theoretical, to do a more practical degree in social work. He thought the social services had treated him so abominably, and had shown such ideological fanaticism, that the only way to reform them was for more normal people to join them and try to change them from within. That is what Val had argued. He felt that if his presence there stopped even one person being treated the way he had been, it would be worthwhile. He knew he had only survived thanks to Val. He wanted to play that role in as many lives as possible.

He had to bite his tongue hundreds of times and swallow their ideological bilge and regurgitate it in exams, but he managed to get his degree (in spite of the open hostility of the teachers who knew of his history with the social services.) Then, after six months working in a pizza delivery place, he landed a job in a children's home in Leeds. It had a large number of teenagers. He got along well with the kids and enjoyed the work. He began to feel a real sense of fulfilment in helping children and adolescents through the various crises of their lives — their broken relationships, their failure at school, their self-doubt, their sense of rejection, their loneliness and their fear of the future after they were tipped out into the world. The only problem was that some of the teenage girls began to get a crush on him.

He was in his mid-twenties but looked much younger, with a boyish face and blond curls even the youngest girls went for. He could not help being nice to them and responding with good humour and kindness to their clumsy, impulsive attempts at seduction. He saw them as harmless kittens trying their claws. But some took his kindness for encouragement and then felt betrayed by his eventual rejection, however gentle. And some girls felt jealous of others and became vengeful and treacherous. One girl accused him to the director of seducing another girl of fifteen called Zoe, whose looks she was jealous of. An internal inquiry was held. Zoe denied they had ever had any physical contact but admitted when pressed that she "liked" him. Kayley was cleared of wrong-doing but given a warning for not taking enough precautions against emotional involvement with him by the girls in his care. He was shaken by the whole ordeal and considered resigning. But by chance a new female social worker came to work there, who became his girlfriend. He used her to fend off the advances of the girl residents. Zoe, who continued to throw him sultry glances, fortunately left a year later. However, his girlfriend was soon caught up in the web of rumours, lies and gossip woven by some of the other girls, and became obsessively jealous. She began watching him like a hawk, and accused him of flirting with every girl he spoke to. After a year he broke up with her and looked for a girlfriend outside the care home. After one or two relationships that didn't last, he began going out with a girl who worked in the local pharmacy. Things stabilized and a couple of years passed.

He was thirty when Zoe, who had not been seen since she disappeared at sixteen with a boyfriend, came back into his life. He was walking home from work and was not far from his flat when he noticed a girl at a bus stop smiling at him. She called out his name. He didn't recognize her but she came up and threw her arms round him.

"It's me, silly, Zoe, don't you remember me?" She kissed his cheek, not a dry peck but a voluptuous pressure of the lips, while his senses were engulfed in expensive perfume. He was taken aback by how much she had changed. She was elegantly made up, dressed in a short skirt and high boots, and her manner had become confident and mature. She invited him to have a coffee with her and he accepted, out of politeness and for old times' sake.

She led the way into a nearby café and they sat near the window. She had become even more attractive than he remembered her. She was part Indian and had sensual, tan skin and flashing dark eyes. He now recalled rumours that had reached the care home through her friends that she had gone to other cities and ended up on the game and taking heroin. He calculated she must now be about twenty. She was openly flirtatious and made it clear she was interested in him still.

Unfinished business, she called it. The conversation soon took a surreal turn. She began to talk as if he had seduced her five years before. This was the very thing she had denied when the inquiry was held. She now claimed she had denied it only to save him and that he owed his career to her. She could have sunk him if she had wanted to.

"All I had to do was say: yeah, it's true, and you would have been finished. Grooming an under-age girl. With a view to statutory rape. How many years? Five? Six? In fact I still could. Lately they're quite keen on digging up these old cases. I reckon if they knew you groomed a fifteen-year-old girl in your care, they'd be keen to talk to you."

"Zoe, this is complete rubbish and you know it is."

"Want to bet who the police and the judge will believe?"

He began to feel uneasy, as if this meeting had not been a chance one.

"Did you just happen to run into me or did you plan to see me again?"

"Let's say it was a bit of both. I found out where you live."

"What do you want from me?"

"Nothing really." She looked coy, glanced down and then slowly up at him again from beneath her long false eyelashes. "I just thought it would be nice to give ourselves another chance. Take up from where we left off. I'm old enough now." She smiled. Her lips with their glossy, scarlet lipstick were perfect. "Don't you like me any more?"

"It's not a question of that," he said awkwardly. She was in fact disturbingly attractive. But there was a gulf between them as people.

"What is it then? You think we wouldn't get along? That I'm too uneducated? I'm cleverer than you think. Why not take me back and try me?" She smiled teasingly, sure of her powers of seduction.

"I can't take you back, since I never had you in the first place."

"Course you did. In your mind. And in mine. You know what we were both thinking. You were thinkin' of me in bed when you wanked. And I were thinkin' of you. And when we looked at each other next day we both knew it. And I knew one day we'd do it for real, not just in our minds. Now it's possible. There's nothing to stop us. So why don't we go back to your place and do it? What we both wanted to then. For real. Now."

He stared at her in confusion. It's true she had been by far the best-looking girl in the home at that time and her image had occasionally slipped into the beauty parade of his nocturnal fantasies. It astonished him that she had somehow guessed that.

"Look, Zoe, you're a nice girl but we have nothing in common and it wouldn't work between us. I've already got a girlfriend and I think you should find someone else and move on. I'm sure you attract boys in droves so what's the problem?"

"The problem is I want you." She grinned mischievously. "There was always something cool and distant about you, even though you were friendly on the surface. I could have them all except you, so you're what I want. You were such a goody-good, like a choir boy, butter wouldn't melt in your mouth. Now I want that mouth — in my muff. Don't you want it there?" She ran the tip of her pink tongue enticingly along her scarlet lips and then flashed her perfect white teeth in a frankly carnal smile.

"I already have a girlfriend. Didn't you hear?"

"Yeah, and I'll soon fix that bitch. I know where she works and where she lives."

"Look, you go near her and I'll go to the police."

"Oh, will you?" she sneered. "And tell them about the fifteen-year old girl you used to rub up against when you were her care-worker, how you used to stick your hand in my snatch and give it a feel every time you found me alone, how I felt like dirt and took drugs and went astray just because of you?"

"Zoe, you know that's a pack of lies, who will believe you?" He tried to sound confident but underneath he was becoming alarmed.

"I've got friends from back then who'll stand up for me in court. You remember Layla, the black girl who accused you back then of shagging me, she'll testify again you did."

"You contradicted Layla to the inquiry at the care home!"

"Only because you told me to, and I was your slave at the time! Now that I know how you betrayed me, I'll tell them the truth. How you seduced me one night, when you were on night duty. And Layla saw it."

"It'll be your word against mine, and lots of other kids who were there at the time and all the other care-workers will back me up that you're fantasizing." He was trying to convince himself of his case as much as her.

"Oh, yeah? You think a bloke's word is worth shit in court today? Against a girl's?" She sounded scornful. "We're the victims today, you male chauvinist pig, and every judge knows it. Statutory rape. Every guy dreams of shagging fifteen-year-old girls! Who will believe you didn't when you had the chance? You're guilty until proven innocent, and how the fuck will you prove what you didn't do? You got an alibi for every minute of your life?"

He was stunned by her determination and how well she had thought this out.

"Why are you doing this?" he said in puzzlement. "What did I do to you?"

"You turned me on." She smiled dazzlingly. "So now you owe me one. You lit the fire. Now you've got to put it out." She gazed at him with the glittering eyes of a cobra. "With your tongue." She glanced around. "You remember that film where the girl took her knickers off in the restaurant and handed them to the guy? Do you reckon I could do that? Without anyone in here noticing?"

She made as if to hitch up her skirt.

"You'll get us thrown out of here!" he said quickly, alarmed.

"So, we could go to your place. You're gagging for it even now, so what's stopping you? Surely not that stuck up little bitch in the chemist's? With no boobs. Look at what I've got, baby, that she hasn't."

She was wearing a low-cut top with an elastic upper edge, and she pulled one strap off her shoulder and peeled the top down to expose one breast to him. It was smoothly tanned and perfectly shaped, with that honey-melon fullness that arouses a suspicion of silicone implants. He couldn't suppress a twitch of desire at the sight. Some other patrons in the café stared in shock as she put the top back in place. The café owner, a middle-aged, stocky man, came over and spoke to her in a low voice.

"Do you mind behaving properly in public?"

"What's your problem, sunshine, haven't had it lately?" Zoe had developed the cool, cutting insolence of the whore. "I was showing them to my boyfriend, not to you."

"Well, I'd rather you didn't show them to anyone in my café. Now out you go, both of you."

Kayley got up and began moving to the door. Zoe followed suit, not without an obscene gesture in the direction of the café owner.

"Up yours, arsehole! Don't want to be reminded you can't get it up, is that it?"

The café owner raised his hand as if to slap her. Zoe reacted by reflex and swung her big shoulder-bag, a cloth bag but with something weighty in it, and hit him in the face with it. He was stung by the blow to his nose. He at once tried to grapple with her. She began punching him in the face with sly uppercut blows that showed a certain experience of street fights. Kayley rushed to separate them and stop the café owner from punching her back.

"Police!" yelled the café owner. "Someone call the police!" He was bleeding from the nose and stared at his bloody fingers, and then grabbed Zoe again to hold her.

Two or three customers were seen stabbing at their mobile phones.

"Let her go! We're leaving!" shouted Kayley, trying to make the café owner loosen his grip on Zoe, at the same time pulling her towards the door.

The café owner, who was of medium height but heavily built, was evidently less inhibited about punching a man than a woman. He landed a straight right on Kayley's chin that sent him to the floor. Zoe picked up her coke bottle from the table and cracked it over the bridge of the café owner's nose. As he reeled backwards she bent over Kayley.

"Get up before he starts kicking you!" she yelled. She pulled him up by the arm, and he regained his feet, still slightly groggy. She dragged him towards the door and managed to get it open as the café owner rushed at them again. They staggered out into the street, and she pushed Kayley in front of her and turned and swung the bag again at their pursuer. It hit him in the face as he came through the door.

"I bet that's my fucking wine bottle broken!" she said as she grabbed Kayley's hand and ran down the street. They had gone thirty metres before she looked back and saw they were not being pursued. She stopped running and began to laugh, panting from her exertions. As he stopped too, she threw her arms round him. She was unsteady on her high-heeled boots and he had to hold her tight to keep her upright as she recovered her breath. She hugged him and then glued her lips against his and he felt a sensual pleasure flood through him that he couldn't resist. He felt something wet against his thigh, and looked down to see that her cloth bag had a large dark stain where the wine from the broken bottle had soaked through. She held the bag out at arm's length as it dripped red wine.

"I need to get cleaned up," she said. "Your place?"

He nodded. Things had been decided for them. He led her to his flat, only a block away, and they ran up the stairs laughing. When they got inside, she dropped the bag, threw off her top, and hugged him to her naked breasts. Then she leaned back and pushed his face down to kiss them. A few seconds later they flopped onto the bed, still entwined.

"So, I've got you, you bastard!" she said half an hour later, looking down at him dreamily, ruffling his hair as his nose nuzzled her crotch. "The choir boy, the innocent, goody-good care worker, who wouldn't touch the girls, no, not him, half the others were getting their end away, but not you, you were the pure-minded, curly-headed angel. And now I've got that angel with his tongue in my muff, lapping me like a dog. What a victory!"

"Rub it in, won't you," he said, coming up for air.

"Sure. And any time you want to leave me before I finish with you I just have to mention: fifteen-year old girl, statutory rape, and back you'll come like a dog on a leash, won't you? I've got you, baby."

She reached out for her smartphone lying on the bedside table, rescued from her wine-soaked bag on the floor. She snapped two or three photos of them lying together naked, his face on her lower belly.

"Evidence for the court case. The paternity case when I make you marry me, or else go down for rape."

She was laughing in a mocking way and he had no idea how serious anything she said was. She picked up the used condom he had just taken off and put on the bedside table. She knotted it and tucked it inside her bag on the floor.

"Semen sample. All useful."

He had no idea whether he should grab the condom and flush it away down the toilet (which was outside on the landing) and grab the smartphone and erase the photos. Her teasing threats of entrapment might just be zany humour, but then again they might not be.

She mentioned casually that she had nowhere to stay and would he mind if she stayed the night till she sorted something out. He had no real choice. Later on he called his girlfriend and explained that an ex-resident of the care home had shown up and he had to look after her as she was a bit fragile. He wouldn't be able to see her for a day or two. He heard a note of scepticism at the other end.

Of course the one night became two and on the third day Zoe was waiting outside the children's home when he came off duty. She was dressed in a pink mini-skirt, black fishnet stockings, black boots and was made up like Liz Taylor in *Cleopatra*. Her hair was freshly washed and brushed and hung down her back like a dark, rippling curtain. She made a great show of kissing him in front of a group of girls hanging about on the large veranda-like porch. When they cheered lustily, she calmly walked over to them and introduced herself.

"I'm Zoe. Some of you may remember me, I used to live here, I was one of you. I had the hots for him when I was fifteen, even got him into trouble for it, and now he's mine. So there's hope for all of you! Take heart, girls!"

There were more cheers and exclamations. She was clearly seen as a star.

"By the way, don't be fooled by that innocent, choir-boy appearance, he fucks really well, and does other things even better. Kayley the superstud, when I've finished with him I'll pass him on to you. But don't you dare touch him till then! Remember, you're still jailbait!"

There were more shrieks of excitement. One or two social workers put their heads out the door to see what was going on. As Kayley and Zoe were walking away hand in hand, the former with burning cheeks, they came face to face with Kayley's girlfriend from the chemist's, evidently coming to meet him as well. She glared at him, her lips quivering.

"You bastard, I suppose you think this is funny!" she said. She slapped his face and turned round and walked off quickly in the other direction. Zoe squeezed his hand and then kissed him hard.

Two days later the director of the home called him in for a little chat. Walsall was a caring, earnest man in his late fifties, who went in for brown cardigans with leather patches on the elbows. He looked worried.

"I'm afraid this is causing something of a scandal. This girl is an ex-resident of this home, who, I have not forgotten, was alleged by another girl to have been involved in a relationship with you when she was only fifteen — though I grant you it wasn't proven. Still, her sudden reappearance now in the role of your girlfriend can only feed rumours that there was something in it. It does look like an abuse of your position of authority. The girls here must not be led to think that sexual relationships with care workers, even after they leave our home, are something we would encourage. They mustn't see this either as some sort of solution for their lives. That would be quite the wrong message to send, God knows."

"Yes, I understand." Kayley tried to sound contrite. He thought it was best to let the tide of moral indignation wash over him and it would perhaps recede again.

"This girl, Zoe, since she left us, is rumoured to have been living a life of ill fame in Manchester. Do you have any information on that?"

The director looked at him severely, as though he was somehow to blame.

"It's just a rumour, and I can't confirm it."

"Again, that is not the message to give the girls — that someone can live like that and then come back and be blithely accepted as a suitable partner by a care worker she had some sort of crush on when she was a minor in this home. I hope you understand how terribly that would reinforce bad behaviour. It is utterly inappropriate."

"I see that. I'm very sorry, things just.... got out of hand."

"I hope you realize how incompatible this is with your position." He was hardening his stance as Kayley retreated.

"Yes, I do, and I shall try to bring the situation back under control."

"I hope you will, because if you continue to be seen in public with this girl, this ex-resident of this home, and sometime drug-addict and prostitute, if I am to believe my sources...." He paused, as if uncertain where this sentence was leading, and then saw the way out. "Well, I shall have no alternative but to ask for your resignation." He seemed relieved that he had got it out, and had put on a show of firmness and authority which he did not feel.

Kayley took this to heart and that evening began looking on line for vacancies in care homes elsewhere. Zoe thought she had scored a major victory by eliminating the girl in the chemist's, who was clearly so humiliated by the incident at the home that she would not pick up any of Kayley's calls or reply to any of his text messages. Zoe started talking as if she had now moved in with him permanently and they were officially a couple. He began to wonder how he could disentangle himself from this relationship without incurring her wrath and provoking wild accusations that could land him in court. He decided the best thing would be to let the relationship die a natural death. She was hardly the faithful type and would probably soon find him wanting in the sexual gymnastics stakes and would move on to the sort of stud he imagined she was in the habit of shagging. The trouble was he found her so exciting in bed he could not help excelling himself. As the days went by she was starting to accompany her bedroom antics with appreciative murmurs and the odd endearment instead of crude jokes.

"What do you feel for me?" she asked him one night in bed. "You've never told me you love me. I bet you don't. You're just in it for a free fuck, aren't you?"

She was kneeling astride him naked and holding his face in her hands as if he was her property, grinning in an impishly domineering manner that was her favourite role.

"And you, do you love me?" he countered.

"I asked you first," she said, as though playing a child's game.

"I'm not sure I know what love is. Do you?"

He had a momentary feeling of shame that this was the kind of evasive remark that must have been uttered by millions of young men in his situation — getting laid quite enjoyably but not wanting to make any commitment that would shut down all other options.

She gave an impression of thinking deeply for several seconds.

"Love? Sure. It's like really liking someone, only a lot more so." She smiled with satisfaction as if she thought this *bon mot* had neatly solved the riddle of the ages.

"So, liking and love — the distinction is purely quantitative, not qualitative?" he said. He was hoping to irritate her with his intellectual pedantry, and so make her sick of him.

"I don't know what the fuck that means. But it's a question like — do you want me forever and ever, or is it just for a few weeks?"

He thought about it. He decided to be tactful and evasive again.

"Well, forever and ever is just a lot of a few weeks end to end, isn't it? So why don't we take it a few weeks at a time?"

She stared at him for ten seconds, as if digesting this. He didn't know if she was going to explode in anger and slap him or just laugh. At last she smiled broadly.

"That's brilliant!" she said ecstatically, kissing him. "You're so fucking clever! You should have been a university professor, not just a social worker." He was astonished she was so pleased by his flippant answer. "That sounds like.... Zen. Forever and ever is just a lot of a few weeks end to end."

Her ability to repeat his sentence exactly surprised him.

"I didn't know you were into Zen," he said.

"I'm not really. But us working-class sluts are not totally ignorant, you know. By the way, you can keep doing that, it helps me concentrate." She began to wriggle her crotch against his idly caressing fingers and leaned down and put her tongue into his mouth.

He found to his surprise that everything he said to annoy her and push her to resent him had the opposite effect. She was also proving to be a lot more fun than he had expected. Her world was, of course, rather different from his. It was ruled by listening to rock music, dancing about to it, drinking wine and smoking hashish (which she had a stash of.) One night she dragged him to a club, where her sexy dancing made her the centre of attention. In short, she was putting a bit of colour into his rather sober social worker's existence. Yet despite her air of Bohemianism, she did not disrupt his schedule. She went back to sleep when he left for work, tidied the place up occasionally, and made no demands for money except for food and cigarettes. He began to wonder if it would be so easy to end this relationship, not just because of her potential as an avenging fury but because he enjoyed being with her more and more.

"So, tell me what you did after you left the home," he asked her one night in bed. Their sexual jousts were becoming interspersed with scraps of conversation about their lives.

"It was all a bloody disaster at first. The guy I left here with turned out to be an arsehole. He took me to Bradford, where he had friends." She lit a cigarette, drew on it and exhaled at the ceiling as she lay on her back. "They were into dope, so I got into that, and we dealt a bit, and then I got into smack. We had a few rows and then the arsehole split, and I found I had to pay for my habit. So I shagged the dealer, and he got me in with a friend of his who put me on the game. I was working for my hits, basically. Not the best thing."

"So how did you get out?"

"I just left. I was under eighteen so he was a bit scared I'd go to the police. I moved to Manchester and got some help getting off the stuff. Then I lived with a guy who worked in advertising. Drove an Aston Martin. I did a bit of club work, pole dancing. It went OK for a couple of years, then he got jealous and we split up. I did some lap dancing, and then I set up as an escort. I got on a website, posted some really hot photos, and I made good money."

"So, how did you find that as a job?" He was genuinely curious.

"It's not bad, if you get normal blokes." She blew out a stream of smoke thoughtfully. "If you get creeps, it's creepy. And the trouble is you can't tell just by a phone call. If you're going to the geezer's place and you're, like, by yourself, with no back-up, and nobody knows where you've gone, it's a bit scary. You can't do it in your own flat because the neighbours call the police. And you can't share a house with other girls, because then they'll jail you for having a brothel. So all the laws are aimed at forcing sex workers to work alone. Anything that would make it safer like in other countries is forbidden. They want a few of us to be butchered each year as a warning. Gives them a good conscience."

"And is it really dangerous?"

"It can be. But only because their bloody laws make it that way. I had to carry a blade in my bag and some pepper spray. I was stopped and searched one day and they found them."

"What happened?"

"Got off with a fine. They told me next time it'd be jail. That's when I stopped."

"Sounds unfair." He thought for a bit. "So, where do you see your life going now?"

"I guess I've got to make my pile while I've still got the body, right? So the general plan is to marry a rich guy and get a good divorce. That's the fastest way for a girl to get rich."

"And in the meantime, what's the short-term plan? As far as work goes?"

"I suppose I'll find something when you get sick of paying all the bills."

"So, what kind of job would you like to do?" He felt a vague urge to reform her life.

"Dunno. Got any suggestions?" She seemed only vaguely interested in the subject.

"Well, would you like to work in an office as a secretary or in a shop? Or work with kids?" He felt slightly depressed at how limited her options seemed to be.

"With kids? They won't let me near kids with my record. As for an office, sounds like some heavy-breathing, sweaty, fat bastard putting his hands all over me as he shows me the computer programme."

"That's probably about it. So what about a shop?"

"Depends. Selling clothes might be OK. Bloody boring though, if there's no customers."

"So what would you like?"

She thought for a moment.

"I like dancing. And I enjoy anything to do with sex. So maybe I'll go back to gogo dancing. Pole dancing. That sort of thing. I find it fun to turn guys on. And I like clubs."

"So you'd be a stripper?"

"Yeah, why not? You're the centre of attention. And it's one way to meet guys with money. Even if they're mostly sleazes." She pulled on her cigarette thoughtfully. "Otherwise, I suppose there's porn. Do you think I should get into that?"

Kayley glanced at her before answering. He chose his words carefully.

"I don't think so. You know at the home the boss was pretty pissed off you showed up the other day and chatted to the girls. He read me the riot act about inappropriate behaviour."

"Meaning mine?"

"Meaning me being seen with you. The scarlet woman. Meant to have a bad moral effect on the kids."

"That's fucking great, isn't it?" She was furious. "What if you were a faggot living with another faggot, even kissing him in public? That would be fine with them, wouldn't it? That would be good for the kids. Teaching them tolerance! But as for a girl who was once a bit wild, who dresses sexy and likes to kiss her boyfriend in public, that's a no-no. Terribly immoral! Scandalous! Not fit for kids to see! What's wrong with this fucking country? Is everyone in charge a fucking faggot?"

"Not far off it. There's a long tradition of it at boarding schools," he said, reflecting. "The entire upper class for generations had their first sex being buggered by a sixth former. Half the members of parliament have been faggots or paedophiles at private schools. So they see all that as normal. The minister who got it legalized, Roy Jenkins, was secretly one himself. What was presented as tolerance towards a persecuted minority was in fact a sect of perverts legalizing their own practices. On the other hand, sexy women are still seen as dangerous loose cannons to be kept under strict control. They're feared by men and hated by other women. Gay men aren't seen as subversive. Sexy women are. You can tell by the fact there have never been any whores in parliament, but it's full of faggots."

She stared at him with an expression of despair.

"How can you live with these people?"

"What should I do? Go abroad? Where? Germany? Holland? France? Italy? I guess the Italians have at least had one whore in their parliament. She used to campaign topless and really drew the crowds."

"Anywhere must be better than here. Here normal sex is criminal and perverts are seen as normal."

"That's Britain. If I want to do social work, I'm stuck with it. But the fact is the people in charge here see girls like you as a class of women to be outlawed and made to disappear."

She thought about that for a moment, pulling on her cigarette and then exhaling slowly.

"So, I'd be really bad for your career, right?"

"It depends. If you became a lap dancer or something, yeah."

"You couldn't marry me then?" She sniggered. "Or even live with me?"

"They'd use it to get me out. As you said, they'd prefer me to be living with a man than with a lap dancer or a sex worker. Homosexuality is now viewed as the middle-class norm. Something to be proud of. We have to teach the kids that buggery is normal and healthy. That two gays or two lesbians make ideal parents. All the intolerance is now directed against loose women and the sex trade between men and women in any form."

"Why?" She looked mystified.

"Because the feminists are in the saddle. And they are all in favour of more men being gay. They see it as a form of voluntary castration. They'd make it compulsory if they could. The whole sexual liberation thing of the sixties was shut down by the lesbian feminists and diverted into homosexual liberation, so they could wage their war on men. What they can't stand is men getting sex from women younger and prettier than they are by paying for it. It makes them feel like the superannuated, dried up, repulsive old sows they are."

"But women go to prostitutes as well. I knew some male prostitutes."

"For women? But most women don't get off on that. They just pretend to, when they're in a drunken mob at the Chippendales. By themselves they're too scared. So, since they don't enjoy prostitutes they're going to make sure men can't either. All over Europe the feminists are making this drive to ban prostitution by criminalizing the client. If a man is old or ugly or handicapped and can't attract a woman he now has to go without sex. Or watch porn and wank. He's not allowed to use his money to get a service that his looks can't. It's the castration of as many men as possible by a man-hating sect that has taken power through the gutlessness and brainwashing of university-educated men."

"You think the feminists hate men that much?"

"Of course they do. They see men as the enemy. My mother's a feminist. I know how they think. She did everything she could to make me a faggot and to kill my father. That's what feminism is. A man-hating, lesbian sect that now controls the universities, the schools, the media, the courts and the social services. They're brainwashing all white girls against motherhood and marriage. They want our race to die out and be replaced by others."

"But how did they get so much power?" She sounded horrified as well as baffled.

"It's hard to say. For fifteen hundred years Europe was ruled by a woman-hating sect. The Catholic clergy. They were a mainly homosexual brotherhood who spent a lot of time trying to persuade men that women were deceitful, lustful, greedy, lying, manipulative, idle cows. So they could get the best-looking boys into the monastery instead. We no sooner got rid of them than a sect of women took over who were largely lesbian: the sisterhood, the feminists, who have tried to persuade women for the last fifty years that men are violent, bullying, wife-beating, promiscuous, vicious rapists, determined to keep them down."

"That's not a million miles from the truth, is it?" she said, trying to keep a straight face.

"You see? They've even convinced you. But their goal is simple: get more girls to become open to lesbianism. So they have a bigger pool of naive victims to prey upon."

"They had a go at me once or twice. I gave 'em a short shift."

"It's amazing that heterosexual people, who make up 97 per cent of the population, can't actually put in place an ideology that promotes men-women relations instead of trying to poison them. For fifteen hundred years we've allowed ourselves to be ruled by the three per cent of homosexuals who are out to sabotage normal relationships between men and women. First the misogynist priests. Then the man-hating feminists and the faggots."

"So why stay in this business?" She stubbed out her cigarette in a saucer by the bed.

"I don't know any other. It took me a long time to find out it's this fucked up. And I still want to help people."

"I guess I'm going to be in your way." She sounded dispirited and stared at the ceiling.

"No, you won't." He answered automatically and then tried to put some meaning into it. "Don't think like that."

He could tell that his own voice did not carry enough conviction and she sensed it. He turned to her and took her in his arms to reassure her, but she resisted for a few seconds, just to show she was offended by his lack of real faith in their future.

The next day he was again summoned to the director's office. Walsall cleared his throat and began pacing the floor as if he was ill at ease and unsure how to begin.

"It's come to my attention that you are still living with the young woman in question. You apparently didn't take my warning seriously. I can't afford the risk of scandal that this poses. I'm afraid I have no alternative but to ask you to resign. If you find a place in another institution, in another city, within a couple of weeks, say, I'm perfectly willing to give you a glowing reference, because in fact your work has been very good. You're very popular with the children. I have no complaints at all except this unfortunate business of a relationship with an ex-resident who was under-age when she met you. What do you say?" He stopped pacing and looked at him hopefully. "Will you look seriously for another post? If not, I shall have no choice but to write a letter detailing the situation and my warnings and dismiss you for highly unprofessional behaviour."

Kayley stared at the carpet for a moment, reflecting.

"And if I were to break up with her?"

"I'm afraid you've had your chance for that and quite clearly you haven't been able to." Walsall spoke a little sharply, but with a sense of disappointment. Then his tone softened a bit. "Now, far be it from me to judge people on their relationships and who they choose to live with. Your relationship with this young woman should cause no problem at all in another city in an institution with which she has no connection. There is no reason to expect scandal to follow you round the country. It's only here this relationship poses a problem, because she is known here from her last incarnation and is hence a morally harmful influence."

That evening Kayley resumed job-searching on line and told Zoe what his boss had said.

"So, he wants to run us out of town?" she said indignantly.

"More or less. We can start again in some place where there's no chance of rumours surfacing that I seduced you when you were fifteen and in my care."

"Which you bloody well did," she said.

"We've been through that."

"Psychologically, emotionally. You played me like a bloody violin."

"I didn't know I was doing it."

"No. Perverts act by instinct."

"You don't seriously mean that word?" He found it disturbing.

"Yes, I do. You're a perv. An absolute perv." She made the word sound particularly erotic. She put her arms round him and kissed him passionately, then she put on a posh, feminine, little girl voice. "You see, you don't understand how vulnerable I was at that age."

"You were a sexy little tart in a miniskirt who tried to get your claws into me as soon as you saw me."

"Exactly. That's what vulnerable means. And you took shocking advantage."

He began applying for jobs in neighbouring cities and got one interview for a position as counsellor for the social services, to provide help and support for couples with relationship problems. He went to their office. The interviewer was a short man of about forty with a mop of chestnut hair ending in a fringe, which looked like a wig. He had brown eyes that floated around behind thick glasses which magnified them, so that they looked like tadpoles in two very small fish bowls. He wore a slight, sad smile that looked sorry for this candidate as if he was clearly wasting his time. He focused his eyes on Kayley's face for a minute, but the eyes still tended to wander in a circle, as if he was picking the spot to aim at on a dartboard.

"Tell me a little about yourself. Are you married?"

"No, but I live with a girlfriend. Perhaps one day." Kayley smiled amiably. He thought this question might have something to do with his competence in discussing marital problems. His answer did not seem to have scored him any points.

"How comfortable would you be giving advice about sexual relationships?"

"Well, I've had a few, and I'm sure I'm a good listener and can try to understand any problems that may be occurring, and discuss solutions." He thought he should project an image of easy-going confidence, which could deal effectively with any case, however bizarre, that might come up.

"Would you be equally comfortable giving counselling to same-sex couples?"

He tried not to bat an eyelid.

"I'm sure the same basic principles apply in all relationships. Listening to each other, sharing, making compromises."

"What about giving sexual counselling to same-sex couples that might be having sexual difficulties? Would you be comfortable with that?" The smile became a little pinched, as if the interviewer was privately convinced he would not be able to answer yes.

"I'm sure there are books on the subject which one can consult, and these things are largely a question of listening to each other...." Kayley felt a little uncertain of his ground.

"Really? Would you be able to give advice to a same-sex couple about rimming?" The question was accompanied by a sudden, fleeting smile that made Kayley think of a carnivorous animal approaching a very small rodent.

"Rimming?" The word rang a bell but Kayley couldn't remember exactly what it referred to. Some sort of sexual act, he thought. Licking some part of the anatomy, wasn't it? But what, exactly? It sounded circular. Round the nipples? Clitoris? End of knob?

"Yes. Rimming. You do know what I'm talking about?"

"I've heard the term but I'm afraid I'm not absolutely sure what it means." He didn't want to hazard a guess and get it badly wrong. That might suggest a warped imagination.

"It's a sexual practice that involves one partner putting his tongue in the other partner's anus." The smile tightened as the eyes seemed to grow larger behind the thick lenses. "It's not confined to gay people. Do you think you'd be able to give counselling to a gay couple, recommending the practice of rimming and explaining the technique?"

Kayley stared back at him. This looked like a deliberate attempt to make him fail the interview. He replied carefully.

"I'm sure I'd be comfortable with whatever policy the social services have on this."

"That's not the question. The question was specifically about rimming. Would you be comfortable recommending it or would it disgust you?" His tone had become slightly hectoring. "We do need an honest answer because we have a gay couple to whom we urgently need to give counselling about this practice as a priority. A young black man and his older white lover, who is also obese, impotent, and incontinent. Would you be happy talking to them about rimming and the benefits of it? As a complement to fellatio, which, in case you're unfamiliar with that term as well, means taking the penis in the mouth and sucking it."

He spoke with heavy irony, as if to underline the shocking ignorance of this candidate.

"I suppose if that was the best thing for them, I could do it."

"You seem to be in some doubt," said the interviewer sarcastically. "I would say you were very hesitant on the subject. You see, that's what we can't have."

His sarcasm quickly turned into disapproval, and then into indignation. The eyes began to spin madly around the double fishbowl, like tadpoles panicking.

"Imagine if a same-sex couple got the impression that sexual relations between them disgusted you. It could have a devastating effect on them."

"Yes, I quite see that," said Kayley cautiously.

"No, I don't think you do. It would make them call in question their whole identity as human beings. As gay persons with equal rights in this country to pursue sexual fulfilment with the full support of the state and the social services. How would you like it if somebody turned up his nose at your sexual practices?"

"I certainly wouldn't turn up my nose."

"You just did."

"I beg your pardon?"

"I saw a definite wrinkling of your nose when I described rimming, another one when I said one partner was obese and incontinent, and a third time when I described fellatio. It was very slight but I picked it up each time."

"I certainly wasn't aware of it."

"Exactly! You weren't aware of it!" His face expressed grim satisfaction, even triumph. His eyes became quite still and sharply focused as if galvanized by a charge of electric current. "I think that says it all. I think self-awareness, especially of one's facial expressions, is the first thing a sexual counsellor needs. Any inability to control an expression of disgust when faced with somebody of different sexual orientation is absolutely inexcusable. It could lead to the social services being sued or you facing criminal charges. We can't take that risk."

"I see." Kayley stared for a moment, rather shocked. He decided to make one last attempt to salvage the interview. "I have always thought I was perfectly capable of treating with absolute impartiality both sexes —"

"Both sexes?" echoed the other in astonishment.

"I meant both sexual orientations." Kayley felt slightly confused.

"Both sexual orientations?" Equal astonishment. "And what about the others?"

"Others? I'm sorry?"

"You said both sexes. So you exclude all those who are transsexual, transgender, bigender, intersex, those in the middle of a sex change, in either direction — they have just been defined out of existence, have they? How do you think they would feel about hearing the sexist binary term 'both sexes'?" He was quivering with indignation. "As for 'both sexual orientations', that will exclude bisexuals, transsexuals, asexuals, sadomasochists, fetishists, coprophiliacs, zoophiliacs, and all the other rich varieties of sexual experience. They have been banished from the world as well, have they? Do you still believe you have any qualifications at all for this job? Besides being totally ignorant of common sexual practices such as rimming and hence being incapable of giving counselling to same-sex couples?"

Kayley sat there stunned. The other began looking at some papers on his desk.

"So, that's it?"

"What?"

"The interview."

"I'm afraid so. I didn't think you were going to be suitable material anyway, so I'm glad we've found that out so quickly. That'll be all. Thanks for coming in."

Kayley stood up to go. The other, who had begun to read a document, looked up again. The eyes flailed about a little before focusing.

"By the way, don't think for a moment about protesting our decision. It'll be a waste of everyone's time. We have already had jurisprudence on our right to sack social workers for not being comfortable giving sexual counselling to same-sex couples. Some black Christian bigot last year confessed to it. It's now a recognized cause for dismissal or refusal of employment. For any position in the social services. It's discrimination. We believe in equal rights in this country."

"So do I," said Kayley quietly. The other glared back as if this was a challenge.

"Do you want some advice? If you can't have a gay relationship yourself, for some peculiar reason, then watch some gay porn. Get familiar with the practices. And learn to see them as normal. As good, healthy, natural and normal. Something young people and even children should be taught about and taught to see as normal. Then you might fit into today's social services. You've got some work to do on yourself. You might be surprised where it leads you. All right?"

Kayley turned and walked out.

He had a few more discouraging experiences with social services where the gay lobby seemed to be in charge before he finally found a job in a children's home in Birmingham. It had been a boys' home, and had only recently been opened to girls as well, so it was still very largely male. He thought this might avert some of the problems he had had with teenage girls, and Zoe was of the same opinion. He applied for the job on line and received an answer to come for an interview. He went there and was shown over the home. A few days later he was offered the job by email. He reflected that it was a bit of a gloomy place but he thought he could always look for something else in a year or two.

He told his director, Walsall, who had already been contacted for a reference and had given a very good one. Zoe agreed to move with him, though as the time approached for the move she seemed more and more preoccupied. She showed little interest in his efforts to find a flat in Birmingham. Finally she told him she had been given a chance to try out as a pole-dancer at the Purple Doors Club, and was hoping to earn enough money to try and enrol at the Northern Dance School so she could learn modern dance and maybe start a career as a dancer in musicals and stage shows. She said she couldn't follow him to Birmingham for at least a year. He came to see her on her first night at the club and he had to admit she was good. She was made for sexy dancing. He felt a pang at the loss of this fabulously sexy body at the same time as he realized that they were simply not part of the same world. She could show off her naked body in a public performance with a provocative insolence that gave him goose bumps. She got on easily with bouncers, pimps, dealers and spivs whom he couldn't even imagine having a conversation with. They said goodbye and he headed off with the feeling that she would probably never join him. But the fact the break-up was not yet definitive made it easier to bear. He even felt a tiny hint of relief that a complication in his life had disappeared — even though it now made his whole change of jobs and cities pointless. In his first month in Birmingham he went back to see her three times, but he could feel she was drifting away. She had a flatmate, another dancer, who didn't like him. He suspected they were probably both on the game part time, entertaining clients privately after hours. He told Zoe it might be better if they packed it in. She agreed it was probably best.

At Gaveston House Children's Home he got on well with the kids, and since there were no girls over thirteen he wasn't pestered by them falling in love with him as he had been before. He became popular with the children, though some were a bit withdrawn. It was the other social workers he found distant, suspicious and rather odd. He felt they all had secrets they were keeping from him. He was made to feel an outsider, and conversations often stopped when he came into a room. He was being studied, analysed, judged, and he felt uncomfortable. That was still the atmosphere when he decided to confide his suspicions about Eric's disappearance to his director. It was only after Marlowe had him arrested that he understood the reason for the strange atmosphere in the home. He had stumbled into a nest of paedophiles, and everybody suspected everybody else, both those who were in the paedophile ring and those who were outside it. And he realized that he had simply been used as the fall guy. He had no doubt that Marlowe was in this too, if not as a paedophile himself, at least as an accomplice who had turned a blind eye to the activities of Brian and other care workers, as well as those of Cyril Jones. And since Marlowe knew after the visit of Viktor's mother and her friends that it was all going to blow up, he decided to find a scapegoat to blame it all on. The newcomer who had no friends to back him up was tailor-made for the purpose. He could get rid of the one potential whistleblower and put him away for a very long time, and even afterwards he would be banned forever from working in that field. The theory of the one rotten apple would be eagerly accepted by everyone in the care home business.

The more Kayley thought about the trap they had laid for him, the worse his chances of getting out of it looked. The assaults upon him had marked a low-point in his mental state. His inability to leave his cell or have any human contact had deepened the feeling of gloom. But thinking over his whole life brought back to him that it wasn't the first time he had been down and had had to fight to get back on his feet again. Val had helped him back up when he was young and needed it most. He had a duty to her to get up again this time. He felt his life was not entirely his own, but partly belonged to those who had helped him survive. This was the mood he was in when on Friday he received a letter from Ekaterina, telling him she was coming to visit him the next day. He was astonished by it and also puzzled. Her statement: "I am your fiancée after all" made his heart leap, because he thought she was a cracking-looking girl. But why would she say that when they hadn't had more than a few minutes' awkward conversation? He guessed she had written it with the prison authorities in mind. Perhaps she assumed they would read all the letters he got, and she wanted to change their view of him. He was touched by her concern, impressed by her intelligence, and eager to find out what she really felt about him when she came to visit. He couldn't wait for the next day.

17

On Saturday morning at seven o'clock Ekaterina went to Bark Place wearing Olga's sexy outfit and rang the bell of Alena's flat. Alena came down and opened the door for her. She was in her dressing gown but she smiled cheerfully and kissed her cheeks and led her back upstairs. She set to work at once putting on her make-up and gave her hair a brush at the same time.

"I want to make all the other prisoners jealous of Kayley," Ekaterina explained as she sat in front of the mirror. "And I'll kiss him at the end so they'll have to separate us. His status among the prisoners will go up as much as if he'd stabbed someone. No one will believe he's a paedophile after that, no matter what the screws say. It may win him friends and help him survive."

Camilla came out of her bedsit to see her, and brought her a coffee. Alena completed her work and both girls pronounced her perfect.

"You'll knock him dead," Camilla said. "And tell him we'll find him a good lawyer. He mustn't worry." She had topped up Ekaterina's Oyster card, and handed her the day return ticket to Birmingham she had bought on line and a ten-pound note for bus fares and a sandwich. Ekaterina gulped down her coffee, hugged them both and ran downstairs to get to the Tube as she was already late.

She caught the train from Marylebone station and sat in the carriage daydreaming and dozing off. She had looked up buses to the prison on the internet and when she got off the train she found the bus stop without difficulty. When the bus arrived at the prison, a dozen mostly middle-aged women got off in front of her and headed towards the gates. As she stared at the huge, ugly, red brick building, which looked like a Victorian factory, the terror came back to her. She had to force herself to follow the other women towards the entrance. She had tried to prepare herself to deal with her fear and she kept repeating some phrases she had written down and learned by heart, like a sort of litany. "They can't keep me here. I am a visitor. I'm not a prisoner. They can't do anything to me. Camilla knows I'm here. I have to think about Kayley. He's the one who's in danger. I am not."

As they let her in, the guards looked at her with a leering appreciation of her sexy appearance. Their attitude contained a hint of the contempt with which they would have treated a whore. Her state of mind changed as she realized she was not going to be treated as a prisoner but as a sexy woman, with everything that entailed — a bizarre attitude that combined slavering attention, vulgar familiarity and calculated disrespect. Her rising anger at this treatment made her fear drop away. She could never comprehend why so many men despised the female sexiness that turned them on. She wondered if young women would ever be free of this strange contradiction — under pressure to appeal to male appetites while being despised for doing so.

She had to submit to a body search by a female guard, who showed her the same cool contempt as the male guards. All the vile humiliations she had endured for eleven years in prison, with liberties from lesbian guards as well as male guards, and insistent advances from lesbian prisoners, came back to her. But now she felt not despair and helpless anger but burning resentment. It made her all the more determined to help Kayley avoid even worse treatment. A dog was brought in to sniff her for drugs, and she had that old feeling that even the dumb animals had been turned against her. She had to show her passport, and then empty her pockets, leaving even her lipstick, her money purse and her return train ticket in a locker. Her hand was stamped on the back with some invisible mark only a machine could read, like a bureaucratic mark of Cain.

She was given a list of rules to read. She glanced at it. It mentioned that a single brief kiss would be allowed between men and women on arrival and departure. Any further kissing or touching was forbidden. No hand holding or passing of objects or papers was allowed. They were to stay strictly on opposite sides of the table and keep both hands on it at all times.

She was escorted into a long room like a hall. Against the long walls were rows of small tables with plastic chairs on either side of them. The prisoners were sitting on the near side of the tables and the visitors, mostly women and a few children and men, were sitting on the far side. Guards walked up and down the middle of the room. She was led to a vacant table and made to sit down on the chair against the wall, in front of a number. Heads turned to stare at her. A few minutes later, Kayley was brought to her table by a guard. He was limping.

She stood up and leaned forward across the table to hold his shoulders and kiss him. He looked a bit taken aback but responded to her brief kiss on the lips.

"Thanks for coming," he murmured. "It's really nice of you."

He looked subdued as he sat down. Ekaterina thought he had aged five years since the week before. He also looked smaller because she was now in high heels. His curly hair was unkempt. His face was drawn as if he hadn't slept, and he had dark purple bruising round the eyes, one of which was swollen and almost closed. Her own fear left her completely and was replaced by fear for him.

"Are you OK?" she asked.

"So so," he said. Then, as if unsure whether she had understood the expression, he added: "I'm surviving, but only just. I can't go out of my cell."

"Who did that to you?" She looked with concern at his bruised face.

"The other prisoners. They think I'm a paedophile."

"Listen, that's why I came here alone, without my friends." She began to talk quickly, as if it was urgent. "Camilla is going to find you a lawyer. But what's important is what happens to you in here right now. We have to act as if I'm your girlfriend, OK? It'll change their view of you. I've been in prison, I couldn't tell you in my letter. I was in for eleven years. That's how I lost my son. I know how it works in here. At the end of this visit when I stand up to go, I want you to kiss me really hard and long on the lips till they run up and separate us. I'll make a scene and yell at them. It may cost you your TV for a week but it'll be noticed by everyone and word will get around. You have a girlfriend. They'll stop thinking you're a nonce. It'll make your life easier."

He stared at her in astonishment and stammered a reply.

"That's really, incredibly — I mean, I don't know what to say. We hardly know each other."

"Let's just say you reminded me of someone."

"Who?"

She blushed and looked down. She thought of the prince on the painted egg.

"Me. I was once just like you. I was also locked up in a horrible place like this, afraid of what would happen to me. I was twenty. I hardly spoke English. I had to fight to survive. I want to help you to survive. You've got to fight. Mentally. Don't let them get you down. Don't let them make you think life is not worth living, why bother, why not just die? People are so horrible why not just check out? People are not horrible. Only these people are horrible." She gestured at the room. "Life is worth living. You've got to hold on to that idea."

"So, why did they put you in prison?"

"A man raped me. And I killed him." She explained the circumstances.

"They shouldn't have locked you up. They should have given you a medal."

"The law is a machine. It doesn't care about individual people. They didn't even believe I was raped, because I couldn't prove it. They are arseholes. But even if they wrongly convict you, you still have to believe it is worth surviving the sentence so you can live happily afterwards and make up for the lost time. You can still be happy. That's the best revenge."

"Are you happy?" It wasn't a challenge; he really wanted to know.

"I'm just beginning. I've only been outside for a few weeks."

"And how has it been for you?" He was concerned about her and how she was coping after so long inside, and for a moment he forgot about his own situation.

"It was hard at first. I tried to find my son. I was alone. Until I found my friends that you saw the other day. They help me. And when you get out, I'll be here for you. However long it is. I'll help you. It's the people that care about you that matter. When nobody cares about you and the whole system is trying to destroy you, you want to die. But when you find people who care about you, you want to live again. Believe me, you will. You really will."

He didn't know what to say. Her green eyes were so beautiful it hurt to look at them. She had touched a raw nerve and he was afraid he was going to go to pieces. He looked down, afraid to look at her in case he cracked and started crying in front of everyone. That would be the end. His right hand on the table closed into a fist.

"You have to always think about people who are worse off than you," she went on, trying to find something to say. She could see the state he was in and wanted desperately to distract him. She wanted to reach out and squeeze his hand but she knew she would be thrown out for it. Then she thought of a subject, and began talking earnestly and quickly.

"When I was in prison I thought every day of the children who disappeared from my class when I was five. In Ukraine, in Lviv, before 1991 the communist teachers used to ask the five-year olds if they had been to mass that Sunday, meaning in secret since the churches were all closed. There was always one child who answered yes. Then they would make a fuss of that one and give him stars in his book and praise him, until other children thought it must be all right and admitted it too. I never did, I had been too well trained by my parents. And a few weeks later the parents of those kids who said they had been to mass would lose their jobs, and then their ration cards, and then their apartments, and if no relatives could take them in they would be out on the street and would be arrested as anti-social elements and sent to a re-education camp. And the children would disappear from class as they were sent to an orphanage in another town, and they never saw their parents again." She paused. Her voice began to tremble with anger. "I imagine the communist teachers felt really proud of themselves that they were stamping out Christian superstition. What they really wanted was to destroy the family. The love and trust between parents and children, and between husbands and wives. Because that's something stronger than communism. How I hated those teachers! And they were never put on trial after communism fell. It was all blamed on the Russians and the Soviet Union and they pretended suddenly to be nationalists, who were against the regime all along." She looked down at her hands, which she had been twisting and turning on the table. "That is what I thought of to get me through the bad days. How much worse some people's lives are. And how much worse some systems are." She looked up again, afraid she had got carried away with her own memories and struck the wrong note. "But I don't want to depress you, I want you to think also of good things, how wonderful life can be when all this is over, what possibilities the future holds if only you make it through the bad times. It's like when you're sick." She seized on the image eagerly. "You can't believe you will ever feel well again. But you do. Life can suddenly be full of fantastic possibilities again."

He had been staring at her beautiful, slim, white fingers which she was massaging nervously and now he looked up at her face again and their eyes met. The atmosphere changed abruptly between them. They were staring into each other's eyes and he felt he was falling into a well. The room around him seemed to recede into a distant background blur and all he saw was her face and her incredible green eyes, which seemed to shine like emeralds, with a glint of tears in them. She was the most beautiful woman he had ever seen.

"You look fabulous today," he heard himself say. "They'll all be mad with jealousy."

"That's what I want," she said. "If they're jealous of you, they won't despise you."

"You're really kind and intelligent as well as beautiful."

"I want to make you feel you're the luckiest man in the world, not the unluckiest. Can I do that?"

"You can. If you mean it."

"I mean it. And you? Do you have a girlfriend?"

"No. I split up with my girlfriend before I came to this city. In fact with two," he added.

"With two?" She grinned for a second. "And your family?"

"My father is dead. My mother and I don't talk any more. She ruined my life."

"Then I'm all you have?" She sounded not so much sad as hopeful. "I'm glad. You're all I have as well. I came here from Ukraine to a strange country where I thought I could be happy and they locked me up before I could even get to know it. When you get out, promise you will take me everywhere, take me to York and Cambridge and Oxford. I have heard of somewhere called the Cotswolds, I don't know where it is but they say it is beautiful. And somewhere called the Lake District where famous romantic poets lived. Promise you will take me to those places. Promise you won't die before you do because then I will have no one to take me and I hate to travel alone. I want you to think to yourself every time you feel bad that you have to take me to the Lake District. You have to live and take me to the Lake District. Repeat that to me now."

"I have to live and take you to the Lake District."

"That is a promise and you have to keep it now, or I will feel you didn't appreciate me coming here, you don't appreciate my friendship, or anything I feel for you."

"Of course I do, I really appreciate you coming."

"And you care about me, as much as I care about you?"

"Do you really care about me or are you just feeling sorry for me?"

She looked suddenly at a loss and her voice changed and began to tremble.

"Kayley, you are a charming and beautiful man, and when I was young you were exactly the man I would have fallen in love with. And I know you would have loved me too. And I just hope that now I'm a lot older and I don't look so good —"

"You look fantastic!" he interrupted. He reached across and grabbed her hand. "You're the most beautiful woman I've ever been this close to."

A guard came down the hall and put a truncheon firmly on Kayley's shoulder.

"Do you mind letting go of her hand? That's against the rules."

"We love each other, surely we can hold hands!" said Ekaterina loudly and angrily.

The whole hall fell silent and heads turned to stare at her.

"There are rules, madam," said the guard, on the defensive.

"How dare you stop me touching my fiancé!" she shouted. "I love him and he loves me! And if we want to kiss as well, we will!"

She leaned forward and grabbed Kayley and kissed him impulsively on the lips. He remembered what she had said earlier and half rose to meet her half-way in the kiss. She slid round the table so they could embrace fully with bodies pressed against each other and they kissed passionately. It was a moment of paradise for him which he dimly perceived would be followed by hellfire. The guard was too taken aback to move for several seconds. It was only when there was a burst of cheering from other prisoners that he sprang to life and tried to pull them apart.

"That's against the rules! That's against the rules!" he shouted, pulling at them.

"Fuck your fascist rules!" shouted Ekaterina, fending him off like a rugby player, and she kissed Kayley again. She was a tall girl and stronger than her slim figure suggested, and the guard, who was fifty and rather thin, was pushed off balance and stumbled back.

Two more guards rushed to his aid and now a truncheon came out and hit Kayley on the back of the head.

"Fascist scum! Murderers!" shouted Ekaterina, clinging to Kayley as he went limp in her arms.

"Now, Madam, you'll have to leave!" said one of the guards and took her roughly by the arm. The other two dragged Kayley away from her and supported his unconscious body as Ekaterina was escorted out without ceremony. Then they half-carried, half-dragged the limp Kayley towards the other door at the opposite end of the hall. Most of the other prisoners were on their feet watching the scene with open mouths. Ekaterina got in one more parting shot. As she reached the doorway she twisted around, despite her captor's grip, and yelled the length of the hall towards the guards holding Kayley.

"If you touch him again, we'll sue you for assault as well as false imprisonment!" Her voice filled the room. "He's been framed, you bastards, and we're going to sue the lot of you!" A burst of applause came from some of the prisoners, as if she had just sung an aria. The guards looked daggers at them and moved to clear the hall.

The next day Kayley woke up to banging on the door of his cell. His head was aching. He sat up. The small trapdoor in his cell door was open and there was a face framed in it.

"Hey, mate, come out and get some breakfast with us," called a rough voice he had never heard. "We'll escort you to the food place. Don't worry, nobody will hurt you. You've had a raw deal."

It was not a guard but a prisoner. The cells were unlocked in the morning for the prisoners to go and get their breakfast from the food servery, but he had stopped going after the attacks the first day. He sat on the side of the bunk and pulled on his uniform trousers.

"Come on, mate, we've heard you're not a nonce after all. And everyone's impressed by that chick of yours. Come with us. We'll look after you."

"I'll just get dressed," he said. He put on his uniform shirt and the cheap slip-on sneakers they had to wear. Then he opened the cell door and went out. There were two men outside, older prisoners who were serving sentences, not on remand. They shook his hand.

"Don't worry, you won't have any trouble now," said one, a giant of a Yorkshireman with a boxer's face and a broken nose. "The fucking screws put everyone wrong about you."

Kayley walked along the corridor with the two men on either side of him. Men called out of the open doors of cells.

"Hey, is that the bloke with the Russian bird? Some bird, mate! What a cracker! And full of guts. She told those fucking screws!"

"Hey, what's she like in bed, man?"

"She's terrific," he said.

Kayley got his breakfast hot for the first time, ordering what he wanted, and took it back to his cell, still under escort.

"If you want to get some exercise in the yard later, Kayley, we'll come along to get you," said the big man, and they walked away.

Later when he went with them to the exercise yard, other prisoners came up and shook his hand and slapped him on the back. It did not matter that the guards disconnected his tiny television for a week, as Ekaterina had predicted. At last the prison was a place he could move in and live in normally. The dull terror that had filled him for days gradually fell away.

Ekaterina was not allowed to come and see him for three weeks as punishment for her behaviour but she wrote letters. Every day a letter came. They were handwritten on pink paper and smelled of perfume. Some had photos of her printed on ordinary paper, which he put on his wall. The letters talked about her childhood in Ukraine in a village by a river, about her grey cat, Mishi, who followed her everywhere, about their move to the city and her years at college, the mother who died, the father who married again, and her decision to leave and seek her fortune in the West by meeting a man on the internet. And they were full of words of love as if all she had wanted to say to a lover for eleven years was coming out all at once. She told him of her dreams, of the life she wanted to live. "I want to have children," she wrote, "because children are the only innocent thing in the world. And I know you love children because you look after them. I am sure you will be a wonderful father."

He sat and read the letters in disbelief, shaking with excitement. She loved him, this stunning, intelligent, brave, generous, caring woman loved him. He kept thinking: "She must be putting on an act, just to make me feel good, to stop me getting depressed. It's a ploy, maybe when I get out she'll explain she wrote all this to save my life, it's not for real." And then he read and reread the letters, and he said: it must be for real. As if lightning had struck twice in the same place, he had found the love of his life.

18

When Ekaterina came back from her visit to the prison, Camilla was eager to find out what had happened. So were Olga and Alena. They had dinner together, this time in Camilla's bedsit, and Ekaterina recounted events, though in a matter-of-fact way. She said that everything had gone as planned, she had kissed Kayley and made a scandal, and the guards had hit him and dragged him away. Then she just shrugged and smiled mysteriously. After she had gone home to her shelter, the other girls talked about her and agreed she was not revealing the full significance of what had happened.

"She's in love!" declared Alena. "But she doesn't want to say it in case it doesn't work out. Did you notice her eyes? They always glowed a bit like opals but now they're on fire."

Ekaterina began cleaning for Mrs Konstantinou and one of her neighbours and for the first time she had some pocket money. Olga wouldn't hear of her giving her clothes back since she would need them again for her next visit to the prison but the two girls took her shopping and helped her buy some things of her own.

"After eleven years out of the fashion world you need to learn again what to wear," said Olga. "And it doesn't have to be expensive."

Gone were the old clothes picked up in a second hand market. New blouses, T-shirts and sweaters replaced them. In Olga's wardrobe they found her some trendy, faded jeans that fit her perfectly, which Olga claimed she no longer wore. Alena insisted on giving her a range of make-up products, which she said she got for free from her beauty salon.

Camilla watched the metamorphosis of Ekaterina the way one watches a peach tree blossom again after a hard winter. Ekaterina seemed full of energy. She insisted Camilla take her to a lawyers' association to get free advice about getting a lawyer for Kayley and about how legal aid worked. Camilla could feel that she was ready to spend her life working to pay for the best defence counsel in the country, but the lawyers' association assured them Kayley would be able to get legal aid, and put them on to a law firm in Birmingham.

Ekaterina spent more and more time at Bark Place, mostly in Camilla's bedsit, using her computer to look for a job on the internet. She was keen to find a part-time job in a local café or shop, and also a longer term one in a social service or association, where she could put her languages to use. She wrote several letters of application and got Camilla to check her English. She was now able to afford a small, prepaid mobile phone, not a smartphone (she couldn't understand them or afford one) but a tiny, old-fashioned one, and Maeve was able to call her when she needed her help as an interpreter. Camilla watched her rebuilding her life with a happy feeling that things were finally looking up for someone who was kind and good-hearted, even if a bit naive, and had not deserved the horrors she had gone through. She was amazed how many letters Ekaterina wrote to Kayley, enclosing photos she asked Camilla to take of her with her smartphone. Camilla marvelled at how love-struck she was and how completely she placed her faith in the future happiness she imagined for herself with Kayley. It seemed incredible that all the violent and depressing things Ekaterina had gone through had not dampened her faith in this simple happiness of true love that she envisioned. Deep down, thought Camilla, she was still a little girl in blonde plaits from a Ukrainian village dreaming of her prince. As she saw her friend doing everything in her power to make her dreams come true, Camilla began to think about her own life and whether it was time she overcame whatever it was that seemed to stand in the way of her finding happiness as well.

Camilla had not told Romain everything about her relationship with her step-father or the effect it had had on her life. But telling what she did made her think back over the whole affair and everything that had followed. She had been at Saint Odile's College for Girls for nearly a year when she received the news of Brendan's death. There was no question of going to a funeral service because they had already cremated him by the time she received the letter from the prison director, which was sent on by her mother with a note of particular coldness. She did receive a visit from the lawyer who had defended Brendan at his trial. He explained the circumstances of his death, how Brendan had been found hanged, but with marks of a severe beating. He felt she ought to know that this was almost certainly not suicide, despite the official verdict, so she should not blame herself in any way. He seemed to want to spare her the worst details, but this only made her imagination run wild. She had no doubt the prison guards had connived in his regular beating by other prisoners, and perhaps worse.

On his visit the lawyer also briefed the Mother Superior about Brendan's death in prison. The grand old lady, whose role was now largely honorific, was one of only four nuns left in the school. She bore the name and much of the aura of the intellectual French nun, Sister Marie-Clotilde, who had founded the school over two hundred years before, as a refugee from the Revolutionary Terror, which had put an end to the tradition of English girls from old, aristocratic Catholic families being sent to France for a classical education. Their order found its inspiration in the seventh century's Saint Odile. Her life was a saga held up to the girls as an example of perseverance in adversity. Odile was born blind, was condemned to death by her father, the Duke of Alsace, was smuggled away by her mother, had her sight miraculously restored, was brought home by her brother, who was killed by their enraged father, before he repented and allowed his daughter to found a monastery, which became famous for its charity and good works. The Mother Superior swept into Camilla's classroom (an exceptional event) wearing her full regalia. She announced to the astonished class (in the Welsh lilt that had never left her, despite her many years in Ireland and England) that Camilla's step-father had died in tragic circumstances.

"We must respect her grief, show her understanding, and pray for her over the coming days and weeks," she told them quietly. "Our faith teaches us to show special care for those who are suffering pain and heartbreak at a difficult moment in their life. The road of life is hard and each of us will be tested at some point along it. It is only in the support that we give others in their time of trial that we will find strength to face our own. When our darkest hour arrives, we ourselves will pass judgment on how we behaved to others during their ordeal. Let us not give ourselves cause to condemn ourselves and bitterly regret what we did or failed to do."

Most of Camilla's fellow-pupils dutifully complied with these solemn injunctions. When she sat alone at break or after class one or two girls came and sat beside her in silence, making a show of tactful support. Whenever she cried or began shaking uncontrollably, her best friend (a Russian girl from a rich family) put her arms round her and held her tight, murmuring softly in her own language. When two older girls from other classes came up to her and probed for information: "Is it true he was sent to jail for abusing you?" or more brutally: "Was he your lover?" her classmates drove them away indignantly. A short-lived attempt by some malicious girls to spread stories about Camilla and her step-father ended badly for the girls concerned. Their mobile phones and computers were mysteriously sabotaged, and their beds were filled with dead rodents (the young caretaker in charge of mousetraps was often seen in the company of an eccentric Russian girl known as the Rat Lady.) Camilla's teachers were respectful of her grief and treated her very kindly over the following weeks. This publicly acknowledged trauma set her apart from the other pupils and it was more than a year before her special status as a tragic victim was forgotten.

She reflected later that going to an all-girls school had taken away the burden of dealing with sexual relationships till she was much more mature and able to handle them. But the absence of any flirtations with boys left her entirely at the mercy of her memories of her love affair with Brendan. There were no romantic events in her life that might have eclipsed those burning recollections. She spent her holidays at Brendan's mother's place in Ireland, a suburban house in Wexford, where she met no boys, or at the country estate of her Russian friend, where they rode horses or went fishing in the river, with only servants for company. In her final year they had some school dances with a Catholic boys' school and she felt a little awkward holding a boy and also surprised that she was besieged for dances. She had paid little attention to her own looks and tended to be sceptical when they told her she was beautiful. She had developed into an intellectual who was less interested in teen magazines about fashion than she was in Hume's sceptical essay on miracles or Kierkegaard's *The Concept of Despair*, which her Religious Studies teacher had lent her when she detected in her a philosophical bent. Shortly after Brendan's death her English teacher had set the class an essay on love in *Wuthering Heights*. In class discussions this teacher pointed out how love, when it is against the rules of society and must be kept secret, can become a fatal obsession. She argued that when Catherine says "I am Heathcliff" she is denying his separate identity, his separate feelings, and treating him as a slave or a possession. To identify totally with the other, she claimed, is to deny the other. Camilla suspected all this was intended for her, to make her think about her own experience intellectually. Her teacher, a fervent Aristotelian, to whom schoolgirl gossip imputed a tragic love affair, told her as much after class one day: "Camilla, when you feel too much, the only remedy is to think."

The closest Camilla came to happy depictions of love was reading Shakespeare's love comedies, which she saw as taking place in an ethereal realm far removed from the crass, vulgar modern world. In her last year, her English teacher gave them T.S. Eliot's *The Waste Land*, and stressed its contrast between a coarse, degenerate modern age and the elegance, refined sentiments and intense passions of a bygone era. In short, Camilla spent her college years in a kind of time warp, at a distance from her own age, in the company of the great minds and great works of literature of the past. It made her despise the real world of her time as a mediocre, grey iron age, which had drastically declined from a far-off golden age that had gone before. And unconsciously the golden age of the past was associated in her mind with the radiant light of that early adolescent springtime where she had found true love, a magical romance with an exceptional being — a world destroyed forever by the harsh reality of narrow minds, vile souls, and brutal, murderous beasts.

When she went to Oxford it was at first a continuation of her sheltered, scholarly existence as she immersed herself in the infinite ocean of human knowledge. She opted for a combined English and History degree, with a vague idea of some sort of career in journalism or writing. She joined one or two clubs, including a yoga club, and became a yoga enthusiast. She also joined a feminist group out of a vague yearning for political activism to defend the rights of the oppressed around the world. At their meetings she got to know three lively, rather boisterous girls who shared a flat in town, and led a freer lifestyle than was possible in her college residence. She was a little surprised that the parties they invited her to seemed to be nearly all girls, but she assumed that sooner or later they would get together with a boys' group and have mixed outings. One night at one of their parties she smoked hashish for only the second time and drank vodka and woke up on a bed half-undressed to find one of the girls on top of her kissing her. She uttered a kind of animal yell and fought her off and leapt off the bed. She got dressed in shock and fury, choking on tears as she searched for her clothes, while the other girl laughed at her sarcastically from the bed and told her to grow up.

"It's about time you understood what you are and why you've been hanging around with us all this time."

Camilla was shaken by the episode and withdrew into herself. Then she began to realize that other students assumed she was a lesbian because she had been friends with those girls, and nobody had bothered to tell her who they were or what was going on. How was she supposed to know? She had noticed girls kissing at their parties two or three times, but thought she had to be tolerant, and never dreamed they were all that way inclined. She felt betrayed and became suspicious of other girls from then on. She thought she should try to find a boyfriend and started going to a popular student pub frequented by some of her classmates. But she felt that the tipsy young male students who began trying to paw her were rather like dogs she had to keep pushing away. She liked them but had no wish to have their tongues all over her. One night after a bit too much to drink at a post-pub party, she went as far as going home with one of them and then ended up begging him not to do anything and slept on his sofa. Her reputation for lesbianism soon gave way to one for frigidity. She was bewildered and angry with herself that she couldn't find a boyfriend. But those unattached males whose looks she liked the most had an attitude to sex that seemed to her so crude, so obsessed with competing to notch up conquests and then brag about them, that it put her off completely. There was no one she found attractive whom she could trust with the stark emotional exposure of herself that for her went along with making love.

It was not until she was twenty that she began to feel a certain affinity, at first an intellectual complicity, and then a degree of personal warmth for her tutor, Miles, who was nine years older than her. He was a slim, boyish figure with a mischievous grin, and he treated her with a humorous, ironical flirtatiousness, while evincing a profound respect for her intellect. Out of professional scruples he waited till he was no longer her tutor before inviting her to see a play with him and then to a weekend at Stratford-upon-Avon. There, after a performance of *The Tempest*, she finally succumbed to his advances in an attic room overlooking the river.

She was astonished at the banality of proceedings and how utterly unaffected she was by all of it. She recalled Brendan's touch as having been electric. This experience made her think of Oscar Wilde's phrase "cold mutton." She became slightly depressed that her precocious encounter with the pleasures of sex as an overwhelming revelation had spoiled her so completely for any enjoyment of it now. But she didn't give up: she thought that a closer emotional bond might be necessary to make her feel anything. She tried to explain her state of mind to her lover and told him about her affair with Brendan and its disturbing effects on her. Miles at once began to treat her as a convalescent emotional invalid who needed time to get over the trauma of abuse and learn to like normal sex. He tried to provide the soothing potion in anodyne, homeopathic doses, but it remained for her something oddly therapeutic, like medicine she had to take for health reasons. She lay awake at night and wondered bitterly why the most wonderful experience on earth had utterly ruined her capacity to enjoy the most wonderful experience on earth. Did intense love at an early age burn itself into the soul like a brand that could never be removed? Would she be forever in mourning for her lost lover?

The affair with Miles finally petered out in long midnight emails of explanation, self-justification and amateur psychoanalysis. He concluded that their tutor-student relationship, clandestine as it had to be, was too reminiscent of the forbidden relationship she had had with her step-father. He was, he speculated, a substitute for Brendan, and she had been driven to this affair as a means of reliving her former experience. But this new forbidden relationship now blocked her libido instead of releasing it — which was, he pointed out, in fact a positive step on her road to recovery. She found these abstruse discussions tedious and concluded privately that he simply didn't turn her on. She resolved never to attempt this sort of therapy with a man again by letting him know her story. After she broke up with Miles, she turned her back on intellectual infatuations and thought she should just go for physical attraction and try to cultivate a taste for pleasure. She went through a period of partying, since she now had a lot more friends to go to pubs and parties with. She drank more, smoked a little dope and allowed herself to be bedded by a succession of eager young men. She usually woke up feeling disgusted with herself and her partner and began seriously wondering if she was frigid.

She expressed her disappointment by breaking off with these casual lovers at once, even though most of them were keen to see her again. Her old fear that they would treat her as a conquest to brag about made her more callous at these moments than she approved of afterwards, and she even caught herself enjoying the minor heartbreaks she inflicted. It was as if she had to get in first and be the one who rejects the other, in order to avoid feeling rejected or demeaned herself. She knew after the first night that this person was not going to be able to understand or salve the deep wound inside her, and she didn't want the empty ache of waiting for emotions she was not going to get. Despite her sybaritic intentions she knew that sex alone was not going to satisfy her while this wound remained unhealed. After enduring some angry recriminations from jilted lovers, she became afraid she was turning into a cold, unfeeling ice-maiden. She gave up sex for long periods, and succumbed only occasionally as a kind of relapse, like a drug addict in the process of withdrawal.

And she knew that, like a heroin addict, her problem was her perpetual disappointment that the new fix never came anywhere near the paradisiac experience of the first one. Every new affair was embarked on in the hope of reliving that first high, and came to an end abruptly when the hope died.

She wrote her autobiographical novel about her relationship with Brendan as a kind of therapy. But the therapy was incomplete because it lacked an essential element: publication. That would have made her see her own account of the affair more objectively, would have made her defend it publicly, explain it, analyse it, and perhaps finally detach herself from it. Instead, rejection by every agent (publishers smugly announced on their websites that they no longer read manuscripts that didn't come from agents) simply led to her own rejection of the world. One agent told her that it would be impossible to publish a novel about a genuine love affair between a fourteen-year old girl and her step-father — that was not the way public opinion on paedophilia was moving. The man could only be presented as an evil predator and the girl as his naive prey — anything else would be seen as a shocking justification of child abuse. It was also unacceptable to have a Serb as heroine, seen as a victim of NATO's bombing, as this went directly against the established political narrative and would insult the memory of the many real victims of Serb atrocities. She reacted with scorn to the intolerance, the blinkered conformism, the ideological totalitarianism of the new age, where dominant political opinion dictated what could be published and what couldn't. In the end she self-published the novel and it sat unsold on Amazon and she was able to forget about it. Since she never got any feedback from readers (one e-book version was sold in six years) she was never forced to rethink the affair in the light of how others perceived it. She kept the vision intact of the romantic idyll destroyed by the vicious bigotry of the world.

The failure of her novel to find a publisher or any readers reinforced a gloomy conviction that she and the world were not made to get along. She would never be understood, and the horrific thing that had been done to two innocent lovers would never be acknowledged or condemned. Despite the distraction of writing her novel, she obtained a first class honours degree, and naively assumed it would open career doors. She applied for jobs on national newspapers, but was soon told they required a degree in journalism, and all she managed to obtain was short-term, unpaid work experience. She tried publishing houses and at last got a low-paid traineeship in a firm in London. She was happy to move back there but she had to take on tutoring work as well to make ends meet. Meanwhile she tried to sell articles to newspapers on a freelance basis. However, the left-leaning papers were hard to crack because she did not share the left-wing intelligentsia's self-righteous, politically correct view of the world. On the other hand, her attitudes to social injustice, a warmongering foreign policy, and the obscene rule of money did not endear her to the right-wing press either. She soon found she could only sell articles that kept well away from anything even vaguely political.

Her inability to find an ideological home was what finally led her to start her own blog. Her alienation from the thinking of the age led her to try to find inner peace through practising yoga more intensively, and she was soon advanced enough to become a part-time teacher at the club she went to in Notting Hill. Two of the women she got to know there were social workers in an association dealing with domestic violence. She became interested in their work. Despite her lack of qualifications in the field, she began to feel the most useful thing she could do with her life was to help victims of various forms of sexual violence or abuse. Through her new contacts she started working as a volunteer in battered women's shelters, and for a while in a battered men's advice centre before it closed for lack of funding. She worked with girls who had been forced into prostitution and escaped, helping their efforts to prosecute the gangsters who had enslaved them. She used her blog to describe these struggles and also to denounce the scandalously short prison sentences these brutal, professional slave-traffickers received (often no longer than the sentences of "date rapists", men who claimed that a girl on a date had consented while she later claimed she had been too drunk.) These short sentences for gangsters (who had committed or organized hundreds of rapes, beatings, sequestrations, and acts of torture) exposed their former slaves to horrific retaliation, and deterred many from testifying. Yet Camilla found herself almost alone in her campaign of protest. Most feminist groups ignored the lenient treatment of violent gangs of women-traffickers (often Eastern Europeans or Africans) just as they ignored the lenient prison sentences (often only four years) given to the brutal Pakistani gangs who raped and enslaved thousands of thirteen year-old white girls from Rochdale to Derby. Instead the feminists organized social media lynch-mobs against non-violent, white English "date rapists" (sometimes men who had been framed by a spiteful one-night stand) to ensure they could never work again after coming out of prison. The feminists, she concluded, campaigned against rape only in order to vilify white Englishmen, whom they saw as the "patriarchy". They were largely indifferent to the many far more violent acts of rape (including child rape) committed by foreign gangsters and non-white immigrants, because the Marxist-feminist ideology saw these latter groups as "fellow victims" of Western men.

Getting to know the milieu of prostitution then led her, paradoxically, to support the struggle of the self-employed majority of sex-workers against attempts to equate their whole trade with trafficking and sex slavery. These women were now the targets of a hysterical campaign against them by feminist organizations bent on banning their profession. The radical feminists, buoyed by the success of their decades-long campaign to destroy marriage and brainwash women against it, were now determined to stop the wretched casualties of that destruction — the millions of divorced, solitary older men — from ever knowing any kind of solace in a woman's arms. The only form of sex the lonely older men were to be allowed from now on was masturbation to the sordid pornography of the internet. If they were ready to pay for the company and sexual favours of a flesh-and-blood woman once or twice a year they were now to be arrested as common criminals or "sex addicts". One prostitute told her: "The feminists want revenge on men by eliminating us." She recounted how colleagues in Scandinavia, who lived under a regime of criminalization of the customer, told her how they had lost all their normal, law-abiding, older clients and were forced to take on criminals and dangerous perverts to survive. And how, despite feminist promises not to criminalize prostitutes, the police harassed them as the instigators of crime or pressured them to entrap and betray their clients. And all of this masqueraded as a struggle against the "trafficking of women" — a real and growing crime, but one which the radical feminists had done nothing whatsoever to combat, and which had nothing to do with the vast majority of sex-workers.

In whatever field Camilla worked to help women victims of violence or abuse, she found herself coming into conflict with the feminist movement, which was trying to exploit the issue for its own purpose — the spread of a cult of hatred of men. She had first been made aware of this by Maeve, one of the pioneers of the combat against domestic violence. Maeve had been the victim of a violent mother, who had assaulted and terrorized Maeve's father as well as the children, so she vigorously opposed the feminists trying to use the issue as proof of the inherent evil and violence of men. Maeve told her how the feminists had vehemently denied for decades that men could also be the victims of domestic violence at the hands of women, and had campaigned to stop male victims getting any help and to have them treated as perpetrators. Camilla came to see the feminist movement as rather like the communist movement in its heyday in the West — denouncing evils not in order to put an end to them, but in order to incite hatred and social division. The radical feminists, she believed, aimed to destroy the family just as the communists aimed to destroy private enterprise. The communists wanted enterprises without entrepreneurs, and the feminists wanted families without fathers. The war against "patriarchy" was a war against fatherhood. Camilla in her blog denounced the blindness of the political and intellectual class in supporting the radical feminist struggle against "patriarchy" — a concept developed by Engels and imbued with all the hate-filled Marxist rhetoric of an endless war against an evil oppressor group.

Her blog articles provoked a violent controversy with feminist bloggers and forced her to define her views more precisely. Of course, she explained, she supported the struggle for equal pay and equal access to all jobs on merit, after the long exclusion of women from most economic and political roles. But she denounced the dishonesty of many feminist campaigns — notably the claim there was a 19 per cent gender pay gap. This, she said, was a carefully constructed statistical lie, arrived at by lumping part-time and fulltime wages together.

If fulltime wages alone were compared, British women earned 10 per cent less than men, but also worked 10 per cent fewer hours, 40 a week as against 44 for men. If part-time hourly wages were compared, she pointed out, women earned 5 per cent *more* than men. The fact that over forty per cent of women worked part-time (which was paid less per hour than fulltime work) was treated by feminists as wicked oppression, as if their choice to spend more time with their children couldn't possibly be a free one. But to regard men as tyrants for supporting their wives by working longer hours was both perverse and a denial of the freedom of couples to choose their own division of roles. Camilla argued it was also dishonest to see the pay gap between kindergarten teachers and engineers as a gender pay gap. Women were not excluded from engineering, and if far more of them chose lower-paid caring professions with shorter hours, that was again a personal choice, often linked to their mother role and their husband's willingness to support them in it. The feminists' denial of a wife's (or a husband's) right to play a greater role in child-raising while her partner worked more and paid more of the bills, their stigmatization of this choice by women as slavery, their virulent campaigns against non-existent injustices constantly stoked a confused sense of female victimhood and sabotaged relations within marriage. It was this feminist victim culture, she argued, that was breaking up marriages and families by recasting every marital dispute as a revolt of the oppressed (seventy per cent of divorces were initiated by women.) In her view, the feminist movement, like Marxism, was committed to perpetual civil war and would not accept peace on any terms, because at bottom it rejected heterosexual relations.

Camilla's critique of feminism was also that of a history graduate. She condemned its distortion of history, based as it was on the fantasized myth of the matriarchy, dreamed up by Engels. The reality, she pointed out, was that most matriarchal (or more correctly, matrilineal) societies were (and still are, since many still exist in Asia and Africa) subsistence horticultural economies where women cultivated the land, using the hoe or digging stick. This meant daughters, being the main food providers, were kept at home and inherited the farm, while sons were cast out into the world, wandering abroad, trading, plundering, warring and philandering, and taking no responsibility for their children, who were raised by their girlfriend's family. The change to a patrilineal system resulted from advances in farming (use of the heavy ox-drawn plough and cattle raising) which required male strength and suddenly made men the key food providers. Sons were then kept at home by ageing parents and inherited the farm while daughters were given in marriage to other households. This change of systems, argued Camilla, was not a male seizure of power, as Engels and feminist mythology fantasized, but a social evolution in response to technological advances. Since these new farming techniques enabled a man to trade surplus food and acquire wealth, it was in his wife's interest (and her parents' interest) to change the inheritance system so that the man's wealth would go to his own children instead of his sister's children (as in the matrilineal system, where his wealth remained in his mother's clan.) This required a closer, more faithful marriage bond that would persuade a man to invest in his wife's children, confident they were also his, as opposed to the casual, irresponsible sex of matriarchy.

Whatever the gender inequalities this patriarchal system led to in various ages and cultures, Camilla argued, it is the basis of the human family — the principle of the investment of the father as well as the mother in the raising of their joint children. To destroy patriarchy is to destroy the family. The feminist attack on extreme forms of patriarchy — the man's sense of "ownership" of his wife and children — might be justified in non-Western cultures where these extreme forms still exist. But in the West, where they no longer exist, this continued war on patriarchy is an attack on the man's sense of responsibility for his wife and children — that is to say, fatherhood. The result, she claimed, is what can be seen in black American ghetto culture, the closest thing to matriarchy in the modern world. In that culture most men do not marry, and do not live with or support their children, who are brought up solely by women at the expense of the state. This backward, failed, crime-ridden culture, said Camilla, is the crazed matriarchal ideal that feminism is working to bring back, and the official promotion of this mad ideology is tearing apart the whole fabric of Western society.

The paradox, she argued, is that the global feminist agenda (pushed by Scandinavian feminists) to impose identical work and child-raising roles on both men and women — condemning any division of roles between them, even for a few years, as "inequality" — is what is straining marriages to breaking point and leading to a fifty per cent divorce rate, so that half of children are now raised in a home without their father. By trying to enforce an unnatural, impractical identity of roles, and constantly inciting a sense of female victimhood, leading to frivolous, mercenary divorces, feminists are destroying marriages and bringing about a de facto matriarchy where half of Western fathers are now excluded from any child-raising role whatsoever (fortnightly visiting rights are not child-raising.) Feminism, Camilla concluded, is the most self-defeating ideology of all time: it proclaims the goal of identical gender roles, and ends up with a far greater difference between gender roles than in the 1950s. She argued that the survival of the family, which feminism is wiping out, is far more important to humanity than the proportion of women directing multinational companies.

These ideas provoked furious attacks on Camilla's blog by the internet trolls of the sisterhood. She tried to get her views published in newspapers, but no editor would accept an anti-feminist article. After a while she simply moved on from this subject to other things. While working with prostitutes she discovered how many of them had suffered sexual abuse as children — to which they sometimes attributed their ability to have sex in a detached, impersonal manner. And this new contact with paedophilia drew her back to her own story like an obsession. She started a new website, *The Paedophile Files*, with the first narratives she collected from sex-workers. She felt that getting to know and help people who had been victims of paedophile abuse might enable her to detach herself from the traumatic events of her own adolescence. By seeing her own experience as exceptional she might learn to live at a distance from it, and finally come to forgive those who had destroyed the love of her life.

Her website led her to pursue an intellectual study of paedophilia as she sought to understand it as a phenomenon. Three years before she met Romain she began to attend the lectures of Professor Peter Rigdon at the Havelock Ellis Institute, which specialized in sexual studies and gave lectures open to the public for a nominal enrolment fee. Rigdon, who had held some high academic posts and been sacked from at least one, had a reputation for contentious, even outrageous views. She was not disappointed. There was one lecture he gave at the end of the series which came close to her own experience and affected her deeply.

Rigdon was a charismatic figure, a vigorous man of about sixty, flamboyant, provocative and never afraid of controversy. He had spoken extensively in previous lectures about paedophilia, homosexuality and sadomasochism. He had also broached the subject of the origin of evil, not as a theological but as a psychological question. This last lecture of the series would, he had promised the week before, make an attempt to draw all these themes together into a unified vision. She went along to hear it with high expectations, which surprised her, given her instinctive scepticism towards gurus of any kind. But his capacity to form an astonishingly connected whole out of disparate parts impressed her. She had a feeling this lecture might have an important effect on her life — that it might open up new horizons, and change her emotional relationship with her own past and with the world.

19

The tall, broad, imposing figure of Rigdon appeared punctually three minutes after Camilla slipped into one of the last free seats at the end of a middle row. He began addressing the rear wall of the auditorium, as was his custom, in a powerful and dramatic voice like that of an orator from another century. He spoke as if he was speaking not for this audience but for the ages. He had a handsome, square-jawed face and a fine head of white hair (with yellowish streaks, like old piano keys) combed back in an impressive mane. He changed his style of clothes and his appearance frequently, and today he looked particularly eccentric. He wore traces of eye shadow which gave him an air somewhere between camp and an old India hand from the hippie era, and he wore a black academic gown over what appeared to be a black cassock, which made him look rather like a Russian priest out of Dostoyevsky. His language was as colourful as his appearance, and his lectures were packed mainly because of the outrageous assertions he enjoyed making. His fans sat expectantly, ready to giggle or laugh uproariously at his more preposterous statements. Many of these faithful followers wore unconventional clothes and hairstyles. Men's ear-rings and piercings abounded, along with tattoos, chains and the odd biker jacket. They seemed to represent a cross section of the more marginal, would-be intellectual elements in society. This unconventional-looking audience, some of whom did not hesitate to heckle other speakers, added to the dramatic atmosphere. Camilla wondered what scandalous pronouncements Rigdon would come out with this time in his ruthless pursuit of what he saw as the truth in the teeth of all pious hypocrisy. She laid her smartphone on the desk and switched on the recording app as he began to speak.

Philosophers have argued for centuries over the origin of evil, but I suggested to you last time its origin is very simple. Evil is merely the natural aggressive response to an injury or a threat, but a response which is disproportionate, misdirected and out of control. There is in an American prison today, serving several life sentences, a man who murdered a series of women and cut out their sexual organs with a razor. This person, from when he was five years old, was used as a sex toy by his mother, who made him perform cunnilingus on her. This fact is not cited to excuse his crimes, but merely to identify their cause. The sexual abuse becomes an obsession. A reflex of violent revulsion is triggered by anyone that calls to mind the perpetrator. Finally, you have the explosion in a series of horrific murders and mutilations of people he didn't even know. It is this disproportionate and misdirected aggressive response to injury that we generally label evil.

A good deal of extreme sexual abuse mimics what was done to the abuser when he was young. It is an attempt to purge the self-hatred caused by the abuse and turn it outwards onto others, who become surrogate objects of revenge. Another American man serving a life sentence for shoving a dildo up a teenage girl's anus was reproducing exactly what was done to him at the age of four by a teenage babysitter — who made fun of his penis and shoved various objects up his anus. There is something about doing the same thing to someone else which seems to relieve trauma, as if one can accept oneself as victim only by acting out the role of the perpetrator — and perhaps identifying with the new victim one creates. One may even guess what abuse a person was subjected to by the acts he carries out in revenge, which are often greatly magnified versions of his own injury. There are reasons to think that Vlad the Impaler, a ruler of Wallachia, now part of Romania, who was pathologically obsessed with impaling his enemies, was raped while a child hostage of the Turks — since impalement is a lethal parody of anal rape. (*There were some guffaws.*) But sometimes an injury gives rise, through the distorting effect of obsession, to a massive project of revenge of a more diffuse and indiscriminate kind. Even Hitler may be seen in this light. His suspicion that his servant grandmother was seduced or raped as a girl by her Jewish employer's son, combined with his youthful indignation at Jewish pimps exploiting poor Austrian country-girls on the streets of Vienna, gave rise to the greatest obsession and programme of mass revenge the world has ever seen. We asked ourselves why this mad, disproportionate reaction of revenge is triggered in some people and not others. And we suggested that injuries of a sexual nature have a greater tendency than others to trigger this magnified aggressive response because they so often become psychotic obsessions. In Hitler's case his alleged single testicle and probable impotence, which (as a fervent Darwinist) he may have blamed on racial hybridization due to the rape of his grandmother, could have fuelled his psychotic rage against the race (and not the religion) which he held responsible.

This led us to examine the close links between the sexual urge and violence. We saw that sexual impulses have no inherent connection with benevolence or affection towards the object of desire. The male sex drive is primarily aggressive, fuelled by the same hormone, testosterone, which drives aggression. The natural outlet of that sex drive is rape. Among animals a great deal of sexual intercourse is indistinguishable from rape. Dolphins, mallard ducks, orang-utans, chimpanzees, bonobos, baboons are only some of the species in which the males are seen to rape the females, sometimes in gangs and to the point of exhaustion. Only in those species that form long-term pairs to raise offspring together are there any marks of affection in the mating process. In much of nature, sex is a casual one-time coupling of a brutal, bullying kind, and not a bonding mechanism. This is reflected in some human behaviour. Whenever there is a return to a state of nature, where the laws and rules of society collapse, as in wartime, rape becomes common, especially in a country invaded by a foreign army. The first impulse of invading soldiers, unless restrained by strict discipline, is to rape the women of the defeated enemy. Now this natural urge to rape is normally restrained in Western societies by a social conditioning to feel respect, sympathy and protectiveness towards women. The idealization of women and of love in Western culture has long played an essential role in counteracting the brutally aggressive sex drive with a social impulse of protectiveness for the weaker sex. This Western tradition is based, of course, on the veneration of motherhood, on which our collective survival depends. (Anyone who doubts this Western specificity, by the way, should try to find a culture outside the Western world where it is the custom for men to step back and let women go first, which is a remnant of the taboo against touching or jostling a woman among the ancient Germanic tribes like the Lombards — similar to the Polynesian taboo against touching a chief.) The specifically Western nature of this code of respect for women means that mass immigration by males from non-Western cultures, who despise our permissive values and consider Western women whores, leads to a huge increase in rape. The city with the largest non-European immigrant population in Sweden, Malmo, now has the second highest rate of rape of any city on earth. Rape in many non-Western cultures is scarcely even considered deviant behaviour, which is why their women must be cloistered, veiled and chaperoned to guard against it. The absence of these protections is seen almost as an invitation.

This perception that the sexual urge is naturally aggressive, and is associated with love or respect not by nature but only by culture, education and conditioning, led us to consider whether there are categories of human beings even in the West who are in no way educated in benevolence towards the people they are sexually attracted to. I suggested this might be true of one category in particular — butch homosexuals. These are homosexuals who play the active, masculine role, and have a domineering character, as opposed to the stereotypical "sissy" or effeminate gay man who plays the feminine or passive role. In the milieu these tend to be known as "tops" and "bottoms", but we will stick to the more traditional terms. (*There was a ripple of laughter in the audience.*) The aggressive sex drive of butch homosexuals is not generally restrained by any social conditioning to feel respect or protectiveness towards sissy homosexuals. On the contrary, butch queers often absorb the prevailing heterosexual attitude of contempt for effeminate males. So the butch homosexual often despises the class of men he is sexually attracted to, and his sex drive is hence particularly brutal. That is why so much "rough trade" goes on in promiscuous, impersonal homosexual encounters: many butch homosexuals want to screw as an act of pure aggression. Effeminate or transvestite male prostitutes often complain of the brutality and violence of their customers. Sometimes this violence is welcomed by masochistic gay men, like the late French film-maker, Cyril Collard, author of the first mainstream gay film, *Les Nuits Fauves,* who advertised for men to rape him as brutally as possible. When we look at the great homosexual innovations of the last half-century of liberation — fist-fucking, often engaged in by total strangers in homosexual bath-houses, where anuses are proffered to all-comers for the purpose, or the mass orgies that sometimes take place in these same bath-houses, where piles of men copulate blindly with any hole they find available in the mass of writhing bodies — what is striking is how aggressive they are, as well as how impersonal and anonymous they are. It is much the same in the gay pick-up scenes of many Western cities, where partners scarcely exchange a word before proceeding to action. This would appear to be a form of casual sex that is largely devoid of any pretence of affection or warmth (such as we may find even between women prostitutes and their clients.) Instead, it is often sadomasochistic, hate-driven or imbued with a death-wish. The gay French philosopher and sexual theorist, Michel Foucault, who went on a sadomasochistic spree in the bath-houses and sex clubs of San Francisco in his last years, actively sought to transmit AIDS to his casual partners. This suggests a murderous desire for revenge for his own infection. This apparent hatred for his fellow-gays has its counterpart in the self-hatred of those masochistic passive homosexuals who seek to be infected with AIDS by having unprotected or "bareback" sex with strangers.

We have suggested that much of this aggression among homosexuals occurs because of the absence of any notion of respect for the feminine partner of the sort we find among heterosexuals. Men in the West have been brought up ever since the age of chivalry to respect women and to idealize femininity, with its greater physical weakness, sensitivity, and timorousness, as well as its superior grace and beauty. Now no man has ever been brought up to respect and idealize sissy homosexuals, however many feminine traits they may display. Such males are half-despised as milksops, namby-pambies and pansies even by the butch queers who are attracted to them. Part of the urge of effeminate gay men to dress up as women and even transform themselves into women may be a desire to gain something of the respect that women receive from men, and even to inspire the bonding instinct women inspire. But this is usually a forlorn hope, except in the case of transsexuals who actually become women through reconstructive surgery and mate with a heterosexual man. The enduring life-problem of many effeminate homosexuals around the world is that they are treated with contempt even by the men who want sex with them. This is not merely because the butch queer has received a typical heterosexual conditioning to despise sissies. It is also because the butch queer instinctively rejects the sissy queer as the thing that he is not. It is part of the butch queer's acceptance of his homosexuality that he prides himself on being a shagger, not a shaggee, and hence sees the shaggee as a lower form of life. In those ancient societies where homosexuality was most widespread, Athens and Rome, the citizen could only be the active, butch partner, never the passive partner, in a homosexual relationship. To allow himself to be penetrated was a dishonour for a citizen, and if known could cost him his citizenship. The sodomized passive partner was always a slave, and usually a child or adolescent slave, since homosexuality and paedophilia were almost identical in ancient times — the object of same-sex attraction was a boy between the ages of twelve and seventeen. So even societies often cited as models of tolerance by modern gay militants contained an inherent bias against the sissy homosexual and a hierarchy of butch above sissy. This is the same hierarchy that exists in violent, lawless prisons the world over, where weaker men may be forced to become the sexual slaves of stronger ones. It is the passive partner (however much forced into this role by rape) who is despised by other prisoners for surrendering to a shameful act. The active partner passes for a real man who is asserting his virility through sexual dominance.

The feminist Kate Millett tried to use this prison culture (as described in the writings of Jean Genet) as proof that our society has a natural, brutal hierarchy of masculine over feminine, and that the female is inherently a slave. But a glance at the elaborate courtship rituals usually required to win the sexual favours of women in Western societies, and the protection they are given by law and custom, compared to the brutal way taken with weaker men in prison, shows how misguided this argument is. The brutal dominance of masculine over feminine, or active over passive, is something specific to homosexual relations, precisely because gay culture — for all its drag queen parody — has no real respect for the feminine. By contrast, Western mainstream culture, however much the feminists have tried to deny it, is profoundly imbued with veneration for women and for the feminine ideal, from the Mother Goddess to the Mother of God, or the idolized mistress of the courtly love and romantic traditions. It is the absence among homosexuals of any trace of this reverence for the feminine partner — perhaps because "she" cannot be a mother and enjoy a mother's high status — that makes so many casual same-sex relations so brutal and violent.

We have, then, in butch queers a class of men whose sexual urge is linked mainly to aggression, and is devoid of any feeling of respect or protectiveness towards those males they want sex with. They therefore find sexual pleasure in aggression and aggression in sexual pleasure. This makes them prone to violence. We know that most of the officer corps of the Nazi SA were butch homosexuals, like their leader, Ernst Roehm. Roehm recruited other butch queers because he believed they were the most violent, sadistic and brutal men on earth. It is probable that large numbers of the football hooligans and street gangs who engage in violence against other males for pleasure are also butch homosexuals, whether they are fully aware of it or not. Most prisoners who beat up, rape and enslave other men in prison are butch homosexuals. We know that many serial killers are butch homosexuals. Many torturers and sadists are butch homosexuals. And many paedophiles are the same. Any butch queer who is attracted to effeminate males will be attracted to young boys precisely because they look more feminine than adult males. The homosexuality of Greece and Rome, which was in large part paedophile, and where citizens were only allowed to play the active, butch role, is the perfect illustration of the tendency of the butch queer to be also a paedophile.

We may ask ourselves finally whether a good deal of evil in the world is perhaps merely the product of a sexual tendency that finds pleasure in aggression, domination, and cruelty. If this sexual tendency is the result of hormonal imbalances at the foetal stage, will we one day find a way of preventing it by intervening in the endocrine system of the foetus? In other words, will we one day see evil as a preventable sexual orientation?

The Boy in Formaldehyde

There was a vague murmur in the auditorium, but to Camilla's surprise it did not take the form of any open challenge to the anti-gay implications of his argument. Instead it was a buzz of murmured comments among the listeners, punctuated by guffaws of astonishment and chuckles of amusement. The professor glanced benignly at the front rows and continued.

This leads us to the question of whether paedophilia, perhaps considered the archetypal evil of our time, can also be seen as a specific sexual orientation.

On the face of it homosexuality and paedophilia have much in common. Both are deviations of the sexual urge along non-reproductive paths, so that if they became universal in a species, that species would at once die out. This has always been the chief argument for considering these practices unnatural or abnormal. How can something be natural in three per cent of a species when, if it occurred in a hundred per cent, it would lead to the immediate death of the species? The fact that homosexuality occurs among animals is no proof it is natural, let alone defensible, among humans. Rape, paedophilia, incest, infanticide, and cannibalism also occur in the animal world, most of them far more frequently than homosexuality. Could they too be justified as natural for humans on the same grounds? Both homosexuality and paedophilia become common among rats when they are subjected to the stresses of intolerable overcrowding, and they play a role in catastrophic population collapses (of the kind Western nations are perhaps in the midst of now.) But despite often occurring in the same animal species (among bonobos, for example), homosexuality and paedophilia have had very different judgments passed upon them. Social attitudes towards them in the West have recently evolved in opposite directions, as have beliefs about their causes. While current fashions in thinking lean towards biological causes for homosexuality, it is generally assumed that paedophilia has only psychological causes. What those causes might be is fiercely debated, though moral condemnation for paedophilia has become universal in the West.

Freud saw paedophiles simply as timid men who cannot feel dominant enough to be potent except with children. If sex is a form of bullying, then the weak will bully the weakest. A more sophisticated theory is that paedophiles are affected by an imprinting process — like Konrad Lawrenz's geese, which remained convinced that their mother was an orange balloon if that was the first thing they saw when they broke out of the egg. Is there something in the earliest sexual experience of the paedophile, his earliest sexual attraction to a childhood playmate, which fixes it forever as an ideal image in his mind, so that it does not evolve as he grows up? Could this feeling be guilt? If this first instance of sexual attraction inspired a strong sense of guilt, or if it were the moment of revelation to him of his homosexual tendencies, it might imprint itself so deeply on his brain that no other sexual object could ever replace that image. He would remain fixated with that playmate and that age-group all his life. This theory sees that initial childhood experience as a sort of epiphany, a vision of an ideal being he will desire forever. But other theories see this first sexual experience as a trauma inflicted on him by someone much older, which he cannot get over but must relive with the roles reversed. This would see the paedophile as somebody sexually abused as a child, who can take control of that experience only by abusing other children in his turn. But this theory would appear to work only if abused and abuser are the same sex, allowing them to swap roles at different ages. This is where we must make distinctions between homosexual and heterosexual paedophilia.

To the vexed question whether paedophilia is a sexual orientation, and if so whether it has a genetic origin, we can only answer by distinguishing the two kinds. In the case of heterosexual paedophilia, a genetic origin cannot be ruled out. It is quite conceivable there is a gene that makes men attracted to adolescent girls, as that would favour higher reproduction through a longer reproductive life. If a wife started childbearing at fifteen rather than twenty-five she would have time to have many more children over a lifetime. Marrying very young girls may also have ensured the bride's virginity, favoured wifely subservience and fidelity, and therefore more stable and fertile marriages. This attraction to adolescent girls would, in short, be a trait rewarded by higher rates of reproduction. The gene thus reinforced may then have taken on a life of its own and gone to extremes, as is often the case in evolution, where successful traits become more and more exaggerated, like the outsize antlers evolved by the Irish stag. The highly successful gene of attraction to adolescent girls may thus have led to an attraction to pre-pubertal girls, such as we find in many parts of Asia and Africa even today (an attraction which would be sterile, but only temporarily, until she reached puberty.)

By contrast, a gene for homosexuality could have no possible reproductive advantage, given the tendency towards sterility of this condition. All claims that such a gene has been found have turned out to be bogus, despite all the hype they continue to receive in the media. It is likely, therefore, that when homosexuality is biological in origin, it is not caused by a gene but by chemicals that are known to block male hormone. Environmental chemicals such as dioxins, PCBs or phthalates in the mother's body may sometimes get through the placental barrier and block the male hormone being produced by the male foetus she is carrying. Since this male hormone is what directs the growing foetus to follow the male blueprint rather than the female blueprint, blocking it feminizes the foetus. We can create homosexual mice or rats in the laboratory by injecting a pregnant female with tiny quantities of dioxin, which blocks the male hormone and causes the male foetus to develop partly along female lines. When these feminized males become adults, they exhibit homosexual behaviour. The fact we can create homosexual animals at will in the laboratory by this method is strong evidence for the chemical hormone-disruptor theory of homosexuality. By contrast, no homosexual animal has ever been created by manipulating genes, so no genetic causation has ever been proved.

To summarize: heterosexual paedophilia may well be caused by a highly successful gene for attraction to adolescent girls. Homosexual paedophilia is more likely to be caused by childhood seduction. And homosexuality, when it is biological rather than psychological in origin, is probably caused by hormone-disrupting chemicals such as dioxin in the mother's body — that is, ultimately, by environmental pollution.

There were gasps and laughter, and one half-serious cry from the back of "homophobe!" Most of the audience seemed to take it as an outrageous joke, as the professor put on a mock poker face that suggested mischief and provocation. But one young man did venture to put up his hand to challenge him. Rigdon gestured slightly with his index finger for him to speak.

"If homosexuality is caused by dioxin pollution, how did it become common in ancient Greece and Rome, long before the industrial revolution?" The speaker sounded rather smug, as if confident he had found a fatal flaw in the professor's argument.

"I'm very glad you asked that question," said Rigdon, to general laughter. The audience looked forward gleefully to hearing him wriggle his way out of this. "Was there any dioxin pollution in ancient Athens and Rome? I dare say there was — due to the heating systems used for their houses and public baths. Dioxin is a by-product of combustion. A major source of it today is the burning of rubbish in backyards. Now the Roman central heating system, the hypocaust, used smoke from furnaces flowing through ceramic ducts to heat the walls and floor. A certain amount of smoke probably leaked into the rooms. We can assume that household rubbish was burned in their furnaces along with wood. High levels of dioxin pollution may thus have existed even in ancient Rome and Greece and contributed to the frequency of homosexuality — especially among the upper classes, who all had centrally heated houses. But of course homosexuality may have psychological as well as biological causes. The seduction of boys is often a trigger for its later development. And Greek and Roman homosexuality was in fact indistinguishable from paedophilia, since the object of desire was a boy between the ages of twelve and seventeen. Now homosexual paedophiles often explain their behaviour as a reaction to their own seduction in childhood. The seduced boy grows up to be a seducer of boys in his turn. Those two factors between them adequately account for the homosexual practices of Greece and Rome."

"Are you suggesting if we get rid of dioxin pollution, we can prevent homosexuality?" asked another questioner in a tone of indignant incredulity.

"Not exactly." Rigdon drawled the words in a comical fashion, which elicited more laughter. "There are many other hormone-disruptors apart from dioxin. I am using it as a generic term for a range of chemicals that can have this effect, from phthalates to PCBs or Bisphenol-A, and we are forever discovering new ones. We can detect these chemicals in urine, and if we manage to develop ways of eliminating all of them from a pregnant woman's body, so as to ensure a normal process of masculinization of the male foetus she is carrying, there is no reason that homosexuality would ever occur as a biological phenomenon. Of course it might still be caused by psychological events, such as childhood abuse, rape, seduction, or being cooped up in a same-sex boarding-school."

"And lesbianism? Can that also be eliminated?" came a woman's voice.

"Of course, by ensuring that chemical pollutants that mimic male hormone and masculinize the female foetus are eliminated from the mother's body in the same way."

"What about paedophilia? Can that be made to disappear too?"

"It is likely homosexual paedophilia would disappear if homosexuality did. It exists largely because butch homosexuals are attracted to effeminate males, and males are at their most effeminate-looking when they are about twelve years old. So, if butch homosexuals no longer existed, there would be no homosexual paedophilia, except for that caused by psychological events."

"Are you implying heterosexual paedophilia would continue?" someone piped up.

Rigdon reflected before answering.

"Very probably. An impulse as reproductively advantageous as a desire to marry an adolescent girl, thereby lengthening her reproductive life and making her more likely to be a submissive wife and prolific mother, is not something that will disappear any time soon. This impulse seems to occur widely in a swathe of territory from Africa, through Arabia, Iran, Afghanistan, Pakistan and on to India. In this entire region girls are traditionally married at puberty. It is also a region with very large families, where social prestige attaches to having large numbers of children — and where they have the highest birth-rates on earth. These things go together, suggesting that attraction to adolescent girls is not merely a cultural trait but a genetic trait, favoured by the higher reproduction it results in. Of course, much of this whole area of the world is also Muslim. The fact that Mohammed married his favourite wife, Aisha, when she was six and consummated the marriage when she was nine is seen by many Muslim scholars as justifying child marriages even today. But while religious beliefs may have reinforced the custom of marrying young girls, the greater reproductive success it results in has probably now made this tendency a genetic trait. This trait is leading these cultures to outbreed all others and dominate the world. Africans and South Asians are expected to make up nearly seventy per cent of the human race by the end of the century, or seven billion out of ten. Those races will, of course, be the majority in this country as well."

A bearded forty-year old with a worried frown raised his hand. Rigdon nodded to him.

"So are you suggesting that heterosexual paedophilia is in some sense natural but homosexuality is unnatural — reversing the usual libertarian argument that all sex between consenting adults is acceptable, but no sex with children is acceptable?" This questioner seemed at ease speaking in public and elicited from Rigdon a glance of respect.

"It is not a question of natural or unnatural, acceptable or unacceptable. It's a question of whether each of these sexual behaviours is genetic or not. One leads to a reproductive advantage, so it may well be genetic, and the other doesn't. That's all. There is no moral judgment being made. But one *may* judge in terms of evolutionary success. To put it crudely, Africa and South Asia have a legalized perversion: heterosexual paedophilia or marrying girls at puberty. The West has a different legalized perversion: homosexuality. Which one do you think leads to a reproductive advantage, more children, and will one day dominate the earth?"

The audience laughed uncomfortably in acknowledgment of the point.

"But if homosexuality doesn't somehow lead to a reproductive advantage, how did it survive through the ages?" countered the man with the beard.

"Precisely because it is not a gene. Homosexuality is a recurrent abnormality, caused by hormone-disrupting chemicals in the environment. Some of these have always been around, and others have been fabricated recently. These chemicals may build up in the mother's body till they get through the placental barrier and disrupt the masculinization of the male foetus she is carrying. There is no gene involved. If, as the gay lobby has suggested, a foetus inherited a gene that blocked the action of male hormone upon it, it would block it at every phase of its development and result in a totally feminized individual. But most homosexual men are not totally feminized. Gay men have a whole range of personalities — some very effeminate, some quite masculine, and everything in between. This can only be caused by something that blocks the male hormone from masculinizing the foetus only at certain stages of its development. In other words, not a gene, which would act all the time, but chemicals in the environment, which may act for short periods only. Dioxins, phthalates, Bisphenol-A. They may reach a critical level in the mother's body only for a short time, and feminize the foetus only at that stage. They may block the male hormone when the mating centre in the hypothalamus of the brain is being formed, thus feminizing it and making the individual homosexual. But at the stage when the appearance or the personality is being shaped, these chemicals may have disappeared from the mother's body, so the male hormone may masculinize the foetus in a normal way. That is the only explanation as to why most gay men are not totally effeminate, as they would be if a gay gene were the cause."

"Then why are they looking for a gay gene and claiming every few years they have found one?" the same man persisted.

"Because something genetic sounds more natural than something caused by chemical pollution. A condition caused by chemicals in the mother's body blocking the male hormone of her foetus seems like something that can be prevented by eliminating those chemicals. But if it is a gene in the foetus itself that resists the male hormone acting on it, that seems like something natural and inevitable. The gay lobby doesn't want homosexuality to be seen as a preventable condition. That's why they're determined to impose their theory of a gay gene and to stop any research into alternative theories. All these mediatized claims of the discovery of a gay gene have been made by gay researchers and have later been exposed as false. But the gay lobby has kept up the media propaganda as if these claims have been confirmed. The political dogma that homosexuality is now known to be genetic is a lie being imposed on the world in the name of political correctness."

A young man at the back ventured in a nervous voice: "But if homosexuality were to be one day prevented by medical techniques, eliminating hormone disruptors and so on, don't you think something would be lost for humanity? What about all those artists from Leonardo to Tchaikovsky who were homosexual? Would you want to lose them?"

"Not at all. But think about all those artists from Raphael to Mozart who were heterosexual. There is no evidence whatsoever that homosexuality has any bearing on artistic ability. What does have a bearing on artistic talent is a certain femininity of sensibility. But this feminine sensibility in men is not caused by homosexuality, because it is formed at a different stage of the foetus's development, long after the formation of the mating centre in the hypothalamus, which determines sexual attraction. The two things sometimes occur in the same individual because they have a common cause but mostly we have one without the other. The vast majority of male artists, poets, writers, and composers in history have been heterosexual but with rather feminine sensibilities. That will still continue if we eliminate hormone disruptors only at the precise phase, in the third month, when the mating centre in the hypothalamus of the brain is formed but not at later stages. A feminization of other aspects of the brain and personality may then still occur, and continue to produce artists of all kinds."

A rather snide, sarcastic female voice asked: "Is it a new trend that defenders of paedophilia are now attacking homosexuality?"

The hostility of the question caused a tense silence in the auditorium.

"As to what defenders of paedophilia do, I cannot comment," said Rigdon quietly. "The laws of the land being what they are." The silence of the audience became more palpable. "But I will say this. The gay lobby for a long time defended paedophiles and saw them as allies, since many people were both, and both were persecuted. Now as the witch hunt grows against paedophiles, some of the newly respectable gays, who have campaigned successfully to pass laws decreeing they are normal, are distancing themselves from their former allies and condemning them loudly in order to prove their own virtue. I think it's useful for them to know that this is a game that two can play." He smiled with a hint of malice. "But I am less interested in any quarrel between the two camps than in their historical and psychological relationship, something denied by the new consensus. I think comparisons between them bring understanding of both, and that is how I would like to end this lecture."

The audience relaxed, and appeared to settle down again after its brief spate of rebelliousness. It listened dutifully as he continued.

"We have suggested that heavily homosexual cultures, like those of ancient Greece and Rome, are inherently paedophile, because the butch homosexual's attraction to girlish-looking males makes him attracted to very young boys, who are at their most girlish-looking phase. That is not to say all butch homosexuals engage in paedophile acts, but they all have that impulse in them. And since we are dealing with men who are often conflicted about their sexual tendencies (their masculine characters despising their own queerness) and they may have a sense of being victims of a quirk of nature, the urge to visit that same condition on other, much younger males may be a very strong impulse in them.

"It is of course a subject of controversy whether sexual preferences are always innate or may sometimes be modified or caused by events in life. Can paedophilia or homosexuality be learned, or are they always inborn? It is often claimed by the gay lobby that homosexuals are born and cannot be recruited or made; hence any notion of gays spreading their cult is homophobic nonsense. This is by no means certain if you compare the number of men in the recent past who came out of violent prisons homosexual with the number who went in homosexual. Given the highly habit-forming nature of sexual acts, paedophile initiation may be a form of homosexual recruitment, along with repeated rape in prison, the army or boarding-school. In all these places sexual submission to the strong is a survival tactic of the weak — in short, an appeasement tactic, as it is among male apes — and it may then become a conditioned reflex. We know that boys sexually abused young often go on to pursue confused and tormented homosexual careers. Once a boy feels he has been used as a sexual rubbish bin, his contempt for himself may lead him to seek punishment — either by self-harm, suicide or by making himself into a sexual rubbish bin over and over again. The same mechanism may be at work in conditioning boys into passive homosexuality which we see in the conditioning of girls into prostitution by repeated rape. After a while they think: I am good only for this, and seek to punish themselves for their helplessness by subjecting themselves to the same violation again and again. This is apparently the mechanism that converts straight young men into passive homosexuals in brutal prisons — a conditioned reflex of submission, which becomes a form of internalized sexual slavery. It may occur in other contexts, such as the army, boarding schools, or even large families with domineering older brothers. A good deal of bullying between boys is symbolic rape, as when one boy lies on top of another pinning him to the ground. This sort of conditioning is far more likely than any genetic cause to explain the slightly higher proportion of younger brothers among passive homosexuals. The more older brothers a boy has, the more likely he is to have spent a good deal of his childhood with a bigger male on top of him. This may sometimes trigger confused homosexual responses, particularly when the bully is also the younger boy's hero."

A hand shot up. Rigdon acknowledged it with a hint of weariness.

"Don't you accept the current theory of maternal immunity, whereby something in the mother's body begins to neutralize the male hormone of the foetuses the more sons she has, so that they become progressively more effeminate and prone to be gay?"

"No, I don't," said Rigdon. "I think your rather confused explanation perfectly sums up the state of research on this hypothesis." There was laughter. "The incidence of this alleged effect is so small, common sense cries out for an alternative explanation, based on nurture rather than nature. Bullying and sexual molestation among brothers. A much under-researched area." He went back to his notes. "As I was saying, the formation of the passive homosexual, like that of the prostitute, may sometimes be a process of conditioning in a form of masochism. This is one of the possible outcomes of sexual abuse of boys. The other outcome is paedophilia. It depends whether the boy reacts to the abuse by later inflicting the same thing on others, or by getting others to inflict it again and again upon himself. Both reactions are ways of taking back control of traumatic experiences. When homosexual tendencies are the result of conditioning by life events rather than by hormones in the womb, they may well be susceptible to therapies to reverse the conditioning. The same is true of paedophilia. It is reasonable to assume that what was caused by psychological events (such as repeated rape or abuse) may be cured by psychological therapies, but what was caused by hormones in the womb cannot be. This principle would mean that paedophilia must either be curable or innate. If it is innate, would this not be an argument for tolerance, as in the case of homosexuality? Or is the argument that whatever is innate should be tolerated inherently flawed?

"Must we see all paedophilia as a predatory, exploitative phenomenon causing psychological damage and suffering? Not necessarily. A good deal of paedophilia is Platonic, like Lewis Carroll's. Many devoted teachers throughout the ages have been gentle, Platonic paedophiles — men who adored children. When it comes to sexual relations, we must distinguish between those with pre-pubertal and post-pubertal children, the latter being more accurately referred to as hebephilia. An adolescent girl of the age of Shakespeare's Juliet, thirteen, sometimes falls in love with a man, and in the case of a profound mutual passion, the lovers should not be prevented by law from expressing that love. It is clear that the dividing line of puberty occurs in this day and age rather younger than the age of consent of sixteen in this country, as other European nations have acknowledged by fixing the bar as low as thirteen or fourteen.

"Let me end on an historical note. Queen Isabelle of France in the twelfth century married at ten and we don't know how long her fifteen-year-old husband King Philip the Second waited before deflowering her. But we know he wanted to divorce her when she was fourteen because she wasn't yet pregnant. She responded by raising a mob of supporters and confronting him on the steps of his palace, where her tears and entreaties forced him to swear he still loved her and would never let her go. They stayed together and she gave him an heir, before dying in childbirth with twins at nineteen. We can only speculate whether sex at eleven or twelve did this passionate, strong-willed young lady any harm. But, of course, then there were no moralistic militants telling her she was a victim of monstrous patriarchal oppression. It may well be the attitude to a relationship taken by society that is more damaging than the relationship itself. In those cases of fourteen and fifteen-year-old girls whose adult boyfriends — not exploiters or pimps but boyfriends — are imprisoned for years in this country as paedophiles, we can see the Victorian Puritanism of this culture still at work. I am waiting to see a production of *Romeo and Juliet* where the police intervene to arrest Romeo for sleeping with a thirteen-year old girl and the entire audience for watching and applauding this paedophile act. Then much of the hypocrisy and self-contradiction, in fact the profound sexual neurosis of this country, will be plain for all to see."

Rigdon descended from the lectern and walked towards the side door at the bottom of the auditorium as the audience applauded. Two young men, who had been sitting in the front row and whom Camilla had always seen as gay, got up and followed him. He turned at the door and smiled as if they were friends of his. They walked out together. Again she was surprised at the apparent good terms he was on with gay students while putting forward views she could only imagine they would find offensive. She felt there was something missing, a part of the puzzle she did not possess.

But what made a deep impression on her was Rigdon's argument that the attraction to adolescent girls, even girls of thirteen or fourteen, was a natural and normal impulse found in cultures all over the world. She clung to this as a justification of the love of her life, a proof that it was not unnatural, not perverted, not warped, not evil. Brendan was not a pervert and she was not a victim — except of the bigotry and murderous intolerance of British society. Whatever Rigdon's theatrical antics or bizarre views on other subjects, she was grateful for this moral and philosophical support. He was an intellectual lifeline in an ocean of toxic vilification of the most passionate experience of her life.

She remembered the enormous relief she had felt when she walked out of Rigdon's lecture that day. The very air seemed fresher, more invigorating, less stifling. Not alone, she had said to herself. And now she had found someone else who had that same effect on her but a hundred times more. Someone who rejected the *pensée unique*, the politically correct thinking, which had been imposed on the West by a sect of narrow-minded, morally arrogant intellectuals — including the grossly one-sided view of the war they had waged on her homeland. She felt a sense of liberation that the dark days of her solitary struggle to keep her sanity were over. She had someone who shared her views. What bliss! She was not alone with a sense of injustice that suffocated her. And hearing Romain quietly, rationally, and feelingly justifying the love of her life, showing profound understanding of it, suddenly opened the doors of love again. If he could understand that, then he could understand her. And if he understood her she could love him. Was that the thing that made his touch so different from others? Did her mind give her body permission to respond to his?

Once on holiday in Ireland at Brendan's mother's place, she had crossed a bridge over a wide placid river where migrating birds rested. Scores of ducks and water birds of different kinds, with bizarre crests and plumage of all varieties, sat on the water as though at a huge jamboree. She saw the truth of the old adage that birds of the same species flock together. And then she noticed one bird, which had a strange gold crest and looked like none of the others, standing alone on the bank. He was gazing forlornly about him, as if in perpetual hope of catching sight of a bird that resembled him. But there were no others like him. He was the only one of his kind. She suddenly felt like that bird and her heart went out to it.

But now she felt like it no longer. She had found her mate. She knew that when the time was right they would come together. She just hoped he would be patient a bit longer and wait till she was ready. Her body had lain asleep for so long. He was waking it up again little by little. But she knew that something special had to happen to wake it up completely. She didn't know what that would be but she had a feeling that it would happen very soon.

20

Bendigo telephoned Wayne the day after he spoke to Romain and set up a meeting. They met in a café on King's Road and sat at an outdoor table a little apart from other people.

"I need another body," said Bendigo bluntly, "for a special order. I need a slightly older boy. Say, three years older, preferably with longish blond hair. And very good-looking. Do you think I could find that somewhere?"

"I do have two boys at the moment who might fit the bill," said Wayne. "One in particular. Would you like to look at them? They're still walking around. We'll have to talk about the price of delivering them in another state. That carries risks and is rather expensive."

"I'm willing to pay. But I only need the one for the moment."

"You can come to my place and look at them now if you like."

They finished their coffee, took a cab to Soho and went up to Wayne's apartment. Wayne led him down a corridor to a closed door. He took out a key and unlocked it. The room had been furnished like a small prison, with four cages like those in which monkeys are kept. There were two boys in separate cages. They were sitting on the floor, gagged and blindfolded, with blankets around them and hands bound behind them. Wayne opened each cage in turn and pulled off the boy's blanket. He ordered them to stand up and turn round slowly. Bendigo studied their naked bodies carefully.

"Can I take photos?" he asked.

"Yes, but not in here," said Wayne. "We'll move each one out."

He took each boy in turn into the living room and placed him against a bare white wall. Bendigo took several photographs with his smartphone, and asked Wayne to remove the blindfold and gag so he could get the boy's face.

"If I do that," said Wayne, "you'd better wear a mask yourself."

He gave Bendigo a devil mask to put on. Then he took off the boy's blindfold and gag, and let Bendigo photograph his face from all angles. Afterwards he took him back to his cage and brought the other one out and the artist did the same.

"Well, what do you think?" Wayne asked when the boys were locked up again and he was pouring a whisky in the living room. "I do have some more, but they're all out on loan. There's one new boy who's quite good-looking. But his hair's dark."

"These two look good. Especially the taller one with the longer blond hair," said Bendigo, studying the photos on his smartphone. "He really fits the bill. Where's he from?"

"I can't tell you that. You'll be getting him as carrion, so it won't make any difference. After you convert them, they don't talk."

"He looks very Nordic."

"All sorts of trash look Nordic today," said Wayne. "The Eastern European effect."

"How old is he exactly?"

"Just turned fourteen."

"Do you hire these boys out as rent boys?" asked Bendigo curiously.

"Yes," said Wayne. "Does it interest you?"

"I wouldn't mind the taller one."

"When? Now?"

"If you don't see any inconvenience. Just a half-hour with him, if you have a place here — with a bed, do you?"

"Sure. I have a guest bedroom."

"It seems almost a shame to convert him, as you call it, without trying him out."

"Be my guest. I've been screwing him for a few weeks, and he's not bad. Make hay while the sun shines."

He told him the price and Bendigo put the money on the table. Then Wayne went and got the taller blond boy and led him into the bedroom. Bendigo shut himself up with him and came out forty minutes later looking tousled but satisfied. Wayne led the boy back to his cage and then came into the lounge again.

"He didn't bite your cock or refuse to swallow?" said Wayne. "I had one last month who started acting up with clients. Had to be disciplined quite severely. Hot poker up the arsehole. These young bastards, they're more and more hostile and bolshie, especially the Eastern European lot."

"Well, homophobia, it's such a disease, isn't it?" said Bendigo. "They get brainwashed with it so young. The extreme right. Pure irrational hatred." His gaze fell upon the skull insignia of the SS Death's Head Division on the wall and he looked away quickly. "Still, we're making some progress in the schools. The media...."

He came to a halt, his eyes flicking nervously over the other SS memorabilia on the walls. Wayne was staring at him with a look of scarcely concealed contempt. If he hadn't known better, Bendigo would have thought he was a homophobe.

"No, the boy was fine," he went on quickly. "Did what he was told. You've obviously trained him well. Fantastic arse. Still very tight. Almost a shame he has to die for the sake of art. But he will be immortal. I'll see to it. I'm thinking of calling it: Narcissus Fallen into his Pool. He'll become a gay icon."

Wayne broached the subject of price. He drove a hard bargain, named a very high figure, and reminded Bendigo that the boy corresponded perfectly to his artistic requirements. This was made to measure, not off the shelf, he said. There were huge costs and risks involved in the conversion process. Wayne pointed out slyly he was welcome to try to obtain a better price somewhere else. Bendigo gave a nervous laugh. He agreed after some hesitation, as if he knew it still left him a comfortable margin. They shook hands on it. After Bendigo had left, Wayne called Cyril Jones.

"Cyril, we need to talk. Remember the piece of carrion I placed for you. It was a great success and they need another one. I have the raw product. Very tasty. I have an idea who might be interested in carrying out the conversion — it's an old friend of yours. I think it might be better if the approach came from you. It would have to leave the product absolutely pristine. Not a bruise."

"Who do you have in mind?"

"The professor. What do you think?"

Cyril was silent for a moment.

"Good God! Would he still be into that sort of thing? Well, I suppose we could give him a try. All right, I'll get back to you." Then he had an afterthought. "By the way, I've been meaning to ask you. You remember that blonde bitch that attacked us outside my place the other day? A Pole or something. Claimed to be the mother of the first boy. Do you think she could be a danger? Should she be tracked down and dealt with?"

"Only if she makes a nuisance of herself again. Let me know if she comes back."

"She has. I've seen her hanging around with a couple of friends. Watching the place. They've come back several times."

"Next time take a photo of them and send it to me."

"I took one already. I'll send it to you some time. I need your email address."

Wayne gave it, and then ended the call.

Cyril paced the floor for a minute, at least two steps of his huge bulk in each direction. Then he picked up the phone again and dialled.

"Peter?" he said. "Cyril."

"Cyril, how are you, old chap? It's been a while."

"I have something really exceptional for you, Peter. A present."

"I love presents."

"You'll love this one. When can we see each other?"

21

After his phone call to Cyril, Wayne sat down and poured another small whisky. Then he felt like shagging the blond Polish boy himself so he went and got him and took him into the bathroom. He wanted to get all trace of Bendigo off him so he took a shower with him and scrubbed him thoroughly, shoving a bottle-brush dipped in liquid soap up his backside. After he dried him he made him bend over the bath and he took him there — a half-hour pounding that was like a high-intensity gym work-out. He appreciated the smooth, alabaster skin of this classical body, but in a cold, impersonal way as if he was a statue. All the same, he couldn't help noticing that the boy was gasping by the end and in tears. In fact, it had become that half-hysterical sobbing and groaning that marked a new phase in his evolution. He hated himself so much for his subjugation and humiliation that he was beginning to enjoy the pain as a release for his self-loathing. Soon he would be engaging in it willingly and asking men to hurt him. His transformation into a fully-fledged, masochistic faggot was coming along well. Wayne was pleased with the progress he had made in training him. He was turning him inside out, as he liked to put it, in record time. Pity the work would never be completed now.

After he locked the boy up again he felt drowsy and went and lay down on his bed for a while. He rolled a joint and smoked it, something he did only occasionally now. He thought about the blond boy and realized that he wouldn't be shagging him for very much longer. He was certainly a good-looking boy. However, he was determined he would never again get sentimental about rent boys. He had learned his lesson a long time ago with Lazlo. It would be a good discipline to watch this one being killed. He anticipated the slight pang it would cause with an odd spasm of pleasure.

It was a strange life he was leading, he reflected, as his mind drifted with the hashish to various scenes of his past. It would have been hard to predict this lifestyle when he was the blond boy's age. In fact at that age he had no idea there was anything peculiar about him. It was fascinating to think how far he had come.

Wayne had had a normal boyhood, and had gone to a primary school in an area in the process of gentrification. His father was an Irish immigrant who had worked his way up from the factory floor to mid-level trade union official, and gradually smoothed the rough edges of his character. He had played rugby when young and encouraged Wayne to do the same. Wayne became good at it. He was fast and tough, and played number 8 with great success. He was a medium-sized kid of powerful build and he became a devastating tackler. His father, who had had a liking for using the belt on the kids when they were younger, respected Wayne's sporting ability as he grew up. His father had also boxed in his youth and so Wayne began training very young at a local boxing club. When he started going to the comprehensive secondary school (a fairly good one but still with its quota of thugs), he was a boy to be reckoned with in the school yard. On the half dozen occasions when he got into fights at school they ended quickly, with him either knocking his opponent down and intimidating him from getting up again, or else pummelling him into submission on the ground. He felt a sense of elation and triumph at these moments that he never forgot. The prestige he won from these exploits was like an aura around him when he walked through the school yard. He became a natural gang leader, surrounded by boys who looked up to him and were ready to follow him in any escapade. Once he led a gang in an attack on some boys from a rival school on their way home. It ended in them robbing their enemies of five watches and fifty quid in cash, and leaving them with bloody noses. He generously divided the cash up with the others but took care of the watches himself, using a connection he had made with an older youth at the boxing club to sell them on the black market. This won him more kudos. The fact that nobody dared snitch when the police came to the school to investigate the affair added to the legend that surrounded him.

Given his reputation for toughness, he naturally despised sissies and cry-babies. There were two kids at school who were spotted early on as sissies — boys with no backbone, who were useless at sport and couldn't fight to save themselves. They got teased and called names — the usual litany from sissy to poof. He did not take part in this bullying but he understood it and vaguely approved of it. Boys had to be pressured to be boys, to follow the rules of male behaviour. One of the sissies, who sported the poncy name Mervyn, had grown lately into a tallish, slender, good-looking boy with a long blond cowlick, a bit like a young David Bowie. He had an insolent, superior manner, and cultivated a decadent look quite openly by wearing mascara on weekends and painting his fingernails green. He took to wearing the green fingernails to school, which caused a sensation. The headmaster ordered him to scrub his nails, but after a threat of legal action by Mervyn's parents for anti-gay discrimination he had to back down. This successful rebellion earned Mervyn a grudging respect from the other boys, who found him fascinating if utterly weird. Wayne tended to ignore him, but he had the uncomfortable feeling when he passed him that the boy was looking at him insistently with his rather lazy, sardonic, mocking smile, as if he knew things that nobody else knew.

Wayne was soon taking an interest in the girls at the school, partly because he was expected to as part of male competition, and they were eager to attract his attention. He took them out to ice cream parlours, fast food places, the cinema and the occasional party, and had snogging sessions with them. Then one evening when he was fifteen, he was snogging on a bench in a public garden with a girl in his class called Lisa, a foxy little thing of Italian origin with black hair cut in stylish side-swept bangs. His hand was on her knee and as he moved it slowly up to the bare thigh above her stockings to see how far she would let him go, she invited him slyly to put his finger "somewhere nice and warm." Her eagerness to go further threw him off his stride. Instead of leaping at this chance to explore the fascinating secrets of the female body, he was seized with panic. She was clearly more experienced than him and he was afraid he wouldn't be up to this. But there was no way out. He went ahead and moved his hand up to her knickers and then slid it into the strange, hairy territory inside them. She opened her thighs a bit more and when his fingers moved between them, she stiffened in his arms and gasped, as if he was touching something sore. He felt not a rush of desire and an urge to push further inside this mysterious, damp place but a reflex of fear and revulsion. He felt he was touching an open wound, a space from which something was missing. Suddenly her arms clinging tightly to him felt not like a turn-on but a kind of trap. She was like a snake coiling around him, pulling him towards this soft centre of her body. He could hardly breathe. Not this, he thought. Sensing his reluctance, she broke out of his arms and said:

"What's the matter? Don't you want me?"

He felt a wave of shame come over him. His voice shook.

"You know, I'm actually a Catholic and we're not supposed to do this," he muttered weakly, feeling contemptible.

"You wimp!" she said witheringly. She moved further away and glared at him. "I'm a Catholic too, who cares? You're scared, aren't you? I bet you're gay, that's what it is," she said with contempt.

"Me? Gay? You must be fucking joking!" Shame was blown away by sudden fear and anger. "I can thrash any guy in this school. You say that to anyone and I'll kill you!"

She looked at him with a hard, defiant stare. On impulse he put his hands round her throat. Rage flooded through him as he imagined the horror of being called gay, the object of every sneering joke by other kids. The humiliation would be worse than death. He tightened his strangle-hold until she began to choke.

"Please!" she wheezed, her eyes filling with tears as she clutched at his hands.

"You're not going to start calling me names, are you?" he said through gritted teeth.

"No!" she mouthed, tried to shake her head, and made signs with her eyes. He let her go.

"We've got our own code, us Irish, don't you forget it!" he snarled. Even though he spoke with a local English accent he liked to play on his ancestry as giving him a violent, lawless streak whenever he needed to intimidate. "We kill those who fuck us about, even girls. You'll just disappear and nobody will find your body."

"I'm sorry," she said miserably, clutching her throat, coughing and beginning to sob. "I liked you, that's all. I liked you. But now I hate you. But I won't say anything, I promise." He stood up. She grabbed his hand, as if she wanted to placate him further, out of fear. "I'll keep your secret, don't worry."

"I don't have a fucking secret!" he snarled, tossing away her hand. "Just because I don't fancy you, it doesn't mean I don't fancy any girl."

"Every boy fancies me," she said coolly. She had regained her self-possession. "I can have any of them I like. But I chose you. To be my first." She looked at him with bitter reproach. "You still can be if you change your mind. But only if you say you're sorry, that you regret it, and that you'll do anything to get me back." She tossed her black hair back, smoothed her elegant bangs with her hand and reasserted her dignity.

"I'll let you know if it happens," he sneered, and walked away.

That night he lay awake in bed and sweated as he thought about what had happened.

"I can't be fucking gay," he whispered to himself. "I'm not a sissy. I'm the toughest kid in the school. What the fuck is the problem? What's wrong with me? I didn't want that bitch. I wanted to push her away, not shag her." Then he thought of Mervyn, the blond boy with the cowlick. "I'm not like him. I'm not a fucking sissy like that. But he looks better than she does. Why does he look better to me than she does? What the fuck hold does he have over me?" And he hated the sissy boy with a violent hatred and fantasized about smashing his face in, and getting rid of that insolent, mocking look that he always wore, as if he knew what others didn't.

After this incident, he didn't have the impression that Lisa had betrayed him, but he sensed a growing attitude among all the girls at school that he was not quite what he seemed to be. He was not the stud or playboy that his good looks, sporting prowess and standing among the boys would have led them to expect. He tried to create a cover for himself by taking out shy or bookish girls of no sexual experience who might be less inclined to rush things. When the relationship developed to the point where action might be expected to follow, he provoked a rupture by flirting with another girl, and was off the hook for another few months until that new relationship warmed up to the critical point. He thus developed a reputation as a boy who changed girlfriends frequently and left a trail of broken hearts, which was not to his disadvantage. It reinforced his prestige among the boys, and made the girls even keener to compete for him. When it was pointed out by rival jocks that he wasn't going for the really hot girls, he affected a contempt for easy lays, and made disparaging remarks about girls who were too eager for it. A certain kind of adolescent misogyny was well accepted, especially among athletic types following a disciplined lifestyle. He felt somehow secure again, and the girl problem did not weigh heavily on his mind.

At the end of the school year there was a school dance. During a late-night break by the dance band a group of older pupils were lounging about with band members, sitting on a low wall outside the gymnasium, drinking beer and smoking cigarettes and surreptitious joints. It was a mild summer night and there was a full moon. Some of them were about to leave school, and conversations were more serious than usual, since it wasn't certain they would all see one another again. The talk at one point focused on Mervyn, who played the saxophone in the dance band and had impressed them all with his solos. One or two of them made attempts to talk to him to bring him out. They talked openly about the fact that he was gay, instead of just slagging him off. One of the boys, a joker named Wesley, a mixed-race West Indian who was skinny and smart and quick-tongued, began teasing him in a friendly sort of way.

"So, you're gay, right, everyone knows that. But what does it mean in practice? Like, do you fancy any of us?"

"Could be," said Mervyn mysteriously.

"Well, if you fancied one of us, who would it be?" Wesley was pushing him to say something that would cause ructions. He was what they called a shit-stirrer.

"I couldn't tell you that," said Mervyn with a grin. "It might embarrass the guy."

"Go on, you can tell us, who do you fancy?" Wesley glanced around at the other boys present, looking maliciously for a victim. "Is it Brodie?"

Brodie looked enraged at this, but Mervyn answered quickly and reassuringly.

"No, too much of a hetero brute."

"Exactly, a hetero brute!" roared Brodie in triumph, thumping his chest like a gorilla. He felt his virility had been publicly vindicated by Mervyn's rejection of him.

"So, who is it? Go on! It's not going to be another sissy is it, you sissies go for brutes, don't you?" Wesley had become morbidly curious about the other and was relentless in pressing him.

"Yes, but it has to be a brute with a weakness somewhere in him," said Mervyn thoughtfully. Perhaps he saw this as a rare opportunity to get a message across. "A sensitive streak. Someone who doesn't quite know himself."

He glanced around and his eyes focused on Wayne as he said this. Despite all his efforts Wayne could not stop himself from looking startled. The full moon, aided by the light over the gymnasium door, was bright enough for them to see one another's expressions. Wesley chortled and hooted.

"Oh, who's he looking at? At Wayne Madden! Who would have thought it?"

"Shut up, you bastard!" said Wayne furiously. "You think you're funny!"

"No need to get upset," said Wesley. "I didn't say a word, it's him who looked at you."

"Bollocks! You're trying to stir shit, aren't you?" Wayne got off the wall and took a menacing step towards Wesley, who was not at all the fighting type.

"Let's ask him if he was looking at you!" cried Wesley, as he prepared for evasive action, ready to run if Wayne came at him. "Were you looking at Wayne Madden?"

"Yes, I was," said Mervyn coolly. "I happened to look right at him."

Wayne stopped, rooted to the spot. He stared at Mervyn in shock. This was a challenge.

"So, he's the one you fancy?" pursued Wesley, on the balls of his feet ready to sprint away if he had to (he was a fast runner) but wanting to milk the situation for its last drop of scandal.

"Yeah, he wouldn't be bad." Mervyn smiled distantly and somewhat dreamily. "I think he likes me, underneath." He leaned back against the wall so his face was in shadow and took a pull on a joint.

"He likes you underneath!" yelled Wesley in ecstasy. "Underneath what? Underneath your clothes?"

"Underneath his knickers!" quipped someone else.

"Wayne likes Mervyn's knickers!" a girl yelled from the back of the group in a sing song voice. Laughter followed.

"Go on, kiss him, Wayne!" somebody urged as a joke.

"No, beat him up, Wayne, don't let the faggot say that!"

"Don't take that from a poofter, Wayne!"

His own friends and supporters were egging him on now to hit Mervyn. He felt his reputation depended on making Mervyn back down.

"Take that back, you disgusting faggot!" said Wayne, stepping towards him. He expected Mervyn to run and let him off the hook that way, allowing him to save face without having to use violence on somebody of much slighter build.

"I don't see why I should," said Mervyn coolly. He took another pull on the joint and handed it to someone else. When he moved his head, the moonlight fell on his face as he slowly blew out the smoke in a cool, insolent manner. "I do fancy you. Why should it bother you? It doesn't mean you're gay, does it?"

"Yuck!" said another boy. "He fancies him! How disgusting!"

"That's an insult! Beat him up, Wayne!" His own supporters were now raring to see him fight.

"I'll give you five seconds to apologize," said Wayne, through gritted teeth, stepping close to him. He hoped to intimidate him into running away or making an apology so he didn't need to hit him. At the same time, there was a look on Mervyn's face, a look of defiance, which made him suddenly feel that if he had to hit him, he would enjoy it.

"Why should I? You know you're actually rather pleased I fancy you, aren't you?"

This was a deliberate provocation. Wayne grabbed Mervyn's collar, sank his fist into his solar plexus, then as he doubled up hit him with an uppercut and finished with a left hook. Mervyn collapsed on the ground gasping for breath, with his hand over his mouth.

Wayne glared down at him. His victim was looking up at him, fear in his eyes at last, but also a peculiar triumph. It was as if he had provoked what he wanted to provoke.

"Enjoying it, aren't you?" said Mervyn mockingly, when he got his breath. He licked the blood off his lips and felt his teeth with his hand to check them.

For a second Wayne nearly went berserk. He saw himself mentally kicking the boy to pulp. But something held him back. Not only the legal consequences, given Mervyn's litigating parents. He also saw an opportunity to inflict a different kind of punishment. He answered Mervyn's mockery with his own, and smiled down at him sadistically.

"I sure am, faggot." He dropped a gob of spit in his face and turned away.

"Be my guest any time," taunted Mervyn, wiping the spit off his cheek with his sleeve.

"I don't need your permission, pansy," said Wayne, turning back with sudden confidence. "I'll beat you up and spit on you whenever I feel like it."

He walked away with a swagger and his supporters cheered.

That night after the plaudits his performance had won, Wayne was feeling pleased with himself. But he also felt a sense of discovery. It was true he felt some strange fascination for the girlish-looking Mervyn, though what he wanted to do to him physically he was not sure. But what he knew now was the pleasure of dominating him, of making him afraid, of seeing him on the ground at his feet. That was suddenly a pleasure all of its own. He knew he could feel a deep physical enjoyment by humiliating and brutalizing another boy. There was no need for sex, which remained a mystery to him; just violence itself was enough. That seemed to him an important discovery. It was as if he knew now he had another sexual organ: his fists.

The next year Wayne didn't return to school. His O-level exam results were not brilliant, but he had applied on the off-chance for an apprenticeship as a mechanic in a motorcycle garage and they suddenly accepted him. He decided to grab the chance. He was sixteen and was now nearly six foot tall, and he felt it was time he was treated like a man instead of a boy. He had always thought most school work was a waste of time. Who needed to know all that crap in the real world? His parents accepted it grudgingly. At least he would be earning money and paying them some board. He liked motorbikes and this was a way of getting to ride them. He soon had a chance to pick up a second-hand bike on the cheap from a customer and he got his licence. He cultivated a Rocker look, fixing his black hair with gel into a pompadour like that of Elvis. His boss was an old biker and an ageing Elvis fan, and he saw Wayne as a new edition of his younger self. He liked to tell him stories of his youthful adventures when he crossed the States on a Harley-Davidson. Biker gangs came to his garage and hung out there. After a year or so Wayne got in with one gang and rode with them on weekends. The bikers were more like a big social club that enjoyed riding together. But among them there was a group of five or six guys who were a bit harder-looking and had an air of recklessness, of being outside society. He got to know them. He found they were into drug-dealing and petty theft, as well as a bit of pimping. They liked the odd fight as well, and he felt they were the kind of people he could identify with. He was soon accepted into this gang, after proving himself by beating up a designated victim in a fast food place. He began to hang around with them on Saturday nights, mainly in the red light district, which was also the queer district of the city.

One of the gang leaders dealt drugs and the other was a pimp with three girls working for him. The rest of the gang tended to hang around to keep them company, and provide back-up for them in case of trouble. They were also interested in the richer, older punters, both queer and straight, who came to the area to pick up, and who could sometimes be lured into alleyways and discreetly mugged. It was a lively street scene with a dozen or so drag queens, and the gang enjoyed taunting them. They saw the drag queens as turf rivals of "their" girls, and since drag queens tend to bully street girls to drive them off their pitch, they pushed them around in their turn. The drag queens jeered at them and they insulted them back, but it never led to any serious violence, just the odd scuffle. Then one night three older members of the gang and Wayne were cruising around in an old Chevrolet V-8. Suddenly the car stopped and two of the others jumped out and grabbed two drag queens off the street. They bundled them into their car and drove away. They ended up in a wood and two of the older gang-members dragged the queens out, made them bend over a tree trunk lying on the ground and raped them. Wayne found the scene wildly exciting: the screams of the queens, the contemptuous curses of the gang-members, the animal rooting among the dead leaves in the dark wood, the blows, the fear, the smell of sweaty bodies and the queens' perfume, the blood on one of their faces. He was also astonished. He didn't know his queer-bashing companions would do that. When one of the gang leaders had finished, he turned to Wayne and offered him the queen, as if it was his turn. She or he was not bad-looking in a decadent, wrecked way, and suddenly Wayne felt this was a chance he'd been looking for. He was feeling the excitement of bloodlust and violence as much as of sex. He felt that if he didn't manage to get it up he could at least beat the bitch to pulp, since it was after all a man.

This thought liberated him from his fear. He got in there as hard as an axle and screwed the shit out of her. He was panting and grunting like an animal as he finished and he spanked her hard three or four times on the bare bottom.

"Hi ho, Silver!" he shouted for some reason. The others laughed. The fourth gang member was taking his turn with the other queen and he also spanked her backside and gave a rebel yell as if Wayne had started a good joke. Then the gang got back in their car and were going to drive away and leave the drag queens in the wood. The queens begged to be taken back to the city, so they didn't have to spend all night walking back. So they let them back into the car and they sat on the others' knees and everyone played at slap and tickle with them, and by the time they got back the atmosphere had become quite friendly.

"You boys needn't be so rough next time," complained one of them. "You can have us any time you want but you've no need to kill us while you're at it."

"Come on, you love it!" jeered one of the gang leaders. "A bit of rough trade."

"Rough trade is one thing but you went too far and you're not even paying, you mean bastards."

"We'll buy you a drink next time we see you, darling," said one.

They let the queens out on the main drag of the gay district. They adjusted their torn, muddy dresses as they walked away, slightly the worse for wear but otherwise unhurt. And a week later Wayne ran into one of them again in a pub and he talked to her and bought her a cocktail, and then they went out the back and did it in the toilet.

It was the first sex he'd had apart from raping his or her friend the week before. He felt the need somehow to talk to him or her and make some connection to mark the occasion.

He wanted to understand the other, to get inside his or her head.

"How do you live with what you are?" he blurted out as they had another drink.

The queen looked at him with a sardonic, knowing glance beneath her long false eyelashes, as she dragged on a cigarette held elegantly between fingers with long scarlet nails.

"I've lived with it all my life, darling. Ever since I was six I knew I was different." She smiled sardonically. "So it wasn't a shock for me the way it has been for you."

"What do you mean — what's been a shock for me?" he said quickly.

"The thing you're still trying to deal with, sweetheart. That's what makes you so violent towards us."

She sucked the green peppermint cocktail through the straw and looked up at him sexily from beneath her bouffant blond hair.

"And you're happy like this?"

"Not like this. I'm not just gay, darling. Not like you. I'm a trannie. I'm a girl trapped in a boy's body. I'll get out of it one day. I've started hormone treatment. I'm getting boobs already. Can't you feel how they're starting to swell?" She took his hand and slowly rubbed her breast with it. "In a few months I'll have real ones. Big, luxury boobs. Like Pamela Anderson." She smiled flirtatiously and fluttered her eyelashes. "Do you think you'll like me better with big boobs?"

He didn't know what to answer. She laughed, a tiny bit nastily, as if she knew she had confused him. Then she finished her drink and walked away.

He had the feeling she knew more about him than he knew himself. Why didn't he know what he wanted? He was not sure exactly what it was he went for in these people, what combination of male and female they had to be. Would he like her better with big boobs? He liked the female face, the mascara eyes, the long eye-lashes. Would he like boobs? But he didn't like real girls. Something about real girls turned him off at the crucial moment. He only liked fake ones. Why? It was a mystery. All he knew was that he had somehow found the form of sex that suited him, not with women, not with men, but with these strange creatures in between. And he had discovered that he could do it with violence or without, that the violence helped but was not really necessary. What counted was to dominate, to feel he dominated completely someone who was at his mercy, someone of a lower caste, a lower species, on whom violence could be used if the domination was challenged. A male who had lost caste by playing the female role, but who had not acquired the aura of untouchability, the aura of having a softer, more delicate nature, demanding protection, inhibiting violence, which a real girl carried around with her. A drag queen was like a girl you could brutalize without feeling shame or guilt. Since she was really a male, you could screw her as an act of unrestrained aggression. It was as if his desire required a female face but his aggression required a male body beneath it. He needed both things, a fusion of desire and aggression, in order to function. And if one urge was inhibited, the other was too.

He tried to talk about it a few nights later to one of the older gang leaders who had been in the car, the drug-dealer, Stan, as they drank in a pub after smoking a joint on the street. Stan wore a Luftwaffe peaked cap and a black biker jacket with swastikas on the collar. He was a body builder and had tattoos visible on his thick neck and wrists. Wayne thought he sounded incoherent as he struggled to express what he had found out about himself and violence and sex and how they went together. But the other stared at him with a grin of recognition.

"Fucking and violence, it's the same thing! Welcome to the world of the butch queer!"

It was the first time he had heard the term but now he had a name for what he was. Stan slapped him on the back and grinned, holding up his beer in a toast.

"We're the greatest club of dominant males the world has ever seen! The master race! The Nazis, they were all butch queers. All the leaders. Not just Roehm. But Heydrich. Hans Frank. Goering, Rudolf Hoess. Von Shirach. Maybe even Hitler. The whole officer corps of the SA, the Vikingkorps, all butch queers! Roehm wouldn't accept anyone who wasn't. Because we're the most brutal, savage, fearless, sadistic, violent bastards on earth! We're invincible! We were the force that smashed the old order in Germany!"

"But didn't the Nazis kill queers? Exterminate them?" said Wayne in surprise.

"Nah! It was all a show! They arrested ten thousand in all. Six thousand died. In ordinary labour camps. Out of a queer German population of at least two million. Does that sound like a programme of extermination? Less than half a per cent killed? When they killed eighty-five per cent of German Jews? They tolerated queers because they knew their movement was full of them. Only the drag queens and sissies got rounded up, and even then Himmler let the artists go. Butch queers were never arrested unless they were traitors. Half the SS camp guards were queer. They had harems of Jewish boys. We would have been welcome in the Nazi ranks. It was part of their cult of the male, the warrior brotherhood. Like the ancient Spartans. Sexual blood brothers are unbeatable. And we're an elite of blood brothers! There's nothing like raping the same slave arseholes to make men brothers. We're a scourge sent to punish the weak! We'll rule the earth again one day!" He raised his beer in a toast and laughed raucously, a laugh which ended in a high-pitched rebel yell and then a growling "Sieg Heil!" which sounded like the snarl of a wild beast.

Stan and one or two other gang members had links with a local firm of football hooligans who picked fights with other firms at football matches. Wayne and the others took part in some of these brawls as guests of the firm, just for fun. They usually took place outside the grounds so as to avoid the cameras, and sometimes they were organized in advance. They were brutal affairs. Some people used big screwdrivers and iron bars, and there were injuries that required trips to hospital. Wayne was arrested after one of these brawls where he took an iron bar off an enemy and split his skull with it, and he spent a year in prison for Grievous Bodily Harm. For Wayne prison was a formative experience. He was beaten up and gang raped by friends of his victim in the first week, and he spent his time getting his revenge. One by one he hunted down his attackers, cornered them alone with a couple of his mates and beat them to pulp. He always broke an arm or a wrist or a finger so they would remember him. He raped two of them for good measure. By the end he was feared.

After he came out, he found his employment opportunities more limited. He was sacked from his job at the garage: his boss was a bit less of a rebel than he pretended. His family disowned him. His father wouldn't speak to him. He took casual jobs as a bouncer at night clubs and sold drugs on the side, working for Stan. The bouncer job kept him in training by giving him one good fight every couple of nights. Sometimes he provoked it just to give himself the chance to smash someone's face in. That was now his chief pleasure in life. There was that explosive moment when he suddenly let go and rained a barrage of punches on his opponent that he couldn't possibly dodge or parry, and he beat through his defences and felt his knuckles smash into his face and break bones. Then there was the other's collapse and the flurry of punches that followed him all the way to the ground, now a soft, slushy target with blood gushing out of him. It was a sensation like orgasm, and he never tired of it. He didn't even need to kick him more than once or twice in the face when he was down, the guy was usually too far gone to think about getting up again. The sense of triumph was even greater than that of scoring a try under the posts. There was nothing that compared with beating another man into submission. It was like a vindication of his life, the supreme affirmation of his existence. He lived to win and to smash other males to pulp.

Sometimes he heard a little voice inside his head at these moments challenging his victim: "Now call me a faggot!" So he knew there was some connection there somehow, some sense of a flaw in his masculinity, which gave him this fury, this rage to destroy, this desire to prove that he was the macho, he was the master, he was the male, not them. He wondered sometimes where this rage came from, if the discovery of how his glands worked had hurt him a lot more than he thought, that somewhere inside himself he couldn't get over it, he had to take revenge on the world for what had happened to him. After all, being queer was a dirty joke, a nasty trick nature had played on him. He had all the physical gifts to be a shagger of thousands of women, except for one thing: he lacked the desire for it. Instead, those he desired were sissies he utterly despised. He was trapped in a blind alley: he could not desire women and he could not love men. So he was going to live for hate, not love. It was his gradual awareness that for certain men like himself sex does not go with love, it goes with hate, with a desire to kill, that made him sink more and more into a permanent mood where he imagined himself as the devil, as in league with evil forces against the world. Sometimes he said to himself as he walked into a pub (not a gay one but a straight one): "Wake up, suckers, Satan is here," and he liked to give a hard look at all the men in there as though issuing a general challenge, trying to detect a hint of defiance, resentment, snide contempt, that would give him the excuse to sidle up to the source of this resistance and pick a fight with him. And when he had the guy on the floor writhing in his own blood he would feel such triumph, he was king of the world, and he felt like saying to the God that had made him the way he was: "Fuck you, you've made me this, and I'll make your entire creation regret it!"

After a couple of years Stan moved down to London but came back from time to time. Wayne kept Stan's drug business going in his absence. One day Stan asked him if he wanted to come down to London and work for him there. He had expanded his London business a lot more and he needed a right-hand man as an enforcer. So Wayne moved down and lived with Stan in a big flat in Camberwell, where there were lots of druggies among the art students and dropouts. They used to go and visit clients who hadn't paid their debts or small-time dealers working for Stan who hadn't handed over the correct amount each month. It often involved beating the daylights out of the guy and Wayne really enjoyed it. Stan and he used to take turns at first but then Stan got lazy and left it to him more and more. Wayne loved the moment when the sucker had stopped his whining excuses and run out of things to say and Stan turned and gave him a nod. That meant he could just attack anyhow he wanted. He liked to step over and take the guy by the hair if he was sitting down and then knee him suddenly in the face so his nose was broken and blood gushed out. And then drag him to his feet and pound his head against the wall. It was the shock on their faces that he loved to see. They couldn't believe he could do it, just like that, go from a cold start, from a quiet, civilized conversation to pounding their face to pulp. He loved to see the look of horror on their face and he always felt like saying: "Yeah, this is life, man! Welcome to the real world! This is what it's like." And he felt that his beating had an educative function, not merely in teaching them not to renege on their financial obligations, but also in teaching them the nature of life.

Sometimes a young drug addict was worth screwing, so they raped him instead, or in addition. Stan usually had two or three on the go who would do it for a fix. Gradually the two of them moved further afield and began picking up young strays as far away as Victoria Station or Piccadilly Circus. Most were young runaways who were living on the street, looking for some way to make some bread, make a connection with someone, maybe sell themselves for a hot meal and a night in a bed. At first they took the boys home and shagged them normally, and then slowly they began to have more and more fun with them. They began tying them to the bed and shagging them all night and all day without feeding them, just giving them a sip of water, while they ate hamburgers in front of them and held them under their noses. Then they'd drag them outside drugged and blindfolded and let them go in the street again so they could never identify where their tormentors lived, in case they had any ideas about going to the police. It was so easy to do and these gullible young kids were so blindly trusting of anyone who approached them that after a while Wayne had an idea.

"Don't you know any people who would pay a few quid to screw these animals?"

Stan thought for a moment.

"Like hold a party and bring a kid out as a party act? Something to fuck in exchange for a contribution to his education fund?"

"Something like that. Or just advertise for anyone to come in, pay a few quid and get his rocks off. We'd keep the kid doped on GHB so as to shut him up."

So began a lucrative prostitution business, and after a couple of years it gave them enough money to move to a flat in Soho, so they could be nearer the main hunting ground for slaves and better positioned for clients. The drug trade in Camberwell was getting heavy, as gangs from Brixton began muscling in on their territory. They were Yardies with guns, and if you didn't want to go down that road and arm yourself to defend your turf, it was best to get out. In Soho they concentrated more on the prostitution business. They found they could rent out boys by the hour or the night and after a while sell them on to one of the networks that specialized in either porn film-making for the internet or selling broken-in sex-slaves to rich masters. These were mostly boys between thirteen and eighteen, so they had no particular qualms about trafficking in children, since they didn't see them as children.

"If it's old enough to come, it's old enough to be fucked," said Stan. "I did it to my own brother once when he was twelve and I was fifteen. He didn't have the guts to tell anyone. He turned out to be a faggot anyhow later on. I reckon I have a nose for them."

Wayne was slightly disturbed by this story, but he understood him. Both of them shared the same contempt for any male who allowed himself to be shafted, even though these were the only partners they had. They saw their prey as born to be slaves, and they were masters of slaves, like the ancient Romans. And slaves could be sold on when you had finished with them, without worrying too much about what their new owners would do to them. They lived in a world which they saw as harsh and pitiless, and to conform to the rules of that world was for them a virtue, a source of pride.

It gave them a sense of stern rigour in the face of life. They covered the walls of the flat with symbols and photos of the Death's Head Division of the Waffen-SS, their heroes — the warriors bringing death, destruction and vengeance on the world. Stan worshipped them as if they were gods.

Stan told him once how he had learned to enjoy violence. When he was sixteen he had been sent to a youth detention centre in Medomsley in Durham for riding in a stolen car. There he had been picked out by the officer who ran the kitchens, a man called Neville Hubbard, who told him he would be working for him. The next day Hubbard took him into a storeroom, smacked his head against the brick wall, tied him up and raped him. Stan never forgot it. Hubbard raped all the boys he wanted and kept them as his slaves. They were all terrified of him, because he was a big, powerfully-built man and the boys were underfed teenage runts, mainly from care homes. Stan was in a blind rage not just with Hubbard but above all with himself for not having been strong enough to fight him off. In order to get over his own humiliation and shame, he raped another boy two days later. He was determined to be among those who did it to others, not those who had it done to them. When the other boy went snivelling to Hubbard about him, hoping to see him punished, a strange thing happened. Hubbard summoned Stan to the kitchen that night. But instead of punishing him, Hubbard told him to hold the other boy's hand on a hotplate for snitching. He did it, and the boy screamed his head off. Hubbard laughed and then told Stan to hold the boy down while he raped him. Afterwards he proposed that Stan should do the same and Hubbard held the boy down while he did. From then on Stan became Hubbard's sidekick. He joined the little clique of prison officers and other staff who helped in holding or tying down boys while

Hubbard raped them. They got a chance to take their turn once in a while as a reward.

Hubbard was a sadist who liked to hold the boys' hands on hot baking dishes or on the hot stove so they screamed while he screwed them. Then he liked to humiliate them by spitting in their mouths afterwards as they lay groaning and sobbing — just to ram home that he owned them body and soul. He would then hold their mouths shut and force them to swallow his foul-tasting phlegm. Stan developed an enjoyment of the same kind of total domination. He only spent nine months in Medomsley but it was those nine months, he said, that gave him his training for life. After that he knew what he was and how to get his kicks. He became a body-builder just to make sure he was never again on the receiving end at the hands of a stronger man. And though he hated Hubbard and would have killed him if he could have got away with it, in a twisted way he admired his evil nature and modelled himself on him. Above all he admired him for never getting caught. He later learned that after raping hundreds of boys, Hubbard had left the prison service and become a minister in the United Reformed Church. None of the complaints against him was ever investigated, because the police saw his accusers as lying, delinquent scum and threatened to send them back to prison if they ever repeated their accusations against a highly-respected prison officer.

Stan continued to run his own drug business on the side, without bringing Wayne in as a partner, just using him as an employee. Wayne thought this was unfair since he had gone halves on his idea of the prostitution business. Stan, who was eleven years older, still saw himself as the boss. Even the lease of the flat was in his name only, though they split the rent. Wayne didn't complain at first — just noted it all and stored it up. After a few years their relations got more and more strained. He suspected Stan was robbing him blind. When he finally came out with one or two remarks to this effect, and suggested stricter accounting, Stan turned surly. Wayne got the feeling he was getting ready to dump him from the business. He didn't see the point of an open confrontation and a fist fight. What would it solve? One day he just hit Stan over the head with a hammer from behind, tied him to his bed, and when he woke up, asked him politely for the pin numbers of his credit and debit cards.

When only a string of curses was forthcoming, he lit the gas stove and heated a frying pan on it and began to lay it lovingly on various parts of Stan's anatomy. With a gag on, his screams became simply a muffled roar, but his eyes gave eloquent testimony to his pain. Every now and again Wayne would lift the gag a bit and ask quietly about the codes. After two days, when Stan was blistered over most of his body, and his skin was starting to fester and ooze a bit, he gave in and said a number.

"If it's wrong, it'll cost you a leg," said Wayne. He went out, tried the card and came back in with a wad of notes. He decided to let Stan have a drink of water and a piece of bread and go to the toilet. Since Stan had accounts in several banks, Wayne got the other pin numbers out of him in the same way. He kept him locked in his room for months while he took the maximum amount out of each account each day. Occasionally he hosed Stan down with disinfectant, using a powerful water pistol. Otherwise he left him with just a bedside bucket and his own muck and kept the bedroom door closed. Letters came from the banks to inform Stan of the balance that remained in his accounts, and at first they were tidy sums that would keep Wayne going for some time. Then the bank balances slowly dwindled to nothing while the stash in the drawer piled up. At last he realized he didn't need Stan any longer, and his bedsores and festering burns and crap were all beginning to stink the place out. He was surprised how low Stan had fallen in his esteem since he had begun wallowing in his own shit. It was hard to see someone in that condition as much more than an animal.

He moved his stuff out in a couple of suitcases to a room in a small hotel with a solid safe, where he stowed the money. He bought a cheap polyester duvet which he judged would be particularly inflammable. That night he gave Stan a bottle of whisky to drink. When he proved uncooperative, he held his nose and tipped half of it down his throat and the rest on his clothes. Then he knocked him out with a hammer wrapped in a thick towel so it wouldn't split his skull, and put the hammer back in the kitchen cupboard. He undid the ropes that bound Stan and put them in the kitchen cupboard too. Then he laid the duvet on top of him, tucking it under his chin. Stan was a smoker so Wayne lit one of his cigarettes and dropped it on the duvet. He watched while the duvet caught fire and the fire spread to the bed itself, and soon engulfed Stan's unconscious body. He retreated from the bedroom when it became an inferno and quickly left the apartment, pulling the door closed behind him using a paper tissue. He walked swiftly down the three flights of stairs. He ripped the bit of paper with his name on it off Stan's letter box. It was going on for midnight so he thought it would take a while before the smoke woke the neighbours. He walked a couple of blocks and went into a crowded pub where he ordered a beer and waited. It was a good twenty minutes before he heard sirens in the neighbourhood. He looked at his watch with satisfaction. "So long, Stan," he muttered, finished his beer and walked to his hotel.

Wayne was now flush with money. His name was not on the flat's lease and had not been given to the estate agency that rented it, so he felt there was little chance he would be linked to the fire. But just to be sure he rented a safe deposit box and put most of his money in it and then took a trip to Amsterdam. He stayed for several weeks, checking the British newspapers regularly. He saw the report on an accidental death in a fire, which police were not treating as suspicious. He waited patiently for more news about it but none came. Meanwhile, he made some contacts in Amsterdam, fellow-entrepreneurs with boy brothels, internet porn companies, etc. When he felt the coast was clear, he came back to London and rented a bigger flat with a view of the skyline. It was more towards Covent Garden where the rents were less outrageous, but he still called it Soho in his mind because it sounded better. He equipped it with cages. He now had the continental connections to sell on the young boys he captured after he had drawn a maximum rental use out of them. He worked with an underworld travel agency specialized in getting them across the Channel when their use-by date had passed. He also linked up with other men who specialized in hunting for boys on a freelance basis for the networks. He became a supplier to wealthy clients with a penchant for thirteen to fifteen-year olds, whom he guaranteed to deliver broken in and suitably drugged, for a very high price. He was not usually involved with pre-adolescent boys, because he didn't have any urge to screw them himself. It was one of the perks of his business to try out the better-looking boys and break them in personally.

He gradually found in fourteen and fifteen-year old boys exactly the sexual partners that suited him. The Lazlo episode, which occurred soon after he began to live alone, put him off transvestites and transsexuals for a long time. Lazlo was twenty-two when they met, and had a lot of experience and a mind of his own. Wayne found that independence galling. Lazlo's final betrayal was a lesson he never forgot: never let sentiment get the upper hand. In time he came to feel that most adult transvestites and sissies in general were tiresome drama queens who talked too much and irritated him with their silly, giggly personalities. What he liked more and more were teenage slave-boys who remained in awe of him and kept their mouths shut. Breaking in his young rent boys gave him precisely the relationship of domination and submission that he enjoyed. He liked to play the role of a demanding coach imposing harsh discipline on his athletes, or a sergeant major drilling recruits to toughen them up. Their looks and characters at that age corresponded exactly to his tastes. They were not consciously aping girlish behaviour the way drag queens or mincing fairies were. They were naturally girlish because naturally childish. But at the same time they had developed the male form he liked — slender, graceful, but with the beginnings of muscular strength. They thought they were heterosexual and had no idea how they were about to be transformed. They were mostly virgins, utterly ignorant of the acts they were going to be subjected to. He loved that innocence. He loved to violate it and savour their shock. He saw himself as their mentor, their guru, showing them what life was really like. He would often joke with them about the things he was going to do to them, and then have them in tears or yelling in pain, and continue to joke. Or else he put on a show of affection for them and then, when he had their trust, treated them with particular cruelty. In short, they were his toys. And as he played with them, tormented them, and broke them in, he developed a whole range of feelings he had never known existed because he had had no real relationships, apart from Lazlo. He saw his own personality blossoming and maturing as the fruit of these sadistic games. He was above all getting these boys to feel the horror for themselves that he had once felt when he realized what he was. He was destroying the smug complacency they had lived in until then, and making them feel the torment and self-loathing he had known. It was a superb revenge on life.

After some years he went back now and again to drag queens just to see if any of them still turned him on. Some of them did. Then one night he picked up what he thought was a drag queen, judging by her height, slightly mannish face and low voice, but when he got her back to his flat and undressed her he discovered it was a real woman. He was so shocked he found himself checking again to make sure (he was a bit stoned and she was a foreigner who spoke only broken English.) Then he decided to screw her anyway, as a kinky challenge, just to see what it was like. After a few preliminaries, he plunged into her as she lay on her back. A number of surprises awaited him. The vaginal lubrication system also serves as a cooling system, like the oil in a piston engine, so the temperature was several degrees lower than the friction-induced heat of an arsehole that he was used to. It was also far less tight — she was rather wide-hipped, and he could easily have put a fist in there. And it was extremely wet, beyond anything he could have imagined. So this is what they rave about, he said to himself. Compared to a boy's arse, it felt like rooting around inside a waterlogged gumboot. To make matters worse the horny bitch wrapped her legs round him to pull him further inside her. He felt a loss of control as if he was being embraced by the tentacles of a giant octopus — a kind of overpowering mother-love which sought to drown his hard, probing tool deep inside this bottomless swamp. And all the while she was urging him in a dramatic whisper and her thick foreign accent to do it harder, to fuck her to death, to come like a stallion — a ploy to make him shoot his bolt as quickly as possible. He felt that if he came inside her it would be like a surrender, a defeat, a giving in to this enveloping body and its desire to draw him into some slushy, wet communion with her.

He abruptly pulled out of her and curtly ordered her to turn over and get on all fours in the doggy position. It was a struggle to get her to understand, and then he got behind her and stuck it into her arsehole. With no more lubricant than her juice on his knob, he had to force his way in and she cried out in pain. He felt immediate relief that he was now the one in charge. He was now completely external to this body and in total control of it. It was no longer embracing him like an octopus. He was the master; this was his slave. There was no longer a face with its intrusive personality, its eyes staring up at him like a mad cow, but merely a blank body, an expanse of smooth back and rump as much an object as a table. He could watch every movement in and out that he made, as if he was engaged in an act of torture. He could watch his own thrusts and grinds like a voyeur. This was pornography in action, and he was both actor and viewer. This was what he saw as normal sex, sex as it is now — detached, in control, voyeuristic, hard, aggressive, narcissistic. He understood why more and more straight men were indulging in anal intercourse as well, in the doggy position, so that they didn't have to look at a face and pretend there was something personal going on. Sodomy was faceless sex — sex without acknowledging the other person's existence, without sharing, without an embrace, without eye contact, without any of those soggy emotions that spoil the pure physicality and exultation of penetrating another body, dominating it, using it and degrading it to object status. No wonder the Ancients practised sodomy chiefly on their slaves and generally their child slaves. No wonder certain tribes inflicted it on defeated enemy warriors. It was the supreme act of mastery, of subjugating another, degrading another, ramming home his abject inferiority. Sodomy was the ultimate act of enslavement.

When he felt he had had enough exercise, he decided quite deliberately to come inside this slag. He quickened his pace and began ripping into her as hard as he could. The traces of dried shit inside her that had been liquefied by friction into a greasy lubricant had long since been absorbed and it was hurting her again. She began moaning and crying in rhythm to his thrusts. "That's it, you bitch, suffer!" he yelled. He hammered her plump buttocks with his pelvis as if he was hitting a punching bag, faster and faster till he came like an explosion. His organ was like a fist and he tried consciously to rupture her. "This is not love!" he snarled as he jerked and jerked convulsively inside her. It was an act of pure hatred, and he had a sense of triumph that he had achieved this degree of aggression with a woman as well. He slapped the bitch on the behind as he had done that first time with that first drag queen. He had a feeling of having scored a victory as he pulled out of her. She was snivelling, to his great satisfaction. He had outmanoeuvred her clinging female nature, escaped her slushy maternal embrace, and reduced her to one of his catamite slaves. He felt glad to be alive in an age which had made sodomy a standard practice, celebrated it officially in nuptial ceremonies, and taught it to every primary school child as normal.

This excursion into the realm of heterosexual sodomy was not something he repeated. He had enjoyed teaching this slut a lesson, but it was nothing compared to the lessons he enjoyed handing out to males. Of course most of his adolescent rent boys were without experience of any kind, hetero or homo, so he was teaching them from scratch. What gave him special pleasure was screwing slightly older youths who had already started on a heterosexual career and never dreamed they could be used the other way. It was teaching a lesson in humility to young bucks whom he found insufferably arrogant, smug and self-satisfied. It was screwing as an act of pure revenge, and for him there was no revenge on life so sweet as raping a heterosexual male.

Once in the Burger King in Leicester Square, one of his favourite hunting grounds, he saw a slim boy with long hair who was trying to make conversation with a foreign girl sitting near him. The girl left and he caught the boy's eye and made a grimace of commiseration. They got talking. He was a Canadian from a small town in Alberta, a cowboy town, he admitted wryly, and after studying English Literature at university he had dropped out of a graduate degree to travel the world and try to write. Wayne gathered he was about twenty-three, though he looked a bit younger. He was in London staying at a doss house and looking for work to finance his next trip through Europe or Asia. The boy told a few stories of his travels, of living on beaches in Thailand and India, and the retro hippie girls he had scored there. They had one of those male shooting-the-shit bull sessions and Wayne enjoyed playing along with this and thinking to himself how he would destroy this self-satisfied hetero jerk — who was just too pleased with himself and having too good a time on earth shagging girls. He was a sissy-looking bastard with his long fair hair and outmoded hippie gear and Wayne was slightly resentful that his glands seemed to work normally. He had an urge to teach him what life was really like. He suggested a beer somewhere and the boy agreed and they went to a pub and continued the bull session. Then Wayne slipped a little white Rohypnol tablet in his second beer when he went to the toilet. The boy, whose name was Will, was soon out of it and swaying all over the place. He fell off his bar stool and Wayne helped him up and supported him with his arm round his shoulders as he guided him out the door and along the street.

As they walked through the bustling streets of Theatreland, the boy started talking a bit, blurting out nonsense in a slurry voice to passers-by. Wayne kept his head down so as not to be recognized later. He got him up in the lift to his flat and laid him on the bed comatose. Then he stripped his clothes off, took a couple of pills and set to work to rape him for a solid two hours. He enjoyed screwing this self-satisfied hetero jerk more than any of the younger boys because he knew that afterwards he was going to have to seriously disable him. When the boy woke up next morning and turned to him and realized where he was and what had happened, he let out a yell. He reached for Wayne's throat to try to strangle him, and Wayne had to punch him a few times to put him out. Then he tied his hands and feet to the bed, gagged him, waited till he woke up and screwed him all over again.

He kept the boy there for two days without food, only glasses of water, and he was near exhaustion when Wayne took his gag off for a moment. It was an old-fashioned bed with bedposts, and he had placed Will on his back, his hands and feet both tied to the bedposts behind his head, so he was trussed up like a chicken and his arsehole was just at the right angle to be easily accessible. Wayne put a knee on his balls and looked down at him.

"Now, are you going to be reasonable or am I going to hurt you seriously?"

"I'll kill you, you faggot bastard, if it's the last thing I do!" The voice was hoarse and shaking with fury and hatred and humiliation.

Wayne shifted the knee on his balls and bore down till the boy yelled in pain.

"I'm not a faggot, Will. You're the one being fucked up the arse, in case you haven't noticed. You're the faggot. I'm your owner. Your master. You're my Kleenex, my rubbish bin, my rubber doll."

"I'll kill you, you fucking pervert, if it takes me twenty years!"

"That's not the attitude, Will. You're going to force me to do something really unpleasant."

"What did I ever do to you that you've done this to me?" The boy was almost crying in frustration, trying to understand why he had been chosen for this ordeal.

"There was just something about you, Will, that gave me the urge to do it. Take you down a peg, you self-satisfied, straight little jerk. And the best thing for you is just to accept it and forget it. You've been fucked up the arse, it happens to lots of people, and there's nothing you can do about it. It's all perfectly natural. Queer is the new normal. Even if you went to the police, you wouldn't be able to prove it was rape. You look a bit like a faggot, Will, did anyone ever tell you? How will you prove you didn't consent? They'll just laugh at you — faggot had a row with his one-night stand and decided to accuse him of rape. They've seen it all before. Now, I'm going to knock you out again, take you to another part of town and let you go. If you come back looking for me, I'll kill you. Is that clear, lover-boy?"

Will lunged his head up convulsively and spat in his face. Wayne wiped the spit off slowly with the sheet, put the gag back on Will, and then got up. He went into the kitchen and got a skewer out of the drawer, and came back with it.

"I think you haven't learned your lesson, Will. You're going to try and find me, aren't you? Well, we'll see how you go when you can't see any more."

He climbed on the bed and held the skewer over Will's face and slowly descended towards his eyes. Will yelled through the gag and tried to move his face away, his eyes widening in terror. Wayne held his head steady with a vice-like grip on his forehead, peeled back a tightly closed eyelid with a thumb, and drove the skewer first into one eye, then into the other. Blood bubbled out of them, ruby drops that squeezed out through the eyelids like big red tears that soon became little streams mixed with some yellow, watery gunk. Will was roaring through his gag with the muffled roar of an animal, bucking violently against Wayne's weight and twisting the ropes that held him. Wayne thought for a moment and then went and got some superglue from a drawer. He carefully glued his bloody eyelids shut.

"I think your tongue might be a problem, too, Will. I'm afraid you're going to talk about this, aren't you? We'll just have to make it difficult to talk clearly."

He got some pliers from a drawer and a sharp carving knife. Then he took off the gag, held Will's nose till his mouth opened, grabbed his tongue with the pliers and pulled it out as far as he could. Then he slit it across with the knife and tore away a good length of it. Will was screaming like a stuck pig. Blood came bubbling out through his lips. Wayne stuffed a tea towel into his mouth.

"They'll have problems understanding what you say now, Will. And there's just one more thing. Your ability to write."

He took each hand in turn and broke the index finger on the bedpost, then cut the webbed flesh between the fingers so it would infect when he rummaged in rubbish bins for food.

"I think this will stop you writing too much crap for a while, Will. It's really a pity about that writing career of yours. But you were warned. You did bring this on yourself."

Will passed out. His tongue was gushing blood into the tea towel. Wayne decided to cauterize the wound by heating the pliers on the gas ring and placing them against the bleeding stump of the tongue. It hissed and smoked. He tipped some whisky into his mouth for good measure. Then he glued his lips half shut with superglue, leaving a hole big enough to breathe through if need be. Will looked a mess, but curiously enough this turned him on so he screwed him one more time. Will woke up in the middle of it and groaned.

"Enjoying it, aren't you?" Wayne said and came with gusto. Afterwards he said: "That was your farewell ride, Will. The last fuck you'll ever have. You'll never forget it, will you? And this was a first for me, Will. I've never fucked a blind man before."

Then he knocked Will out again with a punch to the temple so he could undo the ropes and put his clothes back on. He spilled a bit of whisky on them too. He took good care to remove his Canadian passport and all other identity cards, credit cards and money. Then he picked him up and carried him to the lift. The boy was only about five foot six and slightly built, so it was almost like carrying a child. By the time they got onto the street, Will had come to, and Wayne was able to place him back on his feet.

"We're going to get you to a hospital, Will, so just walk, will you?"

The boy was so totally subjugated by pain and blindness that he obeyed, as though in a trance, holding onto his arm and wheezing and grunting strangely through his partially sealed lips. Wayne walked him for a couple of hundred metres through the dark streets and took a few confusing turns. Then he laid him down in a doorway in a blind alleyway, hidden from passers-by on the street by some rubbish bins.

"Have a rest, Will. I'm just going for help."

Then he walked away and went back home.

A month later he saw Will again. He was sitting in Leicester Square begging with a Styrofoam cup. His eyes were bandaged, as were his two hands. His lips were covered with scabs as if he had torn them apart. He looked very thin and now had a beard. Wayne walked up to him. Making sure there was nobody else close by, he said quietly over his shoulder:

"Hello, Will, you're still here then. You'd be better off going home, wouldn't you? Or maybe dead? There are bridges, Will. You fucked up this life, didn't you? This was all your choice. You had another one. So now, why stay?"

Then he walked quickly away into the crowd before the roar sounded behind him, like that of a madman. The roar went on and on in a series of connected phrases, but they were utterly incomprehensible, as though he was speaking a language of his own. When Wayne glanced back he saw Will had stood up and was making short lunges in different directions, waving his arms and banging into people. Wayne made a mental note that he had found the perfect way of silencing a victim. The police had obviously dismissed Will as a drunken, deranged tramp from abroad who didn't speak English, and nobody had bothered trying to figure out what he was saying. He had no passport or money to get back to Canada, could not tell anyone who he was, or telephone his family. He couldn't even ask the way to the Canadian High Commission or whatever it was called now. He would probably end his days on the street in London, dying of slow starvation or pneumonia. Wayne shook his head sadly over his case. How heartless life was! What sort of a God had made this world? As for the social services, what a total wash-out they were! It did not bear thinking about.

He got to know Cyril Jones as a business partner. Jones was his customer twice for boys of thirteen, but then he learned that Jones was the kingpin of a network of his own, a real paedo network using boys as young as five, thanks to his access to care homes. Wayne found his business model an interesting one. Jones left the boys in their care homes, their food and accommodation paid for by the state, and just had them ferried about to customers. That saved on overheads. It was something possible only with very young boys, too frightened to talk to anyone and too young to memorize addresses or names. Jones wanted to tap into Wayne's knowledge of how to get into the internet porn industry, how to dispose of boys abroad, etc. Wayne in his turn wanted to extend his client base into the higher circles of Westminster politicians that Jones provided services to. Their businesses had a certain synergy that led them to work together occasionally. They respected each other, but warily, like beasts of prey of different species. They sometimes referred clients to each other's networks. Lately Wayne had provided his best-looking boy for Jones to take to visit a special VIP client, a very rich member of the House of Lords, who paid liberally for his pleasures. When Jones suddenly proposed a dead boy to dispose of, Wayne was able to take him off his hands, thanks to his client, Bendigo, who was in the market for one. Jones had assured him the boy had died accidentally. Wayne pretended to believe him but couldn't care less. He tried to keep Jones and Bendigo from meeting each other so as to break the chain of traceability if the body was ever the object of an inquiry. Bendigo had agreed (if the police ever asked) to claim he had found the boy dead in a wood. Wayne had hinted to him of the consequences if his own name ever came up.

"Nobody shops me and lives," he told him with a grin.

He went along to see the exhibition of the *Boy in Formaldehyde*. He couldn't help admiring how this shit of an artist had converted a corpse into something that inspired so much interest. He could see potential here for far higher profits if the success of this installation translated into the insane prices that top art works now commanded. He calculated that he could increase the price for the next body several times over. And then the artist got in touch again with this new proposition. Wayne knew he was onto something here. He could see this becoming the most profitable line of all. And when he decided to get the professor involved, it was, he thought, a stroke of genius. It would not only outsource the murder but raise it from a sordid crime to the status of a work of art.

22

Cyril Jones and Professor Rigdon met in a pub not far from Rigdon's institute and sat at a table with a couple of pints. It was a bit like a reunion of old friends, though they came from very different backgrounds. Cyril was Birmingham working-class and had gone to work for the Tax Office at sixteen. Rigdon was the son of a wealthy City broker and had gone to a private school in Sussex and then Oxford. But their tastes (and their shared interest in children's homes) had brought them together some twenty-five years earlier, and they had kept up an acquaintance ever since. Cyril broke the news of the boy who needed to be converted into an installation and mentioned the kind of money that might be involved.

"I had a sudden flash — a vision of you making this thing into a piece of theatre or performance art, one of those happenings you used to go in for back in the good old days when things were a bit more relaxed."

"Really?" laughed Rigdon uneasily. "What gave you that idea?" He secretly considered Jones a vulgar buffoon but he was a useful ally, and he needed influential friends with similar interests, so he humoured him. He had also become increasingly wary about what he said on the subject of his unorthodox hobbies, even to those who shared them.

"Well, this boy is going to become an art installation, a boy in a tank of formaldehyde, and I think the act of converting him into that shouldn't be wasted. It should be as artistic and spectacular and — what's the word you used to use? — as transgressive as the installation itself will be."

"It's an interesting idea," said Rigdon cautiously. "It depends whether the artist concerned is fully committed to the notion of transgression."

"I haven't met him personally but I'm reliably informed he is. His track record speaks for itself. He seems to have made transgression his personal signature."

"Really? Of course I'd need to talk to him before thinking about any form of collaboration."

Rigdon took a gulp of beer and his expression became meditative. Then he began casually to expound the ideas that passed through his mind, as if the urge to lecture was something he couldn't repress.

"It's true that all modern art is rooted in transgression. If you think about it, all the iconic, landmark works over the last hundred years — the found urinal, the black square, the soup can, the rows of bricks, the cans of the artist's shit, the pickled shark, the unmade bed — they're all essentially transgressive. Transgressive of taste, of aesthetic standards, of common sense, of human intelligence, even of sanity. Transgression is now the norm, the established order in art. If it's not transgressive — that is to say, an insult to humanity — it doesn't stand a chance of being exhibited. But it's all fake transgression. None of it breaks any laws. It is empty, posturing transgression, confined to the phoney world of the art critics. It is all a million miles from real transgression. A lampshade made of human skin — that is real transgression." He smiled grimly. "Blood, violence, murder, rape, child sex. They are what I call transgression. That is the element we managed to introduce into modern art once or twice in the past — an element of.... seriousness." He sipped his beer and put it down. Then he stared at it with sudden gloom. "But that was in another era. I doubt if we could get away with it now."

"I see no reason why not," said Cyril brightly, trying to cheer him up. "Things may have got tighter in some ways, it's true, but don't forget there has been enormous progress since then on other fronts. Who could have imagined even twenty years ago the Tories would legalize gay marriage, eh?"

"Yes, but it's all become so tame and bourgeois, hasn't it?" said Rigdon with disdain. "Poofter couples sitting on their sofas in their flowery dressing-gowns, watching Strictly Come Dancing as they paint their nails. Where's the transgression? Where are the Maenads, the Bacchanals, the Mysteries of Eleusis, the Lupercal?"

"Oh, you're being a bit hard on the age," protested Cyril with a grin. "Parliaments can't organize orgies. But they can make them legal. And they've made life vastly easier for the likes of us. We've achieved so many of the things we argued for years ago."

"Have we? Such as what?"

Cyril looked slightly taken aback by the challenge. His tone became almost blustering in his eagerness to make such an obvious point.

"Lots of things! What about the European law that the age of sexual consent must be the same for homos and heteros? That means in Spain it's thirteen! We can screw thirteen-year old boys in Spain legally! How's that for legalized transgression!"

A few heads at the bar turned to stare. He lowered his booming voice.

"I had one there on my last holiday. He looked ten. Who would have thought that would ever be legal in a Western country back in the old days? You remember the holiday we had in Morocco years ago — and asked ourselves if this would ever be possible anywhere in Europe?"

"Yes, but that's Spain," said Rigdon dismissively. "The Mediterranean. Two millennia of sensual indulgence going back to the Greeks and Romans. Here in this country people have got a paedophile obsession. It's the new acceptable face of puritan bigotry. Chase it out the door and it comes back through the window. And they've become such busybodies, sticking their noses into other people's affairs. The old days of the iron gates that *hoi polloi* didn't dare look behind are gone."

"Oh, I think you'll find that iron gates are still proof against the riff-raff, the bigots, the puritans. It's a question of selecting the guests carefully, restricting things to a circle of the enlightened and the liberal-minded. You remember how it used to be done! We never got infiltrated."

"So, you think all that would still be possible? Masks, disguises, a private carnival for selected guests only? Black masses. Satanic rituals with virgins deflowered and blood flowing." Rigdon's enthusiasm was beginning to be aroused and he smiled nostalgically at the memory. "It's tempting," he said, without much conviction. He sipped his beer.

"In this case blood might not be so appropriate. Apparently they want the product absolutely intact. Pristine was the word. Not a bruise."

"That limits things a bit on the methodology side. What does that leave? Poison? Suffocation? Or drowning?"

"Drowning would be ideal — given how it's going to be used afterwards. I think drowning would be highly suitable." Cyril mimicked a mincing upper-class accent.

"We'd have to think about how to make it exciting," mused Rigdon. "These things always depend on inventing a brilliant scenario, so that people are so taken with the drama that the actual fatality is almost overlooked, as collateral damage. There has to be a narrative, so there is suspense about whether the subject will make it through or not. That way, when he doesn't, there's a sigh of regret, almost as there is in a tragedy or a tear-jerking film where the hero dies. It's sadness and tragedy that make death palatable. And that is really the purpose of great art — to make us accept death. Death after a tremendous dramatic struggle appears natural, inevitable, even beautiful. What makes death ugly is when it is sudden, absurd, without logic." He paused and changed tone. "Of course, our performance, if we ever did such a thing, would be real art, a class above the usual mediocrity of these installations. In fact this work would gain an aura of seriousness only because of the underground legend our performance inspired."

"Oh, I've no doubt the performance will far outshine the work itself. You're a real artist, unlike this trendy charlatan, that's for sure." Cyril's admiration for Rigdon, whom he considered almost as his mentor, bordered on sycophancy. But he also saw that flattery was the right tactic to sway him in favour of this project.

"I do feel I'm going back to the source of tragedy," said Rigdon with quiet pride. He pursued the idea. "That was almost certainly in human sacrifice. For every culture. Gathering to watch the sacrifice of a chosen victim must have been the central ritual of early society. Even when we became more civilized and replaced the sacrifice of the king or the virgin by a drama recounting the fall and death of a hero, we still kept up the ritual of blood sacrifice in public executions. They became the solemn celebration of death in all its cruelty. Such a pity humanist squeamishness has deprived us of that — killing as a sacred, public ritual!"

"Oh, I think it's just changed form, that's all," Cyril reassured him. "It's just moved to the cinema and the internet. Films are a lot more violent and bloody today than anything in the past. They're often just a series of gory killings for people's entertainment. And then there's the whole sexual dimension, the combination of sex and cruelty, which past ages were too prudish to go in for. Didn't you once say that public executions have been replaced as ritual performances by public sex? That's the spectacle every strip club in every city in the West now provides. Penetration on stage. Simulated rape. It's the new form of human sacrifice for the modern generation."

"I agree, I did say that once," conceded Rigdon. "Live sex as the new form of public ritual. But I still think sexual acts alone are never enough to convey an image of life in all its horror. There's nothing like an actual death — a snuff movie, or preferably a live killing — to provide that fateful, sacrificial solemnity."

"Well, we all agree there. Ideally speaking. But how often can it be done?" Cyril found Rigdon's airs of a purist somewhat exaggerated. "You're the expert on that. How often did you achieve the ideal of sacrificial death as the climax of a public performance?"

He was curious for the details of what Rigdon had actually got up to, and his instincts as Liberal Democrat Chief Whip to dig the dirt on everyone were in full cry. But he also thought that evoking the glorious and gory deeds of the past would help bring the professor round to the notion these things could be done again.

Rigdon sipped his beer meditatively. He had a reflex of caution about vainglorious confessions, even to supposed friends and fellow-aficionados.

"I suppose what comes first to mind is the boy we barbecued twenty-five or so years ago. Were you there for that? We held the show at Lord Sodbury's estate."

"No, I missed that one. Must have been just before we met."

"It was not originally part of the programme. But this boy — he wasn't all there but he was very good-looking — had been brought along as a sex toy. He was buggered by dozens of guests, and had to swallow litres of sperm. He literally choked to death on it, or perhaps even drowned when somebody came down his windpipe. We tried patting his back, mouth-to-mouth, cardiac massage, nothing worked. We were stuck with his dead body. So we decided to put it on a spit and barbecue it. We put an apple in his mouth where the spit came out as they do with a pig, and it caused great hilarity. The atmosphere became quite uninhibited — naked dancing around the roasting beast. Heaps of bodies threshing about on the lawn. A real Witches' Sabbath. And the boy actually tasted remarkably good." He paused, reminiscent. "Ever eaten a slice of roast rump of boy with a few baked potatoes?"

"Never had the pleasure," chortled Cyril. "But I was thinking about it the other day, funnily enough, though the image that came to mind was that of mint sauce."

"Cannibalism has had a very bad press," went on Rigdon seriously. "But it is an excellent way of recycling bodies. I should have thought the ecologists would have been onto it by now. Sustainability. The young healthy bodies, car accidents and so forth, could be used for prime meat, or for those frozen TV dinners, lasagne, cannelloni. They use horse meat, why not human meat? The older bodies could be ground up for cat and dog food, animal feed, or even fertilizer. There's such a lot of protein being wasted. We could feed all of Africa with recycled bodies. I mean, they used to do it themselves for centuries, didn't they? Mass human sacrifice followed by days of feasting. We stupidly interfered and they've been on the brink of starvation ever since. Time we learned from other cultures. Instead we cling to these absurd superstitions. Respecting dead bodies. Why? Nobody believes in the soul any more. What's it about?"

"The trouble is we have so many attitudes carried over from religion even though no one believes in it any longer," declared Jones. "If we could stop the teaching of that unhealthy Christian rubbish, things would become a lot more rational."

At that moment a slim, dark-haired, well-groomed young man of about twenty detached himself from the crowd at the bar and approached their table, swaying slightly as if the worse for drink. He was staring at Rigdon as though at a ghost. Another man the same age but a bit taller followed him, trying to hold his arm and restrain him. The first one shook off his hand and began speaking drunkenly.

"Well, if it isn't Professor Rigdon! I was at your last lecture. What sort of homophobic crap was that? Gay people are caused by pollution! Are you telling me I'm the result of diox — dioxin pollution?" he stuttered, hiccupping.

"Not necessarily," said Rigdon with amiable condescension. "Let me look at you." He glanced at his face from both sides. "No, you might be the result of bisphenol-A. Or perhaps phthalates. Or even PCBs. Though I'd keep that quiet — PCBs produce a rather common sort of gay person. I'd tell people it was phthalates, if I were you. They produce an altogether more distinguished class of poofter."

Rigdon judged that the young man was too drunk to fight so he could safely insult him. He was also smaller and more slightly built than the burly, six-foot Rigdon, and the enormous bulk of his companion, Cyril Jones, was an added deterrent, even if the boyfriend joined in.

"You fucking, homophobic, fucking bullshitter — you're not a scientist! What do you know?" The young man was bursting with incoherent, drunken belligerence. "Haven't you ever heard of a gay gene?"

"Yes, and it's been comprehensively debunked." Rigdon remained calm as though he found this diversion entertaining. "If you were the result of a gay gene you'd be so effeminate you'd be sitting down to pee. An anti-androgen gay gene would act constantly to block male hormone from masculinizing any aspect of a foetus at all. You'd have a lisp, limp wrists, and be absolutely hopeless at billiards. You are clearly the result of a hormone-disrupting chemical which only acted on you for a short time, because it was only a temporary resident in your mother's body. In other words, something that came drifting in from the environment, got up your mother's nose, slipped through the placental barrier, blocked the masculinization of the mating centre in your hypothalamus, and then disappeared again. A pollutant. Dioxin. Phthalates. PCBs. Nothing else can explain you, old chap."

"This is fucking homophobic crap!" he snarled. "Are you a homophobe? Do you have issues you can't deal with? Are you in the closet?" His voice rose. He hiccupped.

"Not at all, dear boy. I left the closet long ago. I now reside in a chest of drawers. I'm as bent as a nine-pound note, which makes it easier to fit in. I too was produced by pollution. I'm rather proud of it. It gives me a dirty feeling. But it's curious how your sect is the only one on earth that accuses its critics of secretly belonging to it. Every homophobe must be secretly gay. Not necessarily, old chap. They can be openly gay. But your sect is absolutely right to think: there is nobody more likely to despise a faggot than another faggot. We really do hate one another, don't we?"

"What fucking bullshit! He's trying to avoid the fucking issue, isn't he?" The young man appealed to his companion, who was holding his arm again. His words slurred even more. "You're a fucking homophobe! Who else would say: faggots are caused by pollution!"

"Well, it's a very green conception of your genesis, I would have thought," said Rigdon mildly. "Why is it worse to be the product of environmental factors than to be the product of a gene? I should have thought the environment was far trendier to have as a progenitor."

"So, what about queer paedophile bastards like you? What caused you?"

"Oh, a double dose, beyond any doubt. Ghastly industrial miasma. My poor mother was choking on the stuff. Did your mother tell you the same?"

"I've never spoken to my fucking mother."

"Oh dear, not one of those two-father jobs already?" Rigdon sounded concerned. "Or were you a care home boy? If so, one of us might have played with you when you were little."

The young man stared at Rigdon for a moment, not entirely sure what he had heard but getting the mocking tone. He swayed a little and his lips began moving in a string of swear-words, which were only muttered under his breath in slurred fashion. He swung his arm back to launch a very inept-looking punch. Rigdon was just rising from his chair to defend himself, when the young man's companion pulled him away roughly by the arm he had swung back. He eyed Rigdon with hatred, and hustled his friend over to the bar again. Rigdon sat down looking rather pleased with himself.

"I seem to have scored a hit with those two," he said to Cyril with a wink. "If hostility is a sign of attraction, as they seem to think, then I can't miss there."

"You wouldn't seriously be tempted if he was available, would you?" asked Jones in appalled disbelief. "I've never touched anything over fifteen for as long as I can remember."

"How very Greek of you, Cyril!" said Rigdon affably.

"But you're the same, surely? Young boys only?" He took a deep gulp of his beer.

"Pretty much."

"How exactly did you get into it, if you don't mind me asking?" The incident seemed to have broken a new layer of ice and made Cyril want to move the conversation to a more personal level. "I'm always curious about kindred spirits," he went on. "It didn't come from caning boys, did it? I was terribly envious of you teachers being able to cane boys when I was young. I was convinced it must be an erotic experience. Does caning lead on to shafting?"

"There may be a small connection between caning and buggery," said Rigdon judiciously. "I did go in for both of them quite a lot, but not usually at the same time."

"So, there's no physical link?" Cyril seemed keen to nail this point. "You were never tempted to actually use the cane to shaft any of them, were you? That was apparently Pasolini's favourite thing, you know — screwing rent boys with a stick. He's said to have been in the middle of it in a parked car when he was murdered in a savage homophobic attack — some say by the boy's relatives."

"No, it's not something that ever occurred to me. In fact the two things tended to be mutually exclusive for me at that age — much less so now. I would find a favourite boy I preferred to fondle rather than cane, and soon he began to play on it and turned into a little sex-slave. And with a boy one was so much more in a position of power by comparison with the endless begging required to get inside a pretty girl at that young and callow age. Girls have such a sense of their market value, and they're such sly little prick-teasers, aren't they? Boys are much more naive. I think that's partly what governed my choices." He paused as if reflecting. "Apart from the fact that the ground had already been laid by my history master, who did me the honour of seducing me when I was twelve."

"I must say the two things were more closely related for me, beating and shafting," declared Cyril. He was in an expansive mood, and had an urge to recount his experiences. "I had a somewhat turbulent upbringing, and I got beaten and shafted a few times in care homes during short stays there. It stamped the care home on my mind as a place of erotic adventure, tinged with violence and sadism. That came back to me later on when I realized young boys were by far the most satisfying partners. You mentioned their naivety. I'd add: their helplessness, their embarrassment, their innocence — they really are asking for it, aren't they? That's what made me gravitate towards these institutions as if by some homing instinct." He gazed across the pub lost in thought. "Once I got into supervising children's homes, it all seemed so natural. I was quite a stickler for rules and discipline. I had a strong urge to spank or cane or whip boys, and I found it shaded into buggering them quite naturally. I do think it's a disciplinarian's vice. There's an intimate connection between the desire to thrash an unruly boy and the desire to shaft him. And it does have a calming effect upon them. They whimper a bit but they're impressed by the violence you bring to bear upon them, and they don't dare defy you again. It teaches them submission. After a while they offer it as a substitute for a hiding. They become your creatures. They accept what is done to them as normal, as part of what you have the right to do to them. There's something profoundly satisfying about that."

"Oh, I couldn't agree more. When one can impose rules that give one absolute rights to use a young boy's body as one likes, and get him to accept that as normal, it gives a sense of almost divine power." Rigdon smiled wistfully. "Children are basically terrified and bewildered by sex. But a good teacher can make them accept being rogered as normal, like training a dog to jump through a fiery hoop. I was also on the receiving end in my first year at prep school. I saw it as a form of hazing I had undergone and I was determined others should as well. But I was initiated later more gently by my history master, who was quite fond of me, though he also had the requisite cruel streak. I do think buggering boys is a kind of chain reaction: the buggered bugger. I don't think it's revenge. It's more like being part of a sect. You get initiated into it and then later you do it to others. A bit like vampires, I suppose. You just see it as your kind of sex."

Rigdon sipped his beer and gazed across the pub without seeing the blur of faces. He felt an urge to philosophize.

"What is life for, finally? It's about experience, whether good or evil. The best life is the life that has experienced the most. The most extreme sensations. Love, lust, rape, acts of sadism. Who really cares? The important thing is to feel. And the funny thing is — it becomes more and more difficult to feel anything. We need stronger and stronger doses of sensation, don't you find?"

"I do, indeed. You know, it's uncanny how you can put into words all my own thoughts," mused Cyril. "I think it's the recasting of morality in a new light that I always liked about your lectures whenever I popped into one, or just heard you talk. You were so able to explain and help me justify my own impulses. I felt such moral uplift after listening to you."

"Lecturing is quite a creative performance art," said Rigdon, to distract attention from this embarrassing flattery. "I suppose most of what I say is really meant, but I often weave in ideas that aren't really mine just to confuse any spies. And I love tossing in ideas that will provoke an outcry. Last week, as you may have gathered from our angry young friend, I had one of my periodic goes at the gay lobby — they're such hypocritical, spineless wusses, drivelling on about love and freedom to love, as though they were all choir boys. It's enough to make you vomit. I like to emphasize what a violent, exploitative, brutal, sadomasochistic cult they are. And the gentle, sensitive souls they like to hold up as their poster boys are just the cannon-fodder of the thuggish brutes who rule their world. Who do the liberal gulls imagine shaft these sissies? Other sissies? It's extraordinary how they've managed to airbrush out the very existence of the butch queer — or the paedo queer like us. And this ludicrous obsession with a gay gene — when everybody knows the extent to which seduction, recruitment and conditioning determine what children become. Half the thrill of seduction is to change a child's entire destiny, the way his emotions and sexual urges work. If it was all genetic you'd just pick out the pre-programmed ones and it would be like shooting fish in a barrel. There'd be no challenge at all."

"Absolutely," agreed Cyril with gusto. "The young can be trained up like puppies. Give me a boy at seven, the Jesuits used to say. Paedos could say the same. That's the whole attraction of the young. They have no sexual orientation until you give them one."

"Precisely. But you know what I detest most about the so-called 'gay brigade'? That they are not only in denial of the vicious sadomasochism of their own cult: they're in denial about evil as such. So is the whole liberal-progressive camp.

And yet evil is the very basis of moral and emotional health. We are able to endure the human race only because we can occasionally indulge in real acts of cruelty and viciousness against it. It is evil which keeps us healthy, by exercising our most intense passions, including our moral passions. Without evil our emotions would atrophy and wither away. We would become amoral, emotionless zombies."

"I think you're right. There is a great deal of evil on a vast scale — war, destruction, massacres — which I find immensely stimulating as a spectator. I am always quite disappointed when the evening news turns out to be dull and uneventful."

"True. Vast destruction and mass killing can inspire awe. But on the individual level we are also capable of wonderfully refined acts of evil. Among the most subtle forms of evil we can engage in is to use sex, the ultimate joy, as a means of psychic destruction of somebody weak and defenceless. Goethe expressed this by getting his Faust to seduce and abandon an innocent young woman — something many critics have found rather feeble as a diabolical act. But they fail to appreciate its subtlety, the emotional intensity of the suffering inflicted. Of course today there are so few innocent young women that we have to fall back on children to find the right degree of naivety and defencelessness. That is why paedophilia is becoming the preferred recreation of the powerful and successful."

"Really? So, we have a future then, after all, you think?" Cyril Jones laughed.

"I truly hope so. But above all we have a long, distinguished past. Almost all the so-called gay icons of the last hundred years were addicted to the very young, if not to actual children. Think of Wilde, think of Lord Alfred Douglas, think of André Gide with their little pre-teen Algerian street boys. Isherwood and Auden with their starving teenage Berlin rent boys. The boy in Visconti's *Death in Venice*, who became the pin-up of a generation of paedos. Our predilection for very young flesh is shared by so many cultures, from Arabia to New Guinea. That folk tradition they have in Afghanistan of training up young boys as erotic dancers and sex slaves of the warlords — fascinating for the insight it gives into ancient cultures like the Persian and the Greek. That is exactly what the great classical cultures must have been like — full of child sex-slaves, little dancers drunk on wine, at the disposal of the guests. And our own traditional boarding-school culture offered that same wonderful possibility of being able to cane a small boy for some trivial misdemeanour, and then, if one fancied it, sodomize him." He smiled wistfully. "We English really did have the sadistic, paedophile culture of ancient warlords — in our own lifetime. It's so important we should use the gay liberation movement to preserve as much of that as we can. Thank God parliament still has so many chaps who acquired a taste for buggery at boarding school. They have certainly stood by you, you should be thankful."

"I am, indeed! Of course there's nothing like being Chief Whip to give you the ability to defend yourself against calumny and backbiting. You get the dirt on everyone, so nobody dares to attack you or you can bring down the whole house of cards. And of course the queer brigade, who dominate the media, rally round you out of the same instinctive fear."

"True," said Rigdon. He leaned forward and dropped his voice confidentially. "I must have told a dozen queers and lesbians, some of them in positions of power, that I buggered young boys in my care. Not one of them ever betrayed me. Let's hope that doesn't change with the new generation, by the way."

"It's very unlikely to." It was Jones's turn to wax philosophical. "Queerness is a sort of religion, and we boy racers are seen as part of it, just a slightly more radical sect. All of us are the persecuted martyrs of history. How could we possibly betray one another?"

They both laughed heartily and then sank the greater part of their pints.

"I do hope you'll join me in staging this little happening, which I think I shall definitely organize," said Rigdon. "We could do it in several parts — perhaps have an exhibition by child sex performers as a curtain-raiser. You can help me there with your contacts. And for the climax we must reflect seriously. Maximum drama and entertainment, but without damaging the body. It will require a lot of creativity."

He drained his glass with a thoughtful expression, as if his imagination was already at work on the problem.

"I'm sure it will be no trouble at all to an artist like you," Cyril assured him, and chortled in a way that made his triple chin wobble engagingly.

23

Romain and Camilla had spent several days creating a website for the castle in Bordeaux and a Facebook page and email address in the name of Henri de Lagarde, Comte de Mayne. They knew they would soon have to reveal the cousin's name to Bendigo, and this would lead the artist or his agent to do a web search for it. Romain also called on a friend in Bordeaux from his days teaching there. Nicolas was both a computer geek and a maverick always keen to cause mischief. Romain sent him the material for the website and the Facebook page and Nicolas put everything up on the internet with his own computer. That way the IP address would be from the Bordeaux region if anyone traced it. Any emails to that email address would also be answered by Nicolas, on Romain's instructions, so someone in England would have no way of knowing they were not communicating with someone in Bordeaux. The Facebook page included photos of Henri and his wife, described as a former top model, all stolen from Russian dating sites. The website had a range of photos of the Château Latour Mayne, purloined from the website of a castle in Poitou, and vistas from a vineyard in Burgundy. They hijacked the Trevi Fountain from an Italian tourism site and placed it in the garden to back up Romain's earlier story. The château featured a terrace, where people sat drinking wine and admiring the view, this time borrowed from a castle in Tuscany. Romain amused himself with inventing a potted history of the castle and the Lagarde family. He described Henri's château as the first to offer what was now catching on among major vineyards in Bordeaux: art collections combined with wine-tasting. A list of the famous artists whose works adorned the halls and grounds of the castle followed, and then the opening times when the castle could be visited, starting in September, when the extensive current refurbishment was due to be finished, just in time for the wine harvest. The panoramic last page of the website featured a monumental Henry Moore sculpture of an entwined couple, sitting on a rise overlooking endless rows of vines. The sculpture was lifted from the website of a museum in Martigny, in Switzerland, which had the work in its garden.

Once this professional-looking website was up and running, they felt more confident about their next interview with Bendigo. He soon called them and set up another meeting at his place. This time they were led into a reception room, less cluttered and more elegantly furnished than his living room. Bendigo presented them to the balding man they had met in the gallery, who turned out to be his agent. He was introduced as Simon Caffrey.

"The time has come," said Bendigo after handing them glasses of champagne, "to get down to the nitty-gritty. Price, and the identity of your mysterious cousin, the buyer."

After a bit of small talk Simon Caffrey took the lead.

"We've agreed — having studied market trends for the past year — that we couldn't let this work go for less than eight hundred thousand."

"Euros?" said Romain.

"No, pounds," said the agent.

"I'm afraid my cousin may find that a trifle steep. He won't go to a million euros."

"At present exchange rates, that is only nine hundred and sixty thousand euros," pointed out the agent. "So it is under a million. In six figures, as you specified."

"I shall have to consult him to see if that is acceptable. If you would like an answer immediately I can phone him."

Romain took out his iPhone.

"It would help us enormously," said Simon Caffrey.

Romain pressed a name on his screen to dial a number. Nicolas, who had agreed to play the role of Henri de Lagarde if necessary, finally answered.

"Henri? Ici Romain." He stood up and walked around, approaching the window by instinct to improve reception. He explained the situation briefly in French. Nicolas, who had been primed with the right answers, played the role with perfect seriousness just in case they had some way of listening in or recording it. After Romain ended the call, he went back over to the two men sitting in their armchairs, who looked at him expectantly. He and Camilla had agreed that they should create obstacles on a practical level in order to distract attention from the more fundamental question of whether they were frauds.

"I'm afraid we have a problem."

"Oh? What's that?" asked Bendigo.

"He won't go beyond eight fifty. Euros."

"That is a problem," said Caffrey coolly.

"But he proposes instead that for the new boy in formaldehyde he wants to commission, with the changes we discussed, the hair, the age, no swimsuit, no mask and so on, for that he will be willing to pay a million euros."

"Still only a million euros," said Bendigo, in disappointment. "That's about what in pounds, just over eight hundred thousand? Hirst got offered a million pounds by Saatchi, sight unseen, for that blown up plastic model of some muscle man. Just a children's toy sent to a factory with the order to enlarge it twenty times. Not much originality there, was there? He probably didn't even touch the damn thing. He even got sued for plagiarism by the toymaker and had to settle. Made no difference to Saatchi."

"But that was at a stage when Hirst had already reached a somewhat higher degree of notoriety," said Romain. "It's still early days for you. It's this sale that will make you. You have to climb the ladder before you can stand on the roof."

"A million pounds is hardly excessive. One of Hirst's later works fetched twelve million!" exclaimed Bendigo, almost indignantly.

"I'm sure yours will too, one day," Romain assured him. "It's a question of time."

"I must say a million euros for a boy number 2 does sound tempting," said the agent, looking sideways at Bendigo. "I think we should consider it." He turned to Romain with a slightly impatient air. "Can we know something about this cousin, finally?"

"I think it is probably time to introduce him," agreed Romain. "His name is Henri de Lagarde, Comte de Mayne, of the Château Latour Mayne, near St Emilion. Here you have his website and Facebook page."

He handed Caffrey a small piece of paper with the details. From a briefcase he then took out a tablet on which he called up the castle website. He handed it to Caffrey, who studied it for a moment. Then, as Bendigo leaned over his shoulder to look, he passed it to him.

"The castle has been in our family since the seventeenth century," said Romain, "when the previous owners, who were Protestant, had to flee the country after the Revocation of the Edict of Nantes. It has a fascinating history. Figures like Montaigne, Montesquieu and the Prince of Condé stayed there. Our family got into wine only recently, about a hundred years ago. Henri's late father, my uncle, began collecting art in his last years as a draw for visitors, though the main draw is the castle itself, which is magnificent, as you can see. We now welcome thousands of visitors a year, who come partly for the castle and its art and partly to taste wine on the upper terrace, which overlooks the landscape of vineyards. The combination is good for wine sales. Our top wine is a *Grand Cru Classé* but not a *Premier Grand Cru Classé*, so it's more accessible to a wider public. All this means that you get a certain class of art patron, slightly younger people who are fashionable, trendy, attuned to what is making waves right now. The kind of person who will recognize superb breakthrough works like *The Boy in Formaldehyde* for what they are — and create a buzz. I should add, my cousin's tastes are resolutely modern. He doesn't clutter the place up with minor Impressionists or second-rate baroque hunting scenes. Apart from a couple of dozen portraits of ancestors that go with the decor, and a few classical replicas in the garden, like the Trevi Fountain, everything he collects is modern. It's that rigorous taste that attracts so many international figures from the world of art, cinema, music and so on, as well as the usual run of French socialites, film actors and the like, many of whom are his close friends."

"I think he sounds exactly like the kind of buyer we are looking for," said the agent. He glanced around at the artist. "What do you say, Piers?"

"Me? Oh, absolutely." Bendigo had been studying the website on the tablet. "It does look quite impressive. I do like the Henry Moore among the vines. Very tasteful. But I haven't entirely given up on the question of price. I'd like to show our guests something I'm working on to give them an idea of what the prospects are of a long-term partnership."

"Well," said Caffrey, looking at his watch, "I'm afraid I must run along. Why don't you call me later, Piers, and tell me what you think and we'll meet again, all of us, when we've had time to sleep on this. Let's not rush things." He gave Bendigo a warning glance and took his leave.

Bendigo invited the other two into his atelier again. He led them past a number of the partitions that divided it up and stopped in one of the spaces they formed. On three partition walls was a series of enlarged photographs.

"Have a good look at the boy in these photos," said Bendigo. "That's the boy we'll be using in the new *Boy in Formaldehyde* your cousin wants me to create. He's exceptionally beautiful, as you can see."

"He looks Scandinavian," said Camilla, looking closely at the photographs.

"He's actually Polish. I met him the other day when I took these photos. He told me he ran away from a paedophile stepfather. It was quite a sob story. Can't say I blame him. The stepfather, I mean. And look at these, some of the more intimate photos."

He pointed to some of the photos showing the boy engaged in a sexual act with another male body that remained only partly visible and hence anonymous.

"These photos are actually selfies. That's me, or part of me. You see, the viewer can identify with this other, anonymous body as his own and see himself engaging in sex with this beautiful boy. These photos are intended as part of the installation, to form a backdrop to it, perhaps as three walls partly surrounding it. That way the viewer can enter into the intimacy of the sexual frolics of this young god, and can then see him in the flesh, floating in his glass case, immortalized by death. I'm thinking of calling it *Narcissus Drowning in his Pool*."

He smiled at them. They stared at the photos.

"The boy is certainly beautiful," murmured Camilla.

"Isn't he? This will be an utterly scandalous installation," Bendigo went on, "because of the overt sexual images in the surrounding photographs. This is a dead boy juxtaposed with images of his own last sexual acts. It will be a double breaking of taboos, not only that of boy love — or gay paedophilia, whatever you like to call it — but also of death, the sacrifice of a life for art. The suspicion that this boy has been used for sex and has then mysteriously died will make this the most scandalous work of art ever created. Once the journalists get hold of the story this work will become world famous and the price will be pushed to astronomical levels. And it will be your cousin's, don't forget."

"Yes, but you don't see the police getting involved to investigate this?" asked Romain with a frown. "Surely they will be interested in how the boy came to be dead — since the photos will make clear that this one, unlike the first one, really was a living person."

"I think this will only be a temporary problem. Then life will catch up with art. There are two solutions that come to mind," said Bendigo, pacing about. "One would be to keep the photos in a private exhibition room with admission restricted to special guests vetted beforehand and sworn to secrecy. They would become a privileged elite initiated into the higher mysteries of the work. The other solution, which I would personally recommend to your cousin, would be to fake a death certificate for the boy as the victim of a boating accident. One could then concoct a narrative about the artist's love for this beautiful boy, a sort of *Death in Venice*, only with the boy not the artist dying tragically at the end. The work would then be a memorial to his love, a sort of mausoleum for a dead boy-lover, a gay Taj Mahal. I think the time is ripe for a real breakthrough in the apotheosis of gay love and boy love in particular. It has come out of the closet but it has not yet reached the altar where it belongs, the object of worship of an entire civilization as it was for the Greeks and Romans. Your cousin's château will become a place of pilgrimage for millions of gay people where they can finally see their form of love on a pedestal, recognized as the great inspiration for art that it has always been." He smiled. "This boy will be a gay icon to rival Michelangelo's David. That is the package that I have in mind for your cousin, and the total price of the installation and the photographs, all installed by our care, will be a million pounds."

"Good heavens, that's exactly the price Hirst got for the blown up plastic toy!" said Camilla brightly, with a charming smile.

"Exactly! You've seen through me, my dear," said Bendigo with a bow.

"It does seem very tempting, and certainly looks like a great draw for Henri's château," said Romain seriously. "The gay market is a very important one commercially, and it functions by word of mouth and social media."

"Precisely. And the gay movement is on a roll right now that can't be stopped. Did you see the final of the Eurovision song contest the other night?" he asked with sudden interest. "The vast majority of the viewers voted for those vulgar Sexy Polish Girls, a bunch of cleaning-girls in mini-skirts. But gays dominate the music industry and the juries that control half the total votes, so we imposed our choice! A bearded gay transvestite! And Europe's media hailed it as Europe's choice! What a slap in the face for the homophobic masses! We made them see they no longer own Western culture — we do! And the next step is to glorify boy love as the single greatest inspiration of Western art!"

"I can see that, indeed," said Romain, stroking his chin in thought.

"But you must understand this is not just the next step for the gay movement," said Bendigo, warming to his subject. "It is above all the next step for the contemporary art movement. Every innovation must build on what has gone before and add one vital new element. If you look at the history of Modernist and Postmodernist art, the logic leaps out at you. The great innovation of the twentieth century was the found object. What's more logical than for the next step to be the found person, the found body? You see, artists used to sculpt objects. Then Marcel Duchamp came along a hundred years ago and taught the world that you don't need to sculpt anything. You just find a ready-made object and call it a work of art. You confer on it the status of a work of art, because of who you are, the artist. An old urinal, a snow shovel, a bicycle wheel, as you reminded me the other day. Put it on a pedestal and it's art, because the artist says it is. You were highly perceptive to see Duchamp's work as the key to all this. Have you seen any of it?"

"Yes," said Romain, "I've seen the urinal, signed R. Mutt, a schoolboy pun on mother."

The Boy in Formaldehyde

"Then you understand what a breakthrough that was! It has determined the entire history of modern art all the way down to Tracey Emin's bed — all installations are just elaborate versions of Duchamp's found objects! Now, in exactly the same way, artists used to sculpt people. So the obvious next thing was the found person: find a body and just confer work of art status on that. Piero Manzoni, who became notorious for making cans of his own shit — some of them bought by the Tate Modern, incidentally — did it with living women's bodies in the sixties — he signed them and made them officially works of art. Women queued up to have their naked backsides signed by him. They became walking readymades. But with living bodies there was a problem with selling them or displaying them permanently in museums. You can't put them in a glass case except for short periods. The person gets bored and hungry. It was better to use dead bodies. Hirst began it with animals. Sharks. Cows. Fish. Sheep. Don't sculpt them, use a ready-made. Put it in formaldehyde to preserve it and call it art. So I said: why not extend that to people? What difference is there between humans and animals? Darwin proved there is no difference! We've got to get over this absurd reverence for human bodies, even after they're dead. It's a superstition! There's nothing there, there's no soul you have to respect, it's just a corpse, like any other animal's. So this will be the next phase. It's inevitable! It will be part of the desacralization of everything that is one of the hallmarks of the Modernist and Postmodernist movements."

"Desacralization?" queried Camilla.

"Yes. Nothing is sacred any more. We've already put a crucifix in a bucket of piss. That was a real breakthrough! And we've had a picture of Christ giving a blowjob to the beloved Apostle John. Anyone who objects to that is just a homophobic bigot! Why should a gay Christ be sacrilegious?

Why shouldn't he have another man's penis in his mouth? It's a normal, natural act, approved and celebrated by every civilized, progressive government today, and if you object to it, if it repels you, you're a homophobic hate-criminal who belongs in jail! People have got to get used to the world of now, the world we live in today. Bodies are just bodies. They no longer have any status, any meaning, except the meaning we decide to give them. It's a waste burying dead bodies. They should be burned to generate energy. Made into cat food. Or, why not, preserved in formaldehyde to become works of art. Nothing is sacred! The sacred is finished! No one believes in that shit any more. Read Dawkins! There's no God, no afterlife, no soul, how can there be anything sacred?"

His eyes were shining with an inner light and he spoke faster and faster.

"Bodies are to be used, exploited, recycled, transformed! We can convert them into art, whether human or animal. If you think it's OK to put a shark in formaldehyde but not a human being, you're a bigot! A species racist! You're filled with superstitious prejudices! You're denying Darwinism! There's no difference between humans and animals. There's no immortal soul to make the difference. So an animal body and a human body have exactly the same status. And anyone who denies that is a religious fanatic! It's time we got outdated Christian prejudices out of our system of laws. Christianity was the greatest superstition of all time! Responsible for millions of deaths, wars, persecutions, witch-burnings, untold cruelties! The origin of racism, homophobia, Islamophobia, anti-Semitism, the patriarchal society, fascism, the oppression of women — all of it Christian in origin! They murdered gay people en masse in the Nazi gas chambers! Why shouldn't we piss on Christ? Why shouldn't we fuck dead boys and fuck dead bodies? Nothing is sacred! Let's fuck everything! That's the meaning of my art!"

He stopped, out of breath, but with an expression of rapture on his face. Romain was stunned by the vehemence of this diatribe, but wanted to prod him to keep going.

"So, who do you admire most among modern artists?"

"Marcel Duchamp, obviously! The source of it all. Any piece of junk is art! Because I say it is. Andy Warhol. The same thing. The soup can advert as art. The silkscreen print of a celebrity face, reproduced a thousand times, as art! I designate this piece of pop commercial trash, this advertisement, this media cliché, as art. He updated Duchamp. Duchamp picked real objects as art. A urinal. A snow shovel. A bicycle wheel. Warhol says: no, it doesn't have to be an authentic object. It can be a copy. A mass reproduction! If I say it's art, it is, even if it's a mass-manufactured image! And Hirst went even further. When he ordered a factory to copy a plastic muscle-man toy from a toyshop, only twenty times bigger, and called it an original work of art! The fact he got sued for plagiarism and had to pay up only reinforces the point! He proved that art doesn't have to be original! Just copy someone else's idea and call it yours! Theft is art! Plagiarism is art! If your name is bigger than his it becomes your work, not his. Steal it and make it yours! Fake it and make it yours! Get someone else to do the work and claim it as yours! All that counts is that you decided to do it! The concept! Who actually carried out the work is beside the point!" He spoke like a man possessed and his eyes were staring like the devotee of a sect. "In the Italian Renaissance artists had workshops. They didn't do half the work themselves! What's the difference when you pay someone else to make your work of art for you? All of Judd's wooden boxes — made by someone else! At the Bauhaus they ordered works of art from the factory by phone. They never even saw what they created! Hirst's spot paintings — three hundred of them done by his assistants and signed by him! Am I going to make a glass tank myself? Why? Why not pay a cabinet-maker to do it? Duchamp even delegated his decision-making, his choosing function. He got his sister to choose objects in junk shops and he signed them as his works of art. So his only input was his signature! And that stuff is now worth millions! That's what I value. The power of the magus! To transform junk into art by a signature! He doesn't even have to choose it himself. Just sign it and it's worth a fortune! I want to be able to do that. Find any piece of crap in a builder's skip and sell it for a million just because my signature is on it! That's real power! The power of the magician, the alchemist! To transform shit into gold! Duchamp had that power! Hirst has got that power! I want that power! The true power of the artist!"

He had been speaking faster and faster till he reached his triumphant climax. The others looked at him in astonishment. They had backed away slightly from this torrential outpouring of words but he followed them, as if he was convinced he had found two true disciples at last and wanted to get his whole message across. He tried to sum it up in one final sentence.

"You see, it's not a question of art being hyped. It's a question of hype being art! Hype is art! And art is hype! That's where we're at today."

He stopped. There were specks of foam on his lips. Suddenly he looked drained by his passionate tirade. They stood staring at him in fascination.

"That's certainly a revolutionary point of view," said Romain with an air of wonder.

"I am changing the world!" declared Bendigo. "Art will never be the same again! And you can be a part of that. Or rather your cousin can. If he chooses."

"I shall certainly present your point of view to him. I'm sure he will want to meet you. And I'm fairly confident that your latest offer of this package, as you call it, will be of great interest to him. I'll get back to you."

On that optimistic note they shook hands and Romain and Camilla left. They did not exchange a word till they were out of sight of the windows of Bendigo's building.

"Wow!" said Camilla simply.

"He's as mad as a hatter," said Romain. *"Fou à lier."*

"Barking mad!" said Camilla. "And he's planning to kill that boy, the one Ekaterina tried to save. And I've got the whole bloody lot on my smartphone!"

"Do we take this to the inspector?"

"Of course. And later on to the media. But it'll be our story." She looked at him suddenly with shining eyes as if she had an idea. "This is the story you'll write, the one that will mean something to you at last." She took his hand and squeezed it. "We'll each write a version in our own language. We'll make this madman immortal! And destroy him as we do it!"

24

Rigdon became more and more engrossed in the project Cyril Jones had proposed. He began in idle moments to plan in detail his last great public spectacle, as he saw it. And the truth was he had lots of idle moments. He was doing less and less lecturing. This series might well be his last. He was getting bored with it. The constraints he had to work under were becoming intolerable. The censors were everywhere ready to pounce. He still had the backing of a few old Kinseyites in the Havelock Ellis Institute who remained faithful to Kinsey's idea that there should be no taboos, everything should be explored, including the sexuality of small children, but these views were under fire from a new moralistic generation. Kinsey's achievement seemed more and more incredible to him. The very idea of using paedophile "researchers" to stimulate hundreds of children to orgasm, some of them less than a year old, and record how many minutes each one took, and report on whether the child screamed, cried or otherwise resisted his adult partner, was almost inconceivable in this day and age. And yet it had been done over sixty years ago and published in an appendix to *The Kinsey Report on Male Sexuality*, the book that revolutionized Western sexual attitudes. The fact he had got away with it was extraordinary. That people still quoted Kinsey as a respectable authority on sexuality, in spite of this criminal child abuse, was testimony to the exceptional force of his character. Nowadays he would probably have been jailed for life, but his work still stood, with those passages still in it, reprinted year after year. The Kinsey Institute was still cited as a respectable academic body. In America Kinsey was still an icon of sexual liberation for the entire intellectual class.

Of course most specialists knew that Kinsey's statistics about sexual practices like homosexuality were entirely bogus. He had carried out no random surveys but only canvassed those social groups whose answers would support his preconceptions — an approach that today would be called academic fraud. (His inflated statistics on the numbers of gay men were based largely on surveys done on prison populations — in an age when men were still jailed for homosexual acts — yet the media quoted them regularly as "scientific", in particular the grotesque figure of ten per cent of people being homosexual, when every serious study since then had put it at three per cent or less.) But because his noisiest critics were self-confessed Christians, this statistic-rigging charlatan still retained the respect and admiration of much of the academic world, because he held the libertarian views on sex, and especially on homosexuality, which were still politically correct. In short, for the pro-gay intelligentsia his heart was in the right place and a small detail like academic fraud could be overlooked.

Rigdon too saw him as his hero. He envied his fame and his lasting influence, and admired his buccaneer contempt for orthodox methods. Kinsey had started out as a scientific nerd studying frogs, but his personal sexual experimentation (serial adultery, homosexuality, sadomasochism, group sex, voyeurism) had inspired his life's mission to prove that Middle America was rife with sexual perversions, making his own look normal. Rigdon had in some ways followed a parallel path of increasing sexual deviation — or at least increasing openness about it. And now at the end of his career he felt challenged by the example of his hero to do something spectacular to have a similar impact on his society. If he couldn't do it by writing an academic bestseller, he must do it in his own way — by creating some extraordinary scandal. Then with his considerable fortune he could simply leave the country and settle somewhere else for a blissful retirement. Perhaps the Philippines. Thailand. Some place where sex was viewed with a bit more worldly wisdom, especially the sort he went in for. But he wanted to depart with some panache, leaving behind a smell of sulphur and brimstone. He wanted to go out with a bang.

At sixty-five he no longer felt any huge personal need for sex, except as a trivial amusement. What he wanted was to promote an idea, propagate a practice, change mentalities. He wanted sex with children to be acknowledged as part of the spectrum of human sexual normality. If it was natural for other primates such as bonobos, why not for humans? In certain New Guinea tribes, the men regularly sodomized the young boys. Sexual stimulation of infants in order to calm a tantrum or a crying fit was common in many non-Western cultures. Mothers, nurses or older sisters in those countries regularly played with the willies of baby boys, as a way of giving them pleasure, bonding with them, strengthening the organ, as well as making the girls familiar with male anatomies. A degree of casual incest appeared to follow naturally from the conditions of crowded promiscuity of sleeping arrangements in poorer countries. Children often shared beds with parents and with each other. Nakedness in the family was natural in warmer climates. An exaggerated set of incest taboos had been created by the peculiar conditions of overdressed northern Europeans fearing nakedness and cold air, combined with the sexual phobia of a puritanical religion. In the West even a baby's erections, which were often a response to his mother's caresses, were seen as deeply embarrassing and either ridiculed or punished — as he himself had been for playing with himself in the bath. Why on earth hadn't his stern, puritanical mother taught him to enjoy it? Or joined in the harmless stimulation as no more than a tickling game?

This Western sex-phobia had to be overcome by a concerted campaign. He felt he could play his part not merely by lecturing to the masses but by once again organizing an event that would show the naturalness and harmlessness of sex with children. He felt endowed with a mission in life to break taboos, to shock people out of their prejudices, to show how the very image of evil in the Western imagination was a deluded farrago of ignorance and superstition, demonizing normal sexual practices as though they really came from the devil. The more he thought about it the more he felt this chance of staging a paedophile festival was a fitting climax to his intellectual career.

His good friend Lord Sodbury, a notable paedophile who had collaborated with him on a number of shows in previous decades, had disappeared abroad, rumoured to have taken refuge in a "colony" in South America where he could recruit local children for his lifestyle choices. He had left his large country-house in Hertfordshire to be administered by an association dedicated to vague progressive causes. Rigdon knew their sympathies for Sodbury's habits, and the opaque administrative structure which made it possible to hire the estate for events without anyone looking too closely into what went on there. Pandora House, as it was called, could only be got in touch with through a tangled thread of contacts, which he still had, thanks to his past connections with it. He got through to them and came to a financial arrangement for the holding of a sort of garden party on the 14th of June. He then checked with Cyril Jones for the invitations. The latter put him onto Wayne, the pimp, who was supplying the prime material and selling it to the artist after the conversion took place. They had a long discussion in which Rigdon sketched out his creative ideas for how the thing was to be done. Wayne was positive; he proposed to pay him a fixed fee to cover his expenses and to split the gate with him. He would organize the security and some of the minor acts, and would liaise with the artist for other things. They agreed to meet up with Jones to finalize the details, and to make use of everybody's networks to organize the sale of invitations. At the end Rigdon was satisfied. He calculated he would make a tidy sum from the whole business while expressing his most passionate convictions.

After making these arrangements, he sat in the gathering dusk in his living-room without bothering to put on the lights and listened to some music. Out of principle he chose something avant garde, Morton Feldman's *For John Cage*. Unfortunately, after a few minutes its excruciating disharmonies and brain-gouging infelicities of tone, endlessly repeated, set his teeth on edge. It began to sound like madness, like somebody in a loonie bin pulling out his own hairs one by one. He stopped it. Searching for something a bit less neurotic, he came upon Stravinsky's *Rite Of Spring* and put that on. It had just the right degree of modernist madness, without it actually driving you insane. A savage hymn to human sacrifice! A prophetic evocation of the slaughter of the Great War that was to break out a year later! He listened to it reverently as though to a sacred oracle. What marvellous savagery had been unleashed over the intervening century! Almost as if the artists had called it up out of the deep with their violent injunctions to the world: "Sweep away bourgeois culture! Sweep away civilization! Wallow in primitive barbarism and bestiality!" And it had happened, just as they had decreed!

He gazed out the open French windows into the garden and let his thoughts drift with the music. A slight scent of carnations was wafted on the warm evening air. It was strange, he reflected, the things for which people wish to be remembered — the impact they want to have on the world. This was not one of the things he had planned to make central to his life's work. A general belief in sexual liberation, yes — he thought it was the key to human happiness. But this narrow obsession with child sexuality had gradually manoeuvred itself into the pole position of his ideological drive to convince and convert. Of course his own sexual career had influenced his thinking in this field. But he had also arrived at these ideas by an intellectual path. The crisis in sexual relations that had fallen upon Western society in the last third of the twentieth century had shaped his mental world from adolescence onwards. The sexual revolution of the sixties, the revolt against the Vietnam War and the militarist image of men, the flower-power counter-culture of free love, almost immediately blown apart by the feminist movement, which drove the sexes into hostile camps after their brief sixties idyll and prepared the ground for the homosexual cults that followed — all of this formed the backdrop to his own life and intellectual career. As he witnessed the collapse of all sexual norms and the triumph of the gay subculture, Rigdon, as though overtaken by history, and by his own history in particular, began to focus on the last remaining taboo — that of sex with children. Though he had of course practised it ever since he was seduced at the age of twelve, he had always thought of it as a secret, underground cult bound by a law of silence, rather than a public cause. Then a number of events made him change his mind.

He first publicly broached the subject when he wrote a scholarly article on a controversial feminist called Andrea Dworkin. He realized that the themes of paedophilia and incest were the key to understanding her character. Dworkin was a fascinating case, and her life could be analysed all the more easily because her on-line autobiography made her an open book. As a child she had been sexually attracted to her father, a sensitive, feminist intellectual who doted on her (unlike her cold mother), and his apparent rejection of her childish sexual advances was the trauma of her life. From then on she turned her back on sensitive men and adopted a grunge attitude to sex. She later boasted that even as a schoolgirl she felt up old men on buses to earn pocket money to go into New York to buy books. When she went on to attend an elite university she became a hobby prostitute ("I fucked for food and shelter and whatever cash I needed") while other students waited on tables. It seemed clear to Rigdon that these crude, mercenary encounters (otherwise inexplicable) were a self-punishment for failing to seduce her gentle father, who nonetheless encouraged her and supported her financially throughout her studies. After quarrelling with her parents, she used hobby prostitution to pay for her travels in Europe, but at the end of an excessively violent relationship with a leftist militant in Holland, she had a revelation. All the crude sexual violence she had sought out was men's fault. Her masochism was really men's sadism. All straight men were rapists and sadists, and all heterosexual intercourse was rape. She went back to a sensitive, caring man (like her father) but a homosexual, with whom she lived Platonically in New York.

She became a feminist militant, preached against heterosexual penetration as a violation, but advocated parents having sex with their children. She claimed to be lesbian, cultivated an obese, butch look, denounced pornography, and went back to dreaming of childhood sex with her father and of having sex with the children she never had (in real life falling back on dogs as her preferred sexual partners.) She had come full circle, and Rigdon genuinely felt that her problems had begun with her father's rejection of her sexual advances when she was a child. She spent the rest of her life denouncing the incest taboo and advocating parent-child sex, as well as denouncing all heterosexual men as the brutal rapists she had deliberately sought out among them. Despite these somewhat eccentric views she was hailed as a feminist icon by Gloria Steinem, who called her one of the few writers who help the human race evolve.

Rigdon felt a morbid fascination for this deeply disturbed woman. He saw the devastating effects on her life of the rigid moral taboo against paedophilia that had governed her father's behaviour towards her. A child with a precocious sexual appetite, whose crude sexual expression of her affection for her father had shocked and repelled him, was unwittingly made to feel dirty and obscene. She could never again associate sex with affection. This led her to a schizophrenic attitude to men. She could only have sex with brutal, unfeeling thugs (whom she sought out through prostitution), while she could only relate emotionally to gentle, sensitive men like her father — and since she was forbidden to have sex with them, they had to be gay. It was a sign of how well she understood the root of her problem that she spent her last years advocating parent-child sex and denouncing the incest taboo.

At first glance her neurosis might seem so unusual as to be irrelevant to others, but Rigdon saw it as symptomatic of the age. The inability to connect sex with affection was, he argued, a disease of modern times. Many baby boom feminists had denounced their distant, emotionally inhibited fathers, members of the tough, stoic war generation, for having crippled them emotionally. In Dworkin's case her father was affectionate, but terrified of paedophilia, and this had crippled her by forever separating sex from affection in her mind. And Rigdon saw this as a phenomenon that was on the rise again, as the growing hysteria over paedophilia made men fear that any physical expression of affection for their children might be suspect. In an age where every vengeful wife was ready to accuse her husband of paedophilia in order to gain sole custody of the children — to the point where lawyers now warned fathers never to bath their children alone — paranoid fathers would inevitably return to Victorian distant coldness towards their offspring. Male kindergarten teachers were already instructed never to hug a child. And this paranoia about paedophilia would paradoxically lead to its spread. Children, deprived of the natural affection of the men in their lives, would start to look for it in strangers, and respond gratefully to the proffered bag of sweets.

Rigdon ended his essay with a subversive suggestion. Perhaps the ancient Greek figure of the adult lover of boys might be seen not so much as a predator but as a bridge between parental affection and the erotic initiation the child needed. In the heterosexual (and uninhibited) eighteenth century, he argued, this role had often been performed by a boy's frisky young nurse. In a later academic work he went on to suggest that care home workers might usefully play this erotic initiation role in the lives of their young charges — which caused the first of many scandals in his career.

Rigdon himself had succumbed to paedophile seduction partly, he suspected, because of the affective void left in him by cold, distant parents, which had laid him open to the blandishments of a charismatic history master when he was twelve. Of course, his later understanding of this event did not enable him to reverse any of its consequences. A series of similar relationships had followed, all of them experienced as secret, forbidden adventures. At Oxford he had an affair with a kindred spirit called Clifford, and when the two of them became teachers they embarked on a career of seducing the boys they taught. Rigdon used to keep a diary with the names of his several hundred conquests and what he had managed to do with each one. He gave each a score, ranging from one point for fondling to ten points for sodomy. In this way he could pass the boys on to his friend with a precise assessment of their erotic potential. They both "came out" as gay, partly because that was how they saw themselves, but mainly to profit from the solidarity and support of the gay rights movement and the positive discrimination this oppressed minority now benefited from in every educational and social field. Even though they were known by fellow-gays to be paedophiles, he and Clifford were accepted into the gay fold and never denounced.

Over the years he often wondered what it was that attracted him to boys rather than men. The need for tenderness and affection, he supposed, while remaining in total control, the sole author of the script. He sometimes thought his impulses were frustrated parental feelings. But he wanted the sweets of parenthood only (the physical affection, the emotional closeness) without the downside of dirty nappies, sleepless nights, or the financial and existential millstone. He wanted to be a serial, short-term parent (which is what teachers and care workers often are in practice) but only for the most attractive children at their most attractive phase. And he wanted these relationships to be short but intense emotional affairs, in which he awakened an innocent young boy to the joys of sexual gratification. Why not, he thought. He saw it as simply one of the myriad, wonderful ways human beings could relate to one another.

In fact, he considered the role of guide and mentor, combined with seducer and sexual initiator — the pattern of ancient Greek paedophilia — to be one of the most valuable of all human relationships. He remembered how flattered he had felt by the attentions of his history master when he was twelve. How excited he had been that a man so mature and important should take such a personal interest in his thoughts and feelings — and in his secret ambitions to be a writer and intellectual! That this interest was accompanied by physical caresses he saw at first not as threatening but as comforting. To feel that his own slightly-built, pre-adolescent self was endowed with the power to render this mature, respected man happy or unhappy by a smile, a caress, a kiss, was a heady experience. And when this mentor expressed his passion in the clearest terms as a desire for sexual intercourse, naturally he was frightened of the pain of physical violation but also secretly proud of having conquered a heart and mind more important in the world than his own. This was an authority figure with the power to cane him or fail him, and he was at his feet, begging him for sexual favours. It was the stark inequality of the relationship that made it so irresistibly exciting. And it was this whole experience that he tried to reproduce when he became the older partner, the guide and mentor figure, and young boys suddenly appeared as opportunities in his path. Despite the various conventional views he paid lip service to in his lectures, he had no doubt whatever that paedophilia was a chain reaction, a flame passed on from mentor to protégé, like a baton in an endless relay race. Once you had known this intense, thrilling relationship as a child, you had an urge to recreate it in your turn as an adult.

Was there anything predestined about those who became part of this chain? He didn't believe for one moment that the boys he chose were inherently homosexual. You chose the sensitive, artistic boys not because they had innate gay tendencies but because you could have a greater ascendancy over them by exploiting their need for recognition and encouraging their secret artistic aspirations. That was the hook you used to reel them in — not any inborn predisposition to same-sex relations. Boys craving recognition for their special, secret talents were so overwhelmed by the attention they received from an admired older man that they lost all capacity to say no — or even to fully understand the path they were starting along. And it was precisely because these boys were not naturally inclined to homosexual relations that it was such a challenge and a satisfaction to seduce them. You were leading them along an unknown path, making them explore things they would have left forever unexplored if not for you. And you were doing it against all their natural inclinations, prejudices and fears. It was like taming a wild animal and little by little making it eat from your hand.

Of course this whole process had a violent aspect and he distinctly remembered the horror of violation himself, not only the first rape at prep school but later on his fear and revulsion as he realized that his history master wanted to do the same thing to him again. But boys have a capacity to accept pain as an initiation into a new stage of their existence. They even have a touching faith in mentors who inflict suffering upon them. To be that trusted initiator of innocence was a deeply satisfying role, and one which salved, a whole lifetime later, the original wound of his own brutal initiation. To teach the innocent what life is about and shock them with its brutality, and to see in that shock the image of his own violation by life, to relive at second hand his own far-off initiation into life's cruelty and horror — what could be sweeter? The paedophile was a sort of cruel sentimentalist, full of suppressed self-pity for his own childhood rape and seeking to create a new kindred soul by making him go through the same experience, and thus lessen his own emotional and psychic isolation. He was very much like a vampire, an afflicted one who could only find relief by adding to the numbers of the afflicted. In the grim pity he felt for his violated victims, he allowed himself at last, under the carapace of years, a surge of pity for the violated boy that he had been.

Was the whole vampire myth, in fact, a prudish, half-conscious, coded Victorian parable of homosexual paedophilia? Bram Stoker had been close to a number of homosexuals, including Oscar Wilde, a notorious seducer of young boys after his own rather late initiation by the young Robbie Ross. The pattern of the seduced youth becoming the seducer of others was certainly mirrored in the chain reaction of vampirism. And homosexuality was often seen at the time as a corruption spread by contagion, like a disease. Rigdon wondered if he ought to float that idea or was it too far-fetched? It was a long time since he had published any scholarly articles. He had thought for several years that he ought to write about his personal experiences, about what he really felt in his pursuit of this perversion, how it evolved over his life, as an aid to the world's understanding of it. But now that this vast anti-paedophile frenzy had been unleashed, he knew such a book could never be published. If it ever was, he would be the object of universal vituperation. Why should he subject himself to humiliation and vilification by baring his soul? Better to maintain the image of cynicism and indifference to the end. Even to present it all as an impersonal, intellectual analysis in an academic paper seemed to him futile in the present atmosphere of hysteria. It was more in keeping with his character to stage one more scandalous show to horrify the world and thrill his cult following, and satisfy the itch in memorable fashion. Intellectual articles seemed to him to be sterile and fruitless exercises, compared to real physical acts. Nobody read academic papers any more anyhow; nobody listened to anybody else, there were too many voices, and only those bleating the same dominant ideology got heard. He preferred to leave behind an image of insolent, triumphant transgression, which would live on in an underground cult when all the academic papers had long been forgotten. The morality of the world evolved through entertainment, through shocking performances, through violating taboos, and not through intellectual insights.

He glanced across at the devil mask propped on the back of the couch, which he had got out to try on again. He thought it winked at him in the darkening twilight. He winked back. He had made his choice in life.

25

Simon Caffrey dropped in to see Bendigo. He found him looking at some photographs.

"So, what have you decided? Or haven't you yet?"

Bendigo answered slowly, as if deeply absorbed in the photographs of the juvenile genitalia he was studying.

"I'm leaning towards the offer of a million euros for a second Boy in Formaldehyde, but I'm trying to get him to up it to pounds by throwing in a few extras."

"I wouldn't make too fine a point of it if I were you. I think his offer is a good one as it stands. Assuming, of course, you can produce the goods."

"Do you have any doubt about that?" Bendigo said sharply.

Caffrey looked slightly embarrassed.

"I mean, from a technical point of view I don't know the difficulties involved. He was very specific about what he wants."

"I can fulfil the commission, no problem," Bendigo said rather testily.

Caffrey studied him as if he was seeing the emergence of a new side of the man he considered almost as his protégé. The balance of power between agents and artists, he knew from experience, tended to see-saw wildly with growing success.

"Of course I've never gone into all that with you and I have no wish to," he said carefully. "I don't know if the rumours concerning this latest work have any substance and I don't wish to know. As an agent I am not in the secret of the tricks of fabrication of a work of art. I merely take it to market as it is. I relay the statements you have made about it. My involvement stops there. That's the way I want to keep it. I think you are right to play with the ambiguity of the work and cultivate a somewhat sulphurous reputation. Provided I don't need to know the details of how justified it is."

"Don't worry, your professional integrity is safe with me." Bendigo was attempting a little sarcasm. Caffrey deliberately ignored it.

"On that basis, I'm sure we have a long and prosperous future together."

"I'm sure." There might have been a hint of irony in the tone but it was a small one.

"Then my advice would be: take the offer as it stands. It's as good as you'll get. And it can only lead very quickly to better things."

"I'll think about it."

After Simon Caffrey left, Bendigo sat lost in thought. He had noted the coolness of the other's manner. He was increasingly unhappy with this arrangement whereby his agent had to be kept officially in the dark as to how he had made his latest work of art — in order to keep his hands clean. As if there was any risk somebody would dismantle an installation to find out! Of course Caffrey's stance was pure hypocrisy. He must know this was a real body. He knew Bendigo's talents as a sculptor were zero. Even if he had used another sculptor as a ghost, what material could the boy possibly be made out of? Caffrey's cowardice was irritating. Bendigo needed somebody with more enthusiasm for the moral as well as artistic revolution he was engaged in. He needed somebody he could confide in. Someone without all this moral and legalistic squeamishness, this stick-in-the-mud attitude to what were already the taboos of a past age. He needed somebody willing to embrace the future as he saw it.

This Frenchman seemed to be on the same wavelength as him. The Lampedusa idea was pure genius. The more he thought about it the more that struck him as the way of the future — his future. A steady supply of bodies for a whole series of people in formaldehyde. Where else would you get so many bodies, most of them young, in perfect shape because they had drowned? No wounds, contusions or mutilations to be covered up (no need for a clumsy diving mask to cover up a nasty gash in the temple.) A range of races and skin colours to provide just the right degree of variation. And all of them anonymous, with little chance of a relative showing up from some Third World hellhole and recognizing them. Now that he had become notorious for one body in formaldehyde, why not mine that vein for all it was worth? Repetition in art today was no bad thing. Nearly all the successful modernist artists constantly repeated themselves. Picasso with his faces drawn both full front and in profile. Mondrian and his squares. Rothko and his two planes of colour, one above the other. The minimalists who painted the same stripe down the same blank canvas over and over, shifting it an inch to the left, then an inch to the right, and then (oh, revolution!) changing the colour. Hirst had put a whole menagerie in formaldehyde before he ordered hundreds of standardized spot paintings to be churned out by his staff. Repetition was the essence of modernism. The creation of a signature work over and over. A brand. Warhol had given it a new lease of life by making art into a production line. Endless silk-screen reproductions of Marilyn's face, in rows like cans on a shelf, and then the same with Goethe, Einstein, etc. Like so many different flavours of soup. Repetition was the essence of advertising, hammering an image till it sticks in the mind — totally familiar and totally meaningless. Warhol, of course, came to art from advertising. He used advertising's tricks. And finally that is what he reduced art to. The repetitive clichés of advertising. The same idiot images over and over, signifying nothing.

And he, Bendigo, what did he want to reduce art to? And the answer was: a shock. The shock of a perversion. The murder of a young rent boy whose arse has been banged out of shape. Portrait of a young faggot or paedophile catamite preserved in formaldehyde. In the past, art celebrated love. Now it celebrates perversion. Every form of sadomasochistic, twisted, paedophile perversion. The two things were related. The love and beauty of the art of the past had become the perversion and ugliness of the art of the present. Modern art is to the art of the past what sadistic perversion is to the ideal of romantic love that inspired previous ages. The attempt to distil pure beauty, emotion and harmony by Chopin or Renoir had given way to the obsession with ugliness, psychosis and obscenity of modernist art and music. He wanted to rub people's noses in this fact. To make them see how irrevocably art and the world had changed. How the old ideals had gone forever. The old emotions, the old dreams, the old love of beauty. Nothing was sacred any longer. And least of all a human body, which was no more than an object to be used, abused, perverted, dismembered and degraded. The more he thought about it the more he saw his life mission as putting a whole series of naked bodies in formaldehyde — with suitably pious captions, which would ironically underline the indignity and degradation of their fate. And perhaps a later series of bodies could be mutilated, disfigured or dismembered? What endless possibilities it opened up for cruel, cynical mockery of the whole human circus!

But to do this it became vitally important to cement his relationship with this new associate — the key to the supply of bodies that would make his artistic and moral revolution possible. He had to bring this Frenchman into his confidence, build a close partnership, and ensure the kind of complicity that could get around any legal hurdles that arose. He had to do it quickly, whatever the risk, and put this relationship on the right footing from the start, by making sure that Romain was not only willing to accept ready-made dead bodies but that he would not baulk at seeing how they were made. He had to remove all ambiguity in the Frenchman's attitude by making him a witness to a killing. Romain must not be allowed to linger in the kind of hypocritical limbo that Caffrey was in, perpetually covering his own arse by pretending ignorance. Once he had established that partnership of trust, once he was working out of this count's château in France, with an endless supply of bodies from Lampedusa, then he could tell Caffrey to go to hell. An international network of kinky, edgy and morally progressive collectors would assure his fortune, attracted like flies to the smell of death emanating from his work.

He phoned Romain and asked if they could see each other. He suggested it should be just the two of them, since he was not sure what the reaction of the girlfriend would be. He didn't know how permanent their relationship was or what influence she might have over his decisions. He had the feeling she would be a bit more squeamish than Romain, so he would leave it up to the Frenchman to decide how much to tell her.

Romain showed up at his atelier at the agreed time. Bendigo produced the bottles of beer again and they sat in the cluttered living room.

"I was wondering if your cousin was close to making a decision."

"About?"

"About the offer of a second boy, with the photographs."

"For a million pounds?"

Bendigo nodded.

"He's still hesitating a bit. He'd like to come over and have a look himself before going that far."

"Of course. Be delighted to show him." He tried to hide his disappointment. This would mean very inconvenient delays. "But I thought you had his full authority."

"Up to a million euros."

Bendigo's eyes narrowed.

"Look, if that's a problem, let's cut a deal. Let's do it for a million euros, without the photos. Then when your cousin comes over, I show him the photos, and he decides if he wants them as well by paying the difference. Let's not quibble when I see a bright future of collaboration between us. I haven't forgotten the Lampedusa proposal. Your cousin is still serious about that?"

"Absolutely. That's his main attraction to this whole thing. He wants you as his resident artist, churning out works on the spot. He thinks it'll have huge appeal."

"And the sudden production of a lot of bodies in formaldehyde is not going to pose any problems in France? With the police, or nosey journalists?"

"Who is to know if these are real bodies? How will they find out? There is enormous respect for works of art in France. And there is a love of the ambiguous, of letting mystery surround any object of controversy. They will love writing about it. It doesn't mean they'll ever investigate. It will become one of the great unsolved art mysteries. Are Bendigo's bodies real? Like the real identity of Mona Lisa. Or did Vermeer use a camera obscura? They love speculating but the whole intellectual industry depends on not finding out."

Bendigo breathed more quickly at this thought.

"Then I think we can seal our deal. A million euros. The boy as specified."

He held out his hand. Romain hesitated and then shook it.

"Done," he said.

Bendigo smiled with relief. Things could go ahead after all.

"Of course I understand your cousin may want to see the finished work before he pays. But on the strength of your word, I can start making it, according to his instructions. And what I would like to do is involve you in the whole process of how it is made, so you can see it step by step, and be sure it is following his specifications. And a key stage, the most crucial one, will be the production of the body. Or shall we say, the conversion of the body."

He paused for one last, lingering moment, staring at Romain. Then he took the plunge.

"You have already seen the photographs of the living boy. You have seen how he corresponds to what your cousin has in mind. But of course in this state he's of no use to us. He has to become a body. A usable body. A work of art. Immortal. Dead, in short. And that process of conversion is going to be done as a private show reserved for a few superior souls."

He sat back and studied Romain carefully as he took a swig of his beer. The Frenchman did the same and showed no reaction apart from deep interest in what he was saying.

"There are people who will pay considerable sums to be a witness to a ritual of death," Bendigo went on. "It has become one of the last truly decadent self-indulgences in a world where every chav moron can watch as much live sex as he wants down at his local lap-dancing bar. Watching death has become the vice of the elite, the addiction of kings, the secret indulgence of a highly privileged few — selected not by money alone but by connections. I want you to join that select few — to observe, to feel part of an age-old ritual. I want you to feel involved in it, so that the making of this work will be something you have shared in. This will be the sacrifice of a life for art. For the work of art your cousin has commissioned. It will be an unforgettable experience." He paused. "It is unusual to invite outsiders, but given my own involvement in this project, I can get you an invitation."

"And when is this event to take place?" The tone of voice was neutral.

"On the 14th of June. A Saturday."

"And here in London?"

"Just outside of London. In Hertfordshire. You'll need a car. Or I can take you."

"We'll have our own transport."

"We?"

"I assume the invitation extends to my girlfriend, Melissa."

"Is that wise?" Bendigo frowned. "Do you know what her reactions might be? This will be, let's say, a heavy experience. There will be various unconventional acts of sex. Child sex. And a death."

"She has the stomach of a hyena," declared Romain. "She's used to hunting. She skins and guts deer. She's a savage at heart."

Bendigo stared at him for a few seconds. Then he took another swig of his beer.

"In that case I shall get two invitations for you. I wanted to check with you first before involving her in this."

"Very considerate of you."

"I shall of course accompany you in — you will be my guests."

"Then we'd better meet up beforehand and drive in convoy."

"I'll let you know the details when I give you the invitations. Everyone will be masked, by the way. You will receive a mask with the invitation."

"Sounds very exciting. Quite cloak and dagger."

"One can never be too careful. All sorts of people might try to infiltrate our little gathering and see who's there. Discretion and security, those are the watchwords. No mobile phones or cameras allowed in. There'll be a search at the gate."

"Good, we'll remember to leave our phones at home then."

Bendigo looked at him pointedly.

"I see this as the first stage of our work together in France."

"Absolutely. So do I."

"I'm sure you'll find it unlike anything you've ever seen before."

On this note Bendigo stood up and indicated the interview was over by holding out his hand.

Romain reported back to Camilla, who phoned Inspector Stubbings to let her know the state of play. They agreed to meet and make arrangements. They assumed they wouldn't know the exact venue of this event till the last moment, but things could still be planned in advance.

26

Pandora House had tall iron gates in a high stone wall, on which the name was fixed in rusty metal letters in Gothic script. As they drove through the open gates, two masked guards in black outfits stopped them and checked their invitations. The sun was setting as they drove up a long driveway with woods on either side till they came to a wide area of grass where rows of cars were parked. Bendigo parked beside the last car and Romain followed suit. When Bendigo got out of his Jaguar, they saw he was wearing his mask, the head of a grey wolf. They glanced at each other and put on their masks as well. Camilla became a green parrot and Romain a red fox. They followed some little groups of other guests also wearing masks as they walked a further hundred metres or so to the entrance of a large gatehouse.

As they went inside, showing their invitations again, men dressed as devils frisked them for cameras and smartphones, which signs announced were forbidden. Camilla had taped her smartphone inside one of her high black boots, bought specially for the occasion. The devils groped her thighs and boots but missed it. After that there was a sign saying: "Face control, please remove masks. Our application will detect members of the police and journalists. Your photo will later be deleted." The guests filed slowly through the control point in two lines, passing two guards wearing eye-masks like comic-book bandits, who held up tablets to snap them. Camilla was worried she might be on their data base, even though she had changed the photo on her website for another one stolen from a Russian dating site. She also had a sudden fear that the guard on the right resembled Brian from Birmingham. She whispered it to Romain. They both joined the left queue, separating from Bendigo. As they removed their masks for the photograph they kept their faces turned away from Brian. They were asked to hold the mask beside their face in order to match the two, and this enabled them to use the masks to shield their faces from his view. Camilla breathed a sigh of relief as they were allowed to put their masks on again and were waved on. They caught up with Bendigo, who was waiting for them as they stepped out of the gatehouse.

They followed the other guests along a path through large trees to a lawn bordered by shrubs and overlooked by a grassy slope. On the far side of the lawn was a stage, and beside it a podium equipped with microphones. Further back was a maze of closely cropped hedges, and behind that loomed the imposing bulk of the house itself. It was a vast edifice with a central mediaeval fortress adorned with turrets, which made it look rather forbidding, while the extensions added in various styles over the centuries gave it a rambling, eccentric appearance. Some lights were on in the upper storeys where a few dark figures stood silhouetted against windows. Most people had gathered on the crescent-shaped slope which overlooked the lawn and stage like a natural amphitheatre.

Following Bendigo's lead they drifted with the crowd across the lawn and up the slope till they found a spot in the middle with a good view of the stage. Waiters, muscular men wearing leotards and devils' masks, circulated with drinks on trays. Bendigo stopped one and handed Romain and Camilla plastic glasses of imitation champagne.

They looked around in fascination at the crowd. The animal masks gave it a weird, surrealistic appearance, and reminded Camilla of the host of bestial demons in a painting by Hieronymus Bosch. There were not only masks of wild animals and birds of prey but also monsters, devils, mythological beasts and creatures from fantasy films.

"I'm sure you'd be surprised to know who some of our fellow-guests are," said Bendigo in her ear.

"Do you know of any famous names you expect to be here?" she asked curiously.

He ignored the question and confined himself to vague philosophical observations.

"In ancient Greek drama the actors wore masks. When the spectators wear masks, they too become actors. We all become the play. That is the principle of the carnival, which makes it so exciting and mysterious." He sipped his champagne with an air of satisfaction as he gazed about him.

Camilla felt reassured by the sense of anonymity the mask gave her, along with the growing density of the crowd and the gathering twilight. The atmosphere was festive. There were some figures wearing elaborate eighteenth-century dresses and classical masks like those at the Venice carnival, but she didn't know if they were transvestites. Most of the clearly female guests were mannishly dressed in trousers and high black boots like her own. She noticed a few young boys dressed in mediaeval page costumes and cupid masks. People were surprisingly sociable, forming little groups, and there was an expectant buzz of conversation. As dusk fell, lights came on, illuminating the stage. Music sounded from loudspeakers in the shrubbery. It was Grieg's sinister fairytale music, *In the Hall of the Mountain King*, and after its thunderous climax, someone blew a whistle, as if for silence.

A small troupe dressed as zombies danced out of the maze onto the area of lawn in front of the stage, to the accompaniment of rather stressful and unnerving modern music, which whined and shrieked like souls in torment. As they disappeared again, a master of ceremonies in a tail coat and top hat, with a garish clown face, appeared on the podium and welcomed everyone in a high-pitched voice. Then he handed over to an imposing figure in a grand colourful cloak, somewhere between that of a stage magician and a university vice-chancellor on graduation day. He wore a black mask, shaped like the head of the Egyptian jackal god, Anubis, but something about the way he carried himself struck Camilla as familiar. When he began to speak she got a shock. It took her several seconds to believe what her ears were telling her. The grave, portentous voice was that of Professor Rigdon.

"Welcome to our little happening, ladies and gentlemen. This show is a kind of festival but it is not merely entertainment. It aims to promote a cause — the right to love whoever we choose, without distinction of age, race or sex. In short, Sexual Freedom for All, also known as Sexual Equality." There was a scattering of applause, to which he bowed slightly. "Our little show will be in three parts. The first part will feature some theatrical sketches on sexual themes by highly skilled young performers. They will demonstrate that there is nothing in the world of adult eroticism that children cannot and do not participate in with full enjoyment. The second part will be a little game, in which some very young children will be initiated into the joys of sex in a playful and agreeable manner.

This part will include a brief phase of audience participation for those so inclined. The third part will be a surprise, a game of suspense I can promise you will never forget. I shall tell you more about it when the time comes." He paused and his masked head turned slowly as if scanning the crowd. "It goes without saying that we don't allow any filming of these events, and any mobile phones or cameras that have escaped our vigilance, if seen by our security staff, will be confiscated. The offender, of whatever sex, will be punished in exemplary fashion, by being sodomized over a barrel by the entire security staff, and the punishment will be filmed and posted on the internet with the face and identity of the culprit exposed." There was some tittering at this colourful threat. "But right now let's give a round of applause to our child performers. The first act is called the Prince, the Ogre, and the Sleeping Beauty. It is performed by a Bulgarian troupe. The girl is called Miranda. She is an artist truly to be admired and is only thirteen years old."

Camilla was horrified when she recognized Rigdon's voice. So this was the man whose words she had drawn comfort from, whom she had seen as a figure of wisdom and understanding! Now to see him revealed for what he was — the organizer of a carnival of child abuse! How naive and foolish her judgment seemed! This was the kind of paedophilia he really defended — not the passionate love affairs of headstrong teenagers like Juliet. She blushed at her own gullibility. She wondered if she would have the stomach to watch this show, but realized she had no choice. The plan was that she would call Inspector Stubbings when the murder of the boy was imminent so that the police could catch them in the act. That would certainly be the third part of the show. She stood in the crowd as though condemned to watch an execution, fear in the pit of her stomach at the things she would have to see. She began to feel slightly shaky and discreetly held Romain's hand more tightly.

The lights went out and Camilla recognized the opening chords of the first movement of *The Sleeping Beauty* of Tchaikovsky. A full moon had just risen between bands of cloud and by its light one could make out a small divan being moved into the centre of the stage. As the lights slowly came up again, a figure could be seen lying on it, which revealed itself to be a young girl with long blonde curls. She was lying on her back under a red and gold bedspread and seemed to be asleep. Then a boy of fourteen or fifteen entered, wearing white leotards with a gold-sequined top and moving in the manner of a ballet dancer. He was a handsome boy with longish brown hair. Like the girl, he wore a white eye-mask. He mimed surprise as he noticed the girl on the divan, and went over to her curiously. After gazing at her pretty face, he planted a kiss on her lips. This fairy-tale atmosphere, that of the story of *The Sleeping Beauty*, evoked all the poetry of first love. Then things changed.

The girl remained asleep, so the boy began to pull the bedspread off her slowly, revealing a beautiful, naked, pubescent body. She was slender but with the developed shoulders of a gymnast and only tiny buds of breasts. The boy began to kiss her very delicately from her throat down to her thighs. He bypassed her lower belly and kissed his way down one thigh, as though teasing the spectators, and then he moved to the other thigh and slowly came back up again. When he finally placed a kiss on the downy spot that was the focus of all eyes, the girl awoke with a start. She sat up, stared at the boy in astonishment and then threw her arms round him and kissed him passionately. After a minute he resumed his ministrations to her body while she arched her back in a theatrical display of sensual ecstasy.

They were about to proceed to more erotic caresses when the music abruptly changed. Tchaikovsky's lyrical second movement was broken into by the loud clash of cymbals. Then the strains of Stravinsky's *Rite of Spring* blared out. As these violent, savage chords rained down upon the stage, it was invaded by a mob of near-naked creatures in ghoulish masks, with long, shaggy hair and garishly painted bodies. They seized the two young lovers and flung the boy on the ground where they sodomized him, while others raped and then sodomized the girl on the divan, the whole thing in a violent frenzy as if they were madmen. The audience cheered and laughed uproariously. It was a vision of anarchy and savagery, a tempest of primitive violence brutally annihilating an idyll of romantic young love.

At the height of this frenzy there was another clash of cymbals, a blast on a tuba, and a big man stomped on stage in heavy boots. He wore the mask of an ogre and had a massive, hairy chest. He sat on a chair brought by one of his attendants and barked an order in what must have been Bulgarian. He was apparently calling for the girl to be brought to him. The size of the man made one tremble for the delicate, slender young girl. As the wild men seized her, the young prince, lying on the ground, made an impassioned appeal to the ogre, his gestures indicating that he was pleading with him to spare the girl this ordeal and offering himself in her place. The ogre barked another order and the young prince was dragged before him and made to bend over in front of him. The ogre then stood up and sodomized him while the girl wept piteously at the sight. The ogre, however, refrained from coming and growled another order, whereupon the girl was dragged before him after all. He sodomized her as well, to the delighted roars of the crowd. The young prince went mad at this treachery, grabbed a sword conveniently worn by the ogre's attendant and ran the ogre through. The mob of wild men fell back in consternation, gibbering in shock. The naked girl then began to dance round the ogre's body, at first slowly, then faster and faster, as Stravinsky's music reached its savage climax. It was music intended to evoke a sacrificial virgin dancing herself to death, and her dance became more and more frenzied. The young prince watched her spellbound and at the height of her dance the lovers came face to face and kissed passionately. He lifted her into the air and she wrapped her legs round his head. At that instant the lights went out and the music ended abruptly.

A few seconds later the lights came up again as the ogre, the two young lovers and the crowd of wild men lined up at the front of the stage and bowed deeply to the frantically clapping, whistling crowd. They ran off the stage hand in hand, smiling and waving like actors or ballet dancers, and were cheered to the echo with cries of bravo.

Camilla, who had never seen a live sex-show before, was shocked by this spectacle, most of all because of the children involved and the bestiality of the acts of sodomy and rape. The raucous cheering of the crowd throughout disgusted her. As for the story, it resembled a fable of the destruction of innocent young love by an orgy of sexual violence, which seemed (by some irony, intended or not) to reflect what was happening in the world. The contrast between the delicate, childish body of the girl and the savage assault she was subjected to struck Camilla not merely as a crime but as an image of the times. It symbolized the devastation of childhood by the tsunami of internet pornography, the violation of childish dreams and adolescent romance by a precocious, brutal exposure to violent sexual acts — this she saw as a kind of rape of modern childhood. The discrediting of all notions that the innocence of childhood must be protected, the flooding of children's minds with the crudest sexual images, the indoctrination of young children with the belief that all sexual acts are good and normal — this hodgepodge of gutter "liberationism" was poisoning the minds of a generation. In contrast to her own precocious adolescent passion for the man of her dreams, girls were now subject to a constant social goading into sexual acts not driven by any personal passion at all. The teenage sex act on YouTube was becoming an adolescent rite of passage. The exchange of smartphone photos of their genitalia was more and more the social norm of schoolchildren. It was a collective, herd-like sexual obsession, not motivated by any intense personal feelings for any particular individual. Camilla believed it was undermining the normal emotional experience of boys and girls falling in love — the key to their emotional growth. Behind the criminal exploitation in this live sex-show, she saw the brainwashing of a whole generation to see pornography, exhibitionism and perversion as the essence of sexual relationships.

Most of the sketches that followed had scenarios that were a lot simpler and cruder than the first one. They featured Roman soldiers sodomizing teenage slave-boys, a circle of boy pupils taking turns at fellatio upon a middle-aged Socrates, and a Renaissance artist sodomizing a very young Cupid as he posed naked for a painting. There were some teenage drag queen acts, involving the oral servicing of bishops and judges, where a final strip tease to reveal the true sex of the performers was followed by a brisk round of sodomy, as mock punishment for the dissemblers. What struck Camilla after a while was the trivialization of all these sex acts, and how this trivialization led almost inevitably to their infliction upon the very young, in order to excite the most jaded appetites. When you have seen a hundred sword swallowers, it is only a child sword swallower who can still arouse interest. When a perversion becomes utterly banal, only its infliction upon a child gives it novelty and spice, as the sadistic, degrading nature of the act becomes apparent once again through its violation of childish innocence. And homosexual paedophilia had the added sadistic spice of using the male as a female, an act of symbolic castration, humiliation and degradation, done to a child too young to understand the grotesqueness of his own abasement.

These young transvestites reminded Camilla of junior versions of the wriggling, leering drag queens of a typical Love Parade — that homosexual carnival which had been insidiously imposed on youth culture all over the Western world as a celebration of freedom. The pornographic antics of these junior avatars of liberation seemed intended to prove that they were willing participants, eager to show off their skills without any shame. After years of watching internet porn as a sport, they no doubt saw themselves not as victims but as athletes — and viewed their adult abusers as their trainers. Camilla suspected many of them must perform regularly on a clandestine paedophile circuit or for internet porn. They were part of a new parallel sexual universe, which the ideologues of liberation had brought into existence, as though a new mutant species had been released into the world.

Camilla saw in these grinning, painted children, proudly aping all the feats of porn stars, not just the victims of criminal exploiters but the victims of an entire society and its mad cult of liberation. The spectacle of these young transvestites being sodomized on stage before a cheering crowd was the spectacle of a society devouring its children, like the Aztecs. She saw it as a vision of the future, a sneak preview of the endgame of the liberationists — a cult of sex as a purely gymnastic exercise, with no emotions involved, no hint of a personal relationship that might possibly evoke, as a distant outcome, the tyranny of marriage or the patriarchal evil of family. Camilla recalled what Romain had said of modernist art and music. Human emotions had been sacrificed to an ideological abstraction. Art devoid of emotion had been followed by sex devoid of emotion. She felt she was watching the last throes of a civilization in full decadence which deserved to perish, and whose last sterile descendants would be swept away by the Third World tides within a century. She had a momentary vision of the enormous, old, decaying bulk of Pandora House as a mosque, and its ancient turrets as minarets. In the Afro-Asian future sterile Europe faced, what other destiny would await it, after the debauched aberrations of a suicidal, dying white race had melted into thin air?

After a succession of these acts, Rigdon-Anubis ascended his podium again, like an old magician introducing his next trick. Camilla noticed for the first time he was carrying a staff.

"I hope, dear friends and fellow classicists, that you appreciated this wonderful, liberated display by the younger generation, our future, who are creating before our eyes a brave new world. And now, let me present another little game that has been organized for your delectation. The maze will be the scene of a pastoral mime or masque, a hunt, in fact — the sort of hunt that will no doubt exist in paradise, where there is no ugly slaughter at the end, no scene of horrid bloodshed, but a delicious romp with the most angelic of creatures — little children, whom it will be the task of the hunters to chase and capture. Of course the capture must be rewarded by the sweet fruits of victory: an embrace as delightful as that by which Jove pledged his love to his Cupid-like paramour, Ganymede. In short, dear friends and fellow classicists, you are about to watch a child hunt. As a sign of the very real innocence of the children taking part, they will be dressed as angels, and the hunters as devils. And after the excitement of the chase and the delights of capture, a young queen of the hunt will be chosen and crowned. She will then undergo an initiation ceremony — a sacred ritual of deflowering that will be like the mystic marriage of a virgin in heaven. Following which, a general frolicking will take place in which you are all invited to participate, within the limits of the space available. Enjoy!"

The lights were dimmed again and spotlights were focused on the lawn and the maze behind it. Suddenly a brace of children ran across the lawn from the surrounding bushes and took refuge in the maze. They were dressed in white, with white eye-masks, and had angels' wings attached to their shoulders. The wings were so large and light they resisted the air, and the children thus ran slowly and awkwardly, as though they were only toddlers. At once a couple of adult devils in flaming red costumes ran across the lawn after them and disappeared into the maze as well. Childish shrieks of terror began to echo round the garden.

Camilla was seized with horror to the point of feeling physically sick. These children looked only about six or seven years old, and they were clearly not trained performers like the older ones. What was happening to them was intolerable, and she couldn't watch it. She whispered to Romain she was feeling sick and made her way to the back of the crowd. A short distance behind it she found a tree like a weeping willow, under whose hanging leaves she could make a discreet call on her smartphone. She got through to Inspector Stubbings at last.

"It's Pandora House, as you thought it might be. You must come at once, there's the most appalling paedophile rapes going on in the garden in front of the house, it's an orgy of child abuse." She kept her voice low and close to the phone. Unfortunately the music was so loud and dramatic in the background she wasn't sure her low voice could be heard. Nor could she hear the reply. She wanted to repeat what she had said but she noticed another spectator walking towards her.

"Come at once!" she whispered. "It's urgent!" and turned off the phone, fumbling to put it back quickly into her pocket without looking. To her horror she dropped it on the grass.

"You're missing half the sport," said the person as she got to the tree. She had a low mannish voice, but was visibly a woman inside her falcon mask. She wore a stylish black leather jacket, jodhpurs and riding boots, and carried a riding whip, with which she swept aside the hanging leaves of the tree under which Camilla was sheltering.

"You aren't feeling ill, are you?" She noticed the smartphone in Camilla's hand, which she had just stooped down and picked up again. The voice hardened. "You're not supposed to have phones, didn't you hear?"

"I wasn't filming anything. I just had to check on my children with my babysitter," Camilla said quickly, finding the most obvious excuse for an urgent phone call. She managed to slide the phone into her pocket at last.

"Oh, you have children!" said the falcon mask, in a tone of mocking surprise. "How interesting! And how old would the little darlings be?"

"Oh, they're very small, two and three." Camilla realized too late that this was not a gathering likely to include many parents. She thought she might have made a blunder.

"How fascinating! We don't have too many breeders at our little shows. You may be the only one." There was an ominous pause. "And how does it make you feel, as a mother, watching little angels being given a good seeing-to by wicked devils?"

"I'm a great believer in starting young," Camilla said brightly. "I myself was molested very young and I do think it did me the world of good. I hope my children have that privilege too."

"Molested! That's not a word we use." The voice was suspicious, accusatory, menacing. The riding whip came up and poked Camilla half-playfully between the breasts. It stayed there like a fencing foil threatening her for a few seconds.

"Of course, I used the word jokingly, in the way narrow-minded bigots use it — what I meant was I was initiated very young into the pleasures of penetration, both vaginal and anal, and I can't wish for a more auspicious start to life for my children."

"Indeed? And are you still addicted to penetration or have you found other pleasures since then which are more congenial between bodies of the same sort?"

The woman reached out a hand half covered by a black fingerless glove, with studs on the back of it, and caressed Camilla lightly with a suggestive, serpentine movement down her breasts to her crotch.

"I have developed a very wide range of pleasures, but always with the same persons, whom I must now rejoin, if you don't mind." She backed away.

"I'd like to see you without your mask," insisted the other, clutching her arm.

"I'm afraid that's impossible," Camilla said sharply, pulling away and moving out from under the tree.

"Why impossible?" demanded the other aggressively, moving to cut off her retreat. She snatched her green parrot mask and tore it off. "What a pretty little face!" she exclaimed nastily.

"Give me back my mask, please!" Camilla heard her voice sounding slightly desperate. She knew Brian was somewhere in this crowd and if he ran into her without her mask and recognized her, the game would be up.

The woman laughed maliciously and held the mask behind her, out of reach. Seeing she couldn't get at it, Camilla snatched the woman's mask instead and tore it off.

"Then I'll have yours instead." She fled with the falcon mask, fitting it on as she ran and pulling the elastic over her head.

"Come back, you bitch, you breeder slut!" the woman shouted angrily behind her. "You're a spy, aren't you?"

Fortunately, Camilla was fit and a good runner even in boots, and she slipped back into the crowd easily. By bending low as she wormed her way through it she gave her pursuer the slip. The latter, who was now wearing the green parrot mask, hesitated on the edge of the crowd and peered over shoulders trying to spot her. Suddenly a man gripped her arm. He was dressed in black leather and combat boots and was wearing a devil mask.

"You're coming with me," he said in a low voice. "Security, we want to check up on you."

He pulled her by the arm and led her towards the gatehouse.

"Where are you taking me? What's this about?" cried the woman.

"I told you: Security."

"I don't believe you're Security, show me some badge or something."

She began to resist and put up a fight, grappling with him and slashing with the riding whip. He put her arm in a wrestling hold, made her drop the whip, and twisted her arm behind her.

"Help!" she cried. "Help me! This man's a rapist! He's hurting me!"

He put his hand over her mouth, pushing her mask up to do so, so she could no longer see through the eye-holes. She bit his hand and yelled "Help!" again. He swore and clouted her across the top of her head with his open hand and then again with his fist to the side of it. She sank to the ground, stunned.

"Get up, you bitch!" he said furiously. He began kicking her in the thighs and backside. It was no use, she was unconscious. He sighed and bent down, picked her up bodily and slung her over his shoulder. Two men had peeled off from the crowd and approached him in a stalking, menacing manner.

"What are you doing to her? Who are you?" called one.

"Security. This is a spy," said the man in the devil's mask.

"How do we know who you are?" asked the other man.

"Listen, one of the guards at the gate recognized this woman's face on the photos we just took of everyone coming in. She may be a private investigator, we're checking her out."

The others stopped, uncertain, and let him go. He continued towards the gatehouse with the woman slung over his shoulder. As he walked, he adjusted his mask with his free hand, and smoothed back his black, Elvis-style pompadour, which had been ruffled in the struggle.

Camilla made her way back to Romain. He didn't recognize her at first because of the change of masks and moved back sharply as she sidled up to him.

"It's me, silly. I've changed masks."

"This is appalling," he whispered in her ear in French, indicating the show taking place on the stage.

The child hunt had evidently finished and they were now at the phase of the post-hunt celebration. A large Jacuzzi with transparent sides had been placed in the centre of the stage and boys and girls were being stripped of their angel costumes and thrown into it. There was much squealing and splashing as a number of devils, naked except for their masks, joined the children in the water and played with them. The games were, of course, of an erotic nature and the children squirmed and squealed to escape from the devils' clutches. The crowd roared with laughter at the sport. A dessert trolley was parked nearby, filled with ice cream and what seemed to be sweet alcoholic drinks, which the children were pressed to indulge in. In this way they could be distracted and befuddled enough to make them accept the lewd acts being imposed upon them. Camilla found the scene as surreal as a drug-induced hallucination. It was not so much like an orgy as like the feeding of children to wild beasts. She could not fathom how adults could feel sexual desire for such tiny, immature bodies, yet she knew this was one of the fastest growing perversions on earth and a worldwide internet industry. What she was watching was a mild sample of what was happening on millions of computer screens all over the world at any given moment — a silent massacre of the innocents. What disastrous failure in adult relations was reflected in this perverse displacement of desire onto children? She was struck by the laughter both of the devils and the spectators. The whole thing was an enormous dirty joke, a hilarious game, as sexual acts were forced upon those too young to understand what was happening to them. The children's innocence was the butt of the joke, the object of collective derision. It was as if innocence itself was being subjected to a brutal natural law of sexual violation, whose triumph was being gleefully celebrated.

In the midst of the cacophony of squeals coming from the pool, one girl, rather taller than the others, was proclaimed the Queen of the Hunt by the master of ceremonies, to enthusiastic applause. She was brought out of the pool, dried with a towel and laid on the divan at the front of the stage. Three devils stood around her, like priests officiating at a ceremony. One of them, who was extremely fat and wore a crimson cassock like an Anglican bishop, blessed her naked body with what looked like holy water. A fourth devil plied her with drink, and daubed her belly and slender thighs with ice cream, which he proceeded to lick off. She giggled as if it tickled her. He then placed a white cushion beneath her buttocks, climbed on the divan and mounted her.

Camilla shuddered and looked down to avoid watching. She felt Romain squeezing her hand. The coarse cheers and rhythmic clapping of the crowd formed a hideous, diabolical soundtrack to the act taking place out of her sight. She felt rage and horror rising to fever pitch inside her and she began to shake. She was overwhelmed by a feeling of revulsion for the whole human race, and she remembered vividly feeling the same sensation after Brendan was murdered. She had wanted not merely to die but for the whole human race to die. She had an incongruous flash that this was perhaps at the root of her problem with sex: deep down she did not want to be part of this species, to prolong this nightmare, she did not want to play any part in continuing the whole bestial life process, where the strong prey upon the weak, and the fit survive while the helpless are exterminated, as though all the world was a Nazi death camp. Passages of the Vedas came back to her and she suddenly had a vision of all this as *maya*, illusion, diabolical mockery. She wanted this entire scene of human depravity and viciousness to disappear and the species that produced it to be wiped out by nuclear war. But the hand holding hers kept squeezing it and making her feel part of this species in spite of everything. Of course she recognized there were good human beings, heroes, people who gave their lives trying to save others. But did it make up for this? Did it redeem mankind? Did the good outweigh the evil? She felt tears of rage and confusion scalding her cheeks.

At last a storm of applause seemed to indicate the climax had been reached, and she looked again at the obscene mockery taking place in front of her. The devil was now covering the girl's face with kisses. Another devil passed him a bottle of sweet alcohol and he tipped it into her mouth as she began to sob with shock. She choked and began to cough and he quickly pulled her up and patted her back. A young woman dressed in a nun's veil but in a white dress slit at the side and high heels came onstage and kissed and petted her too, and the whole world seemed to be showering praise upon her for accepting this violation. The girl was so much in shock that she broke off her sobbing and eagerly drank more from the bottle. She was then fed more spoonfuls of ice cream from the trolley, which was wheeled to her side.

The devil who had raped her picked her up and presented her to the audience for applause, which grew even wilder, and he carried her about in a dance step and threw her to another devil and he kissed her too, and then threw her to a third. The crowd called out "olé!" each time the girl was tossed from one to another as though she was a ball in a new ball game. These flights through the air seemed to shock and confuse the child further until she seemed to have difficulty grasping what had happened to her. Meanwhile the young woman dressed as a nun held up the bloodied white cushion in front of the spectators like a trophy or a holy icon. "This is my blood which has been shed for you!" intoned Rigdon's voice solemnly over the speaker system. The MC took the microphone and began chanting the little girl's name: Ashley, which the crowd took up. Some of them apparently misunderstood it and seemed to be chanting "Aisha" until they gradually got it right. The little girl responded to this chanting of her name with pleased surprise, and at last waved and smiled wanly at the applause as she lay half-comatose in the arms of the devil.

"Let's hear it again for Ashley, Queen of the Hunt, deflowered at the age of nine without a tear or a cry!" cried the master of ceremonies. "What a star! What courage! What maturity! What a dazzling, precocious start to a sexual career! How many years of sexual pleasure lie ahead of her! I see great things for her! Actress! Porn star! Child porn star! Reality TV star! Queen of the Night! The future belongs to her!"

The applause reached its apogee. The little girl was crowned with a tinsel tiara and then carried in triumph to the Jacuzzi, and placed in the water again with the other children and devils, who all pressed around her to kiss and fondle her.

The audience buzzed with excitement after this striking demonstration that the deflowering of pre-pubescent girls is so well accepted by them. The mood of the crowd became positively celebratory. They felt they had seen visible proof that sexual acts with children are harmless fun, despite the ignorant bigots who would condemn them. Some of the spectators, both men and women, pressed forward, stripped off and climbed into the Jacuzzi to join in the frolicking with the children. Others embraced children in the audience. The atmosphere of an orgy prevailed for a quarter of an hour, to the wild accompaniment of more Stravinsky. Then one by one the small children in the Jacuzzi were taken out and presented to the huge fat devil in the bishop's cassock, who was introduced by the MC as Beelzebub. Seated on a chair, he took them on his knees like Santa Claus and fondled each one in turn as he dried them with a large towel. Then they were handed over to other devils who dressed them again, amid much giggling and squealing.

Rigdon-Anubis came back onto the podium, waved his hand towards the tableau of contented children, and addressed the crowd rhetorically:

"And to think our patron saint, Alfred Kinsey, has been condemned by bigots for claiming sixty years ago that children were capable of orgasm at all ages and enjoyed sex even in their cradle! What a lone pioneer he was! What a visionary ahead of his time! We see his beliefs vindicated here! What monstrous bigotry and oppression we are fighting against still as we struggle to get the joys of child-love accepted as a normal part of a liberated, tolerant, progressive society! How much Victorian Puritanism remains to be overthrown before we regain that innocent sense of pleasure of the Ancient Greeks, who saw all sex as noble and did not hesitate to make love with children of all ages — the embodiments of that innocent and unselfconscious sensuality that we have lost."

Camilla looked despairingly at her watch. "Did that stupid woman understand?" she whispered intensely in French. "How long does it take them to get here?"

"Depends where they are," said Romain, as applause for Rigdon's speech broke out.

Rigdon-Anubis basked in this homage by the crowd and then made a sign for silence.

"We could say: Our revels now are ended, but not quite. We have finished the joyful part of the games of this evening. Now we are about to witness something more solemn, more tragic, that goes to the very heart of the human condition and the process of evolution, which we know has produced all living things. Although universal love is the deepest expression of life, it is the struggle for survival that is the prime mover of the universe. Human beings are on earth first to struggle to survive and only afterwards, in the plenitude of their survival, to express their love for all other human beings without restriction. We are going to witness a struggle for survival, a Darwinian drama, which will involve the supreme sacrifice, death itself. What we are about to see will be like a solemn ritual, a holy sacrifice, an act of worship of the life principle itself. In this garden will be set up before you a kind of arena in which a struggle to the death will take place — the kind of struggle which was no doubt at the origin of Ancient Greek tragedy. Before the death of a hero was enacted in drama, it was no doubt a real event, the ritual sacrifice of a king. And we are going to reengage with that primitive ritual, from which all art emerged. We are going to sacrifice our own king, or rather our own god, a young boy whose form is as close to the divine as we can imagine. But we will do it without any blood on our hands because we will persuade the victims, like ancient gladiators, to sacrifice each other."

He gave a signal and four men carried a large glass tank out of the shadows beside the maze and placed it on the lawn in front of the stage. It reminded Camilla of Bendigo's tank of formaldehyde, only it was bigger, a two-metre cube, and it had no base. She was filled with a sense of foreboding about what was coming. She crouched down on the ground as if she had had a malaise, and as Romain bent protectively over her she took out her smartphone and again pressed the name Stubbings.

"You must come!" she whispered into it desperately. "They are about to kill a child!"

She thought she heard Inspector Stubbings say: "All right." And then Bendigo was leaning down to see what was happening and she hid the phone quickly inside her jacket.

"Is she all right?" he asked Romain.

"She's unwell. It's the tension," Romain said, straightening up to block his view. "She's rather faint. She's actually pregnant," he whispered confidentially. "She only just told me today. I should have listened to you, frankly, and made her stay home."

"Oh, let her sit down there for a while then, it won't matter, it might be best if she doesn't watch this next bit anyway," said Bendigo, with unexpected kindness. "It gets a bit gory now. We're going to watch the death I told you about. It's absolutely necessary to provide the material for your cousin's installation. And the manner of the death will be wonderfully postmodernist, but it may be a trifle hard to watch, especially for women and other sensitive souls. I thought you said she enjoyed hunting and skinning deer."

"Yes, normally, but this is affecting her unexpectedly, because of her condition," Romain explained. Bendigo nodded and went back to watching the show.

A devil climbed up a step-ladder set up on the stage just behind the glass tank and opened a trapdoor at the top of it. Then a naked boy was escorted onto the stage by another devil. Romain recognized Eric from the photograph they had seen in the care home. He was helped up the ladder and at the top was made to climb in through the open trapdoor and was lowered down inside by his arms. He had to jump the last few feet to the bottom of the tank and landed in a heap. He stood up. The ceiling of the tank was over half a metre above his head. Then another boy was brought in who was slightly taller, with longer, lighter blond hair. Romain was sure it was the boy in the photographs Bendigo had shown them. He had said the boy was Polish and Romain suspected it was the same Polish boy Ekaterina had tried to rescue. He was lowered by his arms into the tank as well. The two boys looked around them warily. The glass trapdoor above them was then closed. The devil climbed down the ladder and came back up again with a thick hose. He poked the nozzle through an oval hole in the trapdoor, about the size of a child's rugby ball. Water began to gush from the hose into the tank, splashing the naked boys below. The crowd stirred and a murmur of excitement ran through their ranks as they began to speculate about what was going to happen.

"We are about to see both a wonderful experiment and a wonderful demonstration of the nature of life on earth," announced Rigdon. "Soon the tank will fill with water. The boys will have to swim. But then the water will reach the top and they will have no air left to breathe. Except in the little oval hole in the roof of the tank. Big enough for one face only to fit into. What will happen? Only one will be able to breathe. The other will drown. Will they co-operate and take turns breathing? Or will it be a struggle to the death between them? A struggle for survival? You may surmise the latter. The only question is: when? How long will it take before any form of altruism is overcome by exhaustion or panic and the fear of death? You may speculate. You may place bets. But above all: you will see."

Romain felt his blood run cold. He had to stop this. But how? If he ran down there and tried to intervene he would probably be knocked out and carted away by their security guards and things would go on as if nothing had happened. The waiters in leotards and devil masks were all muscular and obviously doubled as bouncers.

His heart beat faster and he began to tremble slightly. He felt incomprehension and rage that the police had not yet arrived. Camilla had called them twice, and they were supposed to have a force standing by to intervene. Inspector Stubbings knew where they were. Camilla had told her, even if the GPS on her phone hadn't already informed them. Stubbings had even pointed to Pandora House as a possible location for the event when they pored over a map of Hertfordshire together. She knew the risk they had taken in coming here, and had promised to intervene immediately when she got their call. He and Camilla were now surrounded by a crowd of people eager to watch the macabre drowning of boys. If they tried to disrupt proceedings they would almost certainly pay with their lives. They were doing what they could by being there as witnesses so that if the police arrived too late they could testify in court to what they had seen. But was it enough that their testimony would probably convict the murderers? Didn't they, and he in particular as the man, have a duty to stop the thing happening? Was he not an accomplice if he stood there and watched the actual killing of a child, no matter how dangerous it was for him to intervene?

The more he thought about it the more he felt the adrenalin rush through him. Camilla stood up again beside him and held his hand. She felt it was trembling, and she gripped it tightly. He whispered to her in French: "If I decide I have to act, film everything with your phone." He thought that even if his intervention failed, it would divert all attention away from Camilla and she would be able to film events without being noticed. That would be important evidence in a trial. She whispered back that she was already recording Rigdon's speeches. Then she gripped his hand tighter.

Romain watched the drama before him as though hypnotized. Ravel's *Bolero* was now playing, in low measured tones at first, but slowly growing in menace. The water was now up to the boys' waists and they were beginning to understand what was going to happen. They kept looking at the tiny hole at the top of the tank. But they were talking to each other and it seemed they might have reached an agreement.

"In the first stage," Rigdon commented, "we may expect there to be some rational, civilized agreement to share the precious resource, air, which will save their lives. But then they will see how difficult it is to breathe in this position, to take in enough air, and sooner or later fear of drowning will make the agreement break down. Panic will take over. Then the fight to the death will begin. And one winner, one survivor, will emerge. We will see how fragile is the veneer of civilized response to the threat of death, and at what point primitive survival instinct sweeps away all other impulses. You will witness with your own eyes the proof of the Darwinist thesis, that the struggle for survival prevails over all else — that man is above all an animal."

The water had now risen over the boys' chests and they were soon forced to swim and tread water to keep their heads above it. They looked at each other warily and waited. The water continued to rise and brought them closer and closer to the ceiling of the glass tank. The strains of *Bolero* began to grow louder and more urgent, more sinister and menacing.

"Imagine yourselves in their position." Rigdon's voice was grave and dramatic. "They are beginning to see what awaits them and they must plan their strategy. Will it be to fight or to share? If the latter, can one trust the other to keep his side of the bargain? Or does one play safe and seize the manhole for himself and kick the other away until he drowns? Above all, they certainly realize they are not free beings in a state of nature, but captives controlled by a power which is trying to manipulate them — us. They must be speculating what we want them to do and whether any delaying tactics are futile, since the power that rules will keep trying until he brings them to do what he wants them to do — fight each other to the death. Will any altruistic plans to share be anything but a waste of time and a postponement of the inevitable, with the risk that the decision may go against them? Of what use altruism when the power in control has imposed jungle law?" He paused. "All these thoughts must be passing through their minds. And along with them all the moral conditioning and precepts of a Western, post-Christian education, dripping with ideas of love and generosity, of heroism and idealism. Will any of those values weigh in their minds against the overwhelming and sudden physical terror of drowning, of being without air?"

He stopped for a moment to let them contemplate this, as they all watched the water rising and bringing the swimming boys closer and closer to the glass ceiling. The hypnotic rhythms of *Bolero* grew more urgent and somehow more savage.

"Remember the Roman punishment of crucifixion and what it was based on. The weight of the diaphragm on the lungs of a body hanging by its arms becomes so oppressive, the fear of suffocation so intense, that no matter how much pain he feels the crucified man forces himself up on his nailed feet again to take the weight off his lungs, to take one more breath, even though he knows it is only prolonging his agony. He is unable to will himself to suffocate, to go without air, in order to end his sufferings. Despite all his resolution, he always pushes himself up one more time on the cruel nails through the nerves of his ankles to take the pressure off his lungs, to take in one more gulp of air. Unless his legs are broken and he is unable to, or until exhaustion finally arrives. You can imagine from this the power of the instinct for air, the irresistible need for air, which these boys are going to suffer from in a moment, and how the terror of suffocation is going to transform their moral universe. What you are watching here is the very essence of the life-choice: our life or another's. Do we risk our life in making a generous bargain or save it at another's expense? You are soon going to see, my friends and fellow classicists, the great drama of the struggle for survival. You will see which one of these boys has the ruthlessness and courage to survive by abandoning the other, and which one will perish through the weakness of mind of an altruistic, idealistic, humanist, Christian education. In Nietzsche's terms, which one is a slave, a victim of the slave morality of altruism, and which one is a master. Or which one, quite simply, is the stronger, the harder, and the fitter to survive. That is to say, the more evil."

The boys were now manoeuvring to get their heads into the centre as the air above them reduced itself to inches and then to centimetres and their bodies were pressed against the glass ceiling above them. They had to turn their faces sideways to get any air, and they were now in a competition to get to the manhole. The Polish boy got there first, hooked his fingers into the small oval hole and pulled his face up into it, lying on his back so he could push his face through the hole and breathe the air above the tank. A devil had withdrawn the hose only a moment before as the tank filled to the very top. The boy's nose and mouth were in the clear and able to breathe in good gulps of air, as he held himself in place with his feet braced against the wall of the tank. Meanwhile behind him Eric's arms could be seen flapping in panic as he began to need air. There were a few seconds of terrible suspense in which the watching crowd held its breath. And then the Polish boy took his face out of the hole and pulled Eric's flapping hands towards him so he could take his place. The crowd, despite its predisposition to see a fight for survival, could not stop itself from bursting into applause at the act of generosity. Eric put his face into the hole, gasped, spluttered, and drank in gulps of air with open mouth. Seconds went by. Would he move aside in his turn? The tension became unbearable.

Romain let go of Camilla's hand. At first she gripped his hand again but then she understood and let go. Suddenly he was gone. He was pushing through the people in front of him and weaving his way down the slope towards the tank. Everybody was so engrossed in the spectacle before them that nobody saw him till he broke out of the crowd onto the area of lawn in front of the tank. He had spotted a stone in the garden at the base of a shrub, and he picked it up, ran forward and hurled it against the glass tank. The stone was lighter than he'd hoped and it seemed to dent the glass slightly but nothing more. It was clearly armoured glass. Then a man in leotards and devil mask, one of the waiters, rushed to grab him. Romain seized his outstretched hand and arm, spun him round in a lateral aikido throw and hurled him against the tank. His head struck it and the whole water tank trembled. A small spider's web of cracks appeared in the glass, like in a windscreen. Another bouncer came at him, this one with a baseball bat in his hands. He swung it at Romain, who ducked and then quickly grabbed the man by a wrist and flung him to the ground. He seized the baseball bat, hit the man once over the head, and then turned round to hammer the glass tank. His mask had slipped and was blocking his vision so he tore it off. Before he could swing the bat, two more men rushed at him from behind and threw him to the ground in a rugby tackle. He fought like an animal against both of them, rolling over and over. At last he managed to put one of them in an arm-hold and break his arm. He yelled in pain and stopped fighting. Romain scrambled to his feet and faced the other one, who had picked up the baseball bat.

He ducked as the other man swung, once, twice. The third time the other was more cunning. He swung much lower and a glancing blow caught Romain's ribs. He doubled up, wincing in pain. The other came in, swinging the bat back to land a killer blow. Romain glanced up in time and managed to kick him in the side of the knee. As he lost his balance Romain grabbed his arm and threw him on the ground. He ripped the baseball bat out of his hands, hit him once over the head, and then rushed back to smash the tank. As he swung back, he felt someone grab the bat from behind. Romain looked round and shoved the bat into the other's face in an effort to free it. He hit him in the mouth and felt the bat come loose. When he turned back there was a man in a devil's mask with a Rocker hairstyle standing right in front of him. Before Romain could swing the bat, he saw the right hook coming as though in slow motion. He felt it land on his jaw and he went down seeing stars.

As he hit the ground he had a desperate sense that he had failed. "So close and blew it!" was the phrase he heard inside his head. It seemed to sum up his life. Through a mental mist he heard himself say: "Get up!" and he reached out sideways to brace himself to raise his head and shoulders from the ground. He felt the baseball bat lying beside him. He looked up and saw the Rocker type had torn off his mask to continue the fight with better vision and was about to jump on him with his boots to finish him off. Romain rolled away by reflex. The other hit the ground beside him and at once tried to grapple with him. Romain felt the bat underneath him but he managed to seize it. His mind still in a fog, he rolled back over holding the bat like a spear across his body and ploughed the thin end into the Rocker type's midriff. Then he shoved it twice in his face and felt bone crunch. The other man fell back. Romain scrambled to his feet, feeling the pain in his ribs. To his surprise the way was now clear.

He swung the baseball bat at the tank. It jolted his arms. Water began trickling through a crack in the glass. He put all his strength into a second blow on the same spot, hoping it would not break his wrists. He felt the glass give way under the force of the impact. Water gushed out all over the ground. He staggered from the effort and stared at the jagged hole in disbelief. Suddenly he was surrounded by attackers, five or six of them. He swung the bat at them like a madman, backing up against the water tank. His ribs were hurting and the pain was hampering him from swinging hard enough. He knocked down two, but two more had baseball bats as well. They came in circling, to get him from two sides at once. He thought this time he was for it. Brain damage. Tetraplegic. Dead. He saw his life begin to flash by. A beach. A forest. His father on a boat. Then the images seemed to be tinted blue and there was a blue light flashing somewhere. At that moment he heard a siren. There was a confused sound of engines, car doors slamming and shouts. Then he heard a clattering noise, which he recognized a second later as the sound of a helicopter. Its black silhouette passed overhead like a huge dragon-fly blotting out the full moon. A loudhailer crackled.

"Police! Nobody move! Stay where you are! You are surrounded!"

There was panic and people ran in all directions. Romain's assailants, after staring up and around for a second, abandoned the fight and fled with the others. People were scattering across the lawn and into the park beyond, trying to make it out of the grounds. Police vehicles were charging onto the lawn, engines roaring. Policemen suddenly appeared, uniformed men with truncheons trying to stop the fleeing crowd. Romain saw them catch dozens of people and take them away. He had just hit the glass tank one more time to enlarge the hole from which water was gushing when he was arrested in his turn and ordered to drop the baseball bat. He did so wearily, and allowed himself to be marched towards a police van, saying calmly over and over: "I am the person who called you. Talk to Inspector Stubbings." It was only when he was on the point of being shoved into a police van with a dozen others that a sergeant listened to him, and took him over to Inspector Stubbings for identification. She was standing beside a Landrover-type vehicle looking in command and rather proud of herself.

"You took your time, Inspector," Romain said sullenly. "Children have been abused, raped and two boys nearly drowned. In fact, they're still in the tank, we need to get them out, they may not be alive."

"It's all right, sergeant, this is one of our informers," said Stubbings tersely. "Where is this tank?"

Romain led her and the sergeant back across the lawn to the tank. To his relief he saw the water level had fallen dramatically and both boys were standing up with water to their waists. He gave instructions to a policeman to climb up the step-ladder and open the trapdoor at the top. But there was still the problem of getting the boys out through it, as they couldn't reach it. The hole he had smashed in the armoured glass was jagged and not large enough for the boys to squeeze through. As the remaining water drained out through the cracks lower down, he suggested tipping the tank on its side. He called out to the boys to explain what they were going to do, and told them to crouch in the corner. Then a group of policeman tipped the tank on its side, and the boys, after being sloshed with the remaining water, were able to crawl out through the trapdoor to safety.

Someone put their arms round him and he turned to see Camilla at his side. Suddenly her lips were glued to his, and she kissed him passionately as if she would eat him alive. He felt her tears on his cheeks.

"You saved them!" she said with shining eyes and then hugged him tightly. "And you survived! Thank God!" she whispered in his ear.

The two boys were standing shivering, the policemen were wrapping them in blankets, and Romain led Camilla over to see them, his arm around her.

"You were brave boys," he said. "What they did was bestial and you were heroes."

"You saved us," said Eric quietly. "We saw you with the baseball bat after you smashed the glass."

"And you fought them all," said the Polish boy admiringly. "Like Batman."

Camilla put her arms round both boys and hugged them to her.

"You are the heroes," she said fervently. "You showed you are human beings, not animals like they wanted to prove."

"I was so scared," said Eric. He gulped and began to cry suddenly. "I don't know if I could have moved away again from the hole. Not the seventh time. The first six times I managed. The seventh time I was too scared. I couldn't take a deep breath. I couldn't get enough air. I nearly killed you," he said to the Polish boy.

"I found it hard too. It doesn't matter. We did it."

"If he hadn't smashed the glass," said Eric bitterly, still crying, "I would have let you drown."

"No, you wouldn't," said the Polish boy, trying to reassure him. "No, you wouldn't."

"But you don't understand. They told me. They told me in advance what was going to happen and I should kick you away. I nearly did. If it had gone on any longer...." He choked.

"Everyone is human, Eric," said Romain. "Everyone has a limit."

"How do you know my name?" asked Eric in surprise.

"We went to the care home and tried to talk to you about your friend, Viktor, who disappeared. Viktor is the son of a friend of ours."

"He was murdered," said Eric. "He was raped to death by Cyril Jones. The Member of Parliament. He killed him. I saw it. He banged his head against the wall fifty times as he raped him."

"You can come and say that to the Inspector," said Romain. He turned and looked for Inspector Stubbings. She was standing a few metres away talking to another policeman who had just come to report something. "Inspector, can you just hear this boy for a moment?"

Inspector Stubbings came over, and Romain got Eric to repeat what he had said. She nodded grimly.

"They've just told me they've arrested Cyril Jones. And a Peter Rigdon."

"They were the organizers of this whole event," said Camilla. "Rigdon made the speeches. He's a professor. I know him and I recognized his voice, despite his mask."

"Let's hope this time Cyril Jones doesn't get away with it," said Stubbings quietly, taking them aside. "And we don't get an order from somewhere to drop all charges. If I do, I'll denounce him and the whole conspiracy behind him to the media."

"And the media tomorrow?" asked Camilla. "Are you going to make a statement?"

"We're going to be as transparent as possible and let the public know the whole thing that happened here," said Stubbings. "I'm sorry we took so long to get here, we had a few problems. There was a brawl between football hooligans at the same time, so some of our force were going to be diverted. I had to convince the big boss we needed everybody and we had to get here with maximum strength immediately. It took a bit of time."

"Children have been raped and traumatized," said Camilla. "Romain was nearly killed as he smashed the tank, which saved the boys' lives. I've got everything recorded here on a smartphone. I'll give it to you, but only once I've copied it to my computer, just in case this evidence disappears. Has anyone told you what they did to these boys yet?"

She explained the game of getting the boys to drown each other. Stubbings listened with a sombre expression.

"I swear to you," she said at the end, "I'll make sure these men, Jones and Rigdon, pay. If there's any attempt to cover this up, I'll fight to expose it for the rest of my life."

"And don't forget Piers Bendigo," said Camilla, "who put Viktor in his so-called work of art. The boy they tried to drown tonight was for another one of his horrible installations."

"I'll make sure we get him. Even if he's got away tonight, we know where he lives," said Stubbings, "and we know where his so-called work of art is and I'll have it seized. Don't worry." She consulted her tablet for a few seconds. "By the way," she said, "I persuaded my big boss to intervene on behalf of that social worker arrested in Birmingham, Kayley Burke. He'll be out soon. And the other one who falsely accused him, Brian Spenser, is among those they've picked up tonight — I've just seen his name here."

They spent a few more minutes clearing up details. Stubbings assured them the two boys and all the other children would be taken care of by social services. The Polish boy was now crying quietly and a young policewoman had her arms round him.

"Go home and sleep," Stubbings said to Camilla. "You both did a great job. Come to the station tomorrow and talk to me. And bring your phone."

Camilla and Romain made their way towards their car with a young policeman escorting them. Camilla put her arm round Romain and insisted that he should lean on her to ease the pain in his ribs. He humoured her though the pain was lessening, and they walked slowly with their arms round each other. They got through the gatehouse, past the policemen guarding it, and began walking down the driveway. They passed more officers searching the grounds and arresting fleeing guests and herding them towards police vans. The night air was filled with shouts and the barking of dogs. As they got to their rental car, Romain saw the front door of Bendigo's Jaguar next to it was open. He mentioned to the young policeman it was Bendigo's car. They both noticed the window of the open door had been smashed.

"Hullo," the policeman said, and went cautiously round the car and looked in, flashing his torch. Then he leaned in the open door. There was nobody inside. He looked around and shone his torch over the ground nearby. There were drops of a dark liquid on the grass. He bent down and picked up a white paper which seemed to have fallen out of the car. He turned it over and stared at it.

"You'd better look at this," he said, "but don't touch it."

Romain and Camilla looked at the sheet of paper as he held it out and shone his torch on it. It had been folded in four and unfolded again. There was a photograph printed on it. It showed Romain, Camilla and Ekaterina standing on a street looking upwards at the camera.

The policeman glanced up and shone his torch towards the line of woods forty metres away. Something had attracted his attention and he walked cautiously forward, slipping the photo into his jacket pocket. Suddenly a man jumped up from a ditch about ten metres away. He froze and stared at them for a second. Romain recognized the Rocker hairstyle and the black outfit of the man he had fought with at the water tank. The piercing eyes seemed to have picked out Romain too. The man looked like a wild animal at bay, but something in his bearing suggested he was more naturally the hunter than the prey. His mouth was slightly open as if he was out of breath, and there was blood around it. The image of a werewolf flashed through Romain's mind. Then Romain noticed he was holding something next to his thigh, pointing downwards. It glinted in the moonlight, but only the upper part of it. Before they could move, the man sprinted away and made it to the edge of the woods and disappeared in the darkness.

"I think there may be someone in the ditch," said Romain.

The young policeman walked towards it warily and stared down into it, before crouching down. Romain and Camilla followed him and stood looking over his shoulder. The policeman shone his torch into the ditch. Bendigo was staring up at them, his eyes without any life. His face was fixed in a rictus of horror. A dark stain covered his shirt front inside his open jacket.

"Do you know who he is?" asked the policeman.

"That's the artist, Piers Bendigo," said Romain. "One of the organizers of this event. He owns the Jaguar. He's the guy we came with. Inspector Stubbings will want to know he's here."

The policeman called Stubbings and told her. They spoke quietly for a minute or two. He ended: "And we'll need dogs. He's taken to the woods." Then he turned to the others. He looked at Camilla's ashen face.

"You don't need to wait around for this. Let's get you out of here and home. You can come in and make a statement tomorrow. Inspector Stubbings will call the boys at the gate to let you through. I'll have to stay here now. They're bringing some dogs for our friend." He nodded towards the woods.

They left him staring down at Bendigo's body. They got in their car and drove down the driveway.

At the gate there was a group of policemen and two large vans. Several cars had been abandoned on the grass verge. An officer signalled Romain to stop. He put his head to the window and asked their names. When he heard them, he saluted casually and stepped back.

"Right you are, sir. Thanks for your help tonight. Drive safely and good night."

He waved them on through the gates and Romain turned carefully into the country lane and headed back towards London.

"That guy was one of the bouncers I fought with," said Romain, as though the tension had fallen enough to allow him to speak at last. "I smashed him in the face, which is why it had blood on it. But why did he kill Bendigo? And where did the photo come from?"

"The photo must have been taken by Cyril Jones. And he must have sent it to the bouncer, not Bendigo, otherwise Bendigo would have known we were bogus."

"He must be more than a bouncer."

"Didn't Ekaterina say that the gangster type with the Polish boy had an Elvis hairstyle?" Camilla cried excitedly.

"Exactly! That's it! He's the pimp who supplies the boys! And Jones sent him the photo of people spying on him, and he showed it to Bendigo tonight, after he recognized me when he attacked me."

"And Bendigo confessed he brought us along as his guests. Or maybe he tried to deny it. Either way the pimp was furious."

"Maybe he thought Bendigo would give him away if he was arrested," said Romain. "Since Bendigo was the one who needed a dead boy. Without him they could claim it was all just a game and no death was intended." He drove on in silence. "We may never know for sure. Unless the dogs get him."

"We're still going to write about Bendigo," Camilla said with grim determination. "This changes nothing. Now he's dead we can name him. We've got all his bullshit and his mad ideas recorded. We'll sell the story even more easily now because his death will be all over the front pages."

After a minute she phoned Ekaterina and told her everything that had happened and how the boys had been saved. Ekaterina was overjoyed.

"And guess what?" she said excitedly. "The prison has been ordered to release Kayley. He phoned me an hour ago.

Orders from higher up, they said. I'm going to go and get him tomorrow. I'm so happy! He said he's going to take me somewhere that I asked him to once."

"Where's that?"

She hesitated.

"It's our secret!" she said after a moment, with an odd sound between a chortle and a giggle, like a child bursting with excitement. "But I'll call you from there!"

"That's fantastic," said Camilla. "I'm really happy for you."

After she ended the call she told Romain. He smiled across at her. She suddenly felt emotionally drained but managed a wan smile back. She leaned her head against his shoulder as he drove.

"We're going to your place," she said. "We have to spend the night together, I can't be alone. I'm tired but I feel so awake I'll never sleep."

She put her arms round him as soon as they were inside his flat, and they made love passionately, with many tears on her part as well as much joy. Later they got up and made something to eat, since they were starving. As they sat eating in the poky little flat they began at last to feel normal again. Time slowed down, and they felt that their eyes were filming each other, while they told themselves silently not to forget this moment. They moved carefully around the tiny flat, touching each other whenever they were close, as if to reassure themselves the other was real. And they entered little by little into that strange double life, like a duet played on the same piano, which is the life of couples on earth who have found each other and resolved never to leave each other again.

Printed in the United States
By Bookmasters